"AM I DEAD? OR DREAMING?"

You are not dead. Unless you want to be.

"I want to live."

What will you do to live? Will you kill your own kind under my direction? I need a human to do my bidding in the Great Above. In return I offer immortality. You would be one of the Ageless.

"Can you—?"

Enough questions. Accept or you will be returned to the flames.

"I'll do whatever I have to do."

DARK TIME

"Part immortal, all human, Maliha is a heroine
who will leave readers breathless and craving more."
New York Times bestselling author JAMES ROLLINS

"Edge of your seat, breathtaking action . . .
a must-read supernatural thriller."
DAVID DUN, author of *The Black Silent*

"A passionate, fascinating story packed
with action and history."
DAVID MORRELL, *New York Times* bestselling author of
The Brotherhood of the Rose

"Food for thought on every fascinating page.
Dakota Banks is firing on all cylinders."
STEVE BERRY, *New York Times* bestselling author of
The Charlemagne Pursuit

By Dakota Banks

Mortal Path
Book 1
DARK TIME

ATTENTION: ORGANIZATIONS AND CORPORATIONS
Most Eos paperbacks are available at special quantity discounts for
bulk purchases for sales promotions, premiums, or fund-raising.
For information, please call or write:

Special Markets Department, HarperCollins Publishers,
10 East 53rd Street, New York, New York 10022-5299.
Telephone: (212) 207-7528.   Fax: (212) 207-7222.

DAKOTA BANKS

DARK TIME

MORTAL PATH

BOOK ONE

An Imprint of HarperCollinsPublishers

EOS
An Imprint of HarperCollins*Publishers*
10 East 53rd Street
New York, New York 10022-5299

Copyright © 2009 by Dakota Banks
Cover art by Don Sipley
ISBN 978-0-06-168730-3
www.eosbooks.com

First Eos paperback printing: August 2009

Printed in the U.S.A.

10 9 8 7 6 5 4 3 2 1

To my husband, Dennis,
the wind beneath my wings

ACKNOWLEDGMENTS

Maliha Crayne, her circle of friends, and her quest for redemption are concepts that have been stirring in my mind for several years. As any writer knows, thinking about something is a long way from seeing it realized in print. Without the help of others, you wouldn't be reading about Maliha and her adventures. I'd like to thank my agent, Jill Marsal of the Marsal Lyon Literary Agency, for her vision in seeing a worthwhile story in *The Mortal Path*, and for patiently working with me to get an early version of the manuscript ready for prime time. Diana Gill, Executive Editor at HarperCollins, provided invaluable suggestions and comments to improve this book, helping me rework it and bringing it much closer to the idealized version that exists in my mind's eye.

A reader's first connection with a story is through the book's cover. Art Director Tom Egner drew on his immense talent to create the stunning artwork that graces this cover.

Copyediting is invisible to the reader, but writers recognize its value. Ellen Leach copyedited this book and did an excellent job. She wielded her red pen as delicately as a photographer's airbrush to improve the readability of this book.

To F. Lit Yu, filmmaker, screenwriter, and writer extraordinaire, it's been an honor to work with you. My thanks for your friendship and support, and for the whip sword.

My husband, Dennis, has been wonderful, celebrating the happy times and encouraging me when the words just wouldn't come. He's not only a sounding board for some of the ideas that brought this book to life, but a source of them as well. As for my college-aged sons, Tom and Tim, they think Maliha kicks butt, and they're waiting for the movie.

Good and evil are repaid in kind,
just as shadows follow bodies,
and echoes follow sounds.

—CHINESE PROVERB

DARK TIME

Chapter One

1692

It was well after dark, time to set aside the herbs Susannah Layhem was sorting at the table. Time to blow out the candle and join her husband Nathan.

Nathan had worked since dawn, hard physical labor helping his younger brother build a home. The boy—Susannah couldn't help thinking of Nathan's younger brother George as a boy, even though he was a scant two years younger than her age of twenty—was getting married in a month. It made her smile to think about the couple moving in nearby and starting a family. If Patience, the bride, caught a baby soon after marriage, then she and Patience could raise their first children only a year apart. The two young women had already grown as close as sisters. Patience reminded her of the sister she'd lost years ago, in the rush of a flooded river. Susannah would be the experienced mother Patience looked to for guidance, and that would deepen their relationship further. If Patience could get out from under her mother's broad and smothering wing, that is.

Susannah had been working with horehound, useful for the coughs that came with winter. She'd also fashioned a number of packets of yarrow that could be grabbed in a hurry and used to staunch bleeding from harvest-time accidents. The pungent odor of the yarrow filled her nostrils, reminding her why it was sometimes called Devil's Nettle.

Silly. If the Devil wanted to do a person harm, I doubt he'd need to use a little flower.

She gathered the remaining herbs from the table and placed them into a basket, then scrubbed her hands in a basin of water. Herbs were very useful, but some of them discolored her hands, added a bitter taste to any food she touched, or weren't good to be exposed to for a long time—especially with a baby growing inside her.

After blowing out the candle, she sat in the fading light of a dying fire in the fireplace, one hand on the swollen belly that rounded the front of her nightgown. Looking around the room, she felt warmly enclosed in the place she'd turned into a home. Sometime soon, she would sit and look at the fire while nursing her baby. She hoped that her baby would be born by the time Patience got married. The midwife said it would be so, and Susannah's healer's instincts agreed.

My baby. The name will be Resolved if a boy, Constanta if a girl. I hope a son first, for Nathan, then a girl for me the next time.

She'd thought those words so many times they were practically a prayer.

Nathan had gone to bed more than an hour ago. He'd come home in the dark, smelling of sweat and freshly sawn wood, and gulped the meal she'd prepared. She heard his snoring from the other room with satisfaction. She could go to bed and not have to worry about Nathan's intentions, about his arms wrapping her and fumbling with raising her nightgown.

It was the only thing she faulted her husband for, and never aloud. He wanted to lie with her nearly every night, and at first, she enjoyed it—so much that she wondered about the wifely duty her mother had told her she must endure. It wasn't a duty to her. Nathan was a gentle lover compared to stories she had heard, involving her and not just taking his pleasure. As her birth time grew near, though, it became very uncomfortable for her; yet he kept on, even after she told him that. She secretly dreaded his touch, his whispered, "Come here, wife," in the darkness.

Any other time we can shake the bed, but now I fear for my baby's life. Maybe it's a fear that doesn't make sense, but can't he wait a month or two?

Nathan told her that babies didn't suffer any consequences from a man's natural urges. What did he know?
She hid from him the red stains she found on the sheet in the
morning. Susannah loved her husband and wouldn't do anything to make him think less of her as a wife, so she tucked
her fear away. That worked—mostly—during the daytime,
but at night, worry crept back.

It was the kind of thing that slowly eroded marriages
from the inside, but she didn't want to think about that.
In a little while, she wouldn't have to deal with the issue
for another year, and maybe by then his newlywed's ardor
would have cooled enough that he would grant her a few
weeks' peace.

Breathing a sigh of relief at his continued snoring, she
rose and went into the room. Perching cautiously on the
edge of the bed, she slipped her feet under the blanket and
rested her head on the pillow.

Safe! At least for tonight.

She slept on her side, letting her belly rest on the bed,
one arm cradling it. For some reason, that seemed to be
the signal for her baby to kick. She would lie there unable
to sleep for a while, but enjoying the feeling of life within
her.

A thunderous knocking rattled the front door.

Susannah sat straight up in bed. Nathan was still asleep.
He was so tired she could have clapped wooden plates next
to his ear and he wouldn't have noticed. She shook him,
hard.

"Nathan! Someone's at the door."

He got groggily to his feet. Few things brought a knock at
the door at this time of night, and they were all bad.

A death, a birth going bad, a fire . . .

Susannah's heart pounded in her throat as he crossed the
room and went to the door. She heard the front door's familiar squeak as it swung open, but now it sounded sinister
to her.

Patience! Something's happened to her.

There was a buzzing in Susannah's head, and she was
dizzy. She heard men's voices from the other room, but

couldn't make out the words because of the buzzing. Her dread grew as boots slapped the floor, coming in her direction, the men standing all too soon in the doorway. Three figures were backlit by the fireplace glow, with their faces darkened. She was breathing hard, open-mouthed, staring.

"Susannah!" Her husband's shout broke the frozen moment. "They're here to take you away!"

Two burly men pushed into the room after him. They were men she knew, villagers she'd known all her life.

Take me away?

Susannah pulled the blanket up and held it protectively below her chin, covering herself and her baby. Nathan crossed the distance toward her in the space of one of her gulped breaths. He threw himself across her legs, holding her down, holding his wife and child where they belonged.

"They say you're a witch. Your healing, those herbs . . . You've been accused, Susannah." Her husband stared at her from the foot of the bed. The flickering light painted his cheeks faintly red, but his eyes—his eyes were dark holes in his face. "You're not a witch. Say you're not a witch!" His voice bounced from the walls of the tiny bedroom and seemed to come at her from all sides at once.

She tried to use her voice but fear constricted her throat. All that came out was a low moan.

The men shoved Nathan aside and moved toward her. She gripped the blanket, her fingers locked around the cloth. She was tugged from the bed, dragging the blanket with her. Each man put an arm under one of her elbows, and she was propelled across the room, her feet barely touching the floor. At last a scream, a terrible wail, burst forth from her, and she twisted in their grasp toward Nathan. At the sound, her husband collapsed on the bed and buried his face in her pillow.

Susannah huddled in the corner of the dark, windowless room, awaiting execution. The place smelled of damp dirt and the covered bucket in the corner that held her wastes. It was cold. No warmth drifted through the tightly closed door from the fireplace in the jailer's room.

It had been three days since the men came at night, three horrible days filled with fear, pain, and betrayal. There had been a trial. Her accuser, a young village woman named Alice, pointed at her across the room, and gave details of afflictions she'd suffered from Susannah's practice of witchcraft. There wasn't a bit of truth to it, but Alice played her part grandly, crying, shivering, thrashing her limbs, and shrinking away pitifully if Susannah looked at her.

Not only was Alice afflicted, but she testified that she had overheard Susannah planning to slaughter her husband and use his blood in the practice of witchcraft.

Nathan wasn't given an opportunity to speak on Susannah's behalf. As her husband, he couldn't be expected to give unbiased testimony. Friends and family turned from her, caught up in the swift-moving drama and willing to believe baseless accusations instead of trusting their inner feelings. Every accidental hurt Susannah had ever caused was paraded in front of the crowd and seen to support the claim of witchcraft. When Patience shook her head and left the room in tears, Susannah's heart broke. She cried out, and was swiftly gagged before she could utter any "curses."

The jailers callously mishandled her during the trial, and no one seemed to notice or care. More than once she'd been shoved and had landed hard on her belly, denied even the comfort of cushioning her full womb from the fall. Her arms were tied behind her back and her fingers were wrapped together with rope to prevent her making evil signs.

In her prison, in the middle of the night, birth contractions shook her body. Her muscles cramped and the tendons of her neck strained under her skin. Her hands clenched into fists, the fingernails cutting into her palms. Sweat drenched her clothing and her dark hair clung to her forehead and cheeks. It wasn't her time, she wasn't due until the harvest, but her baby was coming now. When she could breathe after each contraction, she screamed for pity, for a midwife to help her give birth, for someone to save the life of her baby. The jailer stopped his ears against the malevolent cries of a witch.

Hot blood rushed from between her legs. She could smell it in the dark. She was a healer who had helped midwives with births, using herbs and hot water, offering a hand to squeeze and comforting words. Susannah knew the blood was wrong. She cried out her anguish, but no one came.

Please, if my baby dies, let me die here with him.

She couldn't control the urge to push. With her back against the cold stone wall and her legs drawn up, she bore down. Her screams echoed in the room again and again, as she strained and rested. One last mighty push and the infant slipped out onto the floor.

Susanna lay down next to the small body. In darkness as deep as a cave's, she could see nothing, but she could feel that the baby was flaccid, unmoving. Hope dying in her heart, she did what a midwife would do for a baby who appeared dead—try to share her own life with it. She placed her mouth over the baby's mouth and nose and breathed out in small puffs. Each time she lifted her head, she willed the baby to draw breath and begin crying.

After a while she stopped trying. Tears streamed down her cheeks and onto the still form, and she thought she felt the baby's soul fleeing the place of its miserable birth.

Contractions squeezed her womb and the ragged afterbirth slid onto the bloody floor. Unwelcome cramping stopped the flow of blood from her body, keeping her from dying with her baby. Susannah longed to pick her daughter up from the floor that was fouled with dirt, blood, and afterbirth.

She rested her head next to Constanta and tugged, for the hundredth time, on the bonds on her wrists that kept her from pressing her daughter to her breast.

The heat left the small body and the soft, perfect arms and legs locked into the stiffness of death.

The next morning the jailer opened the door to check on his charge. Susannah blinked as clean sunlight spread over the floor of the room. She gazed at Constanta, looking for the first and last time at her baby. Her daughter had dark, curly hair like her own. In the hours since the birth, Susannah had come to think it was a good thing that her daughter died quietly, here in this room with someone who loved her. Constanta wouldn't have to suffer the fate of being burned alive.

The jailer recoiled in horror at the blood and at the dead infant lying next to the witch and slammed the door. A midwife came and gathered the baby in a blanket and shoveled the afterbirth into a bucket, but made no effort to comfort or clean Susannah under the jailer's watchful eye. Susannah cried wretchedly, her body shaking. When the jailer turned his back, the midwife smoothed Susannah's hair and rested a palm against her forehead in a fleeting gesture of empathy. Then the woman stood and carried away her burdens.

My baby, my Constanta.

After that, Susannah's grief was hot and wordless. She rocked herself back and forth, back and forth, feeling a phantom baby suckling at her breast.

When she was forced to leave the room, her dress sagged over the soft belly of recent childbirth and the blood had dried, stiffening the cloth. Her appearance shocked the assembled townspeople. There was a thick silence as Susannah was tied to a post, a freshly cut trunk that would outlast the fire. She twisted her wrists hard, feeling the bite of the rope into her flesh, drawing fresh blood. Her hands were slippery with it. With no past or future that she cared to think about, the narrow present of heartbeat to heartbeat was all that was left for Susannah.

Her body was drenched in sweat, but it wasn't clean sweat from honest work. She was bathed in mortal fear, anger, and bitterness. Even if she could slip free of the stout rope, it wouldn't make any difference. Young men were standing by to catch her if she succeeded. And what was there left for her anyway? She tried to console herself with the thought that her husband still loved her, but she was haunted by the emptiness in his eyes that night in the bedroom as she was dragged away.

So long ago. A lifetime ago. Constanta!

The voice of the magistrate droned on.

"Whereas Susannah, wife of Nathan Layhem of Trenton Village of the County of Essex at a special Court of Oyer and Terminer was arraigned on two indictments for the Crime of

Witchcraft upon the body of Alice, daughter of John Hobbs and Rebecka, wife of John, and on one indictment of Petty Treason for plotting the death of her husband . . ."

The glares of the gathered villagers struck her as if they were casting stones. Among them, hands on hips, face flushed, mouth leering, stood Alice Hobbs, the afflicted young woman who had cried out from the torment of Susannah's evil craft. Or so Alice had claimed. It was a lie.

". . . trial whereupon she was found guilty by the Jury and sentence of death passed upon her for the Crime of Witchcraft and for the heinous crime of Petty Treason . . ."

The only affliction Alice suffered from was jealousy. She'd wanted Nathan as her husband, but he'd chosen and married Susannah instead. Alice would try to claim his affection when Nathan was a widower, doubly bereft of wife and child, and in need of the comfort of a woman in his life and in his bed.

And I'll be nothing but a pile of bones and ashes with my soul moved on, and I'm not done with this life. I want to live, to see Constanta smile, to grow old with Nathan. I swear I would kill Alice if I could get my hands on her. She stole my life and soon my husband.

Susannah sent a blast of hatred toward the woman who'd ruined her life. She, a healer, had been driven to hate and to wish death on someone, and to be willing to deal out that death.

She pulled her wrists until pain blackened the edges of her vision. She saw Nathan as if looking through a tunnel. He seemed so far, impossibly far removed from her, even though he stood within the ring of onlookers.

". . . by the law of this Colony and of England cause her to burn until she be dead."

She saw him fall to his knees and weep, overcome with emotion and shock at the horrible meaning of the blood on her dress. There was nothing he could do now but bear witness to her death.

They would have burned my baby alive inside me. They couldn't even show mercy and wait until Constanta was born to claim my life. Alice probably told them the baby would be born a witch, too. She didn't want my baby around to get between her and Nathan. She wants to be the one to bear his children. Forgive those who injured me? Never!

Alice smirked as one of the magistrates stepped forward with a torch and touched it to the dry brushwood piled around the post. The brushwood caught immediately. Susannah's stomach turned and she gagged. Bile burned her from the inside as the fire moved forward.

The heat, oh no, the heat!

She pulled her feet back as far as she could, pressing them against the post, hoping the sturdy green wood would somehow protect her. The fire reached her toes and the scent of burning . . . *something* filled her nostrils.

I'm going to die. Please, help me, help me, anyone! Help! I want to live!

She shrieked with her mind and her heart and a voice roughened with smoke. Bitterness flowed from her like a defiled river. She screamed her plea again and again, until pain seared her lungs and silenced her. The flames came higher still, and the heat singed off her eyelashes, set her hair afire, and burned her eyes so that she was blind. Coherent thoughts were driven from her mind as the fire began to consume her.

Chapter Two

Suddenly she was elsewhere. Cold, moist air flowed over her and condensed in drops on her skin as though she were walking through a drizzling rain. Her lungs sucked in air untainted by smoke.

Her hands were free.

She lowered her eyes and found that she was naked. Charred bits of clothing stuck to her in places, but her skin was untouched by fire and there was no blood on her body. She pressed both hands to her soft, sagging belly, confirming her loss for the first time with touch.

They would have burned my baby alive inside me.

She bent over and vomited liquid that burned her throat and mouth.

There was fog all around, thicker than she'd ever seen before, so dense she could barely see down to her own knees. Susannah tried to take a step and found that she couldn't command her feet to move. She waited for whatever was going to happen next, alone and naked, wondering in a numb way if her baby would be given a decent burial and what Alice and the others were seeing.

Had she vanished before their eyes? That would do nothing but confirm her judgment as a witch.

Not that it matters now.

Lost in mind and body, she let her grief and anger loose and dwelled on them. They circulated through her veins, heating her, making the fine mist turn to steam when it reached her skin. She felt something shift inside as the healing, comforting part of her was pushed into a small corner and locked away. The woman who had smelled her own flesh roasting was no longer the gentle person she'd been, the wife, the near-mother.

How long have I been standing here?

The fog thinned but didn't clear. Peering ahead, she saw a shape approaching. Wherever she tried to fasten her gaze on it, it slid away. A foul odor came her way, of must and decay, of graves and bones and winter sickness wrapped in the burnt hide of an animal. Malevolent streams of brown and green fog pushed aside the clean air. When the streams came near, they swirled around her as though a huge finger had stirred them. The smell of excrement filled her nostrils. She retched again, bent over and helpless in the throes of her nausea.

When she raised her face, the shape had drawn nearer, and still she couldn't make it out clearly. It was big, twice her height or more, and roughly human shaped. Roughly. There were too many joints, too many places where the creature bent as it moved.

"Who are you?" Her voice sounded strange to her ears. She didn't know if it was some unnatural quality of the fog or a scorched throat. She looked down again, needing reassurance that she wasn't burned.

She was anchored to the ground in front of the terrifying creature, with nothing to do but await her fate. "Who are you?" she repeated.

The answer came inside her head, so loud it reverberated in her skull.

Rabishu.

She understood it to be a name, not a place, although she didn't know why.

"I was burning. . . . Am I dead? Or dreaming?"

No.

She clapped her hands to her ears. The noise inside her head was excruciating. Had she traded one mode of torture for another?

The voice in her head moderated to a tolerable volume.

Dreams I do not understand, but you are not dead. Unless you want to be.

"I want to live." When the words came out of her mouth, she knew it was true. She did have something to live for, but it had nothing to do with motherhood and home, and everything to do with revenge.

You said that in the past. In the flames. What will you do to live?

Susannah tried to focus on the creature's face, or where a face should be. It was hard to tell where the fog ended and the face began, but she had the impression of wet sockets pointed in her direction, empty of eyes but sensing her anyway. Abruptly her eyes slid off to the side, as though the creature had been caught unaware. She had been allowed to glimpse too much, and the correction was swift.

Do not meet my gaze! The voice thundered in her head. *What will you do to live? Will you kill your own kind under my direction?*

Susannah thought about the bitterness that permeated her, the unknown time in the fog with heat in her blood, the key twisting in the lock. She knew what she wanted.

"I'll do whatever I have to do." She was shocked at the coldness in her voice, as cold as her baby's stiff body.

I need a human to do my bidding in the Great Above. In return I offer immortality. You would be one of the Ageless.

Susannah blinked. "Are you the Devil from hell?"

Not as you believe. I am a demon beholden to Nergal, Lord of the Underworld, god of glorious destruction and plague.

"Nergal?"

A being of power and darkness far beyond your understanding.

"My baby. Can you—"

Enough questions. Accept or you will be returned to the flames. You have more need of me than I of you. There are other humans.

"I accept. I choose life."

The fog formed into a tremendous wall, flattened like the gleaming stillness of a lake at sunrise, a vertical lake.

On the surface of the lake, fiery writing began to appear. The characters were completely unfamiliar to her, sticks and three-sided shapes formed into patterns. The luminous writing scrolled upward and towered over her, a dozen times her height. When the writing finally stopped, the characters continued to glow. They had some of the same ability to deflect her gaze as Rabishu's shape did—slippery, as though not meant to be considered for long.

Sign it.

Susannah dropped her eyes, suddenly ashamed. "I cannot write."

A skeletal arm with more than one joint stretched out toward her, and she cringed away as much as she could with her feet rooted. She felt a sudden pain between her breasts, and looked down to find a small wound forming there, a perfect circle, with blood welling through the skin. Her hand moved up to protect herself, but before she could reach the spot, the blood flew away from her like an arrow shot by the bow of her ribs. The blood splashed on the vertical surface and joined the sticklike characters of the demon's writing. As it did, she felt something tugging loose inside her, and a puff of dark smoke emerged from her chest.

Death has left you through the mark I have made. You are now beholden to me, as I am to Lord Nergal. Your first task is a simple one to accustom you to your new role. You must kill your accuser.

For the first time since Susannah was pulled from her husband's bed, she smiled.

Finding herself back in the flames but not feeling them, she stepped naked from the fire. The ropes around her wrists were gone, the injured flesh there healed. Her stomach was tight and flat, showing no trace that she'd been pregnant. Alice's smug look was replaced by one of revulsion, mirroring the faces of the others around her. Susannah walked right up to her.

They would have burned my baby inside me. . . .

Alice was too shocked to run, and a scream died in her throat.

"Come, *friend*, I have something to share."

Susannah's voice had a new timbre, a new power to it. She grasped Alice's hands and pulled her. That startled Alice into acting. The woman yelled and dug in her heels.

"Get away from me, witch! Magistrates, kill her now! Stone her! She's evil."

Susannah tugged harder. All of a sudden it was easy to move Alice, as easy as plucking a berry from a bush. She was aware of the others staring, aghast at both her nakedness and the fact that the fire hadn't killed her. She swiveled her head, looking for Nathan in the crowd. His face showed no trace of the love they'd shared, of the new life they'd built together inside her body. He was repelled by her, convinced now he'd been deceived and that she had planned to take his life. She was indeed a witch in his eyes.

She held Alice effortlessly with one hand, and pressed the fingers of her other hand to the circle between her breasts.

Rabishu's mark. This is my future.

The bloodied skin pulsed with power beneath her fingers, and she caught a faint whiff of the foul odor that had made her sick earlier.

A timidly thrown stone struck Susannah's leg, tearing her skin. Blood welled and a rivulet ran down her leg, but before the blood reached her ankle, the cut healed. Another rock, with some determination behind the throw, hit her soundly on the knee and ripped open a large gash. She traced the path of the rock back to the thrower, and was saddened to see that it was her own Nathan. His face was contorted with a mix of anger and fear.

The wound on her leg closed, the skin pulling together before her eyes as though sewn by an invisible needle and thread, and the pain faded.

Susannah pulled Alice into the fire and grasped her around the waist so she couldn't escape. The woman writhed in agony as the flames took her. When Alice was dead, Susannah tossed the charred corpse aside. She stalked away, enjoying the feel of power that flowed through her, her bare skin feeling warm and vibrant in the morning sun.

The terrified villagers parted in front of her.

Chapter Three

1951

The government agents would have to explain how an intruder had gotten past them so easily, and how they ended up with their hands and feet tied and their service revolvers boiling merrily away in the stockpot on the stove.

The house was in Springfield, Illinois, one of a few dozen like it on a street carved out of a farmer's field. The kitchen was cramped, but judging by the items on the counter, the lady of the house took cooking seriously. Susannah tested the air. Tomatoes, garlic, onion, herbs, more garlic. As she glided across the linoleum, the light of a full moon poured in dining-room windows open to the night air in the vain hope of a cool breeze. The moonlight rippled across her body and glinted from the hilt of a knife at her waist, one of several weapons she carried. There was no one awake to see her move through the house like a shadow cast by Death.

The living room next. A sterile place, a place to sit on facing sofas and utter social banalities. With her toe, she touched something that hinted at the true life within the house: a doll, no doubt dropped on the way through. That's what people did most in this room: walk through it. The comparison to her life was inescapable, a life where friendships were frequently left behind and love was never more than a fling.

Like a doll left behind on the floor.

She shook the feeling, picked her way carefully through a playroom littered with toys and books, and made her way down the hall. The first room on the right, she knew, was Patty's. Easing the door open, she slipped inside.

The curtains were open and a square of moonlight fell on the bed. A young girl was there, blanket thrown off on a sticky summer night, her nightgown twisted around her legs. Patty had turned fourteen a month ago. The faint odor of nail polish hung in the room. The top of her dresser was crowded with hairbrushes, bottles of cream, makeup, and a jewelry box a much younger girl would have, the kind with the dancing ballerina. Next to the jewelry box, in a prominent position, was a framed photo of the family, mother and father beaming as their daughter blew out the candles on her birthday cake. Susannah peered at the photo and counted the candles. Fourteen, plus one for good luck.

Susannah had never had a birthday cake.

Emily's room was on the left side of the hall, the moon-dark side. Susannah let her eyes adjust to the relative darkness, and then stood just inside the room. The sleeping girl wore pajamas covered with sheep. Emily was seven, and the owner of seven times seven dolls. They were all over the room, propped on a dresser, piled on a chair, mounded at the foot of her bed. Sharing the dresser with half a dozen dolls was a photo of Emily with her father, dressed for Halloween as matching clowns, clowns with laughing eyes. The picture had a frame made of Popsicle sticks, glued on neatly except for one that sagged on the bottom. Susannah put her face up close to the framed picture, looking at the latticework of sticks. A few still had traces of orange on them, her favorite as well as the child's.

Emily stirred in her bed, and Susannah backed out into the hall.

Mary's room was next on the left, closest to the master bedroom that was across the hall. The room was dark, like Emily's, and the door was pulled mostly closed. Susannah put her hand on the door, but was suddenly reluctant to open it and enter. Instead she peeked in to see the dark-haired girl baby sleeping peacefully in the crib.

As Constanta should have been.

She pulled her hand away.

A smell drifted from the room. Mary needed a diaper change and might wake soon, crying because of that or hunger or the pure cussedness of being eight months old.

In the master bedroom, Katherine DiNina wore a delicate nightgown that the moonlight turned the color of old blood. She had a few extra pounds on her, no doubt a result of cooking to please a family, and a sweet face that wasn't quite beautiful. Black hair spread over the pillow. Pictures of her family crowded the top of her dresser, but the side of the bed where her husband slept was empty. Her arm rested across the space where he should be. Susannah's gaze fastened on a Moonbeam alarm clock on a stand next to the bed. The lighted clock face said 2:45. Susannah had a clock exactly like it. She closed her eyes and breathed in the fresh scents of soap and shampoo. This woman went to bed clean, ready to embrace her husband.

Thoughts tickled the back of Susannah's brain. From the infant girl to the mother's black hair, this family could have been hers and Nathan's, in a different time. The pain of remembrance coursed through her in a way that it hadn't in centuries.

My job is to destroy this family, so like mine could have been. These people are like piers of a bridge. Yank one out and the bridge is unstable. That's what I've been doing since I became Ageless, I just never thought of it that way. One strike, one kill—but a cascade of ruined lives.

It was time to leave.

As Susannah retraced her path, she understood why the man of the house, Lorenzo "Ledger" DiNina, had made a deal with the Feds to turn on Adamo Tenaglia, a ruthless crime boss. He did it for the four dark-haired females in this house, who meant more to Ledger than his life did.

A week later, she ran on a dusty road, breathing evenly, enjoying the feelings of her muscles moving and blood pumping.

It was half an hour past sunset on a late August evening in Iowa, the darkness beginning to gather, yet the temperature was ninety degrees and so was the humidity. Cornfields

ran on either side of the road for miles, interrupted only by
the occasional driveway marked by a mailbox. The air was
saturated with the intense smell of ripening corn.

In an hour, she'd be invisible under a thin slice of moon.
Her clothing was black from head to toe, the silk fabric snug
against her skin and as supple as she was. Her long, black
hair was braided atop her head and her pale face concealed
by black silk wound around it from the neck up, leaving a
narrow gap for eyes as green as the fields around her. She
wore skintight black leather gloves with padded palms, and
a leather pack snuggled against the small of her back. It was
her killing outfit.

Running with her mind elsewhere, she retraced her path
through Ledger's home to the moment she'd frozen in front
of the baby's door. Her memories of Constanta were so
strong that Susannah hadn't been able to enter the baby's
room.

Not in my killing outfit. Not with a knife at hand.

A doe ventured out into the road ahead, followed by her
spring-born fawn. Susannah maintained her speed, judged
the moment, and launched herself into the air, arcing over
the two deer. The larger one startled as Susannah's foot
lightly grazed the fur on her back.

It was an exhilarating moment, one of the many Rabishu's
gifts afforded her.

The gifts had been beyond her understanding at first,
in the limited life she'd led in Massachusetts when it was
an English colony. After that first time in the flames, she
wasn't impervious to fire. That was something Rabishu
had conferred for a single purpose: recruiting her. But there
were other things, like being able to move so fast that she
appeared as a blur to the human eye. Her body healed from
wounds that would be fatal to others. The irony wasn't lost
on her: Susannah the healer now healed only herself. She
treasured her ability to see auras, reading emotional states
by the colors in the radiance that surrounded people. She'd
been taught martial arts by a Chinese master, at Rabishu's
insistence, and over the years had picked up strikes, defenses, and weapons from various countries around the

world. Her fighting had lost its original eloquence in favor of street techniques that served her well.

She sized up the farmhouse where Ledger was held, guarded by F.B.I. agents. For the federal case against Tenaglia, it was important to keep Ledger alive to testify. She was here to make sure he didn't testify. Rabishu favored keeping Tenaglia and his crime syndicate in business.

Ledger was probably on the second floor, as far from the front door as possible. She settled a throwing star into the wood frame above a second-floor window and tossed a loop of slim rope over it. After tugging on the rope to make sure it would hold her weight, she scampered up it easily.

A typical burglar would use a glass cutter at this point, for a silent entrance. For Susannah, that wasn't necessary. This was going to be a quick assault, lacking in elegance but leaving the agents in the home disabled, and Ledger dead.

She wanted to get her assignment finished. When Rabishu had given her the task, she'd toyed with the idea of turning it down. She wasn't sure what would happen if she flatly refused to do Rabishu's work, but she didn't see him as the forgiving type. At the least, she'd no longer be one of the Ageless.

What would it be like to be mortal again? Would I live out my life from now on, or would all my years catch up to me and I'd age in a flash? Here's Susannah Layhem, a pile of bones—no, dust—on the floor. At least I would be dust that no longer had to kill.

She pushed away from the wall of the house and came swinging in, her body bent, feet leading the way to break the window. Glass tumbled inward.

The noise of her entrance drew an immediate response. Shots zinged past, and she hit the floor and rolled, pain tracing a fiery line on her shoulder. She arched her back, sprang up, and took out her first assailant with a roundhouse kick to the jaw that sent him spinning across the floor, sliding through the debris.

A bullet struck her left arm as she did a handspring toward the other two men in the room. They overturned a table in her direction. Coins, cards, dollars, and drinks went flying. They'd been passing the time playing poker. She sidestepped the rolling table, and saw a flash of recognition in one of the men's eyes that maybe they should have kept the table for cover. Exposed, they scuttled away in opposite directions, knocking over a couple of lamps.

A kick to the stomach and the edge of her hand to the back of his neck turned one of the agents into dead weight, and he slumped against her. The last agent fired at her from across the room. The limp but still living body of the man she'd just disabled took the bullet squarely in the forehead as she ducked to the side. She somersaulted to reach the last agent as he pondered—a second too long—the fact that he'd just shot his buddy. A kick sent his gun spinning across the floor, and another kick sent him flying in the same direction, unconscious before he landed. She retrieved three guns from the room and flung them out of the broken window.

She paused for a moment, looking at the man who'd taken a bullet for her. He was in his mid-thirties and in good physical shape, blue eyes staring, a strong chin, a lock of hair curling onto his forehead. In the prime of his life, most people would think. He wore a wedding band. Previously, she wouldn't have given the dead man a glance, but lately the consequences of her actions lingered in her mind.

He had a wife, maybe kids. Parents, friends. A widening circle of mourners, ripples in a pond. Most likely, the agent who shot him will blame it on me. And why not? If not for me, the man would be in his wife's arms after this dull job, watching some accountant, was over.

She flexed her left arm. The bullet had lodged in the muscle above the elbow and was going to hurt like hell when she dug it out with a knife later. The other spots where she'd been injured vied for her attention with various levels of pain, but none of them was serious. Although Susannah wasn't immune to pain, wounds that might kill a human, like a shot to the heart, weren't a threat to her. The only thing she had to fear was losing her head, literally.

Susannah wiped her bloodied gloves on her pants and reclaimed her knife, sheathing it at her waist. She eased out into the brightly lit hall and tried the knob of the first door. It wasn't locked, and opened with a small creak. She pushed the door fully open, rolled and came to her feet smoothly, a throwing knife poised in each hand.

Ledger's eyes followed her in the dim light of a lamp. He'd retreated to the furthest corner. An aura of dull brownish yellow surrounded him, shot with smudges of gray. The dark mustard color was apprehension of pain and the gray represented dark thoughts, thoughts of a bad outcome.

A man anticipating a painful death. No surprises.

"You're the Black Ghost."

Susannah blinked and paused in her approach. As she blinked, she saw his aura on the inside of her eyelids, but it faded immediately.

"My wife wasn't sure whether to believe her, but Emily was right. You were there, in Emily's room, a week ago. To a seven-year-old, that's what you were. A black ghost."

Susannah nodded. So she'd been seen.

"The Feds denied it. They said nobody'd been in the house. Just covering their asses, as usual. Fuck. You were in my house with my family. Could've killed them all, right under the Feds' noses." Ledger sighed. "And here you are again. Goddamned Feds. You work for Tenaglia? He's using a woman for his dirty work. That's a low one, even for him."

She shook her head. She never bothered to explain whom she was working for, or anything else about herself. No one would believe it.

"You're probably lying. What do you care? I'm going to be dead in a minute. But you tell Tenaglia that Kate and the girls are untouchable. You hear that? He so much as breathes in their direction and lightning is gonna strike his family, especially that rat's ass son of his. Old man Amoretti's taking care of my family. You tell him that."

Do it and get out.

Her hands played out the motions of knife throwing in muscle memory while the blades remained perfectly still in her palms.

"Why did you turn yourself in?" She wanted to hear it from him, hear him say that he loved his family more than his life.

Ledger frowned. "What does that matter to you? Get it over with, Ghost."

Susannah retreated enough to check the hallway, then walked over to him, moving as quietly as a hunting cat, the throwing knives her claws. Although he hunkered down a little, he knew he had nowhere to go and didn't stand a chance against her. Placing a sharp tip over his heart, she leaned in close to the man's ear and said, "I'm curious. Indulge me."

Ledger, who'd been holding his breath waiting for the knife to plunge into his chest, exhaled warmly into her face. He smelled unmistakably of chicken soup.

"I turned forty. My predecessor retired at forty-two. Bullet in the back of the head. Accountants know way too much. They get so they're holding too many secrets and somebody gets antsy. So I figured I'd get out early and make the best deal I could for my family."

A tear slid down Ledger's cheek. "Lately that's all that matters to me," he whispered. "You know. You were in the house."

Years ago, Susannah would have killed him and slipped away. His story of family love would have bounced off her heart. But she'd seen what he had at stake.

Pajamas with sheep . . . dancing ballerina jewelry box . . . black hair on a pillow . . . a baby girl in a crib. A family that could have been mine.

The knife eased away from Ledger's chest.

She thought about Rabishu's order: *The man Lorenzo DiNina must not be allowed to testify against Adamo Tenaglia.* Susannah slipped the knives back into their sheaths. When Ledger saw her unarmed, he tried a last, desperate attempt to save his life. He came at her, fists ineffectually flying. She pinned his arms behind his back.

"Cut it out. I'm helping you."

What the hell? I'm helping?

No time to mull things over. "You're going to have to do what I say to get out of here alive," she said.

"Alive? I thought you were sent to kill me."

Susannah spun him around and firmly gripped him by the shoulders, alert for any muscle tell that would indicate he was going to lash out at her.

"I need to stop you from testifying. You don't have to be dead to do that. You made a deal with the Feds: your testimony for safe passage for your family. I'm offering you another deal. Keep your mouth shut and I'll take you to your family."

They'll get Tenaglia some other way. They got Capone on tax evasion.

Ledger blinked several times, an ocular Morse code, as he processed this. Then narrowed eyes betrayed suspicion. "What's in it for you? I'm not wealthy, you know. I can't pay much."

Not wealthy, my ass. Only an accountant would haggle at this point.

Susannah shook her head. "I haven't figured out what's in it for me. Listen, we're out of time here. Yes or no?"

"I'd be a fool not to take the chance. Even if it's just a joke you're playing on me. Yes. I say yes." His chin jutted out in an attempt to shore up his courage.

Echoes of her first conversation with Rabishu so many years ago flitted through her mind. She'd chosen life; so had Ledger, even with the hope of it surely seeming small to him.

The smell of smoke, of burning flesh, impossibly slipped into her awareness.

Something was chipping away at centuries of indifference to the fate of her targets, bringing back scenes from her past.

She went back to her village at night a few years after becoming Ageless. She didn't go to see if Nathan had taken up with another woman, or to see Patience and George enjoying their married life and sweet child. She went to the cemetery. As powerful as she'd become, the sight of the

*small gravestone felled her and she crawled on her knees
and kissed it. Constanta, it said. If Nathan had done nothing for Susannah in her time of greatest need, at least he'd
claimed his daughter's corpse, given the baby the name
they'd agreed on, and insisted that Constanta have a right-
ful burial.*

Susannah sagged a little. The memory was as visceral as
a punch to the stomach.

"I'm ready," Ledger said.

His words jarred her into the present.

There was an old pickup truck parked behind the farmhouse. A few minutes later, the two of them were on the
road.

Susannah felt almost giddy. She'd found a loophole in
Rabishu's orders and used it to save a life—and it felt good.
The demon's next assignment would be locked down tight
with no wiggle room, but for now, it was plus one for the
Black Ghost.

Chapter Four

1955

Susannah strolled through the summertime exhibition of Pablo Picasso's work at the Musée du Louvre. The multilingual crowd chattered, some offering their interpretations of the paintings, some gossiping about Picasso's mistress, who appeared as *Madame Z* among the paintings. Children brought "for the culture" swarmed in a second layer below the adults' heads, like lizards scampering through the understory of a rain forest.

Susannah listened in on conversations in a dozen languages and studied the great man's paintings. She loved the museum, beginning with her first experience of it in 1810, at the marriage of Napoléon and Marie-Edwarde, his second wife.

Susannah had come to the Louvre every year to study and keep up on cultural trends. Since the Smithsonian Institution had come into existence, in the mid 1800s, she went there for intensive study, too, alternating years with the Louvre. It was an odd feeling to see objects that had been part of her daily life show up in the Smithsonian's American History Museum, including a table that bore her name carved into the top by her husband's hand. She added other museums to her travels, in London, Cairo, Madrid, St. Petersburg, wherever the great collections settled.

A visit to Paris usually lifted her spirits. By day she visited familiar attractions; at night she walked the streets of Paris, taking the pulse of the city. Frenchmen came up to her, boldly asking for her company, and if she declined, they tipped their hats to her and left to try their luck elsewhere.

Leaving the Picasso exhibit, Susanna found an unoccupied bench in a niche at the end of a hall. Here, in a building where the elusive peace she craved seemed closer than elsewhere, she wanted time to think.

On the surface, her life was ideal. Wealthy, beautiful, intelligent, sensuous, secure from physical harm, she could and did travel the world, living high, leaving a trail of lovers who never touched her heart.

Except that someone else died so I could cheat death. Many someones. I'm living the way I do by dancing on their graves.

Taken as a package, the skills Rabishu gave her and the ones she'd acquired resulted in a tremendous—*okay, unfair*—advantage over human opponents. Her assassination targets never stood a chance. In the early days, that had made it easy for her to objectify her targets. But Ledger hadn't been an object. Neither had a target—*victim*—of an earlier assignment who remained vivid in her mind.

She let herself sink into the memories of Loon Lake, the place that had broken the bands imprisoning her heart.

A long time ago now, over thirty-five years . . .

Susannah had been in the town of Loon Lake in upstate New York for two weeks, scouting the area as a young woman devoted to bird-watching and solitude, spending long hours rowing on the lake in a rented boat.

Target: John Henry Sawyer, known as J. H., prominent scion of a New York old-money family. J. H. had leveraged his progressive Woodrow Wilson-style viewpoints, including strong support for the League of Nations, into political wins, and his run for the presidential candidacy was catching fire. If J. H. was knocked out of the running for the 1920 election, the United States would probably not join the League, a situation that would please Rabishu. Even a tenuous prospect of world peace drew the demon's ire.

Crossing the porch of the politician's summer home, she

tested each wooden board for squeaks before putting her full weight on it. Inside, the door to his den was about fifteen feet away, open to the entry hall. She drew her throwing knives from their sheaths, their familiar weight resting in her palms as she moved forward.

A sound came from upstairs, moaning followed by retching. It was so clear and miserable that her gut twisted in sympathy. There was a pause, another moan, then "Johnny . . ."

Susannah froze in the hallway. She'd watched J. H. arrive alone, leaving his heavily pregnant wife in their New York City home. Unaccountably, the wife was here now. A relative or servant must have brought the woman, probably over J. H.'s objections.

A light snapped on in the hallway upstairs and the cry took on urgency. "Johnny!"

She heard papers rustling inside the den, then the sound of a chair scraping back from the desk. J. H. appeared in the doorway of the den.

"Lucy? Is everything all right?"

Susannah reacted automatically and launched her throwing knives. The instant they left her hands, regret stabbed at her.

Death was in the air.

She lunged forward to grab the knives, to retract her decision to kill. A spinning knife nicked her finger, but even with her speed, she was too late. If J. H. had been ten more feet away, she could have caught the deadly blades.

J. H. fell, a knife in his throat, another in his heart. He made no sound, but there was a scream from upstairs at the moment of his death, as if he were a ventriloquist.

She heard shuffling and groaning from the stairway, as though each stair descended was a victory over pain that threatened to engulf.

Susannah dashed to the body. Bending over, she pulled her knives out, wiped them quickly on the dark cotton of her sleeve, and replaced them in their sheaths. She retreated quickly to the shadows near the front door.

There was another scream—much closer.

A woman stood at the foot of the stairs, clutching her very pregnant belly, nearly doubled over in pain. The lower part of her nightgown was soaked. Her water had broken on her trip downstairs. She started to straighten up, but immediately bent over and vomited. Wiping her mouth, she squinted at the shape in the hallway and saw that her husband was on the floor.

"Johnny, oh my God, the baby's coming early, Johnny, get up I need help, oh my God what's the matter with you?"

It came out as one long string of pitiful sounds. Then the woman spotted her husband's blood inching forward on the polished wood floor.

Susannah, flattened against the wall, breathed so shallowly her chest barely stirred. She was the Black Ghost, in her killing outfit that left only her eyes exposed. She could make it out without being seen, and her assignment would be over.

Leave! This isn't my business.

Susannah had her hand on the doorknob when she heard a shriek that packed in every emotion from horror to desperate love to grief. In spite of her strong desire to get away, the scream compelled her to turn and view the scene.

Lucy had collapsed on the floor next to her husband. A powerful contraction gripped her and she wailed. The hairs on Susannah's arms rose and she felt something squeezing her chest, as though Lucy's hand had slipped inside her ribs to clutch her heart.

It was Susannah's memory that was doing the squeezing.

It wasn't her time, she wasn't due until the harvest, but her baby was coming now. When she could breathe after each contraction, she screamed for pity, for a midwife to help her give birth, for someone to save the life of her baby.

The woman on the floor behind her was crying alone in the dark for someone to help her give birth, and to undo her husband's death. Susannah could help with only one of those things.

Walk away. Run away. This is just an assignment, like other times.

Her feet seemed to be out of her control. Susannah walked over and knelt by the woman, who was in mid-contraction. When the contraction eased, Lucy looked up at her. Her eyes boiled with hatred.

"You did it, didn't you? You killed Johnny. Get away from me!"

What am I doing? She doesn't want me here. I'm not the healer I used to be.

Susannah stood up to leave, when another contraction came and Lucy pushed hard. Susannah could see the crown of the baby's head emerging, and with it, something that made her heart sink: a glimpse of umbilical cord. The cord was wrapped around the baby's neck. Vivid memories flooded back of the times she helped deliver such babies. Many of them culminated in a funeral with a tiny coffin, sometimes accompanied by a larger one.

If I leave, Rabishu gets two lives for the price of one. Damn him, and me.

"Your baby may die if I leave. The cord's wrapped around his neck. He'll be strangled."

"Get out!" It was a snarl, a feral order from a female protecting herself and her young at their most vulnerable time.

A contraction rippled through Lucy's body. The tendons in her neck stuck out, every muscle of her body shook with the effort, and sweat poured into her eyes. She screamed. When it was over, she let out her breath explosively. Lucy was panting, her chest rising and falling like the breast of a captured bird whose heart beat wildly. Then her breathing slowed and she focused on Susannah.

"Damn you to hell," she growled. Then, in a defeated whisper: "Don't let my baby die."

Afterward, Susannah wouldn't acknowledge the feeling of holding Lucy's baby, flush with life, in her arms. For her, there were only memories of Constanta, and dealing in death.

After 263 years of killing in servitude to the demon Rabishu, Susannah's work was lying heavily on her heart. She marveled at the Louvre visitors who walked by her as she sat on the bench and didn't gasp in alarm at the foul stench that surely exuded from her. It was the same way that Rabishu announced his presence, with the odor of the Underworld clinging to him. Lately she'd had that smell caught in her nostrils, even while strolling in a garden, even while swimming in the warm, azure waters of the Mediterranean, even while making love.

My mind is trying to tell me something. My heart is rotting.

She touched her dress above the circular wound between her breasts, the place where Rabishu had placed his claw and drawn blood to sign her contract. It was warm under her finger, even through the cloth. When no one was around, she peeked down the front of her dress. That spot writhed with a whirl of black and green, and her skin pulsed in an irregular way.

Like some nasty little creature pushing to burrow in deeper, or even worse, break through from the inside.

Yet no one else saw things that way. Her current lover would surely have noticed such a flaw on her body, and the smell, too.

And what about my eyes?

Lately she'd seen in the mirror that there was an unfamiliar darkness in her green eyes. The irises were barely lighter than her black pupils.

Will I continue to grow wretched in my own view, yet remain attractive to others?

A thought struck her that left her breathless and stunned by the horrid uncertainty of it.

What if my senses are telling the truth, and the beauty that others see in me is just a deception cast by Rabishu? After all this time, I'm beginning to see the real me.

A seed of doubt was planted, joining the others in the garden of regret she'd been working on.

Susannah sat on the bench until a polite guard informed her that the Louvre was closing. Turned out on the street, she couldn't shake her gloomy thoughts.

After Loon Lake, she had begun learning more about her

situation. Researching intensively, she'd thrown herself into a study of ancient Sumer, wondering why she had never been curious before.

The Sumerians had a complicated relationship with the gods they believed ran their world. The gods of Sumer were the *Annunaki*, a race of beings who had traveled to an Earth devoid of humans, from a place in the heavens called *Nibiru*. Anu was their leader, ruling over three hundred major gods and three hundred minor ones. Once on Earth, the minor gods refused to do the labor of maintaining the world, so they created humans to take over that work.

Anu and his consort Antu had seven demon offspring, the *Utukki*. When Anu left Earth to travel again among the stars, he left the *Utukki* in the service of Nergal, Lord of the Underworld. The demons were given great powers to do Nergal's work, powers that approached those of the gods, and they were fractious and hard to control. When Lord Nergal at last left for the stars, he charged the seven demons with continuing his works of evil in the Great Above, the realm of the humans—basically, he left them on autopilot. In the modern world, the demons were all that remained on Earth of the gods of Sumer.

Anu, in his travels, heard that his demon offspring now worked with no one to oversee them, and he worried that they would take on too much control of the Great Above. So he placed rules on them, restricting the ways they could interact with humans and giving them each a fatal weakness. Anu wrote all of the demons' vulnerabilities on an indestructible Tablet of the Overlord, in a language he created to be impossible for the demons to read.

The location of the tablet was no secret, but the only way to read it was by using a translating lens created by Anu. He shattered the lens into seven shards and hid them in the Great Above, out of reach of his offspring. Each demon hoped to possess both the Tablet and the Lens, because then he would dominate the other six demons, literally holding their existence in his claws. Since they could only enter the Great Above under narrowly defined circumstances, the demons enlisted their surrogates, the Ageless humans, to search for the tablet and shards. Rabishu had instructed Susannah about the search, but hadn't given her the reasons behind it.

The demon who dominated Susannah was a child of an absent father. Like any misbehaving son in those circumstances, Rabishu pushed the limits of his power. While she now had a better understanding of Rabishu's role in history, and the collective evil caused by the demon brothers, the knowledge of what she was up against drove her to tears.

Chapter Five

Outside the Louvre, Susannah kicked her shoes off and began running, a blur of motion easily missed in a blink of an eye. Racing out into the lush countryside, she tried to leave her dark thoughts behind. Restless, she spent the summer traveling on foot.

Months after her quick exit from Paris, Susannah was perched on a ledge overlooking a remote glacial lake in Switzerland. Her determination to end her slavery had settled over her like dust coating every surface of body and brain.

"Rabishu," she whispered to the wind. "Talk to me."

She repeated it for hours, waiting through the frigid night. Nothing happened. She tried again, day after day, varying her appeal, eventually ordering the demon into her presence. The store of food she'd brought with her ran out, but she stubbornly waited, expecting to be yanked into the Midworld, somewhere between the Underground that was Rabishu's realm and the Great Above, the domain of humans.

On the seventh night of her fast, she saw a hellish vision.

Far down the mountain, a humanlike figure moved across the deep snow. He didn't trudge through it, he floated above it. The figure was bathed in fire, flames licking several feet over his head. He was surrounded by a swirling ball of heat that distorted everything within. The wind stilled, and outside his glowing sphere, the darkness was unnaturally powerful. The stars blinked out of existence. Snow melted in a wide swath around him as he advanced. Rivers of water coursed down the hill in his wake, and the exposed ground, long buried in snow, was scorched under his feet. Susannah, jerked to a standing position and unable to flee, felt as though her feet were mired in the rock underneath her, and from there, to the center of the Earth.

Susannah's eyes were pinned on the progress of the figure toward her. Her heart pounded, her lungs drew in hot, fetid air despite the frigid mountaintop cold. It was the air of corruption of body and soul. Adrenaline flooded her body, making her muscles scream in agony against the force that made her unable to move. Her mind retreated to the time that she was burning, surrounded by flames at the stake, her flesh catching fire. Rational thought fled, though her body could not.

The figure relentlessly approached. Steam rose from the snow melt that rushed down the mountain and the tundra blackened in a widening area.

He stopped far enough away that the shimmering heat around him just touched Susannah's body. She sank rapidly into the snow as it turned into water.

Slave, why do you call me?

The thought sliced into her head with the force of an axe blade, dispelling her rambling thoughts. Susannah had felt no pull into the Midworld. Another wave of terror swept through her at the thought that Rabishu could enter her world. It was one constant she had been able to count on through the centuries: Rabishu in his place, she in hers.

"Am I still in the Great Above?"

Yes.

His clipped answer did not offer an explanation, as she was hoping. Instead a surge of heat flowed toward her, making his annoyance unmistakable.

"How can this be?"

You called me. You invited me into the World Above and I can remain for a short time. The rules of Anu permit it.

"I've never seen you like this before."

Ignorant slave! Your perceptions are easy to fool. I can appear as I desire. I ask again, why did you call me?

Faced with Rabishu's anger and the heart-stopping image of him in her own world, her resolve had retreated. She dug down deeply for it.

"I don't want to do this anymore."

Rabishu probed her mind, prowling through her experiences, laying open her desires.

So you want to die.

Before Susannah could answer, the melted water at her feet sprang up in front of her and formed a smooth surface. It was in such a surface that she'd first seen her contract so many years ago. This one, though, was filled with a uniform reddish glow, lit from within by Rabishu's fiery presence, and it was reflective. She could see herself in the mirror.

Her face and body were as they had been for centuries. Then her youthful vigor began to drain away, her faultless skin became etched with wrinkles that were fine at first, but deepened and spread as she watched. Her hair went from thick and black to gray, then patches fell out and the remainder hung in lifeless, wiry hanks from her scalp. In the reflection, her clothes dropped away so that she could see her body stooped over with the weight of the accumulated years. Her limbs became bony, her ribs protruded, and fissures opened in her skin, letting loose a thick liquid of decay.

As she watched, her reflected body slumped to the ground, writhed with its last weak life force, and fell quiet.

Susannah was shaken, but when she thought about it, the horrid scene was only a continuation of what she felt had already begun—the rotting of her body from the inside.

"I . . . I accept this," she said, choking out the words. She held her breath, waiting for the process she'd been shown to begin. Instead Rabishu's words penetrated her mind again.

Then let me show you what awaits after you die.

Chapter Six

Rabishu approached her, drawing her into the sphere around him.

She inhaled sharply, expecting her flesh to be set afire. Her body grew hotter, but didn't burst into flames as she had feared. Rabishu reached out and clutched her shoulder with his claws, piercing her skin and then squeezing until the claws met within her body like a pincer. She was as helpless in his grasp as a hooked fish.

She felt the familiar tug into Midworld, and was dismayed that it didn't stop there.

He's taking me to the Underworld!

Suddenly the powerful claws let her go. Her ears were assaulted with shrieks of pain and fear, and in a moment she realized some of those shrieks were hers. She clamped her mouth shut and bit her lip to keep from opening it. Around her were rows of cages, stacked atop one another higher than she could see and vanishing into the distance. Each cage was made of cross-hatched wire and was long enough for a human to lie down. There was some room above each supine body, but not enough to sit up fully.

Her eyes flitted from cage to cage. In them was more horror than her brain could absorb.

Men tried desperately to hold their bodies together as limbs flew off and their abdomens unzipped. For some, the cage relentlessly collapsed on them, pressing their flesh like ripe fruit through a strainer. Women had their skin slowly peeled off by an invisible hand. And then the torment started all over, the same or some new form, countless different ways. The despair of tortured minds and bodies assaulted her from all sides.

Suddenly she was swept up and deposited in an open cage. The door clanged shut. She screamed, her heart and lungs nearly bursting with the effort, as the ceiling began descending toward her. Lower and lower it came, so slowly, as she struggled with mindless fear. The ceiling pressed her against the sharp wires on the bottom of the cage, and she felt the wires digging in, then her skin breaking in hundreds of places from her feet to her head. Unable to breathe with the pressure on her chest, she felt her flesh beginning to bulge through the wires beneath her. . . .

Then she was flung back onto the mountainside in the Great Above, rolling, rolling in snow, unable to stop. She tumbled over the edge of a cliff and managed to grasp the edge before falling. Hanging by her fingertips with her mind in shock, her body drew on primal reflexes and slowly pulled her up. She clawed her way back from the cliff's edge and collapsed. The heat she'd carried with her from the Underground melted the snow below her body. She sank into it, creating a shaft that gave her a narrow view of the sky.

She'd never been happier to see the stars.

Chapter Seven

Susannah Layhem, demon's assassin, was in Houston in a home that had seen better furniture but not more love.

In the master bedroom, homeowners Ellen and Glenn Morgan lay slumped, unconscious, in their bed. Susannah had used a drug—a little needle prick on their arms and the two were out before the fear and outrage that their home had been invaded could envelope them.

The full moon's light came through the master-bedroom window, bright enough to cast a shadow as Susannah moved. There was a mirror over the wife's dresser, and as Susannah passed it, she saw a startling vision: herself. The process of physical decay that she'd noticed earlier now seemed more advanced. She paused, studying her reflection. Her face appeared gaunt, her hair limply hanging around it, her lips thin. Her expression was slack-jawed and her eyes didn't pick up the moonlight—they were flat and unfeeling.

My face isn't even visible, or my hair. I know that. I know it. My face is covered.

It was her hands that startled Susannah the most. Although she was wearing gloves, the view in the mirror showed bare hands, wrinkled, with small protrusions. . .

She leaned in closer.

Oh no, it can't be. Claws!

She pulled back from the mirror in shock and looked directly down at her hands. Black gloves, only gloves.

Which is the real me?

Her shoulder throbbed where Rabishu had pinched her through and through with his claws. An unwanted memory arose of the feeling of his claws brushing against her shoulder blade, sliding off, meeting inside her flesh with a soft *snick* . . . She squeezed her eyes shut and opened them again. In the mirror were small, pointed claws extending about half an inch from the ends of her fingers. As she watched, mesmerized, her reflection shimmered, and there she was, as young and beautiful as she had been on her wedding night with Nathan.

Damn Rabishu! He's toying with me, damn him! Or I'm insane.

She whirled away from the mirror in despair. She had a job to do.

Susannah sat in a rocking chair in the room across the hall from the master bedroom. On a small dresser to her left, a lamp glowed with a soft yellow light. It had a shade that cast patterns of moons and stars on the wall, and across her body.

Dressed in her killing outfit, she held a baby girl in her arms, a knife poised at her throat.

Three-month-old Candice Morgan was her target tonight, the first one she'd had since her time in the Underworld a couple of months ago. For reasons known only to the demon, this baby was marked for death, and Susannah was the instrument of his will.

She'd been unwilling to hold Lucy's baby after delivering it in the Loon Lake cottage, but this time, she'd had no choice but to take the baby, so full of warmth and life, into her arms.

Rabishu was testing her, punishing her, or both. To her shame, the experience in the cage had suppressed her resolve to stand up to him. Fragments of her Underworld experience replayed in waking visions, leaving her breathless and trembling. The frequency of those experiences was decreasing, and she hoped they would end.

The longer I go on obeying Rabishu, the less he will feel the need to remind me of his power over me.

Her life had changed dramatically. She kept to herself,

took no lovers, traveled to no museums, drank in no raucous pubs. She lived in a cycle of fear: actively having visions, then waiting for the visions to begin again. Exercise invigorated her and gave her a glimpse of her old life, so she kept to a punishing regimen, pushing her endurance to the utmost.

Susannah was resigned to her fate. She would remain an Ageless slave, a killer with a dead heart, a woman with marginal belief in her own sanity.

The room smelled of baby powder and freshly laundered clothing. Candy chortled softly and waved her hands at the moving shapes on the wall. She'd awakened at Susannah's touch, but instead of crying, she'd lifted her chubby baby arms to be picked up, somehow trusting that the Black Ghost meant her no harm. There was no telling how Susannah appeared to the baby, if Rabishu was creating an outward appearance for her. Perhaps she looked like Candy's mother, to instill trust until the knife bit.

Why her? To make her parents suffer, break up their marriage? Or as the girl grows, will she do something that threatens another of Rabishu's plans? Somewhere down the line, perhaps generations from now, things will be very different because this baby died tonight. The amount of pain and anguish in the world will increase by just that much—a baby's death magnified over the years.

She'd followed the lives of Lucy and her son John Henry Sawyer II, named J. H. to honor his father's memory. Lucy did her best for the boy. She was a rock-solid support for her son and made sure he knew what kind of man his father was. She saw him through college and cried at his wedding. With her son settled into adult life, she spent a few days at the house on Loon Lake and quietly hung herself.

Chalk up another one for Rabishu, and for me.

It was the first time Susannah had followed through, tracking the effects of one assassination through the years. It was also the last time, since the experience tore at her heart.

The tip of the knife pressed into Candy's throat, drawing a drop of blood that ran down her neck and soaked into the fabric of her clothing. Candy's face screwed up, her mouth forming a silent O at her betrayal. Silent only for a moment, until a scream erupted, one that her loving parents couldn't respond to, couldn't even hear.

For all I know, this baby was picked at random. There's no plan, no reason except to spur on grief. Rabishu once said: I am a demon beholden to Nergal, Lord of the Underworld, god of glorious destruction and plague.

Her cheeks burned with shame. She was glorious destruction, personified.

I could end it. Never take another life.

To end it would be ridiculously easy. All she would have to do was kill herself in such a manner for which her rapid healing couldn't compensate, and she'd had plenty of time to think about how an Ageless slave could accomplish that. If she put some distance between her torso and her head, not even rapid healing could bridge the gap. She dreamed about it, focusing on those moments of relief before the blade bit into her neck and freed her from killing, and didn't dwell on the promised aftermath.

The baby's body trembled and her pulse quivered under Susannah's hands, a rapid beat that reminded her of the clean rhythm of her feet as she ran. She held the knife perfectly still and subdued the baby's movement with her great strength, like a mother crocodile carrying her young in her jaws.

Do it!

She played out the scene in her mind, the familiar slickness of blood on her hands, the silenced crying, the dull eyes of death, the limp body across her lap. The room that no longer smelled baby fresh. The parents waking but thinking they were still in a nightmare. The little girl who didn't grow up.

I was a healer once. A woman who helped the sick and injured, a woman who carried life within me, and this is what I've become: a killer of babies.

Gazing down at Candy, she let the focus of her eyes relax, looking beyond the baby, letting her aura come into focus. There it was: a wide, undulating, red outline, strong and clear, limned in bright yellow. Candy was a natural healer.

A nurse, a doctor, a psychologist, someone who cares for others. I'm snuffing out the life of . . . of myself, as I used to be.

The irony of it made her close her eyes and moan. The baby struggled a little in her lap, but Susannah kept a firm hand on her. This time it was the knife in Susannah's grip that trembled.

The baby suddenly quieted. Susannah's eyes snapped open, fearing that she'd killed the baby with her now-abhorrent strength.

Lying across her lap was no three-month-old, fair-haired baby.

It was Constanta, her newborn, and very much alive.

Susannah almost leaped up in shock, almost dumped the baby off her lap. With great effort, she held still, her eyes devouring the baby she'd never seen alive. Wrinkled and red like most newborns, she was the most beautiful sight Susannah had seen. Her heart jumped through time and the barrier of death to bond with her baby girl.

Rabishu, thank you for this gift.

The knife slipped unnoticed from her hand, and she held Constanta to her breast, burying her face against the baby's warm head, her lips touching her daughter's black hair. The baby gurgled and settled in contentedly.

Constanta, my baby, my baby . . .

She rocked in the chair, lost in the moment, humming mother's tunes to Constanta. Belatedly, she thought to perform the mother's ritual of checking for perfection, of counting fingers and toes, of setting to rest any secret doubts during pregnancy, of finally being able to say *my baby is fine.*

She gently laid the baby across her lap.

Toes . . . check.

Fingers . . .

She gently tried to unfold her daughter's little fist. Under Susannah's fingers, she felt the girl's flesh rapidly losing warmth. In the space of two breaths, the baby's hands were cold. Memories swept into her mind of the night she spent in the village jail, lying next to the pitiful body of her still-born baby.

The smell of blood in the darkness. Constanta's soul fleeing the place of its miserable birth, the heat leaving the small body and the soft and perfect arms and legs taking on the stiffness of death.

It was happening again. Constanta was dying, and this time she could see it, by the light of the lamp. She could see every detail of her daughter's slide toward death, and was helpless to stop it.

When Constanta was dead—again—Susannah was holding Candy, the true occupant of this room. She put the baby back in her crib and picked the knife up from the floor.

She saw her life stretching out ahead of her, the endless years of an Ageless human.

How many times will I hold Constanta only to have her die in my arms?

Bitterness boiled up from inside her as she remembered how she had thanked Rabishu for his gift.

He must have enjoyed that.

She swayed, nearly bursting with the strength of emotion coursing through her. When she was able to walk, she left the home of Ellen and Glenn Morgan and their daughter Candice, who would grow up to be a healer.

Out in the moonlight, she swore that not one more innocent would die by her hand, and she knew exactly what she was going to do to put a stop to it.

There were technical difficulties. She couldn't just phone someone and say, "Would you mind severing my head?"

Susannah lived in a Montana house built by Frank Lloyd Wright in 1909. It was on a ranch of about 250 acres, small by Montana standards but perfect for the privacy she needed. Susannah was the original owner, having worked with the architect, and had "sold" the place twice to herself, as she assumed a new identity every twenty or thirty years.

Rabishu hadn't responded to her refusal to carry out her

last assignment. She hoped he would delay even further, because she was on a mission of her own.

Two of the home's bedrooms were devoted to her weapons cache, a third to her collection of antiquities she'd accumulated during her world travels. Among the rare items was a blade salvaged from a guillotine at the end of France's Reign of Terror, a bloody year in which thousands of people were executed. Already 120 years old at the time, Susannah had been busy elsewhere in the world. The French didn't need any assistance in slaughtering one another during the Terror.

Half a day to get the lumber and supplies delivered, half a day to build the fourteen-foot frame in a clearing behind the house. The blade in her collection weighed almost ninety pounds and was difficult to mount to the crossbeam, but she managed it. She tested the drop by freeing the rope that held the angled blade aloft. It worked.

It was sunset, a fitting time. She sat on her expansive porch and watched the mountains grow darker as shadows climbed their sides. Clad in her killing outfit, she gathered her strength for her last assassination.

Get on with it, before you chicken out.

She crossed the clearing, settled her neck in the hollow of the bottom brace, and yanked the rope.

Chapter Eight

She closed her eyes to greet death, but instead Rabishu pulled her into the Midworld.

"No! Let me go!"

His voice thundered in her head, so loud it was a roar without words. That voice, so intimate inside her, was more of a violation than the blade on her neck would have been. The circle between her breasts throbbed wildly. She put her hand to her chest and felt the warmth of blood seeping into her clothing.

Rabishu's mark. Once it was my future.

Even though her demon master was at a distance, she felt a blast of anger from him that nearly knocked her flat on her back.

It's gonna be bad. I should've slit that baby's throat from ear to ear.

She yelled at the top of her lungs, pulling bravado from somewhere within her. "Get it over with, you damned stinking pile of burnt dog hide! I've had enough of taking your orders! Go find yourself another slave!"

A searing pain burst in her chest. She clawed at the outfit she was wearing and ripped it away from her upper body. A thin stream of blood shot out at least a dozen feet from the wound between her breasts and hung in the air like a horizontal lightning bolt before breaking loose and splashing on the ground. With each beat of her heart, blood flew from the wound and added to the pool that was forming a few steps away.

"You want my blood? Here, let me speed things up!" She fought mightily against the heaviness in her limbs induced by his presence, and broke through it. Tugging a knife from its sheath, she grabbed it with both hands and pointed the tip at her chest. Her hands began the fatal plunge.

The knife froze in the air as Rabishu came into sight, and the bleeding from her chest slowed to dripping that ran down her body and pooled at her feet.

This time he appeared to her in his most horrifying form yet. He was emptiness, a yawning black hole walking on all fours, a hideous parody of a black panther. The fog of Midworld swirled toward him and vanished into the nothingness that was his body. Susannah fastened on the idea that the void was a direct channel to the Underworld where he lived. She felt a slight pull toward him and feared that she would be drawn in like the fog, trapped forever in his foul innards or delivered straight to one of his torture cages.

"Not without a fight." She said it standing straight, as though Rabishu had politely consulted her. "I've got weapons and the will to use them. All I need is a chance."

Susannah dismissed the thought that came to her afterward, that her weapons couldn't damage Rabishu. Whatever was about to happen, she was going to face it with her chin high, and shaking her fist, too.

Eyes the size of eggs floated in his face, bobbing eerily as he walked, and underneath them two rows of teeth were suspended in the blackness. It was a predator's mouth that could grab her and tear a huge chunk from her body effortlessly. His movement was cat-paw silent except for the occasional *snap!* of his long tail, more whiplike than the tail of the animal he imitated.

Rabishu stopped ten feet away. A tongue emerged from between his teeth and he greedily licked up the blood that had spurted out of her chest. Her stomach turned at the sight, and at the thought that her blood was an appetizer and the rest of her would be the main meal. Then her knife, still frozen in midair, whirled toward him. He caught it with his teeth and crunched down on it, with a sound like the snapping of bones. Her defiance wavered.

Brave words, that "chance to fight" business.

"Go back to your Lord Nergal," she said, a little shakily, "and tell him he's an impotent piece of shit, and so are you!"

Rabishu made no indication that he'd heard her, or if he did, he'd brushed her threats off as a human might brush away a buzzing mosquito. Fog rose at her feet and flattened into a wall, and glowing writing appeared on it. She knew now that it was cuneiform; when she first saw it, it looked like sticks tossed on the ground.

Your contract. Rabishu's words thundered in her head. The writing scrolled upward at great speed. Rabishu reached out a large paw, bristling with claws, and touched it to slow the motion.

This section is the way of termination.

A portion of the writing zoomed down and hung in the air before her. Up close, the writing appeared to be made of a complicated system of thin vessels, disturbingly like her own arteries and veins. Liquid the color of pus pulsed through each abstract symbol, and it was shot through with red—her blood, extracted centuries ago when Rabishu pulled her from the flames.

She'd been ashamed at the time that she couldn't write her name, but Susannah had come a long way since then. Reading Sumerian cuneiform was a skill she'd acquired in the late 19th century. Her contract was written in something that preceded Archaic Sumerian, but necessity had a way of elevating her skills. She studied the contract and read part of it aloud.

"Failure cannot be tolerated. The servant will be given a choice: a painful death and passage to . . . to oblivion, or a life spent balancing dark acts with those of the light. Success will bring passage to a higher plane. Failure to balance will result in unending torment."

She paused, considering what she had just read. She wasn't sure she had it word for word, but close enough. "What does this mean? I don't understand the choice."

It means I kill you. It will take you many years to die, as an example to other slaves.

Susannah shook her head. "Don't lie to me, demon. The last time I saw this contract I was an illiterate girl. That's no longer true."

A sudden blast of noise in her mind sent Susannah reeling. Rabishu didn't like to be challenged. She struggled to keep her feet, and the angry outburst wore down.

It is at the insistence of Anu, Ruler of the Sky, that there is a choice.

"We have spoken of Anu before, and the crystal lens you seek."

Speak no more of that, traitor. It no longer concerns you.

"Then tell me of the choice, as you are bound by Anu to do." If Susannah had any cards to play, she was eager to get them on the table.

If you choose to die now, your death will be painful and prolonged—long by my standards, not yours, and I have served my lord for over four hundred thousand of your years—but at the end you will have no further consciousness. Your essence will be divided up and fed to the winds. It is a release from pain, if nothing else.

"And the alternative?"

If you choose to live, you must save lives to balance those you have taken at my behest. You will be mortal, although you will retain pale versions of the powers that I gave you when you entered my service. If you die before balance is achieved, you become my plaything—as long as I exist, with no release.

"If I should succeed in this balancing?"

None of your kind has ever done so. If you are the first, you will join Anu in the third sphere of existence, an honor granted to very few gods. In your words, it would be paradise.

"I thought Anu was gone from Earth."

In the third sphere, distance and time mean nothing.

"Then I choose life, as I did when you first pulled me from the fire and made me your servant. I choose to live and I will beat you at your game!"

It is no game. You will never succeed. I will enjoy welcoming you to eternal torment.

"Stop trying to cheer me up." Having survived the moment, Susannah was feeling better. Anu, wherever he was, was giving her a chance.

She put her hand to the wound on her chest and found that it hurt but had stopped leaking her life's blood.

An odd sensation gripped her, the reverse of the feeling centuries ago that death was leaving her body. The gray cloud of death entered through Rabishu's mark and spread out inside her, trying on her body like a coat. She was mortal.

Rabishu leaped at her, knocking her over. This close, his stench was overpowering.

How does a void have weight?

His teeth parted and out came the tongue, red and obscene. It played lazily over her chest, taking up the blood from Rabishu's mark, then drifting onto her breasts. She felt his agile tail stroking her legs.

She stiffened beneath him, wondering if he was capable of raping her and unwilling to go any further with the thought.

Then tremendous pain stabbed through her middle. She tried to clutch her arms around her stomach, but couldn't. One paw planted on her left arm kept her pinned down, and her right arm was twisted underneath her. She suddenly felt as though her skin were burning. Panic swept through her as she thought he'd put her back where everything began— the smell of her own roasting flesh obliterating all but her frantic pleas for her life.

She was stunned to see Rabishu's claws tracing a design on her skin between her breasts and arcing down over her belly, a thin trail of fire left in the wake of his claws' movement. When it was over, she was gasping for breath, lying on her back, her chest heaving.

Take a good look, former slave.

This time Rabishu's voice was barely audible in her head, taunting her with a singsong whisper. He jumped from her body and stood over her, the panther enjoying the helplessness of its prey.

A towering column of water snapped into existence three feet above her, held back by his paw. Water dripped through his claws. A twitch of his claws and the incredible volume of water would be released, pouring on her, filling her lungs, pressing her body flat. She could barely draw breath thinking about it.

Instead of drowning her, the surface flattened as though sliced by an invisible blade. Smooth as a mirror, it hovered over her, so that she could see her reflection. Blazoned from just below her navel to between her breasts was a scale similar to the one from the Egyptian Book of the Dead, used to weigh the deceased person's heart against the feather of truth. The scale's two suspended pans tipped wildly out of balance. One pan was crowded with small figures, mounded on top of each other, tiny but distinct, weighing that side down. The other pan, empty, was as high up as it could go.

A figure detached itself from the crowd and began moving across her skin. As the fiery, miniature person walked, each small step left a print that was raw and oozing blood. She gritted her teeth and watched, both fascinated and horrified. When the figure reached the other pan and climbed in, the change in the balance of the two pans wasn't even perceptible.

The disk of water snapped out of existence. Susannah's vision blurred, nausea gripped her, and she felt an odd shift, as though she'd been pulled forward while everything around her stood still.

You have taken these lives at my direction. Susannah felt pressure on her raw skin on the full pan. Rabishu was resting a sharp claw there. She gasped as pain radiated out from the pressure point.

This is what you have earned by saving the child's life. The pressure shifted to the other pan with the lone figure in it.

"I get it, okay? Get your paws off me."

Did I mention that you will not age in the same way as mortals who measure their lives evenly in the passage of years?

"No, I think you left that part out. Did I mention that you smell like shit?"

Every time you save a life, you grow a little older, but

*not always the same amount and not in proportion to the
number of lives you save. Nor will you be rewarded one for
one for the lives you save. Those decisions are for Anu to
make. The only certainty is that the more you try to balance
the scale, the older you will get.*

Freed of the demon's unearthly weight, Susannah sat up
and cradled her head with both hands, not knowing which
part of her body to try to comfort first, her seared skin or her
dizzy, throbbing head, which was reacting to being yanked
through time, aging her in a second.

*How much did I age? Weeks? Months? Maybe I should
have gotten more details. I could be years older with just
one life saved, and I won't stand a chance of balancing that
scale before I die.*

"Can I change my mind?"

The demon ignored her.

*Your body will surrender to age or fatal injury before you
achieve balance. Then you become . . .*

"I know, your Torture-Me doll or something like that."
If she'd been tricked, she was going down fighting. "You
won't win. I swear you won't."

As she was speaking, she felt the transfer away from the
Rabishu's presence. She found herself sitting on the grass
behind her home, watching as the guillotine completed its
nearly instantaneous drop without her neck in the way.

Susannah got to her feet and pulled her tattered and
bloody shirt around her, grimacing as the material touched
the carving on her skin. In her immortal days, she would
already be healing, the pain lessening with each passing
minute. Now that she'd chosen the mortal path, she was vulnerable to dying from wounds that she would have shrugged
off before. Vulnerable, too, to payments exacted by time on
her appearance and health.

Rabishu had said something about her keeping some version of the powers he'd given her, the ones that gave her an
advantage over humans. Only time would tell exactly what
that meant. Right now, all she wanted was a cool shower,
followed by as much sleep as she could manage.

Free!

Chapter Nine

Present Time

Maliha Crayne, set afire as the witch Susannah Layhem three hundred years ago, lay atop a thick towel on the blazing sand of a California beach. Other beachgoers danced rapidly across the sand and sank with relief into chairs shaded by large umbrellas. Maliha stretched full length in the sun, the prospect of sunburn or skin cancer tucked away at the back of her mind.

She'd needed a new name to go with her ambitious quest. She picked Maliha, an Indian name meaning "strong and beautiful." She pronounced it Mah-LIE-hah, different from the standard pronunciation to claim it as her own. The stately sarus crane from the Indian marshlands, a gray bird with striking red markings, inspired her last name: Crayne.

Over time, she'd discovered what she'd lost when she became mortal. Her tremendous speed of movement had dwindled to the ability to have short bursts of Ageless-level speed. It had to be used with great care, because afterward she could be sluggish and vulnerable, depending on how long she'd sustained the burst. Her healing ability had greatly decreased. Wounds no longer healed as she watched. Maliha could bleed to death like anyone else, and if she was severely injured, she would die before her slowed-down healing could catch up to the task. Her only hope would be to get away alive and recover in a safe place. Only one ability remained at its full Ageless strength: she could still see auras. She suspected that viewing auras was something she'd had from birth, and that Rabishu had only made her aware of it. It could account for her uncanny ability she'd shown as a healer, even if she didn't know how to control it.

Her satellite phone rang, a distraction from sunny bliss. It was Amaro Reese, one of three people bound to Maliha by deep friendship and one other reason. She'd saved each of their lives.

"You picked out your man on the beach yet?"

"I have my eye on a guy in a red Speedo. Matches my swimsuit. How's Rosie?"

"She's doing great. The doctor says any day now."

His sister Rosie was approaching the due date for the birth of her third child. Rosie's husband, Alex Sharp, had escaped on a business trip, leaving Amaro as the prime target of her wrath.

"How is she really?"

Amaro sighed. "She says she is about to burst like an overripe tomato, and if this baby does not come soon, she will take matters into her own hands. Cut herself open, drag out the baby, and sew herself up with a darning needle."

"A lovely picture."

"I'm going to have to talk to Alex about the convenient nature of his recent travel. How's the work coming on your next writing project?" Amaro asked.

"The novel's coming along fine. I've got thirty-five thousand words to go."

"Title?"

"*A Lust for Murder.*"

"Don't wait until the week before the deadline to write it, like you did last time."

"Don't nag the artist. My editor does enough of that."

Maliha wrote pulp crime novels, like the ones from the 1950s, complete with trashy covers, cheap thrills, and drab yellowish paper like the originals. She hadn't planned on it being much of a success, just enough to lend credibility to certain aspects of her lifestyle. The books' popularity had exploded, and even writing two a year, she wasn't keeping up with the demand from readers.

Maliha took off her sunglasses. Speedo was looking her way. She made eye contact, and then stood up and slowly turned her virtually naked back to him to make sure he got both anterior and posterior views seared into his mind. The hawk tattoo on her back, its wings spread across her shoulder blades, moved sinuously when she stretched her arms overhead. She bent over to straighten her towel, offering a different view, then reclined on it again.

She knew Amaro hadn't disturbed her on the beach to talk about the tomato aspect of his sister. "What's up?"

"A couple of code masters have turned up dead. Luis Fernando de Santos and Harry Borringer, aka Hairy. Nando worked regularly for me up until a couple of years ago, Harry filled in a few times on projects that were behind schedule. They were both executed in dark alleys in Atlanta. Hands tied behind their backs, two shots to the back of the head."

Maliha imagined her finger closing on a trigger, feeling the kickback of the gun, firing again as the person began to fall. She'd done such things in another time, another place. Guilt swept over her because she had handed out the same kind of unfeeling death.

"The media's calling it the Geek Murders. Rosie knew Nando too, and she's going crazy. Not only because a man she knew was murdered, but if there's somebody out there killing off hackers, I could be next. It's no secret I've worked with these men. She is not going to let this drop."

Neither would Amaro. The group of hackers that worked with Amaro knew each other well enough to be family. A dysfunctional family, but still.

"I'll head for Atlanta. Be careful, and give my love to the tomato."

Maliha stood up and brushed the remaining sand from her hips and legs. Earlier, she'd been the target of a sand bomb tossed by a couple of horny teens. She'd shown no response, pretending to be asleep behind her sunglasses. Disappointed—did they really expect her to get up and chase them, tits bobbing?—the two left to prowl another section of the beach.

A glance at Speedo showed that he was heading in her direction.

Too bad I have to leave. It would have been a fine afternoon.

Inside a gaily striped beach cabana, a man held the canvas flaps just far enough apart to watch Maliha. He was grateful for the shelter, but not because he avoided the sun. He was conspicuous on the beach, where his muscular body in a swimsuit would attract too much attention. He wasn't the blend-in type.

Watcher followed the sweep of Maliha's hand across her thigh as she brushed away sand. Sometime, when the other business was taken care of, it would be his hand on her thigh, and everywhere else on her unwilling body. Not that it mattered to him if she wouldn't give herself willingly. Most of the women he lay with didn't.

My right. My reward.

A man in a red swimming suit approached Maliha. Watcher frowned and lifted binoculars to his eyes. In the bright circles, he saw that the man was close to her, touching her hair and neck, fingers drawing near the strings that held the upper half of her swimsuit in place. Breathing deeply, he anticipated the untying of the strings, her breasts swaying loose, to be cupped by his large hands. With the front of his suit bulging, Watcher suddenly grew possessive. The man's intentions toward his woman were clear. The hair on the nape of his neck rose and a growl emerged from Watcher's throat. His eyes raked the man's body, assessing the physical challenge he posed and dismissing it. Watcher could already hear the crack of the man's spine across his knee.

After a lingering touch on her shoulder and down her arm, the red-suited man turned away. She'd rejected him. With a grunt of satisfaction, Watcher saw her fold up her towel and walk away. A couple of minutes later his erection had faded enough for him to be in public. Not that he cared, since his formidable equipment was a matter of pride, but he'd learned that it was easier to go along with the local taboos.

Chapter Ten

Maliha paid cash at Los Angeles International, waited impatiently to board the plane, and checked in at an Atlanta hotel by 7 P.M. The evening manager opened the business center for her and soon she had the autopsy photos and reports that Amaro had emailed to her spread out on a table in her suite.

There are prominent bloodstains on the front upper half of the undershirt and the right leg of the shorts. No belt or jewelry is present. The hands are tied behind the back with white cord approximately one-quarter inch in diameter using three successive square knots. . . .

The crime scene in both cases was unremarkable. The victims were killed near their own cars, with the driver's door open as if they'd been persuaded to step out before being trussed. The locations were a half dozen miles apart but had a creepy similarity: dead-end alleys with several large trash receptacles clustered at the end.

She went through the scene in her mind, focusing on Luis Fernando de Santos, the victim Amaro knew better. Not lovers of nightlife, these hackers turned pro typically would be home asleep, working, or gaming in the early morning hours. Nando lived in Tucson, though. He'd arrived in Atlanta less than a day before his death and stayed at a hotel near the airport.

The dry medical language of the autopsy report created a powerful image for Maliha. The right side of Nando's face had been hit with tremendous force from the inside, blowing out everything from his eye to his jaw.

Maliha took a break, surprised to find it was already 11 P.M. She ordered dinner from room service, and while waiting for it, she sat quietly and looked out her window at the expansive view of downtown Atlanta. A two-day-old sliver of moon, a pale eyelash of light, rested on the orange pyramid atop the Bank of America tower. The stars were washed out near the horizon, brighter higher up, but nothing to compare to the spectacle overhead in the parts of the world far from the lights of modern cities. A sharp memory took her to the border between Mongolia and China, two hundred years ago.

Lying on the cold ground wrapped in furs, she'd watched, mesmerized, as the bowl of the sky seemed to hover close over her, the stars floating inches from her face against a background as dark as the inner rooms of a cave. It was as if all sense of distance was gone, and she could reach out and touch the glimmering lights.

Not so in Atlanta in the twenty-first century.

Sighing, she turned from the window at the sound of a knock on her door. Dinner had arrived.

Later, well after midnight, it was time to visit the scenes of the victims' last moments. She might be able to learn far more there than she could from an autopsy report. She decided to run the miles to the first alleyway, letting her muscles grow warm and her legs stretch from the confinement in the airplane and hotel room. Dressed in a form-fitting black outfit, her long black hair in a heavy braid down the center of her back, she walked across the lobby. She waved to the night-desk clerk, who eyed her in disbelief, as though a fantasy had sprung from his head. Once out on the sidewalk, there were few pedestrians to avoid in the early-morning hours. She had no weapons in sight. Keeping to a steady pace, she reveled in the simple human pleasure of running. Although her surroundings were mundane, the exultation in physical activity was the same as she'd felt when she was Ageless, swimming the Nile from Khartoum to the Mediterranean or pacing alongside wild horses in the pioneer days of the American West.

When she reached the first alley, Maliha stood surrounded

by the trash bins, with her feet, as nearly as she could tell from the crime photos, squarely on the bit of pavement where Nando knelt before the fatal shots. Few windows overlooked the space, meaning few opportunities for witnesses. Narrow windows high up on one wall were covered with cardboard or paper on the inside. If there was to be a witness to what happened here besides the killer, it would have to be her. She was going to reenact Nando's death, based on what she'd learned from the autopsy report.

Kneeling down, she put herself in the position a doomed man would be forced to assume. She held her hands behind her as though her wrists were tied and kept her shoulders hunched, trying to keep her head from becoming such a perfect target.

It was a posture common through the ages. In this time and place, guns were used for executions in the criminal world. In earlier times, different parts of the world, the about-to-be-executed rounded their shoulders in a last, vain effort to protect their necks from the sword.

She adjusted her position until the input to her senses suddenly lessened. She'd found the right spot. Her eyes were open, but she relaxed her vision and let the scene go into soft focus.

When a violent death occurred, it left a psychic imprint, or scar, on its exact location. Some people called the phenomenon a ghostly recording. Maliha thought of it as a remnant of the victim's spirit that didn't have the chance to pass into its next destination, as it would in a natural death. While others would walk through the scarred location and feel nothing, Maliha could detect the imprint. Experiencing the imprints was an unexpected side effect of her ability to see the auras, or psychic energy, that surrounded people.

The fragment of Nando's spirit still clinging to the place he died was drawn to her. It coalesced around her and she was into the imprint. Eyes open, she saw nothing, but felt the pressure of a tight blindfold over her eyes, and heard a voice—no, two voices—having an argument. The wind blurred the words, and then the tone changed, as one person gave an order to the other.

Then there were no words at all. Her time, or rather Nando's, was drawing to an end.

She felt her hands tied, even though no bond existed for her, and struggled against it. She tried to stagger to her feet, but a heavy hand on her shoulder pushed her back into the kneeling position. A piercing scream tore through her mind, a shriek of desperation that drowned out the sound of the shots, and then pain lit up the right side of her head, two bright streaks like lightning bolts her head could never contain. She felt pieces of her skull go flying. The blindfold slipped down over her ruined face, and her intact left eye registered for a fraction of a second someone visible in the night, a blocky shape with a gun still pointed in her direction. She thought she heard a sigh of satisfaction.

Maliha crumpled as Nando had done. Her left eye now shut, there was internal darkness, the rush of her last breath leaving her lungs, the stilling of her heartbeat, and then the swooshing of her blood settling in its vessels.

After Nando's death, Maliha remained prone and watched through her now-closed eyelids as the spirit fragment brightened into a glow around her body, and then faded. She got shakily to her feet. The imprint in the alleyway had been released. Wherever it was, the spirit belonging to Nando was whole.

Heading for the spot where the murder of Hairy Borringer occurred, she knew she would find a dark, bleak place where humanity had turned its back on one of its own. But it was her duty to go through it one more time.

To let Harry's spirit use her as a launching pad into the next world.

Chapter Eleven

The flight back to Chicago was uneventful. She brought with her the melancholy atmosphere of the alleyways and the lingering effect of the brutal reenactments of the coders' deaths. She'd pried herself from her apartment building to get her sluggish body and thoughts revved up.

"Ms. Winters," the doorman said, as he tipped his hat to Maliha. "Beautiful evening. I hope you enjoyed your walk."

He made no mention of the fact that her hair was dripping wet and that the T-shirt she wore was plastered to her skin.

"Mr. Henshaw," Maliha said, nodding. "It was an invigorating walk."

She'd swum about fifteen miles in Lake Michigan in about five hours, no record for her but more than enough to serve as the day's exercise. Deeply chilled from the fifty-degree water of the lake, she was looking forward to some pleasant interaction with warm water in her apartment.

"You have a letter. Came by private courier. Hold on a second."

He went inside and rummaged around in his voluminous desk in the lobby. He handed her an envelope. She recognized it as the type Chicago businesses used to "packet" items from one building to another during the day. It was slim, and she wondered if the contents had accidentally been left out.

"Good night, Ms. Winters."

"Good night, Mr. Henshaw."

She'd lived at Harbor Point Towers for fifteen years, and known Arnie Henshaw for every one of them, and that was a typical conversation. There was an understanding between them, though. He didn't say anything about the way she sometimes dressed, the dual knife sheaths that shouted "armed with a dangerous weapon," the scent of blood that trailed her as she breezed past him through the door, or the fact that she didn't look like the forty-year-old woman she should be by now.

In return, she tipped him thirty thousand dollars a month, plus a hundred thousand at Christmas. The humble doorman was a multi-millionaire—she'd given him a few investing tips over the years—and when he retired, he planned to travel far away from women who didn't age.

It was a great understanding.

The lobby was deserted. Once past the doorman, she hurried to the elevator bank in the central core of the building. All three elevators were awaiting her command. Her residence, a custom combination of two condos, was on the forty-eighth floor. The tower was shaped like a *Y*, with the corners sinuously rounded. Inside, she pressed the button for her floor and leaned against the wall, hoping there would be no intermediate stops.

The elevator spit her out with a melodic tone on her floor. Her unit was at the end of a bright hallway. She loved the place, even though it wasn't the grandest spot by far that she'd lived in. That honor belonged to a sheik's desert compound, a place of sere landscapes, great luxury, silks, spices, and horses that ran as though their hooves touched not sand but the heat shimmering above it. The sheik wasn't half bad, either.

One thing she loved about her current home was simply that it was in Chicago. The city overflowed with raw energy and sophisticated culture. Although she lived near the shore of Lake Michigan, she'd been all over the city on foot and by bus, and under and above it, too, on the pedway and the El. Sometimes she rode the El in the middle of the night, watching the goings-on with hooded eyes, alert but appearing asleep. The passengers never knew that with her slumped form in the last seat in the car, they were utterly safe from harm.

At her door, she entered numbers into a keypad and stood still while her retina was scanned. The neighbors all thought her biometric security was over the top, because the building had an excellent security staff, but they had no idea what was behind her door. In any case, they thought her kinky with all the costumes and props she wore, and Maliha didn't discourage the notion.

When her retina passed inspection, the electromagnetic lock clicked open, and the bomb-hardened, steel-plated door slid aside.

No one knew what was behind her door because no one had ever been inside since she'd fortified the place ten years ago. She had another unit in the building where she took visitors, including lovers who thought they were seeing the intimate side of Maliha when they looked at the spare, modern furnishings and décor in her condo on the thirty-ninth floor.

They were wrong. True intimacy was reserved for the forty-eighth floor, where Maliha had combined two units into a spacious safe room, reinforced, including the ceiling and floor, to be bullet, blast, and fire resistant. The windows overlooking Lake Michigan were coated with a film that strengthened them and prevented flying shards of glass in case of explosion.

Inside the sliding door, an entrance foyer dead-ended after a few feet, with a hallway leading off at a right angle. A couple of spotlights in the foyer came on, one pointing down for general illumination, and one pointing into the eyes of the person at the door. Maliha expected it, so she covered her eyes tightly as the door slid open.

Light bathed her face as if a lightning bolt had struck in her foyer, amplified by a metal floor and ceiling. She lunged across the space and pressed a switch on the opposite wall. The switch turned off the deadly surprise—a cascade of darts controlled by a motion sensor, shot from the ceiling at high speed, filling the air wall to wall. If the darts were triggered, the hall door instantly closed behind the intruder and another one slid into place in front, trapping the person in an airtight, bomb-hardened steel box. A small pump sucked out the air in the box, making for a truly unpleasant experience for any living thing caught inside.

Anywhere the safe room shared a wall with the building's hallway or someone else's living quarters, there was a similar arrangement—a buffer zone, steel-plated on all sides, divided into compartments. Her rooms had added so much extra weight that structural enhancements were needed to spread out and carry the load. She'd had to buy out the tenants on the floor below her for that purpose.

Since Maliha was capable of short bursts of inhuman speed, she'd made sure no human could reach the switch on the wall in time to prevent being skewered in the skull. If an Ageless slave tried it, he could survive the darts, but even the Ageless needed to breathe.

If she opened the door from the inside to greet someone, the darts would automatically be disabled, but the person at the door would be blinded, giving her a few seconds' advantage—an eternity for her. After the blindness wore off, and assuming the person was still alive, he would see a wall the color of eggshells, hung with a soothing, pastel painting of flowers of the type that might appear on the wall of a psychiatrist's office. Except for the exterior door and the floor and ceiling of the foyer, no hint of the surrounding metal showed in her haven.

Cell-phone reception would be nonexistent except for the three-watt amplifiers embedded in the walls that solved the problem.

As the door slid shut behind her and locked with an authoritative sound, she kicked off her shoes in the foyer, took a few steps on the cool metal, and then buried her toes in the thick carpet of the room beyond.

"Soft lights."

Rounding the corner, she moved past one of her weapons caches: all manner of swords, knives, and other implements, like throwing stars, crossbows, spears, and sturdy fighting sticks in a variety of lengths. A shillelagh leaned against the wall, a three-section staff nestled at her feet, and a vicious-looking, double-bladed sword gleamed in the spotlights. A trained eye could see the influence of martial-arts study in China, Japan, Korea, Brazil, Israel, and the Philippines. Maliha could have traveled around the world winning competitions. She'd taken the lesson of humility seriously, though, and had no trophies.

There were automatic rifles, semi-automatic pistols, rocket-propelled grenade launchers, laser sights, and thermal vision and night vision equipment. Guns had their place, but Maliha had been trained with edged weapons and they were still her first choice. She affectionately brushed the hilt of her favorite sword as she walked past.

Beyond the weapons cache was a spacious area, over three thousand square feet, with a wall of windows arcing across into a half circle. Blackout cellular shades that matched the eggshell walls covered the windows from top to bottom. She rarely opened the shades to see the view of Lake Michigan. With the deep carpeting dyed to match, the covered windows, and the black ceiling hung with many low-voltage lights, it was a perfect cocoon.

A place to heal, in body and mind. Her haven.

Scattered around the room were display cases containing pieces that would widen the eyes and quicken the pulses of museum curators and private collectors. She walked past the case containing the Great Mogul diamond, named after the builder of the Taj Mahal. It vanished in India in the midst of a bloodbath as Indian shahs fought for succession. For three hundred years, Maliha's hands had been the only ones to cup the diamond, shaped like half an egg, and tilt it to the light to see its small but distinctive flaw.

Ordinarily she would pause to admire it or another of the unique treasures in the room, but tonight her thoughts were elsewhere. At times she focused on what she'd lost and what she now faced, and even the physical pleasure of a night swim didn't drive away the thoughts.

She dropped the envelope the doorman had given her on the kitchen counter and headed for the bathroom, which was divided from the rest of the space by an opaque screen hanging from the ceiling. A quick check in the mirror showed no outward change in her appearance. But there had been those two alarming gray hairs that she'd plucked out last week. It wasn't vanity that caused her to check the mirror every day. It was concern about finishing her task before she lost her youthful strength.

Maliha feared that she was aging internally faster than her appearance showed, and that appearance-wise, she would take large jumps as age accumulated. She couldn't bring herself to think the worst, that she might start aging ten times as fast as she had been, or more. There was no reason to think that her aging would remain in any way predictable. Rabishu had admitted that she wouldn't age as humans did.

She stripped, tossing her clothes into a laundry bag—it cost thousands of dollars more per year in "tips" for her laundry service to ignore the occasional bloodstains and to repair knife holes, supposedly obtained during martial-arts training—and stepped into the shower.

"Low cycle."

Dozens of jets arranged along the walls of the shower sprayed her with warm water, encasing her body in a bubble of fine mist. A delicately scented soap mixed with the water.

She scrubbed her hair with a shampoo scented with herbs, and stood while the shower rinsed her and then dried her with warm air. The shower could be programmed to be a lot more intensive, but that was for another time. She was looking for comfort.

Running her fingers through her damp hair, Maliha considered meditating but put it off. Underneath one of the windows was her sleeping space, where the carpet ended, leaving an exposed neat rectangle of wood flooring. On it was a tatami mat, woven of straw and ninety centimeters long, as required by Japanese tradition. She'd adopted the mat after a lengthy stay in Japan during which she added to her martial-arts skills. She unrolled a thin futon onto the mat and crawled on.

"Lights out."

In this place, she was free to let her thoughts wander, to be vulnerable.

Maliha's heart held more than the ache for the people whose lives she'd taken. It held the longing for a normal life, the kind of life she'd begun in the seventeenth century. A life enriched by a loving husband, a baby, a home that wasn't an armory, the scent of healing herbs defining her life instead of the scent of blood. As a demon's servant, those thoughts had meant nothing to her. Now her heart was open to the prospect of love, but would it be fair to a man, much less a child, to bring them into the kind of life she lived? To share the uncertainty of her life and the necessity of redemption, the randomness of her aging?

Her three close friends were a family of sorts. Amaro, saved from gang violence in Brazil. Xia Yanmeng, a refugee from the Chinese Cultural Revolution who had been in prison with a death sentence when she spirited him out of the country. Hound, a Vietnam vet whom she had saved in the jungle and protected thereafter. Yes, she loved them, because love had so many ways of expressing itself. But the ways of love and trust between a husband and wife and between mother and child seemed just beyond her grasp.

For centuries she'd walled herself off from a serious relationship with a man. She'd been mortal for more than fifty years, and not a brick of that wall had given way.

Tears leaked from her closed eyes.

Her phone chimed, the landline only a few people knew about. She ignored it, letting the call roll to her answering machine.

"Pick up, Winters. I know you're there. If you don't talk to me, you'll never hear about last night, and it was s-w-e-e-t."

Maliha wiped the tears from her eyes and hesitated. It was her friend, Randy Baxter, whom Maliha thought of as her parallel self in the normal world. Randy was twenty-eight, intelligent, not nearly as devoted to her exercise regimen as Maliha, and tended to take her horoscope a bit too seriously. She worked as a business analyst in a Chicago corporation, but intended to quit her job and start a green company any day now. She claimed to be the Mother Earth type and looked the part, favoring long cotton dresses and letting her naturally curly hair cascade over her shoulders. Randy had a fresh, no-bullshit attitude that appealed to men, and she exuded sexiness like a female moth drawing her mate to her with pheromones. A few blinks of her long, golden eyelashes, and men didn't stand a chance.

"Pick up! Five, four, three . . ."

Maliha rolled off the mat and grabbed the phone before Randy finished her countdown.

"How was your date with Rip?"

"Couldn't stand it, could you?" Randy said.

Maliha sighed. Rip was the nickname of Randy's latest guy, so named for his well-developed six-pack. Randy tended to name all of her men by their body parts.

Maliha foraged in the refrigerator and come up with half a bottle of wine.

What else? Of course. Microwave popcorn. Just the thing with wine.

She took a hit from the wine bottle while listening to Randy begin the date report. The microwave binged.

"What're you fixing? You're not making s'mores, are you?"

"No," Maliha said. She was smiling. "Just some popcorn. We'll have s'mores again soon."

"Damn straight we will."

Maliha perched naked on a stool at the kitchen counter, bottle and bowl at hand, and put Randy on the speakerphone. Warmth started to spread through her from the wine.

Another day gone and I'm still alive. Take that, Rabishu, and stuff it!

"So what did Rip do next?"

Chapter Twelve

The buzz of her intercom woke Maliha at 8 A.M. She buried her face and tried to ignore it.

"Ms. Winters, you have a visitor." It wasn't Arnie's voice.

"Mmm."

Correctly interpreting that she'd asked who it was, the voice answered, "It's Mr. Amaro Reese. He's on your approved list."

She lifted her head and told the bellman that she'd expect Mr. Reese in ten minutes.

"I'm afraid he's already on his way up. He has unconditional access."

Maliha dressed and took the stairs down to the thirty-ninth floor, taking with her the envelope Arnie had given her the night before. There was no one waiting in the hall outside her public condo's door, so Amaro had beaten her there. He had a key and didn't hesitate to use it.

In the kitchen of her condo, she found Amaro licking his fingers, having polished off a croissant.

"You have any more of these?" he asked.

"No, but I can have some brought up. They're from the bakery in the building."

He rubbed his belly. She laughed and placed the order, and then ground some coffee beans. Her favorite, Kopi Luwak, was an expensive, ongoing gift from a former lover who hoped to get back in her bed. The coffee was rare because the beans were hand-collected from the Sumatran forest floor after having passed through the intestines of civets, catlike mammals. Amaro liked it, but she'd never told him the origin of the coffee. Some people reacted negatively to the whole idea.

While the coffee was brewing, Maliha noticed the envelope she'd put on the counter and opened it. Inside was a photo of her in her car that must have been taken before she went to Atlanta. It didn't have the grainy appearance of a photo taken through a telephoto lens, so it must have been taken from close by. Drawn boldly across the image was the letter *S*, in red marker.

Creepy. I've had stalkers before. Must have picked up one, maybe a fan of my books. The poor thing has no idea who he—or she—has targeted.

She tucked the photo into a drawer before Amaro spotted it.

The bakery package arrived. She put the croissants on the kitchen table and poured cups of coffee.

"So what do you have so far?" she asked.

"For one thing, Nando and Hairy were doing a lot of work behind my back. I've turned up four clients for Nando and three for Hairy. They had two clients in common, Advanced PharmBots, Inc., and Shale Technology Services. PharmBots is a North Carolina firm, run by Diane Harvey, that makes equipment used in hospitals. ShaleTech is named for its founder, Gregory Shale, and it's here in Chicago. It makes computerized control systems for power stations."

"It's possible that their deaths had to do with one of the clients they had in common. Were the jobs the dead coders did security tests?"

"Break-ins? Nope. These were straight coding jobs. I had a bid in on that PharmBots one. Nando and Hairy undercut my bid."

"I didn't know you were interested in coding jobs."

"I'm not, but the money was good. If I'd gotten the contract, I would've subbed it out to them anyway. You going to talk to Diane Harvey?"

"Sure, I'll talk to her. The Shale guy, too."

"Ask Ms. Harvey about the lawsuit. Something's going

on with a lawsuit, but as far as I got, I didn't pick up any details on it."

She nodded. "No juicy tidbits about Gregory Shale?"

"You're on your own there. Turn on that patented charm of yours."

Maliha drained her coffee cup. "Are you planning to stay with me while we work on this?"

She saw heat flicker in Amaro's eyes at the thought of staying with her, but he extinguished it and looked away. "Do I have to sleep on the couch?"

"Not unless you want to. There's a perfectly good bed in the guest room. Two of them, in fact."

He frowned, but good-naturedly. He was flirting, hoping for an invitation to her bedroom. Rescued from assault by a Brazilian gang when he was sixteen, Amaro had recently celebrated his thirtieth birthday. Since he'd surpassed Maliha's apparent age, he'd begun flirting with her. She wasn't sure if he was serious or just related that way to every woman.

If I had to guess, I'd say he's serious. Mmm, maybe I should talk to Rosie. Make that, talk to Rosie after she has the baby.

"I already checked in at a hotel, but I'll move my stuff over here when I get the chance. The media's latched on to the Geek Murders, you know. I figure it's my job to stand up for the geeks, even though those two sons of bitches stole my code job. It's not like anybody else will. I'm going with you to North Carolina to look into PharmBots. I've got a personal stake in this one."

After he left, Maliha contacted Yanmeng's wife, Eliu, in Seattle. She gave Eliu a brief summary and asked if she could use her press connections to set up an interview for Maliha with Diane Harvey.

"Your articles stink. You should stick to your novels. Speaking of which, don't wait . . ."

"I know, I'll get busy on it."

Maliha opened up her manuscript on the computer and read it for a few minutes to get back into the story. Then she put herself behind the eyes of Detective Dick Stallion and got to work on *A Lust for Murder*. Eight thousand words, one jilted wife, one dead prostitute, and a suspicious fire in Stallion's office later, she came up for air. The book was shaping up nicely.

On an impulse, she'd added a scene inspired by the way she'd met Amaro and Rosie: Stallion rescued a young brother and sister from a street gang. Her reading public loved that kind of episode, the kind where innocence triumphed, with a shove from Stallion.

Good ol' Dick.

The phone rang and caller ID told her it was Randy. This time Maliha answered promptly, since Randy seemed to have a sixth sense that told her when Maliha was at home but letting the answering machine pick up.

"*Ahoj, příteli*," Randy said.

"Hello to you too, friend. Do you want me to continue in Czech?"

"Nope. Just testing you. I sat next to an interesting guy at breakfast at the diner this morning, and he taught me how to say hello in case I go to the Czech Republic. He's well-traveled."

"So he's not from . . ."

"No, silly, he's American. But it made me think of you, because you're well-traveled, too. In fact, he'd be great for you."

"I don't have any trouble finding men for myself."

"So you say, but are they marriage material?"

"What?"

"Haven't you thought about the big three-oh around the corner, girlfriend?"

"Occasionally." *Except the birthday I'm facing is closer to three three-oh.*

"You want to have your family while you're still young enough to chase after the kids, don't you?"

In a moment, Maliha was back in village jail cell, her wrists tied, puffing her breath into her stillborn Constanta in a dark, hopeless place. In a few heartbeats she leaped through the years, to land in the nursery of Candice, sitting in the rocking chair with her own sweet baby lying in her lap, a cruel vision courtesy of Rabishu.

Setting to rest the secret doubts . . . my baby is fine.

Toes . . . check.

Fingers . . .

Randy took the silence for assent. "See, what you need is marriage material, not just those guys you fool around with."

Could I go through it again? With the right man . . . maybe so. But what kind of man is right for me?

"Hello? Anyone still on the line?"

Maliha was jogged back into the present. "You're a fine one to talk about marriage material. Tell me about Rip again."

"Rip, schmip. I'm talking the ring, the gown, the whole thing. You gotta think about it sometime."

"Remember the last time you played matchmaker, Randy?"

"You mean Ollie? Okay, I'll admit he didn't have good hygiene. I never actually met him in person, only saw his photo on Facebook. I met Jake in person, though. He smells like a man and he's really hot."

Randy's words unexpectedly triggered the thought of sweaty bodies glued together, and Maliha felt a rush of sensation radiating from her lower spine that left her wobbly on her legs. She plopped into a chair.

Wow, it has been a while.

"Oh, God, Randy, you're not trying to fix me up with a guy you just met in a diner."

"I didn't say that. Did I say that? You're putting words in my mouth."

"I'm putting words in your mouth because I know you. You didn't say anything to him, did you?"

There was guilty silence on the line.

"Geez, Randy!"

"Um, I hope you're not busy for lunch today."

Maliha took a taxi to Al's Beef on West Taylor in the Little Italy neighborhood. Randy had picked the place, but Maliha approved of the choice. She got there early, hoping she could check out her blind date as he arrived. As she pushed the door open, she swore that this was the last time—*ever*— that Randy was going to rope her into something like this.

A woman who's danced in the arms of princes, and I'm having a blind date with some guy Randy thought was hot.

Jake Stackman was already there. There was no mistaking the red polo shirt and dark, curly hair Randy had told her to look for. She went to his table and he half rose to greet her.

She had to admit Randy was right. He was hot. He had a powerful physical presence, very fit, with broad shoulders tapering to a tight abdomen and lean waist. His hair was as black as hers, naturally curly and a little in need of a haircut, and he had intense blue eyes. His face was ruggedly handsome but not movie-star gorgeous. A small scar on his chin added a dash of intrigue. In her professional opinion, the scar was from a serrated blade, and she would bet it wasn't an accident while eating with a steak knife.

This guy couldn't possibly have any trouble finding dates. Maybe he's got 'em stacked in the freezer in his basement.

At the last minute, Randy had warned her to be careful in case Jake turned out to be a wacko sex-freak serial killer, not that she'd detected any hints of that, of course.

"I can handle myself. You don't have to worry."

"I know . . . it's just, you know, there's CSI *and all the shit in the newspapers, and I don't want some old lady walking her dog to find your body in an alley."*

"No body in the alley," Maliha said, thinking of the delicate touch of Nando's spirit as it gathered around her body, gaining strength. *"I promise."*

"Marsha Winters?"

"Yes." She put her hand out to shake, something not all women did, but she thought it would start them off on an equal basis. After all, he hadn't fully stood up when she came to the table. He gave her hand a hearty shake, and in return, he skipped coming around to push in her chair.

So we've established he's not a gentleman and I'm not a lady.

"I'm Jake Stackman," he said. "To get it over with right away, I'm an agent of the Drug Enforcement Administration, and I don't care if or what you smoke."

"Okay." She sat quietly.

"Aren't you going to tell me what you do?"

"Is this an interrogation, Agent Stackman?"

"Of course not."

"Good. Because I'm hungry and it smells good in here. Predator senses prey, something like that."

He was smiling, and it made his eyes light up.

"What would you like? I'm buying."

This was where most men expected their date to demur and order a salad and a diet soda, claiming they're watching their figure.

"We're here for the Italian beef, aren't we? I'll have a Big Al with hot sauce, an order of fries, and a vanilla milk shake."

The smile got bigger. "I think we're going to get along just fine."

He brought the food to the table and they dug in. His order was the same. Not much was said until Maliha leaned back, slurped up the last of her shake, and patted her tummy.

"I'm a novelist," she said, "to answer your earlier question."

His brow furrowed. "You're *that* Marsha Winters? Pulp-fiction queen?"

"Guilty. Ever been on a blind date before?"

His brow furrowed as he tried to figure out what answer she wanted to hear. "Nope. I'll bet you're as surprised to be here as I am."

"I've been subjected to a few of these things before. The trick is, there have to be specific points when we can walk away without penalty."

"Escape ramps from the highway."

She was pleased that he got it. "One of them was when we first saw each other, and the next one's right now. If either of us wants to stop now, we can take the off ramp. The bill's paid"—she gestured toward her plate—"and that's that. I report back to Randy that you were a nice man but we didn't have much in common."

"No phone numbers exchanged."

"We'd regret having put on expensive lingerie. Well, one of us would."

She'd been waiting for him to check her out. Unlike most men, so far he'd kept his gaze on her face, but the lingerie remark triggered the visual assessment. He took his time with it, letting her see the appreciation on his face.

No shy boy here.

"Ready for the off ramp?" she asked. Neither of them moved. "Okay. Tell me a little about yourself."

"Thirty-two years old. Nonsmoker, social drinker. I'm devoted to my job. This is the first real date I've been on in a year, mostly due to the job. I like cats and classical music. I dread long walks on the beach and I fucking never walk in the rain. Is that enough?"

"Good start. I'm a nonsmoker, social drinker. I'm more of a leopard person myself, and I've loved classical music, well, a long time."

Back when it was just music and hadn't become classical yet.

"What about the beaches and rain?"

"I've had my fill of rain. Beaches are a different story. No long walks, but I've been known to pick up men in skimpy swimsuits and fuck their brains out all night."

Jake's eyes blinked as he processed this. "What beaches? I'll be there."

Another good answer.

Two hours later, the diner had cleared out after lunch, but Jake and Maliha were still sitting there. His hand rested familiarly over hers on the table. Their conversation was low and cozy, creating a sphere of personal space with room for two.

"When will I see you again?" Jake asked.

"If we stay here long enough, we can just order dinner."

"I'm game, but I have some work to do. How about dinner around seven? At my place?"

"I need to make a trip out of town for a few days. How about Friday at eight?"

He took out one of his business cards and wrote his address on the back. "Shall I pick you up?"

"Do I look like I've fallen?"

He laughed and smiled. "I only mention it because my neighborhood isn't what you're used to, being a famous novelist."

"So I'll beat off the muggers with my books. I'll be fine."

They both rose from the table, and Maliha came around to stand next to him, leaving the next move up to him.

He gently tilted her face up and kissed her. The touch of his lips thrilled her. He put his arms around her and pulled her to him. She rested there comfortably, their bodies in full contact, with her cheek against his chest. He bent toward her ear, and she thought he was going to whisper something sweet.

"You taste like hot sauce," he said. "I just missed all the off ramps for this date."

A customer came in, and they broke apart.

"Don't stop on my account," the man said. "I like watching."

Out on the sidewalk, he kissed her again, lightly, as if to seal some private arrangement between them.

Best Italian beef I've ever had.

Chapter Thirteen

Watcher saw her arrive in a taxi at the building she lived in. He was familiar with taxis—driven by arrogant men who rarely bothered to talk in the local language, except when they stuck their hands out to be paid extra for mediocre service.

He always made it a point to learn some of the local language, even when it twisted his tongue and made his head ache to do it.

She said good night to the door guard. He smiled at her in a way that set Watcher on edge.

It had been easy to get her address. He followed her home to find out the building. Waylaying a cleaning woman on her way home, he half bribed, half threatened her to find out Marsha's room number and provide it to him. The next day she did, and he paid her two hundred dollars in case he needed to use her again.

Moving around to the back of the building, he waited until a delivery truck arrived. When the driver went inside carrying boxes, Watcher grabbed a few boxes from the open end of the truck and took the same path. Inside there was a man at a desk who barely looked up when Watcher came in.

"Better catch up," the man said. "Your partner's gone up in the freight elevator already."

"Thanks. I'll hurry."

Watcher did hurry, at least until he got around the corner out of sight from the desk. He located the elevator and left the boxes there. The driver would wonder who had done him a favor, but probably wouldn't question it. There were many servants in the building.

Watcher found the fire stairs, almost never used in a tall building with elevators. He jogged to the thirty-ninth floor, enjoying the exercise, and sat down to wait.

At 3 A.M., he cracked open the fire door and made sure no one was in the hall. Once at her doorway, he was inside in less than thirty seconds. Watcher was skilled with his hands in small ways, as well as in large, murderous ones.

He stood in the dark, filling his lungs with her scent.

"No need to rush." He liked the sound of his whispered voice bouncing softly off her walls.

He used a flashlight to examine the room and take in every detail. He was capable of assessing a scene quickly, spotting enemies or vulnerable places. It was a native skill honed by years of necessity. He saw it all: the dented cushion on the chair that held the shape of her ass, the blank, dusty face of a TV hardly ever used, the spoon she'd left on the counter after stirring her morning coffee. A barbarian drink. Tea was the only hot drink that passed his lips.

The spoon on the counter had probably touched her lips. He picked it up and pressed it to his mouth, licking it.

She would be his. She was *already* his, but the time had not come to take her.

Watcher's thoughts grew hot. He hurried toward the bedroom.

No need to rush.

She was a capable warrior, and he was in her home den. He had to be careful. Moving with the stealth granted to him, he slid toward the dark form on the bed. He knelt at the bedside and remained there, unmoving, for fifteen minutes to make sure he hadn't disturbed her. While killing her as she abruptly awakened held a certain appeal, he had other plans for this night.

As his eyes grew adjusted to the dark, the faint glow of a nightlight in the open closet allowed him to see her form in detail. Lying on her back, she'd tossed aside her cover, exposing most of her body. She slept almost naked, with delicate underwear covering the mound between her legs. Her breasts were exquisite, and he longed to take them into his powerful hands. Her scent was powerful this close, the intoxicating odor of the wild, primal creature that she was— the one who belonged to him.

He felt the swelling in his sweatpants and slipped them down. With one hand he began to pleasure himself, and with the other he circled his fingertips on one of her nipples and then the other. She moaned a little and shifted, but didn't wake. He did it again and again, light as a feather, and was rewarded with the sight of her nipples responding to his touch.

His hand traveled like a puff of air across her belly and reached the band of her underwear. His fingertips slipped under the band and felt the soft mat of her hair. Inches more, where warmth rose from her and her womanly scent flowed like water from a spring, only inches more to the prize, but he gently pulled his hand back. Even through his sensual intoxication, he knew that touching her there, pressing his fingers inside, would waken her and she'd go for the gleaming knife on the table by the bed. He'd have to kill her quickly and quietly, and that was no good. He wanted his time with her in a place where screaming didn't matter.

Instead he put his hand softly on the outside of her underwear, covering what belonged to him and what, when the time came, he would not touch so gently.

His arousal couldn't wait any longer. Watcher rose from her bedside and slipped out of the bedroom. He sat on the shape of her ass on the chair and gave himself over to sensation.

In the staircase, he waited until she left in the morning. To his amazement, a man left her apartment soon after she did.

There had been no man there when he entered at 3 A.M. He was sure of it. No man's odor had mixed with hers.

One coffee cup. One spoon.

Someone had arrived after he left, then. *Who lets himself in at that time and leaves after she does in the morning? A lover.*

His thoughts filled with anger. He took the risk of reentering her place to check. There was no man's smell in her bedroom, no smell of sex on her sheets. In a spare room, he found a suitcase and a computer.

Not a lover, then. A lover could not have resisted joining her, the way she looked on the bed.

Before he left, he plucked her worn panties from the hamper. Then it was back to discipline. Back to waiting.

Chapter Fourteen

Peru, Present Time

Manco Miguel Serrano sat back on his haunches, pulled out a handkerchief, and wiped his dusty, sweat-streaked face. He wore a wide-brimmed hat with a cloth hanging down in the back to cover his neck. The cloth had started out wet for coolness, but after four hours in the desert sun, it was as dry and stiff as a board. A hot wind swept across the site where he worked, tossing sand and dirt in his face.

Manco was working near the village of Caral, Peru, about 120 miles north of Lima and twelve miles in from the Pacific coast. He was an archaeologist, lured there by the prospect of working on an ancient Peruvian mound-building culture that was turning out to be the cradle of civilization in the Americas, as Mesopotamia was for Southwest Asia, the Nile River Valley was for Egypt, and the Yellow River Valley was for China. The existence of the mounds had been known since 1905, but because there was no gold, no flashy artifacts, no writing, and no pottery, the remote site didn't attract attention. Recent study led to the discovery that some settlements were as old as 2,600 B.C.E., overlapping with the period of ancient Sumer.

Manco was looking for carved, human-shaped figurines in a small group of houses excavated to reveal several levels of "floor," indicating that the site had been used for homes. On his knees for hours at a time, Manco poked through a carefully marked grid with a small trowel, a whiskbroom, and a small brush. He loved it. What kept him going in the heat, with his knees aching, was the idea that the next small trowel of dirt he shifted might reveal an artifact—something shaped by human hands over 4,500 years ago.

He took a few deep swallows from his water bottle and got back to work. He planned to knock off early and catch up on his paperwork of diagramming and formalizing his field notes. Still, he kept at it a little longer. There was always the chance that something would turn up before then. Manco continued his slow digging, then he felt it—his trowel gently touched something, and it didn't feel like a rock. He worked the tip of the trowel around it slowly, and then used his fingers to scrap away dirt and gauge the size of the object he'd come upon. The figurines he was searching for were small enough to fit in his palm. What he was tracing out was big: eight inches tall or more.

Even with his excitement growing, he kept his scientific discipline. He recorded the grid coordinates and his first impressions of his find in a notebook before he went any further. Then he carefully brushed away more dirt and was stunned by the fact that it wasn't a figurine he was uncovering.

It was a piece of pottery.

Manco's heart was in his throat. The Caral-Supe people were preceramic. There wasn't supposed to be any pottery, not at this depth in the excavation, where it couldn't be a random find from a later period. Yet the more he eased away the dirt, the more certain he was that he'd found a pot. He bent over and blew away dirt.

A few inches of rounded surface appeared, with what looked like cuneiform on its surface, from a civilization that had no writing other than strings tied in knots for counting. Manco closed his eyes for a moment and tried to calm his leaping heart. He ran his hand over the exposed area reverently, feeling the marks incised into the clay with his fingertips. The edges were sharp and distinct, so preserved they were almost . . . fresh. He took photographs, and then exposed more of the pot until its rounded shape emerged. The heat forgotten, his discomfort forgotten, he worked to clear the dirt away so he could lift the pot from the ground.

He took one last set of photographs and made comments and a drawing in his field notebook. Then he held his breath, cupped his fingers in the trench of dirt around his find, and lifted it.

There were a few chips around the top edge, but otherwise the pot was in superb shape. It was full of caked dirt, which he dared not remove in the field for fear of taking chunks of pot with it.

Excitement rippled through his body, banishing his fatigue. Manco realized he was holding the discovery of his lifetime, the mark every archaeologist wants to leave on his field whether he admits to such vanity or not. He went over to his collection kit and came back with a padded case compartmentalized to hold small figurines. He tore the internal dividers out, leaving a bigger space, and fit the pot into it.

He had been working in a highly focused way for over two hours since his trowel had first encountered the pot. Tomorrow he would bring the piece to the attention of the regional archaeological museum in Huacho, a dozen miles away—with his name attached, of course.

That was for tomorrow. Tonight the pot was all his. Already he was poring over the possibilities—the mysteries—that lay before him to solve. Instead of returning to the camp with the others, he took the last bus into Huacho to stay in a hotel. He used the excuse that he didn't feel well and might need to see a doctor, and there were better medical facilities in the town. As the bus made its way down the dirt road, the driver honking and gesturing out the window at goats and sheep that strayed across the road, Manco sat with the padded case cradled in his lap and his mind soaring.

Chapter Fifteen

Advanced PharmBots, Inc., was located in Research Triangle Park in North Carolina. Maliha flew to the Raleigh/Durham International Airport, rented a nondescript car, and drove out on I–40. She found that PharmBots shared a building with a pharmaceutical company specializing in treatments for rare diseases: orphan drugs. The three-story glass-and-steel building was surrounded by a band of trees thick enough to be called a forest.

The lobby was decked out with a fountain, chair groupings, and numerous plants that failed to generate the intended hospitable atmosphere. Maliha strode up to the PharmBots desk. She was wearing a conservative skirted suit, had her hair in a polished French twist, and had a leather briefcase with a strap that went over one shoulder. Eyeglasses completed the look. She felt like a female Clark Kent.

The middle-aged woman at the desk looked up from her work at a computer.

"May I help you?" The North Carolina accent softened the fact that she no doubt had fifteen ways to notify security of trouble.

"Marsha Winters, journalist with the *New Age Tech Journal*. I have an appointment with Diane Harvey."

The woman checked her computerized appointment book and nodded.

"Your ID?"

Maliha produced press credentials from her briefcase.

The receptionist glanced at them, compared the photo to Maliha's face, and buzzed her through the door leading to the company's offices.

Too easy.

Behind the door, she encountered a metal detector and several guards who put her false identity through its paces. Fortunately, Marsha Winters's credentials were solid. *New Age Tech Journal* checked out as legitimate, and the photo that popped up on the guard's monitor matched her face, since her Winters identity had a presence in numerous databases, governmental and private. She silently thanked Amaro. Much background work went into the identities she used. It was easier in the old days, when there was no such thing as an instant ID check. But Maliha not only changed with the times, she made sure she was on the leading edge of the change.

A guard's phone call summoned a young assistant to escort her to Diane's office on the third floor. As they went up the elevator, the assistant chatted about Maliha's trip, the great weather, and what *New Age Tech Journal* was all about.

"The title says it all." In response to a request for a sample copy, she shook her head. "We're a startup. First issue comes out in December."

"I'll look for it, and here we are."

Maliha was ushered into a waiting room with a single door to the inner sanctum. Although there were several chairs, she was alone with the camera. She grinned up at it. She'd been looking forward to grilling Diane's secretary, but there wasn't one.

She'd barely warmed the seat of her chair when she was invited into the office.

Diane Harvey was standing behind the desk in her office. As Maliha came in, Diane crossed the room and shook her hand with a firm, testing grip. Maliha tested back, resulting in a slight narrowing of Diane's eyes.

To Maliha's surprise, Diane was dressed in jeans and a soft ivory sweater that followed the curves of her body. No power suit here. Her figure was voluptuous, with red lipstick the only makeup on a pale face with piercing gray eyes. Her hair was long, wavy, and blonde. Diane was less than thirty years old and looked more like a Vegas dancer than a CEO.

Maliha felt overdressed.

"Have a seat. Care for some cold water? I always keep some on hand."

Maybe she was from Vegas. Locals there always had a bottle of water close by.

Maliha nodded. She used the time while Diane retrieved a couple of bottles from a small refrigerator to check out the space. Number one on the list: There were none of the cameras she'd seen in the halls. Evidently Diane didn't want her private conversations to end up as part of the company's security records.

It was a large corner office—third floor, southeast corner, Maliha noted—and was decorated in an office superstore style of furniture, the kind that came flat in a box and had to be screwed together. In startling contrast to the indifferent furniture, a spotlighted display case held a collection of Moche portrait pots. They were clay drinking cups styled after the faces of real people, complete with emotional expressions, created by the Moche people of ancient Peru. If they were authentic, the pots were up to two thousand years old and almost certainly had been smuggled into the United States. She was willing to give the woman the benefit of the doubt and assume the pots were skillful reproductions. Still, the display reminded her of the priceless objects in her own haven, collected over centuries.

Diane didn't seem like a woman mired in the past. She pictured Diane late at night, putting together her office furniture from flat, heavy boxes, screwing together the display case and arranging the pots on the shelves. The images didn't fit.

Even if they were reproductions, the Moche pots didn't belong in this sterile office. Their faces showed the entire range of human emotions, including some that Maliha couldn't imagine registering on Diane's face, like empathy and love.

Her mind flew back to the time she'd spent in the company of an Egyptologist, who told her that the lives of the ancient people he studied were more real to him than those of his own family. When he got a telegram saying that his wife had died, he made a brief note in his journal and went on with his excavating. She'd heard that, years later, when he died, he left instructions to have his body mummified. His surviving relative, a son, couldn't do it. He brought his father's body back to England to be buried in the churchyard next to his mother. The old man would have been heartbroken if he'd known.

Now that was living with both feet in the past.

Was Diane like that? If so, how could Maliha exploit that in turning up any link to the dead coders?

Maliha noticed there were two computers in the office. The one on Diane's desk sprouted the usual network cable. The laptop on a table, its darkened screen showing a company screensaver, had no such connection, although it could be wireless. If not, Diane may keep information on it that she didn't want available to any network. An isolated computer couldn't be remotely hacked, but had to be physically breached. Maliha's curiosity was tweaked by the built-in thumbprint reader for secure access by one individual.

A computer for the office and one for travel? Maybe. Or this one's chock full o'secrets.

Seated across from Diane Harvey, Maliha was given a thorough inspection as she twisted the cap off her bottle of water.

"Have we met before? I have the feeling I know you."

"No, I'm sure we haven't."

Diane shook her head, her small lips pursed in concentration. Before she could pursue that line of thinking, Maliha tossed a little bomb in her direction.

Not literally, although she could lay her hands on the two plastic knives concealed in her briefcase in a split second.

"I've been admiring your display case. Aren't those pots supposed to be in a museum? Did you get them in an auction or something?"

Diane's eyes narrowed. "Why are you interested in those? I thought you were here to interview me about the company's products."

"Just thought it would make a great sidebar to the main article. Personal interest and all that. Is there some reason you don't want to talk about them?" She smiled sweetly.

Diane leaned back in her chair and relaxed. "Of course. Personal interest. My grandfather was a collector when he was alive, bless his soul. He was from a time when people weren't as sensitive to a country's cultural heritage as we are now. When he died, I donated his collection to a museum with the condition that they study the items and then return them to their countries of origin. The pots were his favorites, and I asked for reproductions of them to keep. They aren't stamped 'Made in China' on the bottom, but they might as well be. That one on the third shelf, second from the right— he always claimed it looked like him."

"Great stuff. I'd like to take some pictures."

Diane shrugged. Maliha removed a small digital camera from her briefcase and snapped away.

When she came back to her chair, Diane was peering at her.

"I never forget a face. I know I've seen you."

Maliha sighed. She'd have to own up or risk alienating Diane and losing the rest of the interview.

"I write novels. You've probably seen my picture in the book section of the newspaper."

"That's it, then." Diane stiffened a little, skepticism plain on her face. "Why would a successful author want to come here to interview one about hospital equipment?"

A question I am prepared for, thanks to Clark Kent.

"Since I was young, I've wanted to be like Lois Lane. You know, girl reporter. I was doing a spec freelance article on new fantasy authors and it occurred to me that I could write as well as they could and I have no shortage of ideas. I make a good living now, good enough that I can indulge my dreams. And here I am."

To signal the end of the pleasantries, Maliha took out a voice recorder and placed it on the desk between them.

"Do you mind?"

"You will be sending me the final version of your article before publication, correct?" Diane's voice was still guarded. "The sidebar too?" She hadn't swallowed Maliha's "girl reporter" story, but was willing to play along for the time being.

"Sure. Why don't you start by explaining what products Advanced PharmBots makes? I like to get that straight from the source."

"Ever been in a hospital, Ms. Winters?"

"Yes." Maliha lied. No way could she let a doctor near a body that healed wounds by itself or was carved mysteriously in the front. Too much explaining to do. "And please call me Marsha."

"Diane here. Those little cups that your medicine came in may have been filled by one of our machines. Our dispensing machines are filled by pharmacists with bulk medicines from pharmaceutical companies. Physicians enter drug orders into a central computer, and our machine responds by grabbing one pill from here, one from there, according to the physicians' orders, and putting them in a cup with a patient ID label on it. Trays of cups are loaded into our robotic delivery cart, which visits all the nursing stations. PharmBots machines are robots with a very responsible job—getting the correct medicine to every patient at the right time. We can handle liquids and solids."

Sounds like a waste treatment plant.

"I've always wondered what happens if the nurse drops the cup and stepped on the pills."

Diane raised a finger as though lecturing Maliha. "Ah, a wasted dose. A PharmBots machine can prepare another cup, but we track all the lost medicine. Excess wasted doses can mean the nurse, or someone else at the station, is selling the drugs. Here, let me get you some product literature. They'll help you get the terminology right when you're writing your article."

Diane went to a round conference table and retrieved some colorful brochures. While her back was turned, Maliha switched water bottles. She'd been careful to drink hers down to the same level as Diane's.

"I'd like to see some PharmBots in action." Maliha said, tucking away the brochures. "Mind if I take this with me for later?" She held the switched water bottle up.

Diane waved permission, and the bottle, tightly capped, went into Maliha's briefcase, too.

"We have a demonstration facility on the second floor. When we're finished here, I'll have one of my assistants give you a tour."

Maliha continued to ask questions of interest to her hypothetical readers, such as how pharmacists felt about the whole robot thing, some prominent clients, and costs. Finally, it was time to move into the real reason for Maliha's trip.

First, she examined Diane's aura, which was yellowish orange with a few swirls of brown and dull green that muddied the color. Diane was intelligent, but she used her intellect for gain and personal ambition, indicated by the brown. The presence of the unattractive green threw some deceit into the mix. In other words, a typical aura for a person in her position.

"Diane, what can you tell me about the lawsuit?"

Leaping red flames appeared in Diane's aura. *Anger, big-time.*

A storm gathered in Diane's eyes. She reached out and turned off the voice recorder.

"Is that what you're here for? To splash that around the media? That's not responsible journalism. Nothing's been released. Who hired you—MedSort? Bob O'Day's just the type."

"I don't know any Bob. I just thought you might want to take the opportunity to get your side out to our readers."

"I can't say anything about it. My legal staff would be all over me. You know that, knew it when you waltzed in here." Her voice had grown icicles. She grabbed the recorder off the desk and plunged it into her center desk drawer. "You won't need this."

Whirls of gray and dark green appeared in Diane's aura. *She's afraid of something and she's being deceptive.*

"You don't have to get riled up. I thought I'd be doing you a favor. What are you afraid of? Surely, your company has faced lawsuits before. Everybody in the health industry gets hit with them."

"I want you out. You've deceived me from the start. Girl reporter, hah. Who's paying you? What have you got to gain out of this?" She half rose in her seat. "I'll sue the hell out of you." Diane stabbed a button on her phone. "Larry, send security in here."

Maliha played the role of indignant reporter and protested her innocence. Security arrived in less than fifteen seconds—*do they listen outside the door, or what?*—and escorted Maliha roughly from the building with warnings not to return.

She did return, though, during the still hours when the sun favored other continents with its light.

Dressed in black, Maliha ran in darkness from her hotel to the PharmBots building. She wore a waist pack that carried everything she needed, including a handgun brought along in checked baggage. She was proficient with firearms, but had no love for them. And she'd yet to have a battle-axe or a throwing knife misfire.

The humid air had a velvety feel and carried the sweet scent of crape myrtle—summer didn't give up easily in North Carolina. She approached the building, keeping to the shadows of trees that ran in rows through the parking lot.

Maliha pulled a launching gun from her waist pack and fired it at the band of steel that framed the third-floor southeast-corner window. Black 5.5 mm Vectran cord snaked toward the building, headed by a powerful vacuum cup. When the cup hit the metal, air whooshed out of it and it flattened against the steel band, creating a powerful seal.

Maliha moved up to the side of the building and clipped a cord with a foot strap to the launcher. Slipping her left foot into the strap, she pressed the rewind button on the launcher.

A small, silent electric motor pulled her up the side of the building. From a distance, she would have looked like a black spider rising on a silk strand.

At the third-floor window, she stopped the winder and clamped dual vacuum cups connected with a handle onto the glass. Gone were the days when she would just crash through the glass. Using a pen-sized laser cutter carefully calibrated for depth, Maliha incised a neat thirty-inch circle in the double-pane bronze glass, which she removed using the handle. No alarm had gone off when she cut the glass. Who needed an alarm forty feet aboveground?

Maliha lowered the circle of glass inside the room and leaned it against the wall. Then she kicked off from the foot strap with a powerful thrust of her leg, threaded her body through the opening headfirst, hit the floor, rolled once, and came to her feet.

The Black Ghost was in.

She waited to see if there was going to be any reaction to her entry. If there had been a guard outside in the hall at just the moment she hit the floor, the guard may have heard something. Waiting silently, she counted the seconds by the steady beat of her heart; after 120 beats she decided no one was coming.

Maliha assumed that Diane would have taken the laptop home, and she'd be searching for disks she could take with her, or attempting to copy data from the desktop's hard drive. Instead the prize sat across the room from her, smugly displaying the Advanced PharmBots logo. She approached the laptop as if it were going to sprout legs and take off like a frightened antelope.

She took a small lamp from her pack, fastened its headband on, and flipped the switch. A bright, narrow beam illuminated her work.

There was no lockdown strap on the laptop. She lifted one corner warily with a gloved finger and saw that there was a small cable running out of the bottom and into a recessed area of the table, from which it dropped into the hollow leg of the table and disappeared into the floor. An alarm. If she pulled the laptop toward her or picked it up, the connection would be broken and an alarm would go off at the guard station.

Maliha removed her right glove and pressed her thumb, wrapped in a thin membrane that carried Diane's print, on the biometric pad. She held her breath. Her fabrication woman, DeeDee Barnes, had told her the thumbprint on the water bottle Maliha had taken from Diane's office wasn't of the best quality. Success was not guaranteed. It had cost Maliha several thousand dollars for the rush job and the personal courier service to Phoenix and back, the water bottle going one way and the print shield coming back. She could do this kind of work herself these days in her own condo, but preferred to leave it to DeeDee, who needed the money. When the woman died or became unable to do the work, Maliha would do her own fabrication.

She exhaled in relief when the computer displayed a desktop and said, "Welcome, Diane." She put her glove back on, slipped a palm-sized, portable hard drive from her pack, and connected it to one of the laptop's USB ports. She found that once into the laptop, the files on it weren't password-protected or encrypted.

Very sloppy, but easy for me.

Maliha began copying all the information from the computer's hard drive. While she waiting for the copying operation to complete, she went over to the display case and studied the Moche pots. She couldn't be positive, but on close inspection, she thought they were authentic. One of the sculpted faces looked familiar from an article in an archaeological journal from a year ago about smuggled antiquities.

She was so absorbed in looking at the display case that she barely heard the click of the lock on the outer room, the waiting area where she'd mugged for the security camera. Her logon activity must have been reported—*that cable was more sensitive than I thought*—and noticed by an alert guard, who realized Diane Harvey wasn't signed in to the building but her computer had been disturbed.

Maliha snatched up the portable drive and stuffed it into her pack. The copy process hadn't completed, but whatever she'd captured, it would have to do. To get out of the room, she was going to have to make a jump for the climbing cord through the opening she'd cut in the glass. She ran toward the window, ripping the headband away and flinging the small light across the room. Then she yanked a Sig Sauer P226 from her pack. The familiar weight of the weapon was reassuring.

The office door opened. As she crossed the room, several red dots danced across her chest. At least three men had rushed into the room, weapons drawn. She could make out their silhouettes in the light coming from the hall, dimmed for the night. She lined up the glowing green dot on the front blade of her P226's night sight with the two dots on either side of the rear notch, and squeezed off a shot. She'd tried for a shoulder hit, and saw the impact twist and drop one of the men.

Maliha narrowed her focus to her escape route. If she missed the cord, she'd have less than two seconds of time in the air to regret her clumsiness before introducing her face to the concrete.

Running across the room, she turned around long enough to fire off another couple of shots, then dived through the circle in the window. It had been big enough coming in, but with her hasty exit, it seemed like an opening she could barely slip through.

A bullet grazed her left shoulder and another hit her right thigh just as she launched herself at the open space. The glass shattered and spun out into the night in a shower of fragments. Tossing her pistol ahead of her, she had a fraction of a second to grasp the cord, obscured by the flying glass.

One hand—missed.

Her left hand found the cord and closed on it. Momentum swung her around the cord. She smashed into the side of the building.

A bullet came whizzing through the window opening.

She eased her grip on the cord just a little and began sliding down. Friction began burning away the palm of her glove. The ground was coming up fast.

She closed her hand tightly to slow her descent, and her

palm felt as though she'd grabbed a hot poker. She came to an abrupt stop and let go of the cord for the eight-foot drop onto the glass pieces below her. She scooped up the P226 and took off running, her thigh wound protesting.

Bullets were coming down from the window, thudding into the ground.

She ran toward the trees on the parking lot. There was shouting, and suddenly bright lights were coming toward her—a car's headlights. She swerved just in time, feeling the wind of the car's high-speed passage. Tires screeched as the driver did a 180 to take another try at her, and a bullet flew past her head. She aimed at the driver's side and emptied the Sig's magazine. The car careened wildly, increased speed from the weight of a dead man's foot on the pedal, headed for the side of the building, and crashed. Heat from friction, gasoline vapor from the smashed tank, and oxygen did what chemistry predicted. Brilliant orange and white flames reached high in the air.

Gunfire from the window above reminded her to keep moving. Nearing the woods at the edge of the parking lot, she glimpsed something crouching under the trees and a quick impression registered.

Animal. Big. What?

Pulling her eyes away from the woods, she saw that two more sets of headlights were heading toward her. Any distraction meant she'd be smeared across the pavement.

Time to pour it on.

Maliha called on the burst of speed she still possessed, the supernatural speed of the Ageless, available to her only for seconds. A blur of motion, she ran directly toward one of the cars, she vaulted into the air, right foot landing on the hood, left on the roof, right on the trunk, and then back to ground. She maintained the speed until she slipped under the canopy of trees.

Pausing to rest, leaning against the trunk of a tree, Maliha steadied her breathing. She recalled how effortless the speed had been as a servant of Rabishu.

A doe ventured out into the road ahead, followed by her spring-born fawn. Susannah maintained her speed, judged

the moment, and launched herself into the air, arcing over
the two deer. The larger one startled as Susannah's foot
lightly grazed the fur on her back. It was an exhilarating
moment.

Mindful of the lurking presence she'd seen in the woods, she made sure her movement remained quiet, tracking through the woods without so much as a snap of a branch. The swath of woods gave way to a park with a playground, and beyond that, a city street. When she was certain no one had followed her, animal or security guard, she called Amaro. As long as he'd followed her to town, she might as well hitch a ride from him. He said he'd meet her on a street corner nearby in a few minutes.

She assessed the toll. The shoulder wound was minor and would heal well. The embedded bullet in the back of her thigh hurt and was going to have to be dug out, but she'd had worse since becoming mortal. The skin of her left hand had been abraded by the rope, but the glove had taken the worst of it.

She'd left behind blood when she was shot, and blood and tissue from her palm on the cord. It wasn't a clean operation. If Amaro couldn't ferret out her information in police files and wipe it out, she'd have to give up being Marsha Winters and reinvent herself.

Should she have fought her way out? If she'd taken out the three guards who'd swarmed into Diane's office—she could have—she might have made her exit in a more controlled manner. But extra time that helped her in the office would also have helped whoever was in that car that tried to ram her. There could have been several people waiting for her as she descended the rope.

Diane Harvey couldn't fail to make a connection between the impudent "reporter" in her office in the afternoon and a break-in that night. Security cameras in the building had captured her image during that earlier visit, and as a bestselling novelist, she wouldn't be difficult to track down.

She watched for Amaro to arrive, and when he did, she sank glumly into the passenger seat. They drove in silence to the hotel. Amaro's hand crept over and gently covered hers.

As an Ageless woman, she'd been utterly alone, in spite of her lovers. She kept her hand under his, thinking how good it was to have friends.

Replaying her escape, she focused on the shape in the woods, trying to glean more from her memory.

Could it have been the stalker? Just my luck: I'm being stalked by Bigfoot.

When they were back at the hotel, Amaro dug out the bullet. She took a shower, slapped a 4 x 4 pad on her thigh, and held it on with gauze. Wrapped in one of the hotel's plush bathrobes, she went out to talk to Amaro.

"You okay?"

"Sure. It's going to hurt to sit down, but that will be gone in a few hours."

Amaro asked her about evidence left at the scene.

"DNA for certain. No fingerprints inside. The climbing cord, launcher, and vacuum cup were left behind, but those weren't custom. Pieces of a glove. The vague possibility of a palm print on the cord, but I doubt it."

"I'll scrub out all the info on the DNA, or at least mess with it as much of it as I can," Amaro said. "It's going to be tricky. I have to make it look like you checked out of this hotel and flew back to Chicago right after the interview at Advanced PharmBots. That way, you would have been out of town at the time of the late-night break-in. I can alter all those records. It'll look like you arrived back at your condo, let's say four P.M. so we can get the story straight. The doorman?"

"No problem. Arnie can arrange that even if he's not on duty then. I can't let anyone see me, though, for two or three days. This hand is in rough shape and the bullet wounds will have to be gone. The shoulder's no problem, but my thigh is going to take a while. My skin heals first, though, and then whatever damage is underneath it, so the thigh wound is going to look better than it actually is in a few days. My best alibi is to show no wounds. I'll have to go on a writing trip somewhere, and I'll make sure my editor doesn't know where I am. That's not unusual."

"Okay, it's all shaping up. You need to get some sleep while I get all this started."

Maliha's eyes were closing. She needed rest—she healed faster when she slept or meditated.

Amaro patted the cushion of the couch next to him. "Over here."

Maliha was too sleepy to argue. She went over to the couch and he put his arm around her. She snuggled next to his chest.

The steady warmth of his body felt good. Amaro tenderly kissed the top of her head. She drifted into sleep and back in time.

1994

In the Cidade de Deus, a *favela* in Rio de Janeiro, most people were poor. Sex and drugs were sold on every street corner, and the police were reluctant to patrol the streets because of violence by well-armed gangs—violence that could turn against them in moments.

It was not on the Top Ten list of places for tourists to go.

That didn't deter Maliha. Concealed in a leather sheath around her waist was a flexible sword, wrapped twice about her waist, its hilt disguised as a decorative buckle on a deadly belt. The whip sword had two double-edged blades that uncoiled when she tugged on the hilt. The blades were sharp-edged bands of thin steel that weren't as floppy as a whip or as rigid as a typical sword blade. As Maliha swung them around, the blades flicked at a throat or a wrist. The whip sword was dangerous to its operator as well; one misstep in its use, and the blades could slit her own throat.

Maliha bristled with edged weapons, and she gave off vibes that it wasn't a party costume. Patrolling by law enforcement was light to nonexistent in the *favela*, and no resident would alert them to her armament. Most people she encountered gave her a wide berth. The ones who didn't, who gravitated to her out of a kinky attraction, rapidly learned to keep their urges in check.

She was heading to a meeting with a man and a mandolin.

Davi Luiz Guterres was a descendant of a Portuguese artisan highly skilled in mandolin making. Maliha had bought her first mandolin from that artisan in 1790. She'd lost it during a cholera outbreak in London in 1831, and recently had decided to commission another one from the same family of luthiers, if they were still in business. It turned out the family had moved to Brazil and still carried on the craft. Davi had moved into the *favela* when it was still a respectable neighborhood. Seventy-five years old and stubborn, he had no intention of moving his shop just because there was a little crime on the block.

Davi had had her play several different instruments to get a feel for her skill level, and then told her to leave a deposit and come back in a year. The year was up.

A noisy scene in an alley attracted her attention. The alley widened and dead-ended in a small plaza. A group of young men had a girl of about thirteen on the ground, her blouse ripped off and her skirt hiked up to her hips. As Maliha watched, a man bent over her frightened form and sliced off her panties. She was about to be raped by one or more of the gang members. Off to the side, two muscular men restrained a teenaged boy who was screaming obscenities.

The auras of the two young people assailed her with helplessness, outrage, and fear. The mandolin would have to wait.

Maliha eased into the plaza. With their attention focused on the girl, no one spotted her, and the game continued.

A young man strutted toward the restrained boy and said something that Maliha couldn't make out. The words heated the captive even further, and he struggled furiously to free himself. The man doing the taunting revealed a broken beer bottle and slashed the prisoner across the arm with it. Then he went back to the girl, who was held down by several gang members groping at her breasts. The leader knelt in front of her and made in-and-out motions in the air with the beer bottle. Then he jabbed the broken neck of the bottle toward the girl's vagina.

The bottle never even made it close to the girl's body. Maliha was on the leader before any of the gang members could react. Her knife was at his throat, and she twisted one of his arms behind his back. With her knee, she bumped the man's other hand, and he dropped the broken bottle.

"Anyone moves and he's the first to die, followed by the rest of you." Portuguese wasn't her best language, but she got the point across. "Let the boy go."

The men holding the boy tightened their hold, eliciting groans from their captive. She nicked the throat of the leader, and he shouted to his gang to release the teenager. They did, and the boy ran to the girl's side—*Sister? Girlfriend?*—and knelt next to her.

"You two, get out of the alley and then run. I'll catch up to you." The look on the boy's face told her he was about to do something stupid, like punch out the nearest gang member. "Don't even think of it. Get the girl out of here. She needs your help."

The pair took off down the alley. After they left, members of the gang edged closer to the exit, cutting off the only route Maliha could take. There were at least twenty of them in the plaza, and now they were being egged on by women who'd remained in the shadows around the edge of the group.

No way out without a body count.

She pulled on the hilt of the whip sword and felt it uncurl from her waist like a pent-up buzz-saw blade, the tough, metal-lined sheath preventing it from slicing into her skin. She pictured the motion of the whip sword a fraction ahead of doing it, a trick she'd been taught to help protect her body from the strike of one of the two blades. She kept her wrist relaxed, and then snapped it to send one of the blades slicing through the throat of the man nearest her. She brought the blades down to waist level, and slashed two others across the belly. She stepped around one of the men as he fell, his hands clutching at the sudden gush of blood from his middle.

Leaving a wake of groaning, incapacitated gang members behind her with various levels of injury, she sped down the alley, the bloodied whip sword trailing behind her. A few blocks of a narrow, winding street led her to a kind of no-man's land, a buffer zone ringing the crime-ridden community. She slowed to a trot, pulled the whip sword up, pinched its blades together at the tip, and inserted them back into the sheath. They spun into their safe position around her waist like a measuring tape retracting into its holder.

The teenagers couldn't have gotten much farther. When she passed a corner, a hand snaked out and grabbed her arm.

"You save us," the boy said in broken English. "I, Amaro, this sister Rosie. She . . . she . . ." He couldn't finish that thought, so he switched gears. "We have no one, no go back there ever."

"Come with me, then," Maliha said, using Portuguese and a soothing voice. "We can't stay here. None of us can stay here."

Halfway back to her hotel, Maliha gasped and clutched her abdomen. Two figures were making their way from one pan of the scales to the other, their footprints burning into her skin. She leaned against a building and moaned. Amaro and Rosie supported her, very concerned, not knowing what was wrong or what to do.

As the figures scrambled onto the good side of the scale, the pain let up a bit. The lurch came next, the yank through unpredictable amounts of time. Amaro and Rosie didn't know what happened, but they understood Maliha had not only risked her life but also suffered to save them.

Chapter Sixteen

Maliha arrived home in Chicago on a Thursday afternoon after three days in Hawaii. She had eight phone messages from her editor, Jefferson Leewood. She dialed his number, hoping to find him away from his desk so she could leave a quick message and be done with it. Instead he picked up on the second ring.

"Must you disappear like that?" Jeff asked. "My boss is giving me hell because I haven't seen anything on the new book."

"I'm working on it."

"When can I see what you have so far?"

"You know I don't work that way. You ask that on every book, and every time I give you the same answer. When I'm finished, you'll see the manuscript."

"You going to make the deadline? You don't have much time left."

Maliha sighed. "I'll make it. Have I missed one yet?"

"No, but . . ."

"Then go with the flow, Jeff."

"Can I at least give your paragraph to the art department so they can get started?"

She'd written a few sentences about *A Lust for Murder* that left her plenty of wiggle room to develop it.

"Sure. Can I get back to writing now, please?"

His voice got quieter, conspiratorial. "Marsha, I got a call from the Carey, North Carolina, police department.

Something about a break-in and theft in an office building a few days ago. They wanted to know where to reach you."

"Thanks for the warning. I'll take care of it."

"Well?"

"I didn't have anything to do with whatever it is. I was in North Carolina, but it must be mistaken identity or something. What reason would I have to break in to an office building?"

"I have to ask this."

Uh-oh.

"Are you working for somebody else as a reporter? Some New Age journal or something? Pyramids and all that shit? You could have talked that over with me, you know. You're not planning to stop writing the Detective Dick Stallion books are you?" He paused for a moment, and she could almost hear the next thought click into place. "Are you planning to switch publishers?"

Maliha pushed a laugh into her voice. "Oh, that! I was doing research for a character in the book who's a reporter. I got into the role for authenticity."

There was silence for a minute. "Oh."

"Talk to you soon, Jeff. Bye."

Now I'm going to have to work a reporter into the book. Sheesh.

Maliha had just gotten to her computer, coffee cup in hand and ready to do some serious damage to her remaining word quota, when her intercom chimed.

"Ms. Winters, two detectives from the Chicago PD are here to see you. They're already on their way up to the thirty-ninth floor." It was Arnie, and there was emphasis put on the floor number.

"Thank you. I'll look out for them."

She'd been expecting it. She made them show their badges at the door, and greeted them in a black silk top and tight, low-cut jeans. She knew she looked like the prize every man wanted to find behind Door Number One.

The older one introduced himself as Detective Ron Nobling. Jerking his head sideways, he indicated that his partner was Detective Ace Morgan. It was clear that they were bored with the prospect of checking someone out for a department in North Carolina and hungry for better assignments than this.

Nobling cleared his throat. "Let's make this short. Are you Marsha Winters, the novelist?"

"Yes."

"Did you visit Advanced PharmBots in North Carolina this past Tuesday for an interview with Diane Harvey, posing as a reporter?"

"Yes."

"And did you return that night to break in to her office?"

"No."

"What did you do after the interview?" Ace said. Ron glared over at him, but it bounced off like a mosquito off a charging rhino. Evidently, it was Ron's prerogative to ask the questions.

"As you know, my interview with Ms. Harvey ended abruptly."

They both nodded.

"I left right away for Chicago." She provided the airline and flight number that Amaro had faked for her. "Um, aren't you going to write that down?"

Ace, jolted into action, pulled a notebook from his pocket.

"Then I stopped here to pack a few things and went off to Hawaii. I was behind on my writing and needed few days away to catch up."

She gave them the address where she'd stayed in Hawaii, which Ace dutifully wrote down.

"Are you willing to supply a DNA sample to rule out your presence at the break-in?" Ron asked.

Do they have DNA or are they bluffing? Did Amaro change all the records? Can't take the chance.

"No."

Both detectives perked up at this. "Why not?"

"I live a public life as a novelist. I don't get to keep many things private, but my DNA is one of them."

"We could get a warrant."

"Not without more than the fact that I interviewed Ms. Harvey and left town."

"One of the guards reported that he shot the intruder in the shoulder. Another said there was a possible hit in the leg. A look at your shoulders might clear this whole thing up in a short time."

"No problem." She began unbuttoning her shirt.

"Uh, wait, I think we need to call a female officer."

"Didn't you say you wanted to make this short?" She finished with all the buttons, slipped off the shirt, and let it puddle at her feet. She wore nothing underneath. The smooth skin on her shoulders showed no trace of a wound.

Ace's eyes fastened on her chest. Ron, with a little more self-discipline, attempted to meet her eyes and was mostly successful.

"No wound there," he said, his voice tightly under control.

"I believe you said something about a leg wound?" Maliha's hands moved to the button of her jeans. "Front or back?"

"No, no, not necessary. You couldn't be a suspect."

He looked even more disgusted. If there was something worse than a trip on behalf of a North Carolina PD, it was a wasted trip on behalf of said PD.

She reached down, picked up her shirt, and slipped it on, but didn't button it.

"Anything else I can do for you, Detectives?"

"No. Thank you for your time." Ron turned to go. Ace was frozen in place. Ron elbowed him, and the two left together.

As she was buttoning her blouse, Yanmeng came out of the second bedroom. He was the oldest of her team of three friends—a team that excluded Randy, who didn't know about her exploits.

Come to think of it, neither does Hound. One of these days he's going to get suspicious.

"I doubt they'll be back," he said. "You handled that well."

Yanmeng was in his seventies but wiry and active. They

sparred sometimes, and his martial-arts skills hadn't diminished with age. In fact, his movements had grown more elegant and spare. He was about her height, very strong but not bulky, as though all that wasn't necessary had dropped away from him, in more than the physical sense. His face was solemn and wise in repose, but that impression vanished when he smiled—he managed to look like a mischievous kid. His head was nearly bald but he had a moustache that was white. He could wiggle it back and forth, so that it looked like a caterpillar crawling, and he was proud of that.

He and his wife, Eliu, had never had any more children after a betrayal by their only son. They carried in their hearts a memory of a son who'd condemned them to death, a son whose whereabouts they didn't even know. Maliha had once offered to put her resources to work to locate the boy, now a man in his mid-forties if he still lived. Silence greeted her offer and she'd never mentioned Xietai again. She did wonder, though, if Yanmeng had ever tried to find his son in his own unique way—Yanmeng was a remote viewer—and encountered only the void of the boy's death.

Amaro joined them. He'd been working on the files she'd copied gotten in Diane Harvey's office.

"The lawsuit you mentioned was filed by the family of a young girl named Karen Dearborn, who died in a hospital with a PharmBots account. She was given the wrong medication. Everybody's pointing fingers, and most of those fingers are pointing in PharmBots's direction. They're saying the new robot pill spewer had a programming error. Of course, PharmBots disputes that."

"Ah. Nando and Hairy worked on that system, I'll bet. Do you think they were killed to cover up negligence? Shoddy work?"

Amaro bristled. "I doubt it. They've worked for me before."

"Sorry. Didn't mean to imply that you'd hire losers."

"Depends on how you define losers. Anyway, there are some emails on the disk that implicate the two hired coders. The police confiscated the robot in question and PharmBots is refusing to give them access to the encrypted software that runs it. They claim, and rightly so, that it's proprietary. So far, that's holding off the law and shoring up their claim, but it probably won't for long. Lawyers are scurrying about on both sides."

"Are Nando and Hairy mentioned by name?" Maliha asked.

"Yeah. Numerous times. Seems they were responsible for some of the coding and all of the software quality-assurance testing. Diane kept copies of their certification memos to produce at just the right moment for maximum impact. Her only problem was that she also kept memos that show that she knows the coders are innocent, but she's plotting with the corporate legal staff to blame Nando and Hairy. PharmBots is guilty as hell. It was a mechanical glitch, not a software one, and Diane Harvey knows it. They took a low bid on some parts for their pill robot from overseas and didn't bother to check out the sloppy quality control on the machining specs. The almighty dollar trumps human lives again."

"Anything else of interest on that disk?"

"Now that you mention it, yes. Those clay pot things in her office are real. She's got records on the disk of black-market purchases. And there's one more thing. She kept a diary. She's having an affair with a married employee on the scientific staff. Steamy stuff. Good fodder for *A Lust for Murder*."

"Anything else? She's a shoplifter or something?"

"Nope. That about does it. Ms. Harvey's corporate and private life in a very untidy little basket. What's next?"

"I'm going to a charity event tonight. I invited Greg Shale of ShaleTech."

"You get to dress up and drink champagne and what do I get? A lousy disk drive."

Chapter Seventeen

Maliha selected a deep blue off-the-newly-healed-shoulder dress for the charity event, and paired it with sparkling open sandals with laces that wound up her bare calves. Her hair was piled on top of her head in an intricate weave that demurely concealed a two-inch knife. The same red color that flashed from her toenails brightened her succulent lips.

The event was sponsored by the Vitality for Life Foundation, which Maliha had started fifteen years ago. The foundation supported research into how elderly people could improve the quality of their lives by remaining active, healthy, and independent. Maliha was deeply interested in the cause. She didn't know what she'd face as she aged, and it occurred to her that many other people didn't know that either. Age just snuck up on them. They were vital and going along full steam in their lives and suddenly, it must seem, they were using walkers and wheelchairs and dealing with diminished expectations. There had to be a better way.

Checkbooks were whipped from pockets and evening bags, dollar amounts with a lot of zeros were written, and the checks were dropped into the collections container—a shiny steel bedpan.

The event was in the ballroom of a luxury hotel. The foundation's director, a shrewd woman who could wring a dollar from a beggar, had managed to get not only the space donated but the finger foods and drinks, too. Maliha paid for the string quartet that had finished an hour ago, and for the gaudy champagne fountain featured in the room. It was tacky, but having something tacky guaranteed media coverage.

With the music over, people talked in small clumps, reaffirming their own youthful lifestyles whether they were young or not. Among them was Greg Shale. Maliha watched him from a distance.

Greg had an athletic build and moved with an ease that was more insolent than graceful. He was a little shy of forty, and had a distinctive scar that ran from the base of his left ear to the corner of his mouth. Its shape suggested the ragged edge of broken glass, and it made an otherwise ordinary face interesting. His left hand rose to touch it occasionally, a habit he didn't notice. He had a strident laugh that clashed with his otherwise deep, pleasant voice.

What wasn't pleasant about him was his complex and roiling aura. Dark, dull red was streaked with black and brown, making a swamp of selfishness and hate, with a little dollop of revenge seeking stirred in.

Judging by his aura, Greg Shale was a horrible man.

Still, there were many such people in the world, and not all of them were murderers. It was possible to be hateful and not do anything about it.

Maliha caught Greg's eye from across the room. After she was sure she'd been noticed, she walked over and joined the group around him. Lily Eddings, a friend and frequent donor, welcomed her. Lily was a wealthy widow who'd turned to philanthropy to stay involved in the community and fill the hole in her life that her husband's death had created. She was a welcome fixture at charity events, and a kind, caring woman. Maliha admired the broad range of her interests.

"Marsha, so good of you to join us. Everyone, this is Marsha Winters, local author extraordinaire and hostess of this event. You know everyone here, dear?"

Before Maliha had a chance to say anything, Greg stepped up and introduced himself.

"Greg Shale, Ms. Winters. I've read your work."

Maliha's eyebrows shot up. He didn't seem the type. She couldn't picture him curled in an easy chair, a mug of hot chocolate in hand, perusing the guilty pleasures of books like the forthcoming one—should she ever finish it.

Greg cleared his throat. He'd seen her reaction; no one in the group could have missed it. "That is, I've always intended to read your work," he said, with a disarming, albeit lopsided, grin.

She thawed a little.

Maybe he's not so horrible. He could just be having a bad aura day.

"I'd like to thank you for the invitation to come tonight," he continued. "I wasn't all that familiar with the foundation, but the more I learn from talking to everyone here, the more I think I'd like to become involved."

"Got your checkbook handy?" The small group laughed, included Greg.

"Actually, I've already used the bedpan."

She let him lead her away from the group and get her a glass of champagne.

"I was serious about becoming involved. I've been charity shopping for some time, looking for something that would become the focus of my company's philanthropic activity. If Gates and Buffet can lead the way, I can follow."

"The foundation welcomes your participation at any level. I'll put you in touch with our development director." *Who will milk your company dry, and do it with a smile.*

"I'd rather talk to you."

"I'm flattered. Who's your legal counsel, then? I can have some papers sent over."

"That would be me. I wear two hats. How did you get interested in aging issues?"

"You want the real story, or the one I tell the media?"

"Real, of course."

"I'm over three hundred years old and my age is catching up to me. It isn't other peoples' quality of life I'm worried about as much as my own." Only four people knew the truth about Maliha: Amaro, Rosie, Yanmeng, and Eliu. Officially, there was now a fifth.

Greg laughed that jarring, abrasive bark of his. "And I'm an extraterrestrial from two hundred light-years away."

Wouldn't it be strange if we were both telling the truth?

"I guess I'll take the story you tell to the media. I can see that you want to keep your real reasons to yourself. All of us have secrets."

"I got interested in elder issues about quality of life because I had to face some tough decisions about my own parents."

"Fair enough. Marsha, would you consider paying a visit to ShaleTech? I'd like to get more facts before I put my money where my mouth is."

"Our director . . ."

"No, I mean you. To tell the truth, it's a ploy to spend more time with you."

Aack! I'm being hit on by the bad guy. At least I think he's a bad guy.

She double-checked his aura. Same dismal picture, with the addition of a large splash of deep crimson—sexual urges. She smiled and linked arms with him.

"When you put it that way, how can I refuse?"

Maliha spent the next ninety minutes at the Vitality for Life Foundation's fund-raiser glued to Greg's arm. Now that she knew the approach to use with Greg, she needed to make a strong impression on him. A quick touch on the shoulder, gossip about another attendee whispered in his ear, a brush of her thigh against his when she moved past him, an accidental contact of her breast with his arm. When he was drunk on the ambrosia of sexual teasing, she handed him off to Lily, who knew everyone there and loved to have a newcomer to drag around for introductions.

Maliha had accomplished what she came for, and was about to slip out of the event when the hotel manager approached her. He said that a man in the lobby wanted to talk to her. "He's from the police," he said in a discreet tone, "and he's very persistent."

More likely my stalker.

She patted the knife nestled in her hair and slipped out of

the charity event. Lily had been waving in her direction, but Maliha pretended not to notice.

When they arrived at the lobby, the hotel manager frowned. "He was right there, sitting on the end of that sofa. I'll check at the desk."

He came back a minute later carrying a small box, poorly wrapped in brown paper and tied with twine. "He couldn't wait any longer, but he left this for you."

Maliha eyed the package uneasily.

"Oh." The blood drained from the manager's face as he picked up on the expression on her face. "Oh. You weren't expecting this package, were you? Shall I contact the bomb squad, Ms. Winters?"

Chapter Eighteen

Maliha took the crudely wrapped box from the hotel manager. She'd rather have her steady hands holding it than his nervous ones. Plus, if the situation called for it, she could run a lot faster than he could to get the box away from the crowded hotel lobby.

"What did this man look like?"

"Tall, thin, mid-twenties, dressed . . . dressed casually for this area, if you get my drift. Actually, he looked like a bum. I assumed he was an undercover cop. He did flash a badge, though I didn't get a good look at it. I wouldn't have disturbed you otherwise."

A homeless man had been hired to deliver the package. Maliha glanced around the lobby.

Too many cameras here for the stalker to show his face.

"It's okay. I was expecting a package, but I thought it would be sent to my home. I was just surprised to see it here. Don't worry about a thing."

It sounded trumped up to her, but since it was exactly what the manager wanted to hear, he nodded.

Holding the package as casually as she dared, she asked the manager to have her car brought around. She put the package carefully on the passenger seat, slipped behind the wheel, and eased out on to the street.

She drove to the parking lot of a beach in Chicago's system of lakefront parks. Deserted at night but smaller than she would have liked, the park was her best prospect for getting away from crowds. She called the police and requested a bomb squad intervention. Her claim was credible since she was a literary celebrity, and she didn't have long to wait.

The package was examined by a track-footed robot and determined to be harmless. A technician approached in full gear, despite the robot's affirmations, and gently unwrapped the package. After a tense hour in the parking lot, Maliha was presented with an open box.

Inside was an index card with the now familiar *S* drawn boldly, and underneath it was a pair of her panties, skimpy, black, and lacy, with her initials embroidered on the band. She had a whole drawer full of them. The technician vacillated between amusement and annoyance at having been called out for a piece of underwear. Maliha muttered something about her boyfriend pulling a stupid trick and made a quick exit.

She drove with a steady hand, but inside she felt escalating anger and a horrible, chilling feeling of violation.

I might have been there when he came into the room. Sleeping like Ledger's wife when I prowled around her bedroom. I have to find this stalker and put an end to this.

She'd promised a late-night phone call to Randy, so she told her all about meeting Greg, and the outcome of the blind date, but didn't mention the stalker's unique way of communicating with her. She didn't feel right hiding something from Randy, but Randy would insist on something inadvisable, like moving in with her until the bastard was caught.

"Is Greg handsome?"

"If you don't look too deeply, yeah," Maliha said, thinking of the nasty aura Greg had.

"Rich?"

"Enough. Besides, I don't need any more."

"Shut up! Nobody ever has enough money. Or things. What did he smell like?"

The question took Maliha by surprise. She had to go back over the moment she first met him and remember her impression. Her nostrils widened with the effort.

Cartier cologne, a sporty shampoo, something else . . . a trace of horsey scent, like a polo club.

"Like money."

"You're gonna end up in the sack."

It'll be a crowd. Him, me, and his aura.

"And when you do, I want a full report. But that's just a little fling. Jake—he's different. Wedding bells different."

"How do you know that? You hardly know the guy."

"All right, you wormed it out of me. It's his horoscope. Astrology, baby! In fact, maybe you should dump Greg before anything heats up there. Clear the lanes for Jake, I mean. Now what is it that's bothering you?"

"Um, nothing's bothering me."

"Uh-huh. This is Randy you're talking to, girlfriend."

Maliha said nothing.

"Gonna tough it out alone, huh? You're not pregnant, are you? 'Cause if you are, we need to talk."

"No, I'm not pregnant."

"Greg didn't get hinky on you, right?"

"No hinky stuff. Give me some time with this, okay?"

"You know I'm always here for you."

She hung up without saying good-bye, a Randy trademark.

Lying in the dark, Maliha reviewed the jumble of recent events. Had Greg executed two coders and left their bodies in the alley near trash bins? Nothing in his aura precluded it, and Amaro was certain Nando and Hairy had worked for him.

Was it Greg covering his tracks on something he didn't want common knowledge? The next generation of control switches, ready to sweep the, uh, control-switch market? If the two coders had gone behind Amaro's back for lucrative contracts, why wouldn't they betray ShaleTech corporate secrets? Greg could easily have been suspicious.

The box with her panties in it kept drifting into her mind, but she pushed it firmly away.

Diane Harvey's aura had revealed that she was ambitious, deceitful, and angry about the lawsuit. Could she have ordered the deaths because the coders knew too much and millions of dollars were at stake? Money is behind so many deaths. Corporate development secrets, damaging lawsuits. Take your pick.

And then there was Jake. He was witty and nice to be around, in addition to radiating sex appeal like a supernova. Something else, too—she felt a real connection to him, and she couldn't pinpoint why. She hadn't examined his aura, and wasn't sure if she wanted to. It might spoil the instant attraction she'd felt toward him.

Maliha finally gave in to thinking about the package she'd received, and what it meant—that some hand had pawed through her things, her *private* things. She wondered when it had happened.

Was I here when he came?

As an assassin, she'd used drugs to keep occupants of a home from being aware of her. Could she have been drugged and didn't even remember it? She sat up and clicked on the lamp beside the bed. She was in her thirty-ninth-floor condo. She was relieved to see her knife on the nightstand.

What else could he have taken?

Once the thought came into her mind, she couldn't let go of it. She turned on all the lights and searched the whole condo from top to bottom. Nothing was gone except one pair of black panties.

She'd dealt with stalkers in her long life, but there was something sinister about this one. She had a feeling she was being set up for something, but what?

Maliha slept uneasily and dreamed of one of Rabishu's cages squeezing the life out of her, over and over.

Chapter Nineteen

Friday evening carried a touch of the winter to come. Only a couple of degrees kept the rain from being sleet, and a robust wind drove it nearly sideways. Maliha resisted the urge to run to Jake's apartment in the McKinley Park neighborhood for the dinner date, and took a taxi instead.

Better to arrive dry when having dinner at a guy's place. Saves awkward questions.

His place was on the second story of a four-flat building a couple of blocks from the neighborhood's namesake park. She asked the taxi driver to let her off at the park.

"You sure, lady? Too dark for park."

"I'll be fine."

Just in time for her arrival, the rain stopped and the clouds began breaking up. She had some time to kill and spent it walking through the park to the lagoon. Wet leaves glistened on the path and pale light danced on the water of the lagoon as the wind sent ripples across the surface.

She wondered how the evening at Jake's would end.

Could be nothing but a dull meal and a peck on the cheek. We each take the off ramp.

Remembering the intensity of the kiss in Al's Beef and the feel of his body pressing against hers, she didn't think the night would end with a chaste kiss. She had a happy, almost giddy feeling thinking about his arms wrapped around her, and wondered if what she was feeling was love. It had been so long since she'd fallen in love with her husband, Nathan, that she wasn't sure she'd recognize what it felt like.

She closed her eyes and shook her head.

Calm down. You're starting to sound like a girl with her first crush.

As she walked the few blocks to Jake's apartment, the rain picked up again and she pulled up the hood on her jacket. She wasn't going to arrive dry after all. She found the streets to be quiet. No drug deals, no prostitutes, no gangs. Yet he'd warned her that his neighborhood wasn't what she was used to.

The rain must be keeping people off the streets. Or crime has taken the night off.

Out of the corner of her eye, Maliha caught movement in an alley. Not all suspicious activity had been snuffed out by the rain. Her hand slid into her jacket pocket and cradled the round palm pistol she carried there. The seven-round turret revolver had been a gift from its French designer in the 1880s. It was an antique firearm now, but she'd kept it in its original condition and ordered custom-made ammunition for it. It had the stopping power of a peashooter, but she intended it only as a distraction until she could put some other weapon—or her bare hands—to use. The entire pistol could be concealed in her hand with the barrel barely projecting out. To fire it, she squeezed her hand. It had gained a reputation as an assassin's gun, especially at close range. More than once Maliha had extended her hand in greeting with the barrel poked between her fingers.

In the bad old days.

Now, though, the pistol was strictly for defense, and was ideal for taking on a date that might end in taking off clothing. Most men wouldn't consider a whip sword or knife sheaths or a shoulder holster as attractive feminine accessories.

The door opened to reveal Jake looking relaxed and pleased to see her. Delicious smells wafted out the door, luring her in with gustatory anticipation.

"Come on in," Jake said warmly. "Jesus, you're sopping wet. Get in here in front of the fireplace."

She pulled the gift she'd brought out of the jacket pocket that didn't contain the gun. It was a beautiful box of marzipan, a hand-painted fruit assortment from Italy. Jake wanted to sample the goods now.

"They're for dessert."

"Good, since I didn't make any. Unless you consider a package of cookies from the local c-store as gourmet fare."

"Are they Oreo Double Stufs?"

"Sadly, no."

He hung up her jacket. The small extra weight of the palm pistol in its pocket didn't draw his attention. He guided her to a comfortable sofa next to a crackling fire. His place had small, tidy rooms, a kitchen, dining room, and living room in sight and a hallway that presumably led to the bedroom area. The fireplace was a luxury in an otherwise utilitarian space. The neighborhood had working-class roots. The fireplaces in use in the mid–19th century for heating would probably have been walled over when radiators arrived on the scene. She was pleased that his fireplace had survived.

"It smells great in here," she said. He'd tucked a throw around her legs. The throw felt nice and smelled even better, a combination of male scent and the smell of seasoned wood burning cleanly.

"Beef stroganoff. You're not vegetarian, are you?"

"Nope."

"It's my mom's recipe. Only thing I know how to cook that doesn't come frozen or gets zapped in the microwave."

The more relaxed Jake got, the handsomer he seemed to Maliha. When he was on the job, he probably wore his professionalism like a suit of armor. She didn't blame him. She had her own armor, times three: the real steel kind, the protective sphere of her hand-to-hand combat skills, and the defensive shield around her heart.

Why him? After all these years of protecting myself from serious relationships, why do I feel I'm on the verge of one here?

Jake chatted with her about everything from current politics to the new exhibit at the Art Institute as he worked in the kitchen. She fingered the jade cameo necklace she wore, her own profile carved in 18th-century China—a piece that would fit right in with the current exhibit. He shared her appreciation for fine things, even though he was limited to viewing them in museums rather than possessing them.

He'd go crazy if he saw my forty-eighth-floor collection. A chance to hold history in your hand.

"Jake, you don't talk much about your job. How do you feel about it?"

Geez, that was subtle.

"I love my work. Remember the *Justice League* comics?" Without waiting for an answer, he went on. "I used to get them used. Never did get my hands on the 1960 debut. Anyway, I knew that's what I wanted to be part of. I couldn't be a superhero, but I could still bring the bad guys to justice. Sounds sappy, huh?"

She shook her head. "What's sappy about saving lives?"

He pointed at her. "See, you get it. Lots of women out there don't. Can't cope with a guy whose life doesn't revolve around them."

Passionate about work—check.

He joined her on the sofa, bringing a glass of wine for each of them.

"About half an hour left until dinner. I thought we'd get an early start on the grape juice."

Maliha rarely drank just for the hell of it, but she enjoyed wine with meals and an occasional Samuel Adams Irish Red or two.

He held his glass out toward hers for a toast. "Those who love deeply never grow old."

Surprised by the quote from an English playwright, she finished it to conceal her reaction. "They may die of old age, but they die young."

Their wineglasses clinked. She sipped the wine and found it to be an Italian Barbera. She raised her eyebrows and nodded at Jake in appreciation, still reeling from the impact of the quote he'd used. Those words seemed to hint at knowledge of an issue of prime importance: her mortality after centuries of being Ageless.

Was it accidental, or does he really know something? If accidental, why did he pick such a deeply romantic . . .

She never finished the thought, because Jake took the wineglass from her and set both glasses on the coffee table. He moved closer, put his hand on her shoulder, gently turned her face to meet his, and lightly traced her lips with his fingers.

It was her move.

Off-ramp decision coming up. Ah, hell.

They moved together for a warm kiss that promised more than she was prepared to deliver. She would gladly have moved from sofa to bed with him, except for the toast he'd made.

This is no casual fling for him. He could be the one. I feel . . .

"I feel like dancing," she said.

He pulled back and looked at her quizzically. She kept her face from revealing the turmoil of her thoughts and the flutter of something light in her chest.

Jake picked up his wine and took a long sip. He was changing gears, and that affirmed her impressions about him.

He'll give me some time.

"Slow dance?" he asked.

"Sure. Let's save the tango for another night." She had an intense memory of dancing in a bar in Argentina a century ago, her body crammed against her lover's, legs wrapping around his body—standing sex, he'd called it. She felt blood rushing to her cheeks, but Jake had turned away to put on music and didn't see her blush.

"The Lady in Red" played softly and Jake took her in his arms. Maliha rested her head on his shoulder, his hand laid claim to her hip, and they danced in the open space in front of the fire. When the lyrics got to the whispered "I love you" at the end, Jake's embrace tightened.

Her move, again.

Her body was beginning to melt against his, age quote be damned, when his cell phone rang.

"Shit. I have to get that."

They pulled apart. Jake slid his phone from his pocket. As he listened, his expression changed from serious annoyance to concern. "Give me ten minutes. I'll be there."

He shrugged apologetically as he put away the phone. "I have to go. It's a case I'm working on. I hate to ask, but could you turn off the stove and oven?"

She nodded. "No problem."

"I'm really sorry about this." He disappeared into the bedroom and came back quickly, pulling a jacket over his shirt, which was now adorned with a shoulder holster. The weapon was a strong signal that their evening was over.

He was at the door. Then he turned back and crossed the living room in a few strides, pulled her close, and kissed her.

She closed the door behind him, her emotions unsettled. She went into the kitchen and occupied herself with storing the beef stroganoff and other items in the refrigerator and cleaning the pans. Busywork. She puzzled over what to do with the fire that was still blazing away in the fireplace. She couldn't close the damper yet or the place would fill with smoke, so she pulled a heavy spark screen in front of the hearth that he'd pushed aside for better viewing. When everything passed inspection, she put her gift of marzipan on the counter with a note: *See you soon. Love, Maliha.* Impulsively, she kissed the paper lightly and left a faint trace of lipstick.

Okay, that's too much. Get a grip.

She tore up the paper and wrote a new note: *For next time.*

Better—less personal. I really need to think about this.

She was about to leave when it occurred to her that this was the perfect opportunity to learn more about Jake. She'd studied her victims in depth as a demon's assassin. Why not do the same for a man who might be "the one"?

Any woman would, she told herself. *Well, maybe not, but I'm not any woman.*

A pile of unopened mail on the kitchen counter beckoned. Strolling casually, as if Jake were still in the room, she circled the kitchen until she reached the pile of mail, then carefully flipped each envelope using a table knife. There was nothing out of the ordinary until she came to a greeting card with his name and address in a delicate woman's script. Eyes wide, thinking she'd found evidence of two-timing, she flipped the card over and sighed with relief. On the back was a girlish drawing of a birthday cake, with block letters underneath it that said, "Uncle Jake is old."

He hadn't mentioned having a niece, but she hadn't asked about his family.

How do I explain my *family? Three guys and a pregnant woman?*

She headed down the hall to the bedroom, stopping at the bathroom along the way. It was tidy, with few things out on the vanity. A razor, a can of shaving cream, a few other boring items, like nail clippers. She pulled open the medicine cabinet over the sink. A typical assortment, the Tylenol and Tums basics. No prescription meds in evidence. There was a full bottle of men's cologne shoved into the back, gathering dust. His niece had probably given it to him as a present, and he kept it around in case she asked about it.

No revelations in the linen closet.

Maliha left a half hour later, after finding that Jake favored polo shirts and blue jeans when not dressed for work, that he used down pillows, that he had a large and eclectic book collection, and that he had a locked gun safe built into the wall behind a print of Michelangelo's Last Judgment, not the usual bedroom artwork. She skipped his underwear drawer, figuring she'd find out the answer to the boxers-or-briefs question soon enough.

Chapter Twenty

The lights in Kelly's Pub were turned low. The man across from Maliha was a private investigator, and although Maliha knew his real name, he was always just Hound. He hunched over his beer and rarely lifted his chin to meet Maliha's eyes. She assumed it was because of his disfigurement. He'd left half his face in Vietnam. The pink scars were in vivid contrast to his black skin.

She'd used Hound's investigative services before. She trusted him implicitly, paid him very well, never questioned his methods, and was happy to share a beer with him anytime.

What he didn't know was that Maliha had been there the day he almost lost his life in Vietnam, and she was content to keep it that way.

Hound downed the rest of his beer. He hadn't said a thing yet. She slid a fat envelope full of hundred-dollar bills across the table to him.

"Good to work with you again." His words were a little slurred as he shaped the sounds with half of his mouth frozen.

"Luis Fernando de Santos and Harold L. Borringer." He handed her two envelopes. "You knew these stiffs?"

"No. Not personally."

"I figured. You can read all that background shit yourself. I got only one thing that stirred my interest." He leaned a little closer, and she did, too.

"Luis Fernando came up with a scheme for smuggling heroin inside laptop computers manufactured in India. The smack goes out of Afghanistan, through Pakistan, and into India. Indian companies manufacture and assemble the laptops. Bags of heroin are tucked inside. The laptop can be booted up to demonstrate that it works. Who cracks one of those things open to check for drugs? You wouldn't think there would be room. Inside one, there isn't room for much. Inside tens of thousands of laptops, the amounts are significant. My source says they take out the drugs at central warehouses and then sell the laptops. By now those little smack carriers are all over the country."

"You're saying Nando put all this together?"

"Hell, no. I said he had the idea. He might know his computers, but what he didn't have was the connections in the drug trade to pull it off. I mean, he couldn't score H on a Friday night on the West Side, much less set up a complex overseas operation."

"Who, then?"

Hound shrugged, a disconcerting gesture in which one shoulder went up higher than the other. "Damn if I know. I'm gonna keep at it, though."

She went home with Hound, as she always did. As soon as the door to his place closed behind them, his hands were all over her.

"Wait, take it easy." She pushed him away. One by one, she removed the weapons hidden on her body, and turned the process into a viewer's delight. It was a strip tease done with blades and bullets.

"Jesus, woman, that was the sexiest disarming I've ever seen."

"Your turn."

Two guns and a switchblade knife later, Hound was clean.

Later, they fell asleep in each other's arms. Like always, she left before he woke up in the morning.

Maliha spent hours studying Hound's reports.

If Nando was in on it, maybe Hairy was, too. Two geeks

trying to swim in the deep end of the worldwide drug-trade pool without life preservers.

She decided to let Jake do a little drug investigating for her, and start the process of cutting off the drug importation at the same time.

Even if the smuggling is unrelated to the coders' murders, there's still some justice to be done. Who better than Jake Stackman, intrepid fighter for the cause?

She called the Chicago office of the Drug Enforcement Administration and asked for Jake. Instead of the voice mail she expected, he picked up the call.

"Agent Jake Stackman. How may I help you?"

"Agent Stackman, how many years of experience do you have?"

There was a pause.

"Marsha? Is that you?"

"Pretend I'm somebody you don't know. I'm calling up with an important drug-related tip, and I don't want to trust it to just anybody. Convince me that you're the one I should spill my guts to."

"Is this a joke? Or something for one of your books?"

"No, and no. I'm serious here, Jake."

They had a staring match over the phone. Jake blinked first.

"I joined the agency twelve years ago. I've been with the Chicago Division for eight years, starting with meth cases in downstate rural areas and then working Asian heroin trafficked by West Africans. I do some demand reduction work too, because I think it's important to get the message out to schools and parents that drugs ruin lives. I've been in on a few major operations. Is that good enough?"

There was an edge to his voice that was both defensive and challenging.

"You can put your hackles down now. I know about a smuggling scheme and I wanted to make sure you were right for the case, which you are."

"Kind of you. Details?"

"Heroin is being imported into the country inside laptop computers. Heroin from the Afghanistan crop goes into

Pakistan, then to India. The computers are manufactured in India by a company named SkyDevice Enterprises. They come in through Miami—"

"Wait! Slow down." She heard him rustling papers.

"They come in through Miami and are shipped by rail to a sorting warehouse somewhere in southern Illinois. I don't know the exact location. The laptops are opened up and the heroin bags are stripped out, then the computers are sold online by noolaptops.com. Check out their Horizon Pro line, if you're in the market for a new laptop, and don't forget to ask for the free upgrade to express shipping. Don't rush into it. There are bigger fish behind the first guy you find."

"Holy shit. Who's your source?"

Maliha hung up. Right about now, she figured, he was placing an order for a Horizon Pro at noolaptops.com. In a few days, the machine would be in a DEA lab undergoing testing for heroin residue.

She'd passed the torch and she was sure he'd run with it.

Chapter Twenty-One

1968

Hound looked out from behind a tree at the clearing in front of him. His target was lying fifty feet away, out in the open, vulnerable. He'd heard the soldier shouting for help, but the shouts had faded as the man grew weaker. The guy in trouble was Rod, a nineteen-year-old from Indiana, who'd gotten his nickname from the erections that tented his blanket every morning. Rod had a girl back home, and he missed her mightily. Even in godforsaken Vietnam, the young man could imagine he was somewhere safe and she was in his arms.

Hound's wife, Angel, and daughter Sarana had been killed by a drunk driver on the way to a birthday party. His imagination couldn't compensate for that.

Rod was clutching his leg where a bomb fragment had torn an ugly hole. Blood wasn't spurting, and the wound looked like it was on the outside of the thigh. It wasn't the femoral artery, then, which could bleed out in a few minutes before a medic had a chance to reach the man.

Hound, God help him, had passed by those cases if there were other soldiers down with serious injuries that he stood a chance of saving. He could only do so much with two hands.

As Hound watched, the man's hand slid down his thigh until it rested on the ground, as still as a fawn huddled in the grass.

Hound had to get out there. He couldn't wait any longer,

couldn't wait for cover, couldn't wait for help. It had to be now, or Rod would never make it back to his Jolene.

Bullets flew over the clearing at chest height, like angry metal bees bent on vengeance and looking to sting somebody's heart.

Hound slung his medical kit over his shoulder. He took a deep breath and tried to still the rising nausea he felt at the thought of leaving his place of relative safety. Before he could think too much about what he was doing, he dashed out into the clearing, keeping low, adrenaline powering his muscles.

He followed a zigzag path on legs that shook but held him up. The noise of automatic-weapons fire and shells impacting in the field, throwing up fountains of dirt, the slaughterhouse smell of blood and burst abdomens, all of it made him want to flee. Made him want to be back in bed at home with the covers pulled up over his face. Courage of the purest sort kept him moving forward.

Goddamned stupid thing to do.

A bullet licked the skin of his upper arm.

Hound slid like he'd done on the baseball diamond at home, stealing second on summer nights when the air was so humid-thick that running through it was like parting the Red Sea. His boots tore up the grass as he slid, and he thumped into Rod's side, opposite his wound. Hound grabbed the man's wrist and felt a pulse. It wasn't too late.

He tried to shut out what was going on around him and get to the quiet place at his center where he could think. Still lying on the ground, he reached over and felt the area of Rod's wound with his hand. His fingers sank into a ragged, bloody hole. He grimaced as he felt bone.

Bad, real bad, but not enough to kill if I can get him out of here, unless he's ripped up inside, too. Maybe he'll even keep the leg.

Internal bleeding was the bane of medics. Hound could try to keep the outside from bleeding with everything from the palm of his hand to a pressure bandage to a tourniquet. The inside was the realm of surgeons.

Hound pulled his kit around where he could reach it,

took out handfuls of 4 x 4's, and stuffed them onto the wound. They reddened immediately, and he piled more on top of them. He slapped a large adhesive patch over his handiwork.

Best I can do, buddy. The docs'll patch you up better.

Hound heard shouting, and out of the corner of his eye, he saw VC threading their way through the grass, crouched low. He had to move now and get this soldier out of here, or they'd both die. It was a wonder they hadn't already. There were shouts to fall back, which meant air support was on the way. He didn't have long before he'd hear the *thwack-thwack* sounds of Cobras that preceded their arrival over the trees, their painted shark eyes and teeth the last sight Charlie would see.

Hound inched around to the injured man's head. He grabbed the back of Rod's shirt behind the neck and tugged, sliding him across the ground a foot. At this rate, he wouldn't make it out of the clearing in time. Hound was steeling himself to stand up, pull the man over his shoulder in a fireman's carry, and make a run for it when a grunt came toward him, hurrying for cover. Two men could do the crawl-and-drag much faster.

"Hey!" Hound shouted. "Help here!"

The man didn't hear him or didn't want to hear him and ran past toward the woods.

Fuck. C'mon, then, Rod, it's just you and me.

He got to his knees, and that's when the blast came. A mortar round exploded on the edge of the clearing, near the edge of the woods the soldiers were falling back to. Hound saw the man who'd run past him cut in half by bomb fragments spinning through his body like a buzz saw.

No flak jacket gonna stop that.

Some of the fragments reached Hound, carved his body like eager knives attacking a block of cheese, and threw him backward. Before he slipped into unconsciousness, he thought he felt his wife's hair slide across his ruined face. With tremendous effort, he reached up and touched her cheek.

"Angel," he croaked.

Love you, Angel.

Maliha sped into the firefight and crouched over Hound to make sure he was still alive. To her astonishment, the man was conscious enough to react to her, and lifted his arm to her face, touching her tenderly. His fingers left a trail of blood across her cheek.

He must think I am the angel of death come to claim him, yet he reaches out for me.

Then his head lolled to the side. She gathered him up and took him to his platoon, leaving him on the ground so that one of the men tripped over him. She went back to the clearing, but the man Hound had been working on was dead.

Chapter Twenty-Two

ShaleTech had its headquarters in Chicagoland's Technology Corridor, which flanked Interstate 88 in DuPage and Kane Counties. It shared the general area with the likes of Argonne National Laboratory and Fermilab.

It was a splendid fall afternoon. Maliha retrieved her car from the private garage she'd had built inside the building's main garage. She drove a black McLaren F1, until recently the fastest street-legal car in the world with a top speed of 250 miles per hour. Although she knew the car's speed record had been surpassed, she loved everything about it, from its elegant butterfly-wing doors to its center driver's position. She'd had a number of customizations made by the British manufacturer. Several of them had to do with theft prevention, since the car was worth over a million dollars. The rest had served her well during pursuits.

She tossed her high heels on one of the passenger seats and slipped on the worn pair of athletic shoes she left on the floor. Driving a stick shift in heels wasn't practical, and she didn't do it if it was avoidable. Getting into the center seat shouldn't have been easy in a dress, but Maliha made it look easy. Traffic on I–88 kept her from taking the McLaren on a real romp, but the time behind the wheel was enjoyable anyway.

She wore a long-sleeved black dress that ended modestly at the knee, but that was all that was modest about it. The silky material clung to her curves and the dress dipped low in front and back. Her red high heels would set her ass in motion with every step she took. Her black hair curled into luxurious waves that framed her face. Subtle makeup highlighted her great cheekbones and green eyes. It was an evening outfit, but she didn't mind surprising Greg and putting him off balance. She was as much dressed to kill as when she went out with her black outfit and knives.

Maliha arrived early for her 1 P.M. appointment. The ShaleTech building didn't go for aesthetics. It was a brick cube nine stories high, sparingly decorated with tall, slitlike windows. It looked like a Borg spaceship that had fallen to Earth. She pulled off the road and took a good look through binoculars. There was a double set of peripheral fences about thirty feet apart, with the land in between patrolled by pairs of guards with dogs.

Definitely a tougher nut to crack than PharmBots.

At the first gate, her car was checked by a bomb-sniffing dog and examined underneath with a mirror. She had the distinct impression that the guard wanted to examine underneath her with a mirror, too. At the second gate, her fingerprints were taken on a hand scanner and checked, along with her photo, against law-enforcement databases and against ShaleTech's private list of personae non grata.

Maliha had accessorized her clothing with her Marsha Winters fingerprints today, collected from an unclaimed corpse eighty years ago. She had a large supply of prints from an era before their widespread use for identification that Amaro used to set up her identities.

Inside, her purse was hand-searched as she went through a metal detector under the watchful eye of the chief of security, an emotionless man whose badge simply said CHIEF CLARK. He looked like a man who, in other circumstances, would have been a torturer. Had probably been a torturer in his military stint. She knew the type.

Her cell phone was placed in a small wire basket and a tag was wired to it with the number from her visitor badge. If she wanted to make any calls, she'd have to use a company phone, and snapping photos was out of the question—at least, using the phone.

The slim purse Maliha carried had a tiny camera in its lining, and she was snapping away by squeezing a certain spot near the clasp. The camera showed up on X-rays in the shape of a cough drop, and she carried several real ones in her purse to confuse the issue. Her escort took her to the seventh floor. Greg met her outside his office, preventing her from getting a look at his workspace. He appraised her frankly with his eyes, and appeared to like what he saw.

"I'm glad you could come. It's a pleasure to see you again."

"The pleasure's mutual. Shall we get settled in your office to talk?"

"I thought we'd talk over lunch."

"How about we go out for lunch, then?" What she'd wanted was a good, long look at his office. A restaurant would be second choice, to get him out of the comfort zone of his home territory. "I'm in the mood for Italian."

They walked a couple of doors down the hall to a small dining area with expansive views of the grounds.

There were a few late-lunch stragglers in the dining room, executives talking to their counterparts, one table of white-coated scientists in a vigorous, hand-waving conversation.

"Let's sit with them," Maliha said, indicating the scientists. "They look lively."

Greg smiled and waved her ahead of him into a private room with a door that closed out the voices from the main room. There were no windows. The lighting was dramatic, pinpointing works of art on the walls and statuary on pedestals. On a table topped with black marble was a stand containing a traditional display of Samurai swords—the tanto, wakizashi, and katana—in their sheaths. Maliha wandered over to them. They were old, authentic.

Soul of the Samurai. I wonder whose soul this is in front of us.

Greg had followed, and was standing too close behind her. Any closer and his groin would be on a first-name basis with her ass.

She ran her hand over the curved sheath of the katana,

doing her best to make it seem sensual. The catch in Greg's breathing told her she'd succeeded.

"You're a collector. Twelfth century?"

"Thirteenth. I never would have taken you for a sword expert."

She turned around to face him, and Greg remained where he was, putting them very close together.

"I dabble in the martial arts," she said.

Greg put his hand on her shoulder. "I'm a practitioner, too. I've been told I'm pretty good."

She swiveled her hips slightly. "Really? Maybe you'd like to show me a few of your moves after lunch." She almost winked at the innuendo, but refrained.

"I'd like nothing better. I have a dojo right in the building. I'm a strong believer in the mind-body connection, and I do my best work when my body's needs are attended to."

There was just a touch of a leer in the last part of what he said.

You'll have to drink at another trough, Mr. Horny Stallion.

She filed the thought away to use as a line in *A Lust for Murder.*

A waiter entered. Greg told him to have the chef do something Italian, and asked for wine to start.

"I'll send out the sommelier," the waiter said. The word rolled off his tongue beautifully.

"I guess this isn't the usual company cafeteria," Maliha said, when the waiter had gone. "Not many of them have chefs, much less sommeliers."

Greg made a gesture of dismissal with his hand. "I need a place like this. A lot of high-powered people come through here."

"Is that what you consider me? A high-powered person to wine and dine and get concessions from?"

"I like the sound of that last part. We could put some offers on the table, so to speak."

I think he's saying we should do it on the table before the sommelier arrives.

A quick check of Greg's aura revealed sharp spikes of

dark crimson, representing sexual passion. She looked away to let the aura fade.

"Offers for the foundation?" She decided to play it straight. "I'm eager to hear what you have in mind."

Mild disappointment showed in his eyes, but then they hardened, business-style.

"To put it simply, I have a public-relations problem. I need to soften the corporation's image. You look around, everybody's into philanthropy like it's the flavor of the month. Your Vitality for Life Foundation fits the bill. It isn't oversold in the market. Others are going for photo ops with sweet-faced kids. I'm going to do those photos with Grandma and Grandpa. A lot of folks out there are dealing with care of their elderly parents. It should strike a chord."

"We don't talk about it in such mercenary terms. But, yes, 'striking a chord' is an apt description. Caring for elderly parents is a common experience, and as more of the baby boomers come on line, thinking about aging issues is very popular. I think you're making a forward-thinking decision to go with the old folks over the sweet-faced kids."

She hadn't been able to keep the sarcastic tone out of her voice entirely, but Greg didn't pick it up.

"Forward-thinking. Good sell. I'll use that with the board. That's enough business for the day, don't you think?"

She excused herself to freshen up before lunch. In the swanky restroom, she reached into her purse and took out a large compact. While powdering her nose, she pressed a button to take a reading on the GPS device built into the compact. She might not know where Greg's office was, but at least she'd be able to find the restroom.

Lunch was delicious. Maliha ate lightly, remembering her appointment to do a little sparring after the meal. She asked for and received a tour of the seventh floor, which housed busy executive offices, with Greg showing off but keeping his own office off-limits. She took pictures, filed away her impressions and memorized the floor plan. Maliha turned heads wherever she went, but when the men saw she was with Greg, they turned back to their work. It wasn't part of the corporate culture to lust after the boss's new toy.

Outside the dojo, Greg sent her into a dressing room where she changed into a karate *gi*. An assortment of belts was available. She picked black and went to the dojo, where she bowed and entered. Greg was already inside, wearing a black belt. She gave him a courtesy bow.

Though he should be bowing to me, for both age and experience.

"I see you're not wearing pads." Greg was referring to the helmet and the chest, arm, and leg pads worn by students for sparring. "Sure that's okay?"

"Not a problem. If you can do without, so can I. Open hand or weapons?" The dojo had a well-equipped weapon wall.

"No weapons. I wouldn't want to hurt—"

She swept his leg, vaulted over him, punched a strike at his throat, stopping her hand a fraction of an inch away from his Adam's apple, and ended up standing on the other side of him as if nothing had happened. She offered him a hand up from the floor, but he didn't take it.

"Okay, let's get serious."

Yeah, let's.

Maliha kept him on edge but didn't dig deeply into her set of skills. It was clear he'd been trained by someone with an eclectic style similar to the way she fought: whatever works. They switched to eskrima sticks and then swords. Greg called a halt after twenty minutes of testing. He was red and sweating. Maliha's heartbeat had barely ticked up a notch.

"You're certainly a match for me," he said, puffing a little. "I thought you said you dabbled in martial arts. How'd you get so good?"

"Years of practice, I guess. I started when I was a lot younger."

"You must have started as a baby, then." He laughed at his own joke. "What do you think about taking on someone with more experience? My trainer's here today. I'm sure he'd love to work with a more advanced student than I am."

I've got better things to do than this. Like carve a bar of soap into a dragon or something.

"Sure, I'm up for it."

The trainer turned out to be a taciturn man from Central Asia who didn't say a word. She placed him as Mongolian.

Wind howled outside the small ger. *Inside, in the sweaty aftermath of fierce lovemaking, Susannah lounged naked in front of the fire. Wood smoke rose to the open hole in the ceiling. Snowflakes from the storm outside drifted down into the hole, met the rising column of smoke, and winked out of existence. She ran her hands across the furs beneath her and listened as her man sang and played the* morin huur, *a two-stringed fiddle with a carved horse's head on the handle. The instrument produced the sounds of a horse galloping across the steppes, and his voice rose and fell to match the rhythm. He set the fiddle down and turned to her, his eyes hot with lust, hotter than the fire. Her smile was all the invitation he needed.*

The trainer was a man about her height, well-muscled, compact, with a low center of gravity. He'd be harder to take down to the mat than Greg, but all that was needed was a feel for how much force to apply where, and she'd find that out the first time she tried.

She gave him a traditional bow, but he inclined his head slightly in return.

Arrogant son of a bitch. This is going to be fun.

Her first few attempts to throw him to the mat failed. She couldn't seem to use his weight against him, so she adjusted her strategy to swift, powerful kicks and rapid punches. He blocked everything she did, and answered her attacks with more-effective ones. Tempting as it was, she didn't want to get into it and show skills that were exceptional. She called it quits, admitting that he was too much for her.

Greg looked smug. A win by his trainer was a win by proxy for him, and it was apparent that Greg didn't like to lose. He excused himself, saying that he had to make a few phone calls and would meet her after she changed clothes. He hinted that she should shower in the dressing room, and she wondered if he had a peephole in there.

As soon as he left the room, the trainer spoke for the first time.

"Shall we continue?"

The trainer's voice was like a blast of cold air. She shivered and the hair rose on her forearms.

Before she could answer, he launched an attack that drove her back to the edge of the mat. In defense, she began to move faster, strike harder, use the walls as springboards. He was relentless, and the blows he used would be lethal if they connected. All pretense of a sparring exercise had vanished.

What is this? Who is this?

He came away from the weapon wall with a sword, leaving her no choice—she chose a sword, too. The pace of the fighting accelerated. He drove past her defenses and slashed her right arm, a stroke to weaken the muscles there. Instantly she spun to keep him from inflicting damage on her other arm, switching the sword to her left hand before her blood even hit the mat. She ended the spin in a crouch, an unusual position that she thought might take him off guard. His blade whistled above her head, a stroke that would have cut her in half if she'd been standing. She found an opening, and jabbed upward toward his armpit. It should disable him enough for her to put a stop to this contest. She had to stop it, because very soon she'd have to reveal skills that had taken more than one lifetime to acquire.

He blocked her unexpected jab, but a fraction of a second late. The blow was deflected downward into his arm. She was off balance, leaning forward into the movement, and struck harder than she meant to. The sword bit into his wrist, nearly severing his hand.

Horrified at what had happened, she pulled up on the next strike she'd launched, and stood motionless, as did he. He was bleeding profusely from the wrist, and his hand was hanging by thin band of skin.

Going to be hard to explain to Greg. I come for lunch and chop off somebody's hand.

The Mongolian pushed his hand back into place and held it there. She stared as the bleeding stopped and the flesh rejoined. In a minute he flexed his wrist with no sign of damage except red stains on his clothing.

He's Ageless.

The realization hit her hard. She was standing a few feet away from a being like she'd been, a servant of a demon. She couldn't breathe, couldn't move. All the blood seemed to have left her limbs, leaving them cold and immobile. Like her first days as a martial-arts student, she was in the presence of someone who could strike her dead at any moment. Her heart thudded against her ribs with a force that had nothing to do with physical exertion and everything to do with fear.

"My name is Subedei. We'll meet again on another battlefield."

He was gone in a flash. Or was he? The dojo was silent and threatening. At any moment, he could reappear behind her and slash her throat, or in front of her and run her through with the sword. With a running leap from the edge of the room, he could decapitate her, and in that second she would enter Rabishu's unending torment, her goals on Earth unfulfilled. The thought made her ill.

Subedei. S. My stalker, who put his initial on my photo like I belonged to him, who violated . . .

She pictured the black panties, then herself wearing them, and gasped. She didn't know how she knew it, but she knew for certain that Subedei's hand had rested on them between her legs. He'd done nothing more, but the touch was to claim her.

In the dressing room, still trembling, she stripped off her uniform. The wound on her arm wasn't serious. She ran water over her arm to clean off the blood, then wrapped the area tightly with gauze she found in the room's first-aid kit. She put her black dress back on, glad now for the long sleeves that hugged, and hid, her arms. As she stepped out into the hall and saw Greg walking toward her, she remembered that there was blood on the mats in the dojo, both hers and Subedei's.

Let Subedei deal with it. He wouldn't want it known, either.

On the way home, the pleasure of driving the McLaren forgotten, she pulled off the road and vomited into the grass when the fear of what could have happened in her encounter in the dojo hit her. Of what already had happened, some night in her home, his powerful hand resting on the most private of places.

She'd had better days.

Chapter Twenty-Three

After his guest took her leave, Greg Shale moved into the room adjacent to his office, which resembled a war room. In the dim light, monitors mounted on the walls surrounded his chair, a swiveling black leather seat that gave him a wide view of the screens. The changing displays showed a variety of information. Some were charts, some maps with gleaming pinpoints, like diamonds scattered on a spider web. Others were interior views of bright and busy rooms with uniformed people in motion. He could see himself in several of the monitors angled just right to catch his reflection. The colors and designs on his reflected view made him look machinelike, a robot with its electronic workings exposed. He was pleased with the look.

The bulk of the Mongolian blocked his view. It was startling, like a black cloud passing over the sun out of a sky that had been clear moments before.

"Shit, don't sneak up on me like that!"

Subedei gave no hint that he'd heard the complaint.

He needs to work on his fucking people skills. If he wasn't such a damned good bodyguard and trainer, I'd chuck him out.

Greg didn't mean that. It was a spot of luck that Subedei had come along right after Greg's former chief bodyguard was killed in a car crash. Being around Subedei somehow gave him a feeling of invincibility he'd never had with a bodyguard before. On the whole, the benefits of having

Subedei around seemed more than enough to compensate for the fact that the man wasn't the kind of deferential employee Greg liked.

Never said one goddamned "sir" to me in all these months, but he takes the personal-protection crap off my mind and lets me concentrate on important things. Like the Winters woman. Damn, she's hot. The way she moves on the mat . . . I can hardly wait until I get her moving under me.

"How was she, then? What did you think of her?"

"She's good, very good." Subedei's voice was deep, and there was a catch in it Greg hadn't heard before.

"Good, but no threat to us," Subedei continued. "You can forget about that and just enjoy her."

"Just what I wanted to hear. If you want her when I'm done with her, go ahead." His bodyguard didn't seem to mind Greg's castoffs, although Greg was sure that supply alone wasn't enough to satisfy the man's immense appetite for sex. For a moment he imagined what it would be like to be the powerful Subedei, who was uninhibited by social restraints and took what he wanted, when he wanted it. The thought aroused him.

Not only a bodyguard, but a role model as well.

He decided it was a good time for a little afternoon delight with Fawn, his current personal—and extremely loyal—assistant.

When he looked up from his reverie, Subedei was gone.

Before he could call Fawn, the special phone rang—the one he didn't dare ignore.

He listened for a minute. "I'll be right there."

No longer in the mood for a romp with Fawn, he headed to his private parking area. It had just turned into a shitty afternoon. He had to give a progress report to the boss, known to him as B. T., since he had some unpronounceable Chinese name. Mentally, Greg called him Big Turd.

Fucking Chinese are taking over the world.

Greg drove to Morton Arboretum, where he'd met with the boss twice before. Walking through the East Woods, Greg had to admit that the woods were beautiful in October, with the brilliant gold of the sugar maples as a backdrop to a scattering of oaks, with their deep crimson leaves. It was a place where peace could soak into a person's bones. Greg wasn't there for peaceful meditation, though.

He rounded a bend in the trail and spotted the old man sitting on a bench, wearing a floppy hat to protect his nearly bald head from the sun. He had binoculars to his eyes, staring into the trees looking for some damn bird or other. It was quite a trick, since at other times Greg got the impression that the old man was blind.

Greg sat down on the bench and neither of them said anything for a few minutes. B. T. finished his observation, put down his binoculars, and made a quick notation in a journal.

"A cerulean warbler. Rare in this area. This little one should have left for South America already."

Greg shrugged. The man's voice sounded like paper crumpling, and his body looked as though a good kick to the belly would snap him in half.

Subedei spoke of this man with humility, even a twinge of fear, and Greg couldn't imagine his bodyguard bowing his head to a weakling. Subedei had once called him Grandfather, but Greg didn't think there was a literal relationship. It was a respect thing. Taking his bodyguard's warnings to heart, Greg stayed on his best behavior and refrained from making the smart-ass remarks he might direct at a weak old man. Subedei had warned him not to speak until B. T. asked him a question. He had also hinted that Greg should sit on the ground at the boss's feet and that he should keep his eyes lowered, but all that was too much. Did his bodyguard think this was the Middle Ages or something?

This is America, and we don't do that peasant shit.

"The sun is pleasantly warm today," the old man said.

Does that call for an answer?

Playing it safe, Greg nodded. He noticed that the man's clothes were summer-thin, and he wore no coat. Greg was wearing a sweater, and a jacket on top of that, against the fall chill in the air.

"I believe you have diverted some of the project's development funds for your own use in propping up your corporation. Is that true?"

How the hell did he know that?

Greg hesitated. With anyone else, Greg would lie. With B. T., he tried to gauge whether he could get away with it or not.

The man suddenly fixed Greg with eyes as hard as stone, ancient and cruel and supremely confident, and full of utter disregard for human life.

Nope, not blind, unless he could turn it on and off.

Greg shivered as he realized that if anybody were to be broken in half with a kick here, the two bloody pieces lying on the ground would be his own.

Without quite realizing it, he dropped his gaze respectfully to the ground.

"Yes, sir, that's true."

"You will remedy the situation immediately." There was an unspoken *and it will never happen again.* "Now tell me about your progress."

Greg told him in detail about the work on Project CESR, and when he was dismissed, he hurried away. His previous meetings with the old man hadn't made much of an impression, but this time Greg knew exactly where he stood: on shaky ground that could tip him into hell at any time.

Chapter Twenty-Four

Maliha wanted to sort out her thoughts about Subedei in private, but when she got back to her building, Arnie pulled her aside before she could get through the door.

"There's a DEA agent in the lobby waiting for you, Ms. Winters. I told him you weren't home and I couldn't buzz him in, but this guy doesn't take no for an answer. I think he's prepared to sit in the lobby for days. He had a sandwich delivered from Dave's Deli and read the *Tribune*."

"You'd think he'd have better things to do with the government's time. Thanks for your efforts, Mr. Henshaw."

Arnie stretched his neck to look around her at the lone figure sitting in the lobby and shook his head. "You want to go up the back way?"

He meant the loading dock and a service elevator.

"No, I'll take care of it. I wouldn't want him to grow roots in there." She turned to walk inside.

"Wait. Ms. Winters, you've got a little spot of . . . er, paint under your right ear."

She held still while he dampened a blindingly white handkerchief from a bottle of water and dabbed at her face. The handkerchief came away streaked with red.

"Don't worry. I'll take care of the, er, paint rag." He folded the handkerchief and tucked it in a compartment of his desk.

She approached Jake, knowing that his eyes were appraising how she filled out the sexy black dress she'd worn to meet Greg Shale. She knew she looked damn good. She'd braided her hair when she began sparring at ShaleTech. In the car, she'd loosened the braid and run her fingers through her hair, so it had a mussed, come-fuck-me look.

"Want to come up to my place?"

It wasn't an invitation a man would turn down. She walked toward the elevator bank, leaving him to stand there and watch her receding ass or follow her. He caught up with her, but not as rapidly as he could have.

When the elevator doors opened, an elderly woman tenant who lived on Maliha's floor stood there, her little poodle in her arms. She was taking the dog for a walk, as she did every evening. Maliha nodded at her. She nodded back and winked, her eyes stuck on Jake.

"Have a good evening, dearie," she said, as she got off the elevator. "Don't do anything I wouldn't do."

Then, in a whisper that was intended for Maliha's ears but was loud because Mrs. Haplinger was mostly deaf, she said, "This one looks like a keeper."

After she was gone, Maliha looked at Jake and shrugged.

Way to go, Mrs. Haplinger. You've got him thinking I bring men home every night.

She took him to the condo on the thirty-ninth floor and plopped into an upholstered chair, breathing a sigh of relief that her two houseguests were asleep in the guest room, or at least quiet. She wanted to close her eyes, ignore him, and think about her encounter with an Ageless one, but Jake started in right away.

"So where did all that information come from?"

What happened to the sweet talk at Al's Beef?

"What have you done so far?" she countered.

"I ordered half a dozen computers under different names. I got the upgrade for express shipping, like you said. I should have them in a couple of days."

"Good service."

He shrugged. "My main concern is getting those machines into the lab right away. According to your information, is every computer affected, or a small percentage?"

"Every one."

"Jesus. What a scheme, if it's real. How come you know so much about it?"

He'd come full circle and was back to his original question. Time for some creative fibbing.

"I had a friend who worked for SkyDevice."

"In India?"

"Yes. An Indian friend. In India. Something wrong with that?"

"No. Would you mind if I used your bathroom? That sandwich I ate . . ."

"Of course not. Down the hall, first door on the left."

It took him too long to find and use the bathroom, so she knew he was searching all the areas down the hall.

"What makes you think I'd keep my drugs in the bathroom if I had any?" Maliha asked when he returned. He ignored her jibe.

"What's in the locked room at the end of the hall?"

Oh, two men living with me. The rooms inside her condo had locks keyed by fingerprints. She'd added Yanmeng and Amaro to the guest bedroom's lock.

"My sexy underwear and leather-and-whip collection. Wanna see?"

The rims of his ears turned red. "Nothing in the medicine cabinet, nothing stashed in the toilet tank," he reported. "Don't you ever need an aspirin?"

"Rarely." She raised her eyebrows. "And I thought we were becoming close. We'll always have Al's."

He missed the reference to *Casablanca.*

It was time to check out this man who could pivot from sexy flirting to prickly questioning, just because she'd mentioned a little drug-smuggling case. She looked beyond Jake, let her eyes go unfocused a little, and waited for his aura to show. There were splashes of blue for high ideals and desire to help others. Thick coils of yellow for intelligence and self-knowledge. There was more: red tendrils of buried anger, ribbons of black for negative, probably murderous, deeds. Jake was not a simple do-gooder. He had a bad past, a present guided by a sense of justice but defined by violence, and an uncertain future.

We're two of a kind, kind of.

She understood that his life today was defined by something bad in the past, maybe truly evil—something he'd overcome. She could relate to that.

"Getting back to this Indian friend. Would you put me in touch with him? Or her?"

"If you'd like to try a séance. He died last month."

Sounds weak, even to me.

"Details?"

She didn't say anything. She preferred to remain a woman of mystery when she was making things up as she went along.

"You know I'm going to have to investigate your background and the possibility of your involvement in this scheme."

"Why would I tell you about it if I'm involved?"

"Could be lots of reasons. Maybe you want out of the smuggling and you were threatened. Maybe you're betraying a boyfriend who screwed around on you and you want to get back at him."

"Creative. You should be the novelist, not me."

"Maybe you were trying to get close to me so you could use me somehow. Just a means to an end."

He didn't bother to conceal the hurt he was feeling that made him say that. It touched a nerve for Maliha, too.

This is what I get when love enters the picture.

"Go ahead and investigate. Knock yourself out."

Her voice had hardened, along with her resolve. Her Marsha Winters base identity was rock solid. Marsha was gainfully employed, paid her taxes, had no police record, and had parents (deceased) and a sister (alas, also deceased). She had a good credit record, a B.A. in Fine Arts (emphasis in creative writing) from the University of Iowa, and an M.B.A. from Harvard. She'd started a charitable foundation, didn't gamble, didn't use drugs. She drove a flashy car, but could legitimately afford it on her reported income from her writing career.

Maliha was ready to wrap it up. She didn't like his scrutiny directed at her.

"I'll be talking to you again."

"I'm sure you can find the door to let yourself out. After all, you have pictures of my bedroom. I'll be sweeping for bugs after you leave."

He pursed his lips, which meant that she actually had to follow through with her threat. He put his business card on the kitchen counter as he left. "You can reach me twenty-four/seven if you want to talk."

She raised one hand and waved bye-bye.

He took with him the sex-charged energy that had permeated the air between them in spite of the conversation. When he was gone, she did a meticulous search for listening devices, kicked off her shoes, and fell asleep.

He called at 6 A.M.

"I've accomplished a lot overnight."

"And this is my business because?"

"You'll be happy to know your background's rock solid," Jake went on. "In fact, you're a little too squeaky clean. You almost have a minister's wife thing going."

"Did you know it's six A.M.?"

"Just keeping you apprised of my progress. I found the downstate warehouse."

"You did? Tell me about it."

"Tell me the name of your friend from India."

"Oh, we're into 'show me yours' again."

"What's your interest in this, Marsha?"

"Can't I just be a citizen doing a good deed?"

"You'll be hearing from me. I can't wait until our next enlightening conversation."

"Yeah, and I don't like beef stroganoff."

It wasn't the best retort she'd ever come up with. She hung up.

Maliha considered moving up to her place on the forty-eighth floor. It just seemed like too much trouble, though, and she wanted to get an early start this morning. Yanmeng and Amaro, whom she'd heard come in after midnight, were giving her some much-needed privacy. She started some coffee, and while it brewed, took a quick shower. As the warm water streamed over her body, she reviewed the phone conversation and thought about the black ribbons in Jake's aura.

In such a short time, a blossoming romance had turned into an acrid standoff.

I'm out of practice with this love thing. I could have kept my mouth shut about the drug smuggling, at least long enough to find out if there was something serious between Jake and me.

When she was dressed, her phone rang. She was sure it was Jake again. She picked up the phone.

"If you're going to keep being so suspicious of me, you're never going to get to first base, much less home plate."

"Uh . . . Ms. Winters, this is the doorman."

"Oh."

"A friend is here to visit you. Ms. Randy Baxter."

"Oh. Thank you. Send her up. I . . ." He disconnected before she could apologize for her tirade.

Randy knocked and Maliha let her in. They hugged at the door. Randy smelled of Ivory soap and clothes hung in the sun to dry.

"Mmm. I smell coffee." Randy swept past her toward the kitchen. She was in full Earth-Mother mode, with long-sleeved peasant's blouse over a tiered skirt long enough so that only the toes of her shoes showed when she moved. It produced a gliding effect.

"Don't you get cold in that? It's October."

"Cold? Nope. I'm layered, see?" She tugged her skirt up and revealed thermal underwear.

Randy found the coffee, poured each of them a cup, and settled at the table.

"I got some bad vibes from you the last time we talked," Randy said. "Something's going on and I want to know what it is. Then I want to know what I can do to help."

Maliha considered where she stood with Randy. Her friend knew nothing about her age, what she'd done as a demon's slave, or the scales carved on her body, or redemption on a grand scale. Randy didn't know about crystal shards or what it was like to be helpless in Rabishu's claws.

There was a whole world of things Randy didn't know. It was as though Maliha lived in many dimensions but presented only a two-dimensional view to Randy: a cardboard cutout that fit neatly into the twenty-something lifestyle. Maliha treasured Randy's friendship precisely because it was outside the complex, dangerous world of her quest.

She thinks we're alike, but only a little slice of me is like her.

"Hello?" Randy put her hand in front of Maliha's face and waved it back and forth.

"Uh, sorry."

"You were like zoned out. C'mon, open up. You can tell me anything."

Maliha made a decision. *Not ready to open up. Status quo, for now.*

"I went to a charity event. It was okay but boring."

"Music? Dancing?"

"Only if you count a string quartet. They had one of those tacky champagne waterfalls."

Randy made a face. "Tell me something important, like what you wore."

"The new blue dress, those sandals with the ties . . ."

"Those are sooo sexy. What about this Greg guy?"

"I already told you about him. Could be we're going to hook up."

"So what's the problem?"

"He's just a little . . . off. Like he's got a dangerous side."

"Dangerous like dark and mysterious or dangerous like psycho serial killer?"

Maliha laughed. "I don't think he's a psycho."

The verdict is still out on that one.

"Okay, then. You need to get your head out of those books you write. Have some fun. Take a walk on the wild side, isn't that what they say? If things get weird, you call me and I'll come over and beat the shit out of him."

"I'd like to see that. He's into martial arts."

"I guess I'll have to let you handle him then, Miss Black Belt Smarty Pants."

"Wanna arm wrestle? I'll give you a two-second head start."

"Are you kidding? The last time you almost dislocated my shoulder."

"Three seconds?"

Randy reached over and punched Maliha lightly in the arm. "So enough of this serious crap. You haven't lost track of Jake in all this mooning about Greg, have you?"

"No." It was an honest answer. Randy waited for her to elaborate.

"Nothing to talk about, huh? In that case, let me tell you about Rip."

"Don't you have to get to work?"

"I took the day off. I was worried about you. Didn't want to have the clock ticking while we talked."

Maliha checked the time. "Listen, I've got a thing I have to do, but I could be back for a late lunch. How about three P.M.? You can tell me all about Mr. Corrugated Abdomen."

Randy laughed. "I can make it. I'll give you a call later and we'll decide where."

"What are you doing on your day off?"

"What else? Shopping and the spa, girlfriend. Come with?"

Tempting. I could use a decadent day.

Then Maliha thought about lying in the alleyway in Atlanta, feeling her life—*Nando's life*—slip away. It took the glow off the spa idea.

"I'd love to, but I've . . ."

"Got that thing to do. See you later." Randy glided to the door.

Maliha drove the McLaren northwest on I–90. She crossed into Wisconsin, keeping a light foot on the gas pedal and enjoying the fall scenery even though it was raining off and on. About 10:30 A.M., she pulled in to Madison.

She didn't want to enter the house that was the object of her drive until closer to lunchtime, but she parked a block away and observed. The McLaren kept attracting the attention, though, so she moved away a mile and walked back.

The modest house under observation belonged to Samantha Dearborn, mother of Karen, the nine-year-old girl who'd died after receiving incorrect medication from a PharmBots machine. The girl who was the reason for lawsuits for five million dollars against PharmBots and an equal amount from the hospital. Amaro's research had demonstrated the corporation's culpability.

Samantha Dearborn was a widow with no other children. She and her husband were both schoolteachers, but he had died in a car accident when Karen was a toddler. Karen had had a serious heart defect that had just been repaired. It had been the third time her daughter had been in the hospital that year. Samantha had no insurance and no resources left. She'd put every penny she owned, and some that she didn't, into her daughter's care. The medical bills had mounted steadily, but she fought for the best care for Karen.

She still had the medical bills and other loans, but no daughter.

The hospital would have considered writing off the large bill as a compassionate gesture and good PR, but they were holding off to use it as a bargaining wedge in case of a judgment in the lawsuit against them. The whole situation was a mess, with both parties willing to escalate the fight and a grieving mother at the center of it all.

Maliha decided on a direct approach, walked right up to the front door, and rang the bell.

A woman answered through the wooden door.

"Who is it?"

"Mrs. Dearborn, I'm the grief counselor from the, er, school district. May I come in?"

"I've already spoken to . . . oh, all right, I suppose so."

The door opened to reveal a sallow-faced woman in her thirties in a worn housedress.

Maliha sat for two hours at Samantha's kitchen table, drank tea and ate grilled cheese sandwiches with her, looked at her photo album, absorbed her bitterness and saw through it to the loving woman underneath.

In spite of her loss, Samantha had had something Maliha

wondered if she would ever have—a child to gather into her arms.

Maliha began formulating plans that PharmBots wasn't going to be happy about.

There were four messages on her phone when she got home, the first from Randy. She begged off on the late-afternoon lunch, saying that she'd met a hot guy at the spa, some chauffeur waiting to pick up his employer. The next two were from Jake. He'd had Interpol look into SkyDevice employees who'd died in August or September.

There weren't any, and he wanted to know why not.

The third message was from a friend of hers, archaeologist Manco Serrano. They'd met at a symposium in Lima, and she'd conveyed her interest in unusual artifacts that raised questions about their origins. It was an intensely personal quest of hers, something that might mean she could avoid the whole Rabishu-plaything business if she died before atoning for all the lives she'd taken.

Years ago, she had deceived Rabishu into revealing the location of the Tablet of the Overlord, an object all of the demons knew how to locate. She convinced him that Anu might have hidden one of the diamond shards in the same area. It was a plausible idea, since no one would think to look for it there. He agreed to have her search for it and gave her the location. After a suitable period, she told him she'd checked and there was no diamond shard there. She hadn't even made the effort, but she'd filed away the location of the tablet.

In truth, when she was Ageless, she had searched for the shards halfheartedly or not at all, because she had no interest in helping Rabishu in his attempt to become all-powerful.

Since she'd left the demon's service, Maliha had intensified her search. Her plans were vague at first—maybe something to blackmail Rabishu with—but settled into a goal as much a part of her as the carving of the scale on her body. She wanted that lens not just to keep Rabishu or one of his brothers from finding it, but for her own use. Maliha intended to get rid of the demons by wielding the Tablet of the Overlord against them. With each one she vanquished, a portion of the misery the human race suffered would be gone.

What would Earth be like without war, suffering, and disease? Did they serve an essential purpose in giving humans something to strive for in their elimination? Or were they the ball and chain around the ankle of the human race, preventing the achievement of its fullest potential? Lord Nergal may have left those demons behind on a whim. If he'd taken his servants with him, life could have been very different for humans.

She had a network of archaeologists looking, in a casual manner, for artifacts that just didn't fit into the location or time period they were working on. She reinforced their interest in staying in touch with her by making them into characters in her novels. They were as thrilled as kids on a roller coaster when they spotted their names. She got an image of a whole squadron of academics hunched over their dusty pot shards, fragile textiles, and canopic jars with contents of mummified livers and intestines, taking lunch breaks and sticking their noses into one of her sexy pulp novels, scanning the pages for their own or colleagues' names.

"Marsha, this is Manco, at the Caral site. I've found something . . . something odd. I have this piece I've been studying, and I've been putting off registering it. I think you're going to want to see this. I sent you a photo by email. Talk to you soon."

His message was intriguing because Manco wasn't one to go out on a limb, keeping a find hidden. Methodical and by the book were more like it.

She eagerly checked her email, found his message, and looked at the photo. It astounded her. The simple pot was covered with what looked like Sumerian cuneiform, even though the image wasn't very clear. Manco's hastily handwritten note across the top of the photo indicated that the pot had been found in the vicinity of figurines carbon dated to be 4,650 years old, comparable in time with the ancient Sumerian civilization—but over eight thousand miles away from Sumer.

The photo wasn't high resolution, but Maliha could make out some writing that was larger than the rest. Filling in the blanks for what was illegible, she came up with a translation.

Anu, son of Anshar and Kishar, leaves this for the children of the Great Above, should their wisdom grow.

She closed her eyes and took a few deep breaths to control the surge of excitement she felt. Maliha fired off a response to Manco, urging him to delay revealing the existence of the pot a little longer, until she had the opportunity to make a rollout, a digital image formed by placing the pot on a turntable and snapping photos as it rotated. The images were blended together by software to form a flat, complete picture of the entire circumference of the pot. A high-resolution rollout could be printed as a large color poster so the detail could be examined. An archaeologist no longer had to travel to the physical location of an artifact to study it. He or she could just get the disk.

After she had her rollout, Manco could turn the actual pot over to an antiquities director and get credit for his find. Getting that rollout in her hands couldn't wait. When she found out that she couldn't get a commercial flight to Lima until the next morning, she chartered a private jet that would be available in three hours and threw some clothing and weapons into a suitcase. She was a regular customer of the charter agency, so no one would be screening her luggage. They'd already verified that Marsha Winters was an upstanding citizen, meaning one with deep pockets.

After the whirlwind of activity, she had nothing to do until she took a taxi to the airport.

Plenty of time to return Jake's calls.

Instead she sat down for a writing session, incorporating the inept and annoying but sexy rookie cop Jackie Stacked, named in honor of Jake Stackman, into her book.

Chapter Twenty-Five

Responding to the intriguing summons from the Peruvian archaeologist, Maliha was onboard the jet that had taken off from Chicago. She called Amaro to let him know about Jake's involvement in the drug investigation.

"I already know. He checked parts of your ID that triggered a warning. I've been looking into your man Jake."

"He's not my man."

"Caution is the word here. Jake looks okay on the surface, but parts of his service record have been expunged. That typically happens when an agent has crossed the line but is too valuable for some reason to shitcan. Or he's got the goods on somebody higher up. It could be your man Jake is only halfway one of the good guys."

"He's not my man. Stop saying that."

"Touchy, hmm? Do you get PMS at your age?"

"How rude."

"I've got news on ShaleTech. I've been chatting with the administrative assistant to Edward Rupert, ShaleTech's chief financial officer. Her name is Betty, and she's a member of a salsa dance club. The chat room's associated with the club. I told her I was planning to join soon so I could meet her."

"You dance?"

"Hell, yes. Don't you?"

"You'll have to teach me the modern stuff sometime. My dance technique never got past 'Rock Around the Clock.'"

"I find that hard to believe. Dance salsa with me, and you can wear one of those sexy dresses with all the fringes."

"Can't. I'm on a plane to Lima. Tell me more about Betty."

"Betty is thirty, a little shy, and joined the dance club to try to be outgoing and meet people. She took gymnastic lessons as a girl, so she thought that maybe dancing would be her route to the man of her dreams. Why are you going to Lima?"

"One of the shards might have turned up. Betty told you all this stuff in a public chat room?"

"Tsk tsk. I would never have a conversation like that in public. I set up a secure, private chat for us. She was a little reluctant to open up about herself, but when she did, it all came out in a rush because she's worried about something. She found out that the ShaleTech CFO is keeping two sets of books. She's afraid Greg knows that she knows, and she could get fired or a lot worse. The lead on the shard looks solid?"

"Very solid. I have a preliminary translation that mentions Anu. I still can't get past the fact that she told you all this without meeting you."

"She checked me out on MySpace. I guess that makes me trustworthy."

Amaro is worthy of trust. I trust him with my life. Betty has no idea who she's stumbled into, though it was no accident on Amaro's part. Probably saved her life.

"Anyway, we met in person for lunch, and things took off from there."

Amaro 1, Maliha 0. So far, my lunch date hasn't taken off.

"I hope you're taking that 'fired or worse' part seriously. Especially the 'worse.' How could Greg find out?"

"Betty's boss was working with Greg in Greg's conference room. Betty came in to deliver some papers her boss had requested for the meeting. She saw a wall safe standing open in Greg's office. She found the ledgers, and without thinking she locked the safe after she'd seen them, instead of leaving it open as she'd found it. Greg and her boss came back and found her in the room. Neither of the men said anything, but she's pretty sure Greg remembered he left the safe unlocked, and that's why he returned so soon—to check on it and lock it up. Plus, she's a CPA, and he knows that whatever she saw, she'd understand the significance of it."

"Betty's nosy. She's also on borrowed time."

"I know. I already did something about it. I put her in my own private witness protection program."

"Good for you. You didn't break her heart, did you?"

"Much as I'd like to think I break the heart of every woman who can't have me, no. I wasn't her type."

"I need a look at that second set of books."

"Breaking and entering is your thing," he said.

Can't argue with that.

"Do me a favor, will you? Find out whatever you can on a guy named Subedei."

"How do you spell that? What's the last name, or is that the last name?"

"How should I know? I'm asking for information on him, aren't I?"

He started in on the PMS thing again, and she hung up on him, then remembered she had been going to ask about Rosie's countdown to baby number three.

Best I not raise the subject.

She reflected that her excuse about getting away had been at least partly true. She did need to get away. The contrast between the sexual and emotional attraction she felt with Jake and the suspicions that had arisen made her edgy. It was good to be unreachable. She wanted him to proceed with his investigation of the heroin smuggling and see what he turned up on his own. That was the point of getting him involved in the first place. She was disappointed that he'd become fixated on her as a party to the smuggling.

After the refueling stop in Miami, Maliha slept until the pilot announced the approach to Jorge Chavez Airport in Lima. She rented a Land Rover. After all, the jet charter to and from Peru cost her $100,000. The Rover seemed in keeping.

She drove up the coast and got into Huacho about ten in

the morning. Manco didn't answer a call to his cell phone, so she went to his room and knocked on the door.

No answer.

Out? No, he was expecting me.

After slipping on a pair of gloves, she picked the lock and pushed the door open a few inches. It was dark inside, with the drapes tightly closed. The scent of blood reached her nose. She crouched and drew a knife, and pushed the door open wider with it.

When she was sure no one else was in the room, she turned on the lights. Manco was dead, face up on the floor, his throat slit. Very recently dead, so recently that the killer might have walked right by her as she entered the hotel.

She couldn't stay long, but she sat on the floor next to him and put her hand on his chest. He was a good man, and it was likely he'd died because of what he discovered, or even because he phoned her to tell her about it.

From the blood pattern in the room, it was evident he'd been sitting in the chair at the desk when he was approached from behind and killed. Checking the window behind the drawn drapes, she found that a hole had been cut in the glass and the window raised.

She slid his body across the floor and sat down in his chair, shifting around to find the exact position he'd been in as he worked at the desk.

Nothing happened for a while and then she felt herself sliding into the imprint left behind when Manco died.

She was Manco, sitting at the desk gazing down at a pot surrounded by foam in a hard case. He had a sheet of paper on which he'd copied some of the cuneiform, and a reference book open to a page on Sumer. He'd been getting close. Maybe he'd deciphered the first sentence, as she had.

Her head was yanked back, and she felt the sting of the blade as it was drawn across her throat. She raised her hands to her neck, then pulled them away to see them covered with blood. Toppling out of the chair, she landed face up and saw her attacker. As her life's blood spilled on the floor, she lost feeling in her arms and legs as her body was shutting down.

The attacker was wearing a black hood that covered his face with crude slits cut for his eyes, and he was holding the case containing the pot. The hood didn't matter to Maliha. She was looking at his aura, which no piece of cloth could hide.

Black, black, streaked with a foul blend of the muddy green of greed. The man had done many wrongs, and would do many more, and his aura was repulsive to see. Maliha's eyes closed as Manco died. She felt the cool, tingling sensation on her skin of the wisps of spirit that remained gathering around her. She waited until it had dissipated and opened her eyes. It was a relief to her that Manco was now whole.

The pot and the notes he had been making were gone from the desk. Searching around the floor, she found what she was looking for: the faint trace of the aura she'd seen and could recognize. The killer had left behind aural footprints. She concentrated on them until they brightened a little, bright enough to follow. She could track the ugly black-and-green trail of footprints as surely as a bloodhound could follow a scent. She set off after him on foot.

He hadn't gone far. She found him about half a mile away in a tumbledown shack that stunk of vomit and urine. Many of the other villagers here were poor, but they were good-hearted and didn't turn to crime. She wondered how much the man had been paid for ending Manco's life. Probably some pitiful amount like fifty dollars.

Controlling her anger, she got the story out of him. He'd been paid to silence Manco and obtain the pottery case. Manco must have talked to someone, dropped some kind of hint that he had something valuable in his room. Maybe an observant hotel clerk just guessed it from the way Manco clutched the case.

The case wasn't in the murderer's shack. A man had taken it away, the same man who paid for the murder. He was a stranger, American, who came in on a plane on the airstrip about thirty miles down the coastal highway, and was leaving the same way.

After she got the information she wanted, Maliha snapped the killer's neck and didn't hang around.

Let his spirit find its own way. Or not.

She ran back to her car and sped down the highway toward the airfield she'd seen on her drive to Caral. It had to be the one. She got there in time to see a man get on an old, battered twin-engine cargo plane with a suitcase big enough to hold the pot.

It wasn't Subedei, as she'd feared, but a pudgy older man, his bald head gleaming in the sunlight.

She slipped into the unattended cargo hold seconds before the loading door banged shut and was secured from the outside. She'd made it just in time.

With the plane in the air and her hiding place undisturbed, Maliha used a flashlight she found strapped to a metal strut to examine her surroundings. The cargo was innocuous but had a strong odor; it was sacks of onions grown in the Supe Valley.

By this time, I smell like a sack of onions, too.

She couldn't tell, because her nose was overloaded. Maliha found a hatch that led upward into the passenger compartment, but it was locked from the other side.

Thinking she might have to stay in the smelly hold area the entire time, she felt a lurch as the plane started climbing higher. The hold, already chilly after takeoff, began dropping in temperature. She'd figured the plane was going to make a short hop to Lima or some other nearby city where the passengers would take a flight out of the country, but instead it was going to cross the Andes. She'd done it a number of times, but never in a dark, freezing hold. The mountain crossing could be tricky. She hoped the pilot had a lot of experience. The likely destination was Iquitos. Although surrounded by rain forest, the town had an airport large enough to handle the cargo plane. It was the launch point for Amazonian expeditions, and its airport served the coca plantations carved out of the rain forest, although that wasn't in the tourist brochure.

Maliha had her own idea of a destination. She wanted to go back to Lima, where she had a jet with the meter running that could get her home with the prize. It was time to hijack the plane.

Her flashlight revealed another hatch. This one was unlocked, but there was something heavy on it keeping it from opening upward. She pushed harder to open it, sliding the obstruction off the top. It slid into something else with a metallic clang loud enough to reveal her presence. She ducked down and concealed herself among the onions.

Nothing happened, so after a while she raised the hatch lid again, just enough to see out. She was at the rear of a large, open passenger compartment that held a dozen seats up front. It wasn't a creature-comfort flight.

Two of the seats were occupied. The bald man she'd seen striding toward the plane was there, along with a much younger woman. Maliha opened the lid wider and crawled out on all fours. The object that had been holding down the hatch was a rolling cart that should have been secured to the floor to keep it from moving. It was a serving cart used by a flight attendant, but there was no attendant for two passengers.

Along with creature comforts, basic safety rules had been discarded.

Maliha silently opened the door of a restroom in the back of the plane and slipped inside. She needed a few minutes to plan the hijacking.

Pilot, copilot, two passengers. Probable handguns. No sweat.

Sitting on the toilet, she was rehearsing the plan in her mind when the door opened.

The woman passenger was standing there, and it was more than probable that there was a gun in her hand.

"I told you I heard something back here," she yelled.

Maliha came flying off the toilet with a lunge at the woman's midsection. She hit the woman squarely in the stomach and knocked her to the floor. The gun went off, a wild shot that penetrated the hull of the fuselage over the right wing. The shrill sound of air whistling from the pressurized cabin through the bullet hole distracted the bald man, who'd turned at the sound of his companion's voice.

Maliha got to her feet, stomped down on the woman's arm, and sent the gun sliding across the floor. Her next kick went to the woman's hip, breaking it and putting her out of commission, unarmed and injured.

Or so Maliha thought.

The woman started dragging herself across the floor toward the gun.

Maliha kicked her in the shoulder, spinning her around and cracking her head on the hull. The woman fell into the stillness of death, eyes open, blood seeping from her ears and the wound on her skull. Maliha regretted that she hadn't had time to do something less drastic.

A bullet whined past her head. Maliha could see daylight entering the plane through two holes. A few more and things could get dicey.

The bald man had recovered from his surprise. She did a handspring, then two more, to cross the distance between them, ending with a whirling kick that shattered his forearm and sent the gun bouncing off the side of the fuselage. As she came out of the kick, Maliha pulled a folded throwing star from her pocket and flicked her wrist to open it. The six-pointed star with serrated blades was a gleaming blur until it bit into the bald man's neck.

There was no time to observe as he collapsed. The cockpit door opened and a man barreled toward her, carrying a fire axe. She sidestepped and then tried to trip him, but he veered away from her outstretched leg, hit the hull at speed, ran partway up, and flipped to come out behind her. The axe sliced her calf and slid out of his hands. Her opponent was still in motion, and as he moved by the fallen bald man, he plucked the throwing star from the dead man's throat with a practiced motion that confirmed he was formidable.

Ignoring the pain from her leg, Maliha picked up the axe and used it to block the throwing star that came spinning toward her.

Confined in the narrow space of the fuselage, the man was using a path of motion that was too predictable. He was good, but not good enough. Maliha aimed the bloodied axe at his projected location and launched it forcefully. As her fingers let go, she slipped in her own blood, and her aim went awry. The axe just missed him and crashed through one of the windows in the compartment. The emergency oxygen masks dropped and air howled. The man was sucked toward the window and ended up with his shoulder pressed against it, his arm hanging outside. He screamed and blood spattered the adjacent windows. Air rushing by at over three hundred miles per hour, twice the speed of the winds of a category five hurricane, had ripped off the lower portion of his arm.

Maliha ended his misery with a knife to the heart. He remained in place, his shoulder joint jammed into the window opening like a cork.

The plane was tilted downward, descending rapidly, and it shouldn't have been. The copilot in the cockpit should have adjusted to the change in pressure by now, since the pilot was doing a fine job of plugging the leak at the window. She approached the cockpit door, which was banging open and closed.

When the door swung open, she leaped in, ready for anything in this bloody airplane. There was no fourth man. The plane had been flying its dangerous route without a copilot.

Should've guessed. Yet another violation.

The view out the window was alarming. A mountain peak was coming up fast on her right. She threw herself into the pilot's seat and struggled to pull up and turn. The right wing clipped a snow-covered outcropping and broke off, leaving a huge hole in the fuselage.

The plane hit the mountain with terrific force and broke apart. The front section of the fuselage slid on the snow, while the rear smashed into the side of the mountain and disintegrated. After sliding for some distance down the side of the mountain, the front section came to rest.

Maliha lost consciousness when the plane hit, and came to, shaking in the cold. Her wounded leg was numb, which in her experience wasn't a good sign.

Not trusting her leg to hold her in the uncertain terrain,

Maliha pulled herself around within the wreckage, going from handhold to handhold.

The nose of the plane was stuck against a rock outcropping, and the flight deck was crumpled. The radio didn't work and the emergency locator transmitter was smashed. She wasn't ready to try hiking out. Her leg needed recuperation time, and in this harsh environment, time was something she couldn't count on.

Maliha the Ageless assassin wouldn't have worried about the situation. The leg wound would have healed within minutes, and she could have run down the mountain. Maliha the mortal—that was a different story. She survived the crash only to face a slow death on the mountaintop.

A search of the wreckage turned up something very important, though. The suitcase holding the pot had been trapped under a twisted metal seat that held it in place like a seat belt.

Opening the suitcase, she found Manco's hard case centered inside, ringed with packing peanuts. The wind picked up some of the peanuts and created a miniature unnatural blizzard that moved off down the slope. Unwilling to open the case and find her prize shattered into dust after lives had been spent to get it, she set it aside and searched for food and emergency supplies. She found a few energy bars in the cockpit, jammed under the flight stick, and then a bag of onions from the hold.

A pillow tossed from the plane yielded strips of cloth from the pillowcase to wrap her leg wound. The rest of the pillowcase she fashioned into a hood for her head, with thin slits in front of her eyes, allowing her to see out but decreasing the likelihood of snow blindness.

The deep blue sky seen at high altitudes had become covered with heavy, gray clouds, and as Maliha searched the wreckage, she felt the first snowflakes on her shoulders. Approaching a shape already lightly dusted with snow, she found the body of the bald man. She stripped off his clothing and layered it on top of hers, then stuffed pieces of his underwear into his boots, slipped them on her feet, and tied them on for extra insulation. As heavier snow fell, she went back to the fuselage and worked her way into an area out of the wind. It was the best she could do.

When a plane exceeds its flight plan's arrival time, a search should be initiated. Given the propensity for violation of rules, however, she doubted that a flight plan for this trip existed. Maliha peeled the skin from an onion with her knife and bit into it like an apple. Darkness fell quickly under the cover of the snowstorm, and with it came bitterly cold temperatures. Maliha wouldn't let herself fall asleep during the coldest time. She hadn't lived more than three hundred years to succumb to hypothermia in the Andes. She meditated, helping her leg to heal, and when she wasn't doing that, she huddled in the wreckage and pulled the bald man's shirt over her face for warmth. It didn't smell very good.

She let her mind roam, found a warmer place and time in her memory, and dwelled there for the night.

Chapter Twenty-Six

1971

I love you," Yanmeng said.

Maliha nearly fell off her camel.

"I have never had a friendship so profound."

Whew!

What he'd just said meant a great deal to her. Over her lifetime, she'd heard many professions of love from men, including some that were sincere. That's when she fled the relationship.

With Yanmeng, his love was of a different type, and when she tested her own feelings, she found that she returned the emotion. Having a deep, close friendship was a new experience for her. The closer she got to someone, the more lying and skirting the truth she had to do. Plus, hanging around with her could be hazardous to one's health. It didn't feel like it was going to be that way with Yanmeng. For one thing, he did a good job of taking care of himself.

He wanted to experiment with remote viewing her. He hadn't done so in the years since his escape from a Chinese prison, feeling that it was too much of an intrusion without a person's consent. Maliha had resisted, because she had many secrets. Having someone peer over her shoulder while she ran with inhuman speed was bound to raise questions.

"Let's talk about it tonight," she said.

They were six days' camel ride into the Taklimakan Desert. The desert was a six-hundred-mile-wide wilderness of shifting sands and dunes five hundred feet high in Central Asia. The Silk Road divided when it came to the desert—

called a sea of death—taking a northern and southern route and leaving the vast, desolate area to the wild camels who roamed it. The Uygur people lived on the rim of the hostile land. They had started out as nomads, but then had settled into villages, some of them large and prosperous, and some consisting of a few adobe huts. Their lives centered on oases and rivers that flowed from the Tibetan plateau, sank into the sand, and vanished into the desert.

It was past the heat of midday. The temperature was about 115 degrees, and the sun was low on the expansive horizon. When darkness fell, the temperature would plummet 80 degrees or more. Several times, she'd seen dust tornados in the distance. The Uygurs hadn't seemed alarmed, so she took her cue from them.

The dunes looked like giant ocean waves frozen in time, although they did move, slowly, driven by wind. That same wind created dust storms that spread Taklimakan sand outside the basin of the desert, although the "desert creep" phenomenon wasn't as marked as with the Sahara Desert. In more than 5 million years, the only change was the pattern of the dunes. Some said it was the most hostile environment on Earth, and Maliha wouldn't argue against it.

Maliha wore a light-colored cotton gown that fell to her knees, and loose trousers underneath so she could straddle the camel, wrapping one leg around the saddle horn and letting the other leg hang down along the camel's side. She had a head wrap that left an opening to see through. Although the wrap kept moisture that escaped in her breath close to her face, her lips and eyes were painfully dry, and the lining of her nose crackled in the heat.

Yanmeng's camel was behind hers, yet she could hear him talk in the quiet of a desert sunset. The camels walked one behind the other, so face-to-face conversation among their human passengers occurred only during meals and at night. With the exception of the caravan master, who was riding out front connected to Maliha's camel by a long rope, the Uygurs who tended the supply camels lagged behind in their own group. The camels sometimes got on a grunting binge, drowning out conversation, but this wasn't one of those times.

Maliha's camel came to a stop. The animal's instinct told it that the time to hunker down for the night had arrived. She tapped its neck with her camel stick, and held on as the camel lurched down to its knees. One of the Uygurs took her camel to be hobbled with the others, and Maliha went over to help prepare dinner. Wrapped in heavy robes against the increasing cold, she and Yanmeng shared bowls of rice with a few chunks of lamb. The wind was still, and sand that had risen during the day gently drifted down from wind-borne heights, giving their faces and clothing a light dusting. Once the sand had settled, the air was incredibly clear, lacking the pollutants of modern societies. They looked up in wonder at the beauty and intensity of the stars in the desert night.

A strange path had brought Maliha to this desert. She was looking for the Tablet of the Overlord, carved by the hand of the Sumerian god Anu, father of all gods. After that, she intended to search for the shards of the diamond lens, unite them, and use the lens to read the tablet, destroying all of the demons.

In Sumerian stories, the lives of their gods and demons stretched back about 450,000 years, when the oldest forms of *Homo sapiens* first walked the earth. Who was she to dream of stamping those demons out? It was a lofty goal for a humble village healer once tied to a stake and set afire, but she was determined to do it, as she was determined to beat the ticking clock of her aging body.

Amid all the world-changing, super-sized plans Maliha was contemplating, there was one small and very personal thought. With Rabishu and his kind wiped away like an ugly smear from humanity's future, would there be a time when she could feel an ordinary woman's simple joys once again?

First—and it was a giant step—destroy the demons.

If she could find all the diamond pieces.

If she could find them before she balanced the scale and joined Anu among the stars, leaving behind the concerns of Earth.

If she didn't die first and ruin everything.

The Uygurs drifted away from the communal fire. Maliha stayed a while longer, poking the dying embers. She had mixed feelings about fire. She knew what it felt like to be devoured by flames, but in the course of her years and global travels, she'd found herself in this situation—crouched in front of a fire built for cooking and warmth—many times. A final jab at the glowing remnants, and she headed for the tent she and Yanmeng had put up before eating dinner.

They'd zipped their sleeping bags together for warmth inside the tent. Disappointed to find him awake, she slid in on her side. She'd promised that they would talk that night about his declaration of deep friendship, and if he'd been asleep, she could have postponed the talk. He was onto her scheme of waiting around after everyone else left the fire.

Yanmeng reached across her and clicked off the flashlight that lay on the tent floor.

"There are some things I need to tell you about myself." At least the darkness made it easier to talk to him. She told him about her past, everything except her quest to collect the shards of the diamond lens. The time didn't seem right for that. He had enough to absorb as it was.

He didn't interrupt, and she wondered what he was thinking about the revelations she was exposing, which must sound like the product of an active, or demented, imagination.

"For someone born in 1672," Yanmeng said when she was finished, "you look pretty good."

She could sense him smiling in the dark. That's when she knew it was going to be all right. She felt a tremendous relief. She let her fear slip away, the fear that he was going to freak out, not believe her, sell her story to a gossip newspaper like she was a two-headed alien baby, or some combination of those. He could put them both at risk.

I did it.

She fell asleep with tears welling in her eyes, tears that shouldn't be shed in the desert.

In the morning, she woke with a lighter heart. She had a true partner. Yanmeng had been lying there waiting for her to wake up.

"You will let me use remote viewing, right?"

She nodded. She'd never asked him about how it works, and this seemed like the time to know. "How do you do that, anyway?"

"It isn't anything I can explain clearly. I develop a 'tag' for a person, and once I have the tag, I can go to where that person is. The stronger the tag, the more likely I can find him. When I view, I see the location from a vantage point above, so I have a wider field of view than the tagged person. It's worked for me before to tag a place rather than a person, but that's much harder. When it's successful, then I can visit that place anytime I want."

"Can you interfere with what's happening?"

"You mean like mess with time or kill somebody from above? No. It's taken me many years just to develop a way to tell someone I'm viewing them. My wife describes it as a feathery touch on the head or shoulder. There's no telling what I could do given enough years, but my progress is slow."

It occurred to Maliha that having someone view her from above could be awkward. There were times when she definitely wanted privacy.

"Can I tell you to break the connection?"

"Sure. You can use a hand signal, anything we work out that's not used in conversation. Hold your hand out parallel to the ground and make the signal. I can see it from above, and I'll go away."

"No questions asked?"

"No questions asked."

"How about this?" She lifted her left arm, formed a fist, and then extended her index finger and thumb at right angles to each other, forming an L shape. "It's an L in sign language, except I'll be doing it horizontally instead of vertically. L as in, 'Leave me alone.'"

Yanmeng lifted up his hand in the same gesture. "Got it."

"Do I have to be close to you, within some range?"

"No. I haven't had the chance to try viewing someone in space, but as far as I know I can see worldwide. It isn't like I have to fly there. I cross the space between us instantaneously. Where can I get one of those teeth implanted with cyanide in it?"

"What?"

"A fake tooth. In case I'm captured and tortured." He said it matter-of-factly.

"You can't be serious."

"I've never been more serious in my life. There's too much at stake here. Consider what I have been through in my life, taken to prison, interrogated, and condemned. I would rather die than give away anything you've told me. And from what you say, you've got some nasty enemies."

A surge of emotion, several emotions, struck her. Yanmeng was saying he'd die for her, and he'd said it with the utmost sincerity. He was propped up on one elbow, watching her.

"I . . . I'm touched," she said about his proclamation that he wanted a suicide tooth to protect her. *Touched* was an understatement. "It can be done, but we'll have to talk about it again, after you get a chance to think about it. A lot."

She hadn't mentioned something the night before.

"There's one thing you may not have thought about. You'll get older and die, and I'll still look young. I think. I'm not in control of aging any more than you are, but I can have jumps forward that could be years long. I can't say for sure about how long I'll live, just that it will almost certainly be longer than you."

"I know. But my life, however short compared to yours, will be full of purpose."

He gently reached inside her clothing and ran his hand over the scale carving. She jerked away, then relaxed. It wasn't at all sexual. It was his way of telling her that he accepted their situation. An affirmation of everything she was trying to do.

She sighed. "There's one last thing you need to know." As his hand rested on her skin, she told him about the diamond lens, and the Tablet of the Overlord, which she was going to snatch from the heart of the desert.

The next morning, over the protests of the camel drivers, Maliha filled a backpack with dried food and water and a few special supplies she'd brought along, and walked out of camp alone. An American going off to die, they thought. As she was getting ready, she'd heard Yanmeng reassuring them, through the one man who spoke broken English, that she'd be back.

They must think we're both crazy.

The Uygurs agreed to wait for Maliha until the supplies ran low enough that they had just enough to make it out of the desert themselves.

Out of sight of the camp, Maliha took off running. She could make better time alone on foot than on the back of a camel in the company of others. She knew she had to pace herself in the extreme environment, but she'd determine that as she went along. The night before, she'd sighted the moon and navigational stars using a sextant. During the day, she'd use the sun. She was adept with celestial navigation. She'd crossed oceans alone, and since this desert was an ocean stilled in time, she knew she wasn't going to get lost.

She intended to cover forty miles in a long day, spend the night at her destination, and return to camp before the sunset the next day. It was a challenge, but she hadn't wanted to leave the others behind and head off on a camel. She sped over the trackless sand as lightly as she could, like a lizard skittering, barely touching its feet to the hot surface. Hours of sameness passed: run, rest, drink, use the sextant, run again. A few hours out, she knew she was far enough from camp and from other sources of help that if anything went wrong, she would die. Break a leg, and she wouldn't be able to heal fast enough, before her water ran out. Spill some of the water, and there wouldn't be enough to fuel a return trip.

It was frightening, but also exhilarating.

She saw no other living creature. There were no scrublands in the area she was passing through to support birds, snakes, and rats; there were only lizards and insects, and they were nocturnal. The sand shielded them from the worst of the daytime heat, and they would come out at night to kill or be killed or to carry on their species. Maliha's thoughts attuned to her body, narrowing down to the next placement of a foot, the angle of a swinging arm, or a slow, deep inhalation.

Every now and then, she felt a faint touch against her mind and wondered if it was Yanmeng, using his remote vision. More likely, it was fatigue.

The sun traversed the sky as if on a chariot pulled by horses with flames at their heels.

Near sunset, she spotted her destination, a mountainous

projection of rock that rose above the dunes. Sandstorms had filed its sharp edges away, so that it looked almost melted. The north side, which faced the prevailing wind, was riddled with small caves dug into the rock by the wind. She found what she was looking for about three hundred feet above the highest dune that broke against its side, a cave entrance so small she had to crawl in on knees and elbows, distinguished from a hundred other caves by the moist scent within.

The passage widened until she could walk hunched over, and it led downward. Her flashlight at first revealed bare rock sides, but as she went further, there was a pale growth on the side of the tunnel, like fungus. She was sure she'd gone down below the level of the sand outside. It was at once a secure and claustrophobic feeling. Secure because the sand outside wrapped the space like a heavy coat with the collar pulled up. Claustrophobic because tons of sand were pressing the sides of the mountain, and she had one small way out, an insignificant straw of a tunnel holding back sand that was eager to rush in and entomb her.

There was air movement in the passage, a gentle push against her face. Her flashlight picked up something quick and flexible scurrying on the walls. She was astounded to hear the sound of running water ahead of her, and quickened her pace. The air carried a clean scent, unexpected in a place that had never seen the light of day.

The tunnel expanded into a cavern whose ceiling rose ten feet above her head. At her feet was an underground stream, water from spring thaws in the mountains that tumbled into the desert basin. The water reached the edge of the sand and filtered down through it in hundreds of places, poured into cracks in the bedrock below, and traveled for miles, sheltered from evaporation by the sun. The Uygurs called them ghost rivers. The water was cool and fresh, unlike the salt-laden puddles that sometimes formed on the surface in the channels of dry rivers.

Maliha tucked her flashlight back in her pack and touched a button on her belt. Small, powerful lights came on, creating a bright sphere of light around her for hands-free working. The lights drew a lot of battery power but they were nice while they lasted. She squatted next to the stream, cupped water in her hands, drank deeply, and cleaned the dust of travel from her face. She waded across, holding her belt and pack over her head, but the water never reached higher than her thighs. On the opposite bank was a room off to the side, and as soon as she stepped into it, she knew she'd reached the end of her journey.

The walls of the cave were smooth and vertical, as if they'd been sliced with a knife. Her belt lights revealed torches on the wall, so she lit them and switched off her lights to conserve the batteries. Torchlight flickered on the walls and reflected in the water at her feet. On the wall opposite the entrance, thirty feet away from her, was a thin tablet embedded in the rock. It was a foot high and eight inches wide, smaller than she'd expected. At the top was a large carving of a star, Anu's symbol. The rest she was too far away to make out.

The problem was getting there. In front of her was a wall-to-wall pool with a glassy surface, and a few inches below the surface was sand. She had a bad feeling about that sand. Pulling a rock-climbing stake she hadn't needed from her pack, she tossed it gently into the water. It settled on the sand, and she waited. The stake sank with a powerful sucking noise. She tried it with another stake, this time counting the time until it sank.

Two seconds.

She squatted and pushed a stake into the water. She couldn't penetrate the sand, exerting as much force as she could. But after two seconds, the surface softened and the suction began. She also noticed that the surface of the water radiated heat. Holding the stake in place, her hand grew hotter than the desert sand outside. This was no cool cave pool, as its smooth surface had led her to believe.

Maliha turned over plans in her mind. She could use a burst of speed to cross the pool before she sank, but she was going to have to stand at the other wall and chip the tablet out of the surrounding stone, and that would take more than long enough for the sand to switch from solid to treacherous and suck her under. She needed something to stand on above the water's surface.

Digging into the pack again, she came up with a set of five throwing spikes. She threw the first one across the pool and was dismayed to see that it bounced off the rock wall and sank into the sand. She tried again, closing her eyes to concentrate. She imagined the motion in her mind, feeling the cool familiarity of a spike in her hand, seeing it traveling through the air, the tip sliding into the rock. Then, eyes still closed, she took a deep breath, held it, and fired off the remaining four spikes.

When she opened her eyes, the spikes were as she'd envisioned them, stuck firmly into the rock wall in a horizontal line, neatly spaced with enough length sticking out of the wall that she could balance on them. She took from her pack a small steel hammer and some chisels she'd brought for just this moment and secured them on her belt. Slipping off her shoes—she could grip the spikes better with her toes—she planned her moves and launched herself into the pool.

At the first touch of her foot to the water's surface, she realized the water wasn't just hot, it was more than scalding hot, unnaturally superheated. She couldn't let the shock slow her down. As soon as she felt the firm sand under her foot, she surged forward.

One second.

Two.

She threw herself at the wall, hoping she wouldn't bounce off like her first spike. Her feet settled onto the embedded spikes, and the tablet was right in front of her. Up close, the writing on the stone was blurred to her eyes, and parts of it shifted and crawled into new positions constantly. The constant motion was dizzying to watch, so she stopped examining it.

Balancing on the spikes, ignoring the pain from her burned feet, she chiseled around the edges of the tablet. It didn't take much effort; the thing threw itself into her hands. She dropped the hammer and chisel into the water, since she no longer needed them, and heard them being sucked under, beneath her feet.

Then it dawned on her that she was facing the wall with

no room to maneuver, especially clasping the tablet. She could think of a way to get both herself and the tablet out, but it was risky. Then she laughed aloud at the thought.

This is a fine time to think about risk, when you're setting out to kill seven demons. Go for it!

She raised her arms, flinging the tablet over her head and backward toward the safe edge of the pool, hoping it wasn't fragile. Pushing down hard on the spikes under her feet, she flipped into a powerful backward handspring away from the wall, and her hands entered the heated pool. The water roiled in contact with her skin.

One second.

She completed the handspring, this time coming down facing the door of the cave, both feet in the water. She bunched her legs underneath her and leaped for the water's edge. If she didn't make it now, she never would. The sand would soften under her feet and claim her.

Two.

She landed there solidly. But the tablet was still in the water, about three feet from the edge. She dropped flat and stretched out over the water for it. She got the fingers of one hand on the tablet as it was about to disappear under the sand. Grabbing with the other hand, the water searing her hands and arms, she strained against the powerful pull of the sand that wanted to claim her prize. Her muscles quivering with the effort, she inched the tablet toward her, then out onto the rock floor of the cave.

Inspecting the tablet, she saw that it was unharmed by its immersion in the water. She stretched out and let waves of pain sweep through her, giving herself over to it now that she was safe and the tablet was hers. She had the sickening feeling if she'd spent any longer in the superheated water—or whatever it was—flesh might have fallen off her bones.

She went to the underground stream, pulled off her clothing, and immersed herself in the cool water. Relief was a long time coming. She couldn't stay in the 60-degree water for too long, for fear of having her body temperature dip too low and becoming lethargic. Finally she dragged herself back onto the bank, wrapped up in her clothes, and huddled on the stone, drinking from the cool stream to replace fluid loss from her burned skin. Hours passed and she slept fitfully.

The Tablet of the Overlord went into a padded bag slung across her back. Making her way out through the tunnel, she emerged into a desert night.

Which night? How long have I spent here?

She began her run back to camp with raw, blistered feet crammed into her shoes and her hands wound with cloth. The sun rose and her burned arms felt the harsh weight of sunlight through the fabric of her clothing. She appeared at the camp just ahead of nightfall and the gathering dust of a storm. She collapsed into Yanmeng's arms, needing recovery time.

Crammed inside one larger tent with several others as the wind shrieked and drove sand into every narrow crevice of the tent's flaps, she let the camel drivers rub their pungent salves on her burns, and she downed the thick, snow-white fermented camel's milk she was offered from a leather skin bag. When the storm passed, she retreated to the tent she shared with Yanmeng to wait out the rest of the day and the cold night following.

Yanmeng described everything she'd done, even chiding her for bouncing a spike off the rock wall. She challenged him to do better under the circumstances.

He'd been traveling in the astral plane, seeing her and her surroundings as though hovering above her. It was fascinating to think that the distance between them meant nothing.

Fascinating and disconcerting. How was she to know if she had privacy? He reminded her that she would notice a light touch, the brush of a feather, as he reached down and dipped into the reality of her situation. When she thought back on her trip, she had felt such a thing, several times.

She dozed through a day and night, and then was healed enough to attempt travel, but their guide insisted on waiting another day, since their food and water were adequate.

Mounting her camel, she felt an odd tug, as though this desert wasn't done with her yet.

Chapter Twenty-Seven

When the storm outside the Andean plane wreckage brightened into a uniform grayness, it was morning. It was snowing hard, and the wreckage of the plane looked like snow-covered boulders strewn across the mountain. She knew there would come a time for hard decisions, such as stay or try to hike out, starve as long as possible or eat the frozen, preserved flesh of the bald man, but she wasn't there yet. For now, she was just happy that she'd made it through the night and that her leg was feeling better.

She tugged the suitcase toward her, unzipped it, and smashed the lock on Manco's case with the handle of a knife. She opened the lid of the case without giving herself time to think better of it.

The pot was in pieces, some of them small, but not ground into dust. The dirt packed inside the pot had supported it somewhat. The writing was visible, and with patience and a big bottle of glue, she could fit the pieces together and make the rollout.

She began removing the larger pieces, thinking that she could lay them out in front of her and get started deciphering the clue. Her fingers touched something hard and slick, like glass. She carefully pried pieces loose from the dirt that had filled the pot until the slickness was exposed.

Then she had in her hands a diamond, the first of the seven pieces of the lens that Anu shattered.

She cleaned it with snow. It was beautiful. It had perfect

clarity and a surface like highly polished glass. Below that glossy surface were thousands of faceted cuts—it was a gem carved throughout its interior. She didn't understand how that could be done, but marveled at the fact of it. The weight in the palm of her hand seemed too great for the size, which was about three and a half inches long and a quarter of an inch thick. She'd pictured the shards as equal wedges of a pie, but her first discovery made it clear that wasn't so. The shard had an irregular shape. Assembling the lens was going to be more like fitting puzzle pieces into a whole rather than putting the neatly cut pie back together. The completed shape could be up to seven inches in diameter: an incredible, unworldly platter of a diamond.

As she held the shard, marveling at it, she felt a feather-light touch on her shoulder. Yanmeng's touch. He was remote viewing her, and she knew everything would be all right. He would send help. All she had to do was make it through the storm alive, even if she had a terrible case of onion breath.

She wasn't going to have to eat the bald man.

Chapter Twenty-Eight

Maliha was back in North Carolina, skulking in the line of trees that ringed the two-acre lawn of Diane Harvey's pretentious home. It was around 11 P.M. The landscaping provided plenty of cover as Maliha, dressed in black, moved toward the house. The burglar alarm was child's play. She picked the lock on a basement door, went inside, and clipped the telephone wire. Not sufficient these days. She had to locate Diane's cell phone. Walking through the darkened house, she approached the master bedroom on the second floor. The door was open and she could hear water running. Diane was taking a shower.

Maliha searched the bedroom, listening to Diane sing "Wild Thing" at the top of her voice. She found a Blackberry and tossed it out the second-story window. A gun found in a desk drawer went into her waist pack.

The bedroom was large, with a reading area that held a comfortable chair, a good lamp, and a set of bookshelves. Nearby was a desk with a computer with a screensaver that flashed close-ups of flowers, one after the other. Maliha inserted a CD that Amaro had given her and installed a program on the computer. Then she sat in the chair, flipped on the lamp so she could be seen clearly, and waited. She had a busy night ahead of her, with travel back to Chicago and a task to do there, and she hoped Diane wasn't the type who drained all the hot water from the tank when she took a shower.

Maliha had some doubts about this venture. As far as she was concerned, PharmBots was off the hook for the murder of the coders. If they'd been planning to use Nando and Hairy as scapegoats for their own negligence, then it was much better to have live scapegoats. If the coders turned up dead, PharmBots would just look like it was covering its tracks clumsily, which would have been true.

Maliha could have walked away from the story of the lawsuit over Karen Dearborn's death in the hospital. There must be hundreds of thousands of other individual needs that went unmet, and Maliha wasn't expecting a boost toward redemption from this one. She hadn't intervened before Karen died.

The manufacturing flaw had been quietly repaired, so the pill robot wasn't menacing anyone else. The murder investigation had shifted elsewhere.

Why this one, then? For the warm fuzzies?

Pictures from the Dearborn photo album played in a slideshow in Maliha's mind. The happy couple at their wedding, husband Sean patting his wife's pregnant belly, a lock of baby Karen's fine reddish hair taped next to a picture of her in the hospital. Years of learning to walk, going to school. An obituary clipped from the newspaper: *Local teacher dies after truck crosses median.* Then the discovery of Karen's heart problems the doctors were working on.

If only she'd had another year, the doctors had said. *Another year and she would have been a normal girl.*

Diane wailed away in the shower, reaching a crescendo, and then the water was turned off.

Okay, admit it. Warm fuzzies all the way.

Diane came out of the bathroom naked and nearly jumped to the ceiling.

"Jesus Christ! What are you doing in here? I'm calling the police."

"You can try to call the police, but you won't get far."

Diane lunged toward her nightstand and pressed the emergency alarm button that sat there. It failed to light up, even though she pressed it a number of times.

"Surprise. Alarm's off."

Diane retrieved a bathrobe from a hook over the door and sat down in the desk chair. Maliha saw her eyes scanning the room, looking for the missing Blackberry. Then she edged closer to the computer, probably thinking about getting a message off to someone. It wouldn't work, thanks to Amaro's program. No programs could execute other than ones he'd specified, and the computer could reach websites he'd allowed. All the paths of communication had been shut down for Diane, and there was no way Maliha would let her leave the room.

"What is it that you want?" Diane's voice was tight with anger and a tinge of fear.

Maliha pulled a mini-CD from her pack. "On this disk there are records of the illegal purchase of twenty-two Peruvian artifacts, the Moche pots on display in your office. Names, dates, places of purchase. Verifiable information. You didn't vet anything for legal importation. The U.S. National Stolen Property Act frowns on that."

Diane said nothing.

"I'll destroy all this information if you'll do a couple of things for me. I have an offer that expires in about"—she looked at her watch—"twenty minutes."

"Such as?"

"First, pay the hospital bills for Karen Dearborn."

Diane shook her head. "I won't do that. It would be an admission of some level of guilt."

"Then you're not going to like number two. Settle the lawsuit outside of court. Pay Samantha Dearborn five million dollars and everything will go away. This disk and all your headaches. It's not like that's going to bring Karen Dearborn back, but at least the mother will get an apology."

"You're crazy! I can't do that! PharmBots . . ."

"Who said anything about PharmBots? I'm talking about paying from your personal account. I know you've got the money."

"No. I won't do that. You can leave now, I'm not talking about this anymore."

Maliha stood up. "You'll be spending years in federal

prison, but it's your choice." She was halfway to the door of the bedroom when Diane spoke.

"Wait. Everything goes away? The Moche pots? The lawsuits against both PharmBots and the hospital? No publicity? The woman will sign a non-disclosure statement?"

Maliha nodded. "She's a practical woman with a crippling debt. Good for your company, good for the hospital, good for Karen's mother. And it keeps you out of jail."

"Why doesn't the hospital have to pay half? Blame hasn't been assigned."

"I'm blaming you. You're vulnerable, Diane." She waved the mini-CD containing the incriminating evidence in her direction. Maliha hadn't mentioned the memos Amaro had concerning the PharmBots plot to place all the blame on the dead coders. That was her backup plan. Besides, Diane must have known that the same theft of information that covered the Moche pots also had damaging information about the lawsuits. Maliha had the winning hand.

"This is blackmail."

Maliha nodded solemnly. "In a good cause. Karen's mom didn't have anything to do with planning this, by the way. It's all between you and me."

Diane frowned. She was clearly weighing the benefit of letting the hospital off the hook, as far as future marketing to that and other hospitals was concerned.

"What guarantee do I have that you won't blackmail me in the future? I'm sure you have copies of that disk."

"Of course I have copies. You have no guarantee except my word."

"This isn't going to surface in one of your stupid books, is it?"

"No, it's too mundane for one of my plots. Transfer the money now. I have a Swiss bank account number you can use." It was a virtual account number, one that would be translated by the Swiss bank to her real account number.

"No way. This is going too fast. I don't have any written guarantees the suits will be dropped. I don't have the Dearborn woman's non-disclosure."

"Is that all that's holding us up? I've got the documents

right here." Maliha pulled a roll of papers out of her waist pack. She hadn't planned to give them up unless she had to.

Diane took the papers and switched on a desk lamp, then started going over them. Maliha watched the woman's right hand inch toward the desk drawer. She was going for the gun.

"Are you looking for this?" Maliha pulled the gun from her pack. Diane yanked the desk drawer open and scowled when she saw that her gun was missing.

She went back to reading the documents in the light of the desk lamp. When she sat back in her chair, Maliha could see that the agreement looked all right to her. It should. It was drawn up by one of the highest-paid attorneys in the country, Maliha's.

"I'd like to have my legal staff go over this."

"I'd like to have a lot of things. The offer's about to expire." Maliha put her finger into the center hole of the mini-CD and twirled it around.

Diane hesitated, then made a decision. "All right. Tell me what to do."

Maliha had Diane log on and visit the Swiss website to enter the virtual account number, then Diane's banking information and password, and the amount. Maliha made a point of politely looking away while Diane entered her personal information, but she did count the zeros on the amount.

A screen came up that said validation of the account numbers was complete, with a notice:

Click the Enter button to confirm and begin the transaction. Click Cancel to stop. Warning: Once confirmed, the transaction cannot be halted or canceled. If you should confirm in error, contact the owner of the destination account to inquire about a reversal.

Diane stared at the screen, her cursor poised over the ENTER key.

"No. No, I don't trust you. It's not as if you've given me any reason to. You're trying to push me into acting before I think the whole thing through. Why is there an expiration on the offer? We can talk this over in my office in the morning, and get my personal and corporate attorneys involved. The lawsuit is a corporate matter, so the funds should come out of the corporate kitty. I still think the hospital should fork over half. Their reputation's on the line, too."

She canceled the transaction.

"You're willing to have your smuggling activities discussed in front of all those people?"

"No reason to. As you've pointed out, I have the signed agreement in my hands." She opened a desk drawer and put the papers inside with a satisfied look on her face. "If you try to raise the smuggling issue, you're admitting to blackmail. You've done yourself in, Ms. Know-it-All Winters. If that's even your real name."

Maliha pulled a knife from its sheath. "I thought there was a good chance of this. I can take those papers back."

"You'll have to come through me. I know self-defense."

Maliha kept herself from laughing. Instead she sheathed the knife and took out her cell phone. She had another deadly weapon in mind: Amaro.

"You have everything you need?" she asked.

"Yeah. It's a go, then?"

"Go." She disconnected the call.

Diane stood up, a petite woman quivering with anger in her voluminous bathrobe. "Go. Get out of my house. That disk's useless to you. You can't blackmail me."

Maliha stalled for a minute, using a verbal boxing match to keep Diane huffy.

"Turn around."

Frowning, Diane turned. Then her eyes grew wide. "What the hell is going on here?"

Transaction complete. US$5,000,000 transferred. Please print a receipt for your records.

"Your computer's been hacked. Everything you entered tonight was collected with a keystroke recorder and fired off instantly to my trusty computer expert. I installed a program that took control of your computer remotely. While you've been railing at me, your money was zinging along the wire to Switzerland. You did the right thing for Karen and her mother."

"You can't do that! You can't take my money without my approval!"

"But you did approve. Your cursor clicked Enter. Of course, you didn't have your hand on the mouse at the time."

Enraged, Diane shoved the computer and monitor from her desk. The monitor burst and sent a shower of glass over the carpet.

"The maid's not going to like that. By the way, you should get dressed." Maliha checked her watch again. "The FBI will be arriving very soon. They've just served a warrant at your place of business to confiscate the stolen antiquities. The FBI Art Theft Team already has all your records."

Diane's face grew red. "You bitch! You fucking bitch! I'll sue you! You can't blackmail me. I want my money back now."

"What money? By now all records of your transaction have already been wiped out. No one can follow the money trail because there isn't any. What blackmail? The Black Ghost was never here."

Maliha turned on her heel and left, with Diane's eyes stabbing her in the back.

A few minutes later, in the taxi on the way to the airport, Maliha squirmed, squeezed her eyes shut, bit her lip, and struggled to keep from outright groaning as a single figure left fiery tracks across her body. The taxi driver, hearing muffled sounds from the backseat, asked if she was all right.

A gasp of pain escaped her, and she stretched it out. "I'mmmm fine." He shrugged and stopped looking in the rearview mirror. He cracked his window a bit, probably figuring that she had a monumental case of gas.

The lurch through time was dizzying and left her panting. She held up a newspaper a previous passenger had left in the taxi to block the driver's view of her face as the reaction passed. She had been rewarded with a small upward nudge of the "good" pan on the scale. The only thing she could figure out was that, without her action tonight, Samantha Dearborn would have continued a spiral of grief and hopelessness and taken her own life.

Straightening up in the airport restroom, Maliha noticed that the movement of the scale had cost her more years. Barely discernible crow's-feet at the corners of her eyes were starting to make themselves known. Studying her face in the mirror, she figured the cost to be about three years. She'd left home with the physical appearance of a woman in her mid-twenties; she was going back to Chicago as a woman in her late twenties.

Samantha and Karen were worth it.

Back in Chicago, Maliha was wearing white out of season. She told herself, though, that any season was okay for a wedding gown.

She'd carried it in a duffel bag and taken a taxi to an allnight restaurant within a mile of her destination. She ran the rest of the way with the bag slung over her back, moving along in the still hours before dawn.

Outside the home of Edward Rupert, CFO of ShaleTech, she disengaged the alarm and went in a back window. Amaro's information was accurate. Edward went to bed—alone—at 10 P.M. on weeknights. On the weekends, he was a man about town, enjoying his bachelor status and drawing women with a display of free spending.

Edward was also, according to anecdotes, a man who believed in the supernatural. Maliha was about to take a page from *A Christmas Carol* and visit him as a ghost.

Edward had been engaged to a woman named Caroline Martin. His third marriage, her first. She was twenty-five years old and a teller at the bank he frequented. The ring was bought, the date was set. Caroline began to feel tired, weak, and bruise easily. A skin rash and an odd shortness of breath sent her to the doctor. The diagnosis was AML, acute myeloid leukemia. Caroline didn't respond to aggressive treatment and died four months after her first visit to the doctor. It would have been a tragic love story, the kind that sends women reaching for the tissue box, except that

Edward had taken back his ring and turned his back on her. Caroline, a woman with no living family, had died holding a nurse's hand instead of her beloved's.

He couldn't spare a mere four months of his life to see her through to the end.

Maliha put on the wedding gown and slipped a two-carat diamond solitaire on her left ring finger. Edward's bedroom was on the first floor. His snores greeted her as she pushed open the door. She unplugged the lamp by his bed, then went up to him and whispered in his ear.

"Edward, darling, why did you do it?"

He brushed at his ear and turned over. She went around to the other side of the bed, stroked his arm, and repeated her question a little louder. He sat up suddenly, but Maliha was across the room by then, standing in front of a window. The moonlight streaming in outlined her body and kept her face in the shadows.

Edward saw Caroline standing there in a wedding gown.

"Mother of God. It can't be!" He reached over to turn on the lamp.

Gotcha.

Maliha glided away from the window. "When's the wedding, Edward?" she murmured. "Isn't it almost time?"

"Keep away from me!"

Maliha shined a pale light downward, illuminating her gown in an eerie way, with deep shadows on the full skirt. Then she flicked off the light, moved faster than a human could to the other side of the room, and turned the flashlight on again.

Edward's head swiveled to follow her. To him, it looked like she disappeared from one spot and reappeared in another. She waved her hand in the beam of the light, so he could see the diamond ring.

"You made me give it back to you. That wasn't nice. It made me feel bad and I was already sick. I came back for my ring."

She moved again. Edward's face, lit by the moonlight, was a mask of fear.

"And I came back to ask why you left me, Edward," she said.

"I . . . I . . ." His voice was nowhere to be found.

She moved close and brushed the edge of the bed with her gown. He cowered back from her against the headboard, holding the blanket up in front of him.

She had him going now. She took a running leap toward the bed, let her foot drag across the covers and landed soundlessly on the other side.

A wordless moan rose from Edward's shaking mass. It was time to get tough.

She threw back her head and screamed for all she was worth. When the sound died away, she spoke. "I was scared when you left me, but you didn't care."

"I cared. I still care." It was a small, frightened voice, a child talking about the monsters under the bed, a nightmare come to life in his own bedroom.

"I don't believe that." She appeared on the other side of the room.

"Yes, yes, I care. I shouldn't have left you. That was wrong of me."

"Then why did you do it? It must have been what happened at work. It was too much stress for you, my poor Edward."

He seized on the idea. "That's it. It was problems at work. I never would have left you if it wasn't for problems at work."

"Poor thing. What problems? Why didn't you let me help?"

"I couldn't tell you, Caroline. I couldn't tell anyone."

"You could tell me anything, you know that. You can tell me now. Was it about money?" She moved and ran her fingers across the blanket where his feet were. He pulled them up like a turtle retracting its feet into the shell. "That's what you did for the company. Take care of all the money."

"The company was in trouble," he blurted. "We were about to default on loans, and Shale wanted to hide it. So we could get more loans."

"He made you do it, didn't he? He's the one who's responsible."

In the next few minutes, she found out the extent of the financial trouble ShaleTech was in, and the reason why Shale was eager to conceal the problems and fend off creditors for a little longer. He had a project, something called Caesar, spelled CESR. It was supposed to make the company whole again, with money beyond their dreams for new development, and no one would have been the wiser about the temporary double set of books.

Edward had come through with the goods, and she decided to let him off the hook a little. "I'm glad we had this talk. I feel better now."

She made her way to the door.

"I did love you, Caroline honey. I really did. I was weak. I didn't know what to do around a dying person."

It had the ring of truth to it. She checked his aura. There was genuine sorrow, and deep shame for the way he'd acted.

"I loved you, Caroline." The moonlight showed the gleam of tears on his cheeks. "Please forgive me."

She came back over to the bed, caressed his cheek, and kissed him lightly on the forehead. She'd gotten what she needed, and in some measure, so had Edward.

Maliha stuffed the wedding gown back into the duffel bag, slipped on the clothing she'd worn to Edward's house, and ran back to the restaurant. It had started to rain, and by the time she reached the place, she was tempted to go inside and pass the time until the rain let up. She thought she'd feel too out of place carrying the duffel bag, though, and she didn't want to leave it outside in the rain to be ruined.

No telling when I'll need a wedding gown again.

At the door to her building, Arnie accepted the duffel bag without comment. She told him there was a wedding gown in it that needed cleaning. He nodded and said he'd take care of it.

"You look a little tired, Ms. Winters. It must have been a very long walk this evening."

"Very." When he said it, she noticed that she *was* a little tired.

Feeling my age.

"You get some rest, and take care now. I wouldn't want anything to happen to my favorite resident."

She was in the elevator halfway up to her floor when she realized he'd meant it. She'd just processed the look in his eyes. He really did care about her.

For money or for real? You be the judge.

Chapter Twenty-Nine

1698

⚖ Susannah traveled across China, taking time to perfect her knowledge of the language. Rabishu had ordered her to go to the Xichan Monastery to learn martial arts. She asked at the monastery for the teacher Rabishu mentioned, Master Liu. The abbot indicated that the master lived like a hermit on a mountain nearby.

She searched the mountain for days with no luck, until one afternoon she came across a naked man washing his robe in a stream. It was raining steadily, a cold rain that would freeze by nightfall, but he showed no sign of noticing. She couldn't see him clearly through the rain, but had the impression he was emaciated, with wrinkled skin that draped loosely over his bones, and almost no hair. She called out to see if he would answer to the right name.

"Master Liu!"

The man continued to squat and rub his robe in the cold water.

A pang of concern struck her. She approached him, and he made no move. When she was within twenty feet of him, he sprang up and disappeared into the trees. Suddenly afraid of an attack from this mysterious person, she spun around and saw him standing behind her. At least, she thought it was him. This man was in his mid-twenties, with shoulder-length black hair plastered to his skin by the rain, a handsome, unlined face, penetrating gray eyes, and a naked body in superb condition. She shook her head. Her eyes must have been playing tricks on her about his age, with the rain and fog.

"Master Liu, I was sent to you by Rabishu."

They stood silently, in the rain. Finally, Susannah pulled back her traveling robe's hood so that he could see her clearly.

"A woman. The demon sends me a woman to train?" There was scorn in his voice.

Susannah was tired, wet, cold, and hungry. Having scorn heaped on her inflamed her anger, both at the man in front of her and at Rabishu, who had sent her to wander far from home.

He was only ten feet away. She lunged at him, using the speed Rabishu had granted her. Instead of grappling with him, Susannah found herself on the ground, looking up into the falling rain, blinking. She quickly rolled away, came to her feet, and tried again. This time she threw a knife at him.

He casually picked it out of the air and stuck the blade in his thigh. Blood poured down his leg, washed to the ground by the rain. He pulled out the knife and in a smooth motion sent it flying inches from her head to thunk deeply into a tree behind her. She saw that his wound was rapidly closing.

"You're Ageless!"

The corner of his mouth curled up in another gesture of scorn. "Did you think you were the only one?"

"You must breathe!" Master Liu walked around her and adjusted her wrist, tucked her elbows in closer to her body, and stood back to watch.

"How many hours must I endure this?" she grumbled. "Hand out, twist wrist, pull back, tuck in. You are teaching me to wring the neck of a chicken, not fight a man!"

He said nothing, just widened her stance by inserting a fighting cane between her feet and whacking her ankles.

She stood from dawn until after dark in his school on the mountain, a large wooden pavilion open to the weather. A school for one, apparently, because she saw no other students. There had been snow overnight, but she wore only a thin training uniform.

"Your hands stray from your center line." He stuck the cane insolently between her legs and traced a line upward to the base of her throat. "You must guard the center or you will never succeed. The demon must see a potential in you that I do not. You are not devoted to learning the ways of the assassin."

"Is that all you are, a mindless thing to kill people?"

She stopped moving and faced him, regretting that she'd spoken her thoughts aloud. He did nothing, but his eyes, already hard to read, completely shuttered his thoughts. It was as though light tried to penetrate but died at the threshold instead. She suddenly saw herself from his point of view: an impudent, whining, unfocused student who had little respect for him or the art he was trying to pass to her. She bowed her head.

"I'm sorry, Master."

A year later, her body and mind were responding to the training. There was beauty in the motions, in the slow, rhythmic breathing that accompanied them, in the clarity of thought demanded.

Then the passage of years blurred in her mind. The spare living, the starkness of the mountaintop, the simple task of sweeping the pavilion daily, the intensity of her training—there was no room in her mind for anything else.

There was a time when pain was her constant companion, intentionally inflicted by Master Liu as part of her training. She learned to cope and keep moving, a mantra in her head: *Pain kills only if I allow it. Pain kills only if I allow it.*

More and more, Master Liu pursed his lips and nodded as he watched her do forms, or when she sparred with him. The throwing knives Master Liu had custom-made for her flew from her fingers like hawks striking prey in midair. When she mastered the technique, Master Liu tattooed a hawk across her back, its wings spread in flight. An exquisite artwork, it was also a sign of his growing respect for her.

*   *   *

Waking suddenly at the sound of a gong, Susannah leaped up for a lesson.

Instead she saw a line of people standing across the middle of the pavilion, people who must have arrived while she slept. That she hadn't sensed and reacted to feet walking toward her on the bare wooden floor was disturbing. They were dressed in black killing outfits, and had black scarves wound around their faces. She had the distinct feeling they were there to kill her if she didn't measure up, but to what, she didn't know.

She turned around and saw Master Liu sitting in an ornate chair, as the hermit she'd seen years ago at the edge of the stream. He was an old man, impossibly old, arms and legs as thin and brittle as sticks, a few white hairs on his head. His face was as wrinkled as a dried lingonberry, though not the same color. He was pale, like a person who'd lived indoors all the time, something Susannah knew was not the case. Rheumy white eyes were locked in her direction, yet she realized that in this form he was blind. He was wearing a gown of gold cloth embroidered with red, far different from his usual training clothing. A man dressed in black with delicate lines of gold trim stood on his left.

"Come here, student."

She hesitated, not sure he was talking to her. No one else moved, so she walked forward and knelt.

"You have proven yourself worthy. Today you become a disciple of this school. My other disciples"—he indicated the line of people standing behind her with a nod in their direction—"have gathered from around the world to witness this ceremony. Let me hear your pledge."

Pledge? I don't know any . . .

Her mouth opened anyway and words tumbled out. "I swear to honor you as my grandfather, to do nothing to bring shame to you or the school, and to never stray from the teachings of this school."

The senior disciple, standing next to Master Liu, approached her, and suddenly she saw that he had a glowing branding iron in his hand.

"This is the character *shou*, meaning 'long life,'" the senior disciple said. "It is the symbol of this ancient and proud school." He pulled up her left sleeve and pressed the iron high on the outside of her shoulder. Pain jolted her, but she didn't cry out or move. Her Ageless skin didn't heal the branding mark, nor was her pain diminished after the brand was removed. There was a price to becoming a disciple of Master Liu. She knelt, dry-eyed, as wisps of smoke rose from her flesh.

"I accept you as my daughter," Grandfather said.

Chapter Thirty

Maliha arrived at Kelly's Pub early the next day. She bought a large glass of orange juice and sat at their table.

Hound had requested a meeting, which he never did unless he had something to say concerning a case. She would have seen him other times than on a case, gone home with him, but these were the rules he set, and she abided by them.

It was raining outside, a persistent, cold rain that would turn into sleet with a little encouragement. She spotted Hound as soon as he came in, a broad-shouldered man in a raincoat, with a wide-rimmed Indiana-Jones–style hat. He said it protected him from the rain, but he wore it sometimes when it wasn't raining, too. She'd once seen him cavorting around in front of a mirror wearing only the hat and a hard-on. She wondered if he thought of himself as a dashing adventurer. She knew so much about him, and so little.

He took the hat off, tipping the rainwater in its brim on the floor and stepping over the puddle. Hound wasn't the type to call for a wet cleanup in Aisle Four. His chin was tucked into the open collar of his shirt as usual, but then he raised his face to look for her. He spotted her, and she acknowledged him with a nod. There was a flash of something halfway between lust and love in his eyes. She didn't want to view Hound's aura to see how he felt about her. She was sure there were things there she didn't want to see, and it was easier to get along with Hound without delving into how he felt about her, or what he did for his other clients.

He pushed students aside to get to the bar. Most of them had edged away from him anyway. He brought his bottle of beer to the table and sat down heavily. Hound was limping tonight, but she didn't say anything about it. Even from her, he would have taken it as an expression of pity.

"The drug smuggling. I looked into it some more. I got the address of the warehouse in Illinois."

Hound hadn't taken off his raincoat. He unbuttoned it enough to pull out a large envelope from the area of his waist.

Does he stuff those in his pants, or what? Another thing I don't want to know about Hound.

He put the envelope on the table and slid it toward her. "I also found out who put Nando's drug-smuggling plan into action. Guy named Gregory Theodore Shale. Local entrepreneur, made it big with a tech company that has a lot of government contracts. There's photos and a full report in there."

"ShaleTech?"

"Yeah. You know the guy?"

"Local philanthropist, interested in the Vitality for Life Foundation. Nando and the other dead coder did some work for his company."

"This whole herd of motherfuckers is starting to stink. Somebody's been sniffing around about you, too. Some DEA prick."

Maliha sighed. "Jake Stackman."

"You know the guy?"

"Yes. I went out on a date with him and things got a little strange after that."

"You fuck him?"

She blinked. It was a typical, straightforward Hound question. "No. We haven't gotten that far."

"You need somebody to run him off, I'd be happy to. No charge."

"I'll keep the offer in mind."

"On the drug smuggling, the thing that bothers me is there's no reason for this upstanding citizen Shale to get involved in moving smack. On paper, he looks like one wealthy guy."

"Things might not be as rosy as they seem. I heard he's keeping two sets of books for the company, deceiving his creditors and shareholders."

"Damn, woman, what do you need me for? You're putting all this shit together yourself. Guess I don't get my bonus."

She leaned forward and covered his large, misshapen hand with both of hers.

"Of course you'll get your bonus. I don't have it with me because I didn't know you were going to drop this delicious piece of information in my lap. I thought maybe you just wanted to . . . talk."

"Yeah, well, I want to do that, too."

"Let's do this. I'll stop off at my place and then meet you at your apartment."

"Sounds like a plan." He stood up and left.

When Maliha left the bar, she caught a glimpse of someone a few doors down, sitting on the sidewalk, resting against a brick building. One glance summed him up: dressed in layers of ragtag clothing against the cold, he was homeless. She started to walk away, then turned back. She might be able to get him into a shelter. The temperature had dropped rapidly after dark, and in the Windy City, exposure was a major problem.

As she approached, the man levered himself to his feet. She could see now that he was older than she'd originally thought. Homelessness plus age equaled heightened vulnerability, from the elements and from sickos who thought beating up a helpless old man was fun.

"You need to be inside tonight," she said.

At the sound of her voice, the man turned and walked away from her, first shuffling his feet, then speeding up when she continued to follow.

No sense scaring him off any further. She stopped her pursuit. She couldn't help thinking that something about him was familiar, though. A certain set of the shoulders, the way he'd risen almost effortlessly from the pavement for a man of his age. It was a puzzle, but she had to get moving. She'd promised Hound she'd need only a short time before meeting him.

She was already in the taxi when it struck her.

Grandfather. The homeless man could have been Grandfather. I think . . . I think he was. What's he doing here in Chicago? I thought he didn't leave the mountain in China.

Maliha retrieved twenty-five thousand in cash from her forty-eighth-floor condo, where she kept a large amount of cash, gold, and precious jewels—the Big Three. Hound opened his door before she had a chance to knock, and pulled her into his embrace.

Afterward, when he was asleep, she stayed next to him for a long time, resting her hand on his chest, enjoying his warmth and closeness while listening to the sleet pattering against the windows.

She slipped out of his bed, showered, dressed, and took a taxi home.

In the taxi, she checked her cell phone. It had been turned off while she was with Hound. No messages.

Jake hasn't called.

As she walked over a particular part of the floor of her haven, she thought about what was beneath it. She'd installed a floor safe, doing all the work herself. Inside rested the Tablet of the Overlord and the first diamond shard. Just knowing they were here, that she could put her hands on them whenever she wanted, made her quest seem more attainable.

The apartment's phone rang. Caller ID told her it was Yanmeng, and she picked up.

"Subedei. Amaro mentioned that you wanted to know about him. Do you still?"

"In a minute. I got some news that's weighing on my mind."

"You go first, then."

"I found out that Greg Shale is the one behind the drug

smuggling. That may have been the reason Nando and Hairy got killed, if Hairy was in on it, too. Poor coders got into something out of their league and lost their lives for it. Thought they had it all under control, no doubt. Greg's company is in financial trouble. He's using the drug money to keep things afloat, maybe to feed a special project he's got going."

She told him about hearing the name Project CESR—she spelled it for him, at his request—from the ShaleTech CFO Edward Rupert. "Does CESR mean anything to you?"

"You don't suppose he's smuggling salads into the country now, do you?"

She laughed. "I doubt it."

"I'll look into it and see if I can turn up anything. Amaro will, too. Back to Subedei. May I ask why you want to know?"

She hesitated, then told him about her observation. "He's Ageless. I saw him heal right in front of me. I cut his hand off and he just stuck it back on. What have you got on him?"

"I have a historical reference. Subedei Bahadur was a Mongolian warrior of the Reindeer People clan, a brilliant general, and one of Genghis Khan's infamous Dogs of War. He was a practitioner of Kung Fu and a master swordsman and archer. He died in 1248 at the age of seventy-two. Toward the end of his life, he could no longer ride a horse and had to be carried in a cart to direct a battle. This doesn't sound like a fighter who could defeat you. Number one, he died over 750 years ago. Number two, he was old and unable to move around well on his own."

"The man I fought was Mongolian. Assuming he's Ageless, being 750 years old isn't an obstacle. I'm almost halfway there myself. As far as being dead, who's to say that a demon serving the Lord of the Underworld can't pull a deceased man from his grave and return him to life with all his youthful vigor?"

She had a sudden insight. *Is that what happened to me, too? I must have died in those flames. When Rabishu pulled me out of there, I was already dead. He gets his recruits from among those who have died with bitterness in their hearts. I should have been in that graveyard with Constanta. No—as a witch, anything that was left of my body would have been tossed into a river, not buried in the churchyard. No peace with my baby, even in death.*

"We don't know the limits of Rabishu's power," she said. "Or it might be one of the other demons besides Rabishu."

I was already dead. She couldn't let go of it.

"No wonder Anu worried about what the demons could do if they all stroked the oars in unison. Why doesn't he come back and put them in their place?"

"You'll have to ask him that. I have to mention something else. I saw someone today who could have been Grandfather. A homeless man. I'm not positive, but I think it was him."

"Something big's brewing, it has to be, to draw him out. How are we going to fight this Subedei?"

She noticed he said "we." She had a feeling that was something she'd have to do alone. She didn't downplay the importance of the contributions of Yanmeng, Amaro, and Hound in her life. But none of them stood a chance against the being she'd fought in Greg's dojo. She didn't want her friends anywhere near Subedei, who'd already died and was far stronger for it.

Why does Subedei associate with Greg Shale? He's either using him or guarding him. Or both.

"Very carefully. I fight Subedei very carefully."

Chapter Thirty-One

The McLaren ate up the road as Maliha drove to the ShaleTech compound. She reviewed her plan as the miles sped by, because she didn't want this incursion to have an ending like the PharmBots break-in. If she had to fight her way out, that's what she'd do, and leave a slew of bodies behind.

The wild card was Subedei. Would she encounter him?

A better question: Am I afraid of him, or just being cautious?

Maliha drove the McLaren down a gravel road to a barn that had shown up on an aerial view of the property. She pulled the car inside the barn and left with the covert entry kit she'd assembled. She took off cross-country, and when she got to ShaleTech at about midnight, she circled around to the back, away from the manned security gates. She climbed a tree and observed for two hours.

Her first obstacle was the pair of fences with guards and dogs patrolling between them. There were lights at intervals that never allowed the guards to be in total darkness, although there were areas that were dimmer than others.

A pair of guards proceeded clockwise around the fenced area and another pair went counterclockwise, so they were in sight of each other every few minutes for verification. In addition, they reported via radio to a central security area inside the building every hour. Walking at a good rate, the dogs keeping up easily, the pairs passed each other about every seven minutes. That was her time window, and it was a generous one for someone with Maliha's speed.

Maliha picked a time when the pairs had just passed each other and reported on their radios. She dropped down from the tree and sprayed her feet with a bottle of rabbit urine sold as a hunting lure. At the fence, she disturbed the ground with a knife, making it look as though a rabbit could have squeezed through. She climbed the first fence like a lizard scurrying up a wall and dropped down from the top, landing with a small puff of dust. Pulling a tuft of rabbit fur from her pocket, she dropped it on the ground. Dashing for the other fence, she was up and over, and then she crossed the distance to the building. The landscaping was illuminated with upward-pointing lights for a dramatic effect, but she found a place of darkness and pressed against the wall of the building.

When the dogs came around, they went crazy over the rabbit scent. One of the guards shined a flashlight at the fence and saw the small tunnel and scrap of fur.

"What is it, Jenson?"

Jenson kicked at the dirt with his foot. "Nothing. Rabbit got under the fence."

"Again?" He turned to his dog. "Enough, Sport. Let's move on."

Both dogs quieted. A guard talked on the radio, and although Maliha couldn't hear it, she was sure the other guards were being told the reason for the commotion. As Sport was leaving, he sniffed Maliha's footprints enviously, no doubt dreaming of the day when he would be free to chase rabbits.

Maliha turned her attention to the building. From her vantage point, the brick edifice with few windows looked like a fortress.

Fortresses I know.

She took advantage of the shadows to wait out the passage of the second pair of guards, whose dogs reacted to the rabbit scent but were quickly pulled along by the guards, who'd been alerted to expect it. After they'd passed, she used a compact crossbow to launch a grappling hook to the roof. She tested the rope and began climbing, a straightforward walk up the side of the building. When she reached the roof, she pulled up the rope and took it with her.

On the roof were several ventilation shafts, vertical drops that ran through the core of the building, joined at intervals by smaller horizontal vents. She picked the shaft that was closest to Greg's office. The louvered cap wasn't locked on. She lifted it and propped it up on a rod, like a car's hood. Peering over the side, she could see utility lights shining up from the bottom, where a large exhaust fan turned lazily. The rest of the shaft was in darkness.

Maliha put on a headband light and switched it on. She fitted the grappling hook onto the lip of the shaft and let the rope slide down the inside. Over she went, into the darkness. Bracing her back against one side of the shaft and her feet on the other, she inched her way downward. She passed the first set of branching vents that served the ninth floor, then the second set, and paused at the third set, for the seventh floor. She picked the vent that headed toward Greg's office and crawled in.

Moving along on hands and knees, she passed several grates. Gazing through, she could see that she was near the ceiling, as she'd expected from studying the photos she'd taken. There were side branches that went to individual rooms. Unclipping a GPS device from her belt, she checked her location using the light from her headband. The special device boosted the reception of the satellite signal. Her target was the restroom attached to the private dining room, where she'd taken a location reading during her lunch with Greg. Once there, she'd have to rely on the blueprint she had in her head to find Greg's office.

It all worked as planned, and in a few minutes she was in the vent with a good view of Greg's office. She looked through the grill of the vent to check for cameras in the room. There were none. Greg, like Diane Harvey, didn't want his private doings on film. She used a clever, U-shaped ratcheting screwdriver to remove the screws holding the grill, and lowered herself into the room.

She was here to find information on Project CESR and the financial troubles Greg was keeping under wraps. She picked locks on desk drawers and file cabinets, to no avail. The good stuff must be in the safe. While searching, she also kept an eye out for anything that looked like a safe combination. Some people wrote the combination somewhere nearby in the office, maybe trying to disguise it as an invoice number or a date or something similar. There were no notes that appeared to have a number casually written on them.

A door on the side of the office was heavily secured. It had a palm-print reader, a retina scanner, and a microphone for voice recognition. She hadn't come prepared to break into it and would have to do it by force if she wanted to see what was in the room it protected.

First things first: the safe.

It was where Betty said it would be, behind a painting. It had an electronic lock with a keypad to enter the combination.

Maliha licked her lips. If procedures were careless, it might be easy to get inside. She was prepared to blast the safe open, but why do that if Shale would open it for her?

She removed from her kit a fingerprint brush that looked like a tiny feather duster and a small bottle of green-fluorescing fingerprint powder. She gently dusted the safe's keypad with a thin coating of powder. From a case that looked like it would hold a pair of eyeglasses, she pulled a device the shape and size of a pen and attached an amber shield to it. The device was a portable Alternate Light Source, ALS, that generated ultraviolet light. She snapped off her headband light and turned on the ALS. Looking through the shield, several of the keys on the keypad glowed with fingerprints: 8, 4, 3, 2, and Enter. The 8 key was more heavily printed than the others, indicating that the number 8 was used more than once in the combination. She sighed in relief. The keypad hadn't been wiped clean after use. She turned her headband light back on and got to work on the keys.

Greg was thirty-eight years old, so she pressed the 3 and 8 keys first, then various combinations of the other numbers. When she punched in 38248—age thirty-eight, two times four equals eight—the red light on the keypad turned green. Greg hadn't been very imaginative with the combination. She pulled down on the handle and the safe was open.

She removed the ledgers and sat on the floor behind the desk with them. She photographed the pages, returned the ledgers to the safe, and locked it. With a clean cloth, she scrubbed off the fingerprint powder. Mission accomplished.

Now for that intriguing door across the room. Her choices were blow the door lock mechanism off or leave without seeing what was behind it. If she blew the door, she would have to fight her way out, because there was no way that was going to escape the attention of the guards.

Blow the door. All that security has to be hiding something important.

She took out a small brick of C4 and rolled it into a snake shape, which she wrapped around the door's locking mechanism. She inserted a detonator, played the wire out until she was across the room and behind the desk, and pressed the detonator's control button. The explosive blew, and the lock with it.

She'd been counting seconds in her head since the blast and now ran over to stand behind the door to the hallway. The guard at the end of the hall would have heard the noise, and she figured the door was wired into central security and her actions had sounded an alarm, too.

First, the guard from the hall.

The office door opened slowly and a gun barrel entered the room. The guard wasn't rushing in. She didn't have time for his caution, so she grabbed the end of the gun, yanked him into the room, and knocked him out. She'd gained more seconds of precious work time.

Beyond the door was a room with a panoramic view of numerous monitors. In the center was a swiveling chair surrounded by computer equipment. The view from the chair would allow a person to track activity on all the monitors and respond to the changing displays using the computer. She walked up and examined the monitors, which varied in purpose.

There were scrolling charts with multiple lines of spikes and troughs, like an EKG readout. There were maps that reminded her of airline routes and views with banks of dials and switches. Those views were in a rapid rotation cycle, and some of the views had people in them, caught in still shots with their mouths open while speaking, in mid-stride, and in one case, mid-stroke, with fly open. She took a couple of photos of the room in general and then close-ups of a few of the monitors. It seemed to be a control room, but for what?

The timer in her head went off. She had to leave. There was another tempting door across the room from her, another secure door that she'd have to blast, but she didn't have the time.

As she exited the control room, the office door slammed open, hitting the wall, and several men came in. They had their guns drawn, ready to shoot first and not have to ask questions later, because the target would be dead.

Maliha hoisted herself into the vent, moved inward a dozen feet, and stopped to pull a tube from her pack. She pulled the pin and slid the flashbang backward through her legs into the room, squeezed her eyes shut, and pressed her fingers into her ears as hard as she could.

The vent lit up around her, the bright light reflecting from the metal surface and visible through her protected eyes. Then the powerful noise rattled her surroundings and her ears too, in spite of having them stopped up. The unprepared guards behind her were incapacitated. She had a few seconds before their eyes would readjust, even longer before they regained their balance, lost due to inner ear disturbances. She made the most of the time by scurrying along in the vent.

Sooner than she'd hoped for, there was a scraping noise behind her—someone else was in the vent. She switched off her headband light and flattened her body against the metal floor. Several bullets flew over her back, through the space where she'd been moments before. When the firing stopped, she scrambled ahead and rounded a right-angle bend. She drew one leg up under her body and waited in the dark. She could hear the man's uneven breathing as he closed the gap. Light moved erratically on the vent walls; he was pushing a flashlight ahead of him. When he got close to the bend in the tunnel, the noise of his motion stopped. He was thinking about what to do next. Finally he stuck his gun hand around the right-angle bend, finger on the trigger. He was going to shoot to make sure no one was waiting for him around the corner.

She kicked her drawn-up leg backward, landing a powerful blow on his wrist. The gun flew out of his grasp. The flashlight snapped off. He fumbled for the gun in the dark, moving his body forward a little. She landed a solid kick to his arm and heard it snap. Moaning, he began to slide backward in the vent, pushing back with his good arm. Satisfied that he wasn't coming after her, she didn't try to finish him off. Instead she moved forward, heading for the main vertical shaft.

She could hear shouts echoing in the vent, bouncing off the metal so that they seemed to come from everywhere. Up ahead there was a light moving around in front of her. Someone had taken off a vent grill and was shining a flashlight in. Her way was blocked.

Shit, shit, shit.

She stopped and loaded an arrow into her crossbow. It was cramped, but she managed it. She lay down on the floor of the vent and waited. She heard a dragging noise, and envisioned a chair being pulled up to the vent. A man stuck his arm in and waved it around to draw fire if someone was lying in wait for him. She kept still.

Having tested for safety—he thought—the guard's head appeared in the opening and she released the arrow. It buried itself in his temple. Without uttering a sound, he toppled backward on the chair and crashed to the floor. She hurried past the opening and soon arrived at the vertical shaft. Her rope dangled there. She grabbed the rope, climbed into the shaft, and started moving upward. She looked up and could see a patch of sky with stars.

Past the eighth floor, heading for the ninth.

Noise reverberated through the shaft. The fan at the

bottom had come on and was whirling rapidly, sucking air from the interior of the building and blowing it out toward the stars. Maliha was buffeted by the strong blast of air. Her feet slipped on the metal wall of the shaft and she slid down several feet until she caught herself with the rope. Planting her feet firmly, she struggled upward as the powerful wind tried to tear her loose.

Ninth floor, out onto the roof.

Maliha used a mirror on a telescoping rod to look over the side of the roof and check out the situation on the ground. Guards were moving around the building, looking for a point of entry. She wouldn't be able to go over the side of the building on the rope, unless she wanted to be a bullet pincushion.

Maliha moved to the part of the roof where the fewest guards were posted below. She stepped up to the edge of the roof and then stepped off it.

Chapter Thirty-Two

 BASE jumping: an extreme sport involving leaping from a fixed object with a parachute. The acronym comes from **B**uilding, **A**ntenna, **S**pan, **E**arth, the four places a jumper leaps from to launch.

An ultra-compact ram-air parachute nestled on Maliha's back, running from shoulder to waist and tightly compressed in a pack. She deployed her pilot chute manually as soon as she jumped. There had been no time to attach a static line to the building, which would have automatically opened the pilot chute as she jumped. She had only ninety feet of air space to the ground—giving her a dangerously short, almost impossibly short, amount of time to slow her descent. Most BASE jumpers preferred six or eight times that height in order to enjoy tracking in freefall, opening their chutes when they got closer to the ground.

Maliha had no tracking time at all. The main chute snapped open partially and she half fell, half glided, unable to maneuver well. She tucked up her legs as she passed over the fence closer to the building, then made it over the outer fence, but the fence snagged the chute. Her shoes were a few feet from the ground, but she was held in place by the harness.

A bullet from behind her snapped one of the harness straps above her head, and she cut the other one with a knife. She ran into the woods with bullets chasing her, heading away from the barn. The last thing she wanted was to have someone trail her to her car, or even worse, guess where she was going and arrive there first.

She ran for miles in the night, the moon lighting her way, forest animals acknowledging her passage with a blink of their eyes or the flick of a tail.

When she got back to the barn, she was feeling good about her mission that night. She'd gotten what she came for, photos of the ledgers, and a bonus: a glimpse behind the secure door.

She flicked on a flashlight in the dark interior of the barn, and was shocked when another one winked on nearby. Instantly, she threw her flashlight at the source of the light. It went spinning end over end, aiming up and to the right of the second flashlight's beam, where the chest of the person holding it should be.

Her flashlight struck the wall of the barn hard and dropped down.

"Ouch! What the hell, what are you doing?"

It was a familiar voice. Her flashlight, now lying on the ground, illuminated the lower body of Jake Stackman. He'd been sitting on the floor of the barn, waiting in the dark. Her flashlight had bounced off the wall and hit him in the head.

"Christ! I'm going to have a bump the size of—"

"What are you doing here? And roll my flashlight back over to me."

"I followed you here. I've been watching ShaleTech." He kicked the flashlight in her direction, but it rolled to a stop eight feet from him. Cautiously, she went to pick it up.

"Don't try anything. I'm armed," she said.

"What a coincidence. So am I."

She retrieved the flashlight and played it over him. He had his back against the wall of the barn and was rubbing the top of his head with one hand. The other hand held a gun pointed at her midsection.

She was eight feet away. She could knock that gun out of his hand before he could squeeze the trigger with his vulnerable one-handed grip.

"Why'd you visit Shale? Picking up drugs? Which is it, resale or personal use?"

"You have a one-track mind. I have nothing to do with Shale's drug operation."

"Then tell me the source of your information. You're going to, one way or the other."

He threatened me. This is getting ugly.

She lunged forward, planted one foot and used the other to flick the gun out of his hand. Before he could get up from his seated position, she snatched up the gun and ended up fifteen feet away, with his own gun pointed at him.

He frowned. "Well, shit."

"Any more weapons you want to threaten me with?" She couldn't keep a smug tone out of her voice.

"Shucks, I left my phaser at home. Who are you, anyway? You look like Emma Peel in that outfit."

I should just shoot the guy. I'd be putting him out of his misery.

She didn't act on the thought, no matter how tempting. Instead she sank to the ground, put the gun on the floor behind her, and sat facing him.

"You don't know how much I regret that I ever gave you that tip about smuggling drugs in computers."

"I'm not regretting this. My name's going down for the credit on this operation. I'm getting a promotion out of this, in addition to taking a lot of drugs off the street. All I have to do is figure out your role. Are you a bad guy or not?"

"Why can't you just believe me that I'm a good guy?"

"Lame. I need proof. Nice car you have there. Nice, expensive car."

"I didn't get that car with drug money. You know that. You already know how much money I've earned in the last few years."

Jake levered himself to his feet. Startled, Maliha did the same. He walked toward her. She kicked his gun across the floor, so it landed underneath the McLaren. She drew a knife, but he kept coming.

"Stop! I'll cut you."

"You're beautiful."

"What?"

He was close, too close. *What was going on? Did he want to be killed?*

"Dangerous. The most beautiful woman I've ever seen and dangerous, too."

When he was three feet away, he reached for her knife arm. She blocked it easily, knocking his flashlight to the ground, and she was about to bring her flashlight around in an arc to hit the side of his head. He grabbed both of her shoulders, pulled her to him, and kissed her passionately.

Her first reaction was indignation. Her second was to pull back from his embrace. Her third was to melt into it.

Her flashlight slid to the ground, and she threw the knife she was holding toward the barn wall, where it stuck, quivering. Moments after that, when they'd frantically taken off each other's clothing, Maliha wrapped her legs around Jake and took him inside her. His hands and mouth couldn't get enough of her. He walked forward, his hands under her thighs, and then braced her ass on the McLaren's front fender.

They were breathless, panting, moaning in time with the thrusts. Jake crushed his body against hers, flattening her breasts against his chest so man and woman couldn't be any closer as they both cried out with release. Then she rested her head on his shoulder and ran her fingers across his sweaty back until he peeled himself away from her. She slid her feet to the ground and stood in front of him. With the light of two flashlights on the floor casting deep shadows, his hands explored her body. His touch was electric, so that everywhere on her skin that he touched she imagined he was leaving bright trails of sparks.

He leaned over and nestled his face into her neck, then whispered in her ear.

"I've wanted to do that from the moment I saw you."

"Me, too." She was surprised that it was the truth. "Does this mean I'm a good guy now?"

"Mmm." He was kissing her neck, licking her earlobe. His warm breath excited her, and she felt his hardness growing.

They came together gently, moving slowly, tenderly, until they moaned with pleasure.

Afterward, Maliha pulled on her clothes with Jake's eyes following her every move. She couldn't stay around. The experience had been too intense, and she had to get away to think.

Chapter Thirty-Three

The morning after Maliha's incursion into the Shale compound, her mind was thoroughly occupied, but not with what she'd learned at the compound. Instead she was vividly replaying her unexpected and fierce lovemaking with Jake. Her coffee grew cold in the cup. Photos she'd taken of the ledgers were scattered across the table, unexamined. Her laptop's screen-saver was put through its paces.

The computer chimed, and she saw an invitation to view Randy's webcam. She accepted and the connection was made.

"Randy! What the hell happened to you that afternoon? A chauffeur? Really."

Her friend was in violet silk pajamas, with a silly grin on her face and a radiance that came from sainthood or sex. In Randy's case, Maliha guessed it wasn't sainthood.

Randy peered at her through the screen. "Put your face up next to the camera."

Maliha complied.

"What the hell happened to *you*? You so need Botox. Could do something with your hair, too."

Pulling back, Maliha said, "Just tired, that's all. Need to catch up on my sleep."

Randy's too observant. She picked up on the Dearborn age jump. What am I going to do about her?

Randy switched the subject, apparently accepting Maliha's trumped-up story about fatigue.

"Take a look at this, girlfriend. C'mere, Rip."

A man stepped to Randy's side within camera range. She turned her webcam toward him and the screen filled with a gorgeous six-pack. Randy rubbed her hand across it like a washboard and continued downward off the screen.

Maliha was caught between wishing the camera would tilt downward and being glad that it didn't. On top of what she'd already been thinking about Jake, it would have been too much to process. She hoped Yanmeng or Amaro didn't stray in, because this little interchange would be hard to explain.

"Well-defined *rectus abdominus*," she squeaked out.

"Hey, I'm not talking about his asshole here," Randy retorted.

"Forget it. Listen, I was in the middle of something. You two go back to whatever. Call me later, Randy, I've got news of my own."

Randy's face lit up. "Marsha slept with Jaa-ake, Marsha slept with Jaa-ake," she said in a singsong fashion.

Maliha cut the connection before Randy could ask any questions.

I don't know why I mentioned that. I'll have to make up some news, because I'm not ready to say anything about Jake.

The morning's thoughts of hot sex and abs were swept from her mind when she heard that two U.S. senators had been killed in their homes overnight.

While she was still absorbing the news, Maliha got a phone call. She hesitated, then answered it. It was from Deputy Secretary of Homeland Security Joe Manning, aka Cocomo. Only his good friends used the nickname. Maliha wasn't in that category, but he'd insisted, establishing a false closeness for purposes of his own. She'd met Cocomo once and he'd contributed to her charitable foundation. In the hothouse of D.C. politics, that meant he was a bosom buddy, and he treated her like one on the phone. Underlying his friendliness, she could detect a lot of tension.

The small talk fizzled out, and he came to the real reason for his call. He wanted to meet with her as soon as she could get there. She demurred, and he said that he had information about the two coders that tied them to the senators' deaths.

That did it. She took the first flight out and rented a car in D.C.

Late-afternoon shadows slanted across Woodrow Wilson Plaza, within walking distance of the White House. The curved walls of the Ronald Reagan Building were an interesting architectural background to the open area of the plaza. Trees sported fall colors, the sky was a brilliant blue, and the food in a plaza café was delicious. A heavy sweater pulled over her blouse was perfect for the chill in the air. She'd gone to the plaza straight from the airport and dawdled around, waiting for the meeting time.

While she waited, her thoughts roamed, and kept turning to her time with Jake in the barn.

Does he love me? Or is this just a physical thing for him? So many times before, that's all it's been for me.

Was love something she could trust? Her husband, Nathan, had stood by and done nothing while she was dragged from their home, accused of witchcraft. Yet she thought she'd loved him. Since then she'd given her heart to no one.

What if I fall in love with Jake and lose him? How do people cope with this kind of uncertainty?

Maliha coped by remaining closed off, and the fact that she couldn't get Jake out of her mind worried her.

If I don't drop this right now, I'll be in new territory. Serious relationship territory.

She could've easily pushed out of her mind any other man to whom she'd made love only once. Or for that matter, a dozen times.

There's just something about him. Maybe it's his mysterious past, a kind of kinship I feel with him. He's done something in the past, something bad.

She caught her breath. *He could be like me, formerly Ageless.*

The thought went around and around in her head as if her brain were a clothes dryer, and it was soon joined by another.

That could be why he has five "lost" years Amaro discovered. Jake uses that time to reinvent himself, like I do.

She wondered if he could read her aura. There was a chance that she was born with sensitivity to auras and had only refined an ability she already had. Rabishu may have had nothing to do with it, so Jake might not have that gift. Plus, there was no reason to believe that the demons handed out an identical benefits package to each of their slaves. Grandfather could change his appearance, something Maliha couldn't do. Jake might have gotten super vision or something.

She gasped. *Or mind reading. Or remote viewing. Oh, shit.*

The toast he'd made in his apartment came back, the reference to aging and love.

Her waiting time, spent thinking about Jake, passed quickly, and left her with the slightly queasy feeling that he knew too much about her. At a few minutes to four, Maliha sat on a half wall in the area of the Wilson Plaza Cocomo had designated, within sight of a large metal rose sculpture.

He arrived, a tall man in a suit that looked slept in, with an aura that said he was frightened.

"Walk with me," he said, after thanking her for coming. It was Saturday, and there were tourists milling around, so the two of them didn't stand out. They strolled the plaza like a pair of lovers, shoulders brushing together occasionally. She approved of the device of looking like a couple as long as he didn't want to hold hands.

Cocomo was close enough that he could speak for her ears only. He was slightly out of breath, and it wasn't from the exertion. The nervous way he looked around made it clear he was worried. He didn't waste any time.

"Senators Kosiorek and Lewiston. You've heard about their deaths?"

"Very little. I heard on the news that they'd been killed in their homes, that's all."

"Throats slashed, both of them. Lewiston was in his bathtub, fully clothed. Kosiorek was in his office, leaning back in his chair, like someone had come up from behind and . . ." He trailed off.

"How does this affect you and me?"

"The senators and I were involved in obtaining a lucrative contract for a company. Not that the company didn't deserve it—their research was solid—but we handheld the whole thing, fended off some competition, and put down some last-minute questions about it."

"The three of you took bribes, in other words."

"I'm not proud about that. I know it's hard to believe in this town, but it's the first time I've been involved in anything like that. I had my reasons, but looking back, nothing is reason enough."

He stopped and checked the surroundings again. "Two of the people I worked with have been murdered. The police don't have any clues. I have to assume I'm next on the hit list. I haven't been home since I got the news."

She studied Cocomo's aura again, and found a desperate honesty clinging to the edges of the churning emotion of fear.

"What's the company involved?"

"I'll get to that. First I want to talk about you doing something for me."

"And that is?"

"Making me disappear. *Poof.* New identity, out of the country. Before whoever got to Lewiston and Kosiorek comes after me."

"What makes you think I can help you with something like that?"

Cocomo's eyes kept moving around and he swiveled his head. His hands were jammed in his pockets to keep them from shaking. He took off walking again, and she hurried to catch up.

"You and I have a mutual friend, a private investigator named Hound. I use his services every now and then." His voice steadied for a moment. "That's classified."

Hound does classified work for the government? Gee, something else I didn't know about him.

"My lips are sealed."

"I'm serious. You're taking this all too lightly. It's my life we're talking about here." His voice was strained. If he was in private, he would probably be crying.

"Sorry. I'm listening. What have you got to offer for this favor?"

"Do we have a deal?" His feet moved mechanically, his pace a little faster as he got closer to the kernel of truth of their meeting.

"Because I trust Hound, that's a tentative yes. I can arrange your disappearance. First you have to tell me what you know. What's your bargaining chip?"

"The two dead coders in the news worked on the same project that the senators and I did. That's four people dead, and those are the ones I know about. It's a cleanup operation. Everybody who knew about the project is being eliminated."

"I asked before and I'll ask again now. If you don't spill it, we're not going any further and I wasted a trip to D.C. What's the company involved? What's the project?

"Shale Technologies, in Chicago. Have you heard of it?"

"Oh, yes."

Cocomo tilted his head sideways and looked at her, picking up something that wasn't neutral in the way she answered.

"Gregory Shale?"

"Yes. I know him."

He blinked rapidly. Fear radiated from him like heat waves off hot asphalt. "You're not working for Shale, are you? Here to kill me?"

She put a hand on his arm. "No. If so, you'd be dead already."

He stopped walking. Her touch on his arm was a comfort, a switch that turned off the compulsive movement of his feet and steadied his eyes and voice.

"We all worked on Project CESR, C-E-S-R. It's . . ."

A streak of motion, and blood spattered the entire front of Maliha's sweater. Cocomo, a look of shock on his face and a gushing slash on his throat, sank to his knees and then pitched forward.

She knew there was nothing she could do for him. Maliha moved away, hoping that no one had seen them together enough to identify her. As she was moving, she pulled the sweater carefully over her head and dropped it in a trash can. At first glance she didn't look like she'd just slaughtered something.

Someone had slaughtered the deputy secretary of Homeland Security.

In the pandemonium, she looked for a center of still-ness, someone too calm, too familiar with death to react with horror to a slashed throat. She spotted him across the plaza—Subedei. She raced toward him and he waited for her.

As she approached, his hand moved at lightning speed, and she felt a sharp flash of pain high on her right thigh. A throwing star was deeply embedded there. She yanked the star from her leg and threw it back at him. By the time the throwing star reached the spot where Subedei had been, he was gone from the plaza. His mocking laughter lingered in her ears.

He was toying with her, and enjoying it. It was going to take all of her cunning just to stay alive. Her determination to defeat him solidified.

Back off? Never.

She let her rented Taurus take her to the airport, driving on automatic as she mulled over the unusual experience of having someone within arm's length drop dead, and she hadn't done it.

Greg was in the dojo practicing forms when Subedei walked in. The Mongolian watched him for a time and then made some suggestions and went through a few throws with him. Subedei took down a couple of swords from the weapons wall and put Greg through a short but intensive lesson.

Greg bowed, and they were ready to talk about how things had gone in D.C. Everything went smoothly and the deputy secretary was dead. When Greg was alone again, he used his cell phone to call Fawn and tell her to meet him in the dojo.

Fawn had an official job as his personal assistant, but he didn't even know where she spent her time in the building. Her real job was to be ready for him whenever he called her, which lately was often. And to perform unsavory tasks such as delivering bribes, where there was a direct risk of being caught. She arrived in a few minutes, and his eyes devoured her.

Still looks damn good to me.

Fawn had been his point of contact with the two computer consultants, to keep Greg a level removed. She'd done everything right, although he still wondered if she'd slept with Nando. He was quite certain she hadn't slept with Hairy. The girl did have standards.

He went up to Fawn, put one arm around her shoulders, and unbuttoned her blouse with his other hand. He had her clothes off and she was doing her part, untying his black belt, pulling down the loose pants of his karate uniform, rubbing him with her hands, whispering the things he wanted her to say. He pushed her down to her knees on the mat and let her pleasure him. Before he came, he stopped her and told her to get down on all fours. She did her cat stretch that he liked and he kneeled behind her.

As he entered her, he flashed back to a time when he'd been doing the same thing he was doing now and Subedei walked in on the two of them. It was the first and only time he'd seen his bodyguard angry. The Mongolian had picked Greg up while he was putting it to Fawn and thrown him across the room like a child might do to a stuffed animal, yelling that it was disrespectful to the dojo. Subedei ordered Fawn out, and she was happy to skip out in a hurry and leave Greg to face whatever was coming alone. Dealing with a pissed-off, mountainous bodyguard wasn't in her job description.

Subedei hauled him to his feet, tossed him a stick and demanded that he fight. Greg was still naked, and Subedei pressed him hard, landing blows carefully controlled for maximum pain and bruising, while not breaking bones or knocking Greg's head open. The bodyguard avoided all of

Greg's angry attempts to score a hit, as though Subedei were sparring with a six-year-old student.

Subedei had thought the lesson would outlast the pain, yet here Greg was again, in the dojo, enjoying Fawn and thumbing his nose—or his prick—at Subedei.

Of course, Subedei wasn't there to see it, and things were fine as long as it stayed that way.

When he finished, he told her to stay where she was, that he liked the view. She was obliging; where else could she earn ten thousand dollars a month as an assistant something-or-other? Greg had a knack for finding women he could manipulate. To be honest, he was well aware that Marsha wasn't one of those. She'd be a conquest of a different sort, one that would involve violence or trickery or both. He wasn't fooling himself that a donation to Marsha's charity would get her on her back.

Greg went to the weapon wall, took down a sword, whirled it around feeling powerful, and brought it down on Fawn's neck.

Fawn couldn't be allowed to live. She was a link between him and the dead coders, so she was part of the cleanup. He'd known it would end this way with her from the start, but he'd had a good run with her.

It was his first kill with the sword. Appraising the results, he thought he did a good job. He could only get better with practice.

Chapter Thirty-Four

Maliha was cautious on the way back to her home in Chicago, but the trip from Washington, D.C., after the murder in the plaza went smoothly. She arrived in the early hours of Sunday morning. On the way up in the elevator of her building, she felt a touch on her shoulder, Yanmeng saying hello from the astral plane. She stuck out her tongue in greeting.

She jabbed the button for the thirty-ninth floor instead of heading for her private rooms higher up, where she'd been anticipating unwinding.

Amaro greeted her at the door of her place wearing boxer shorts and several days' growth of beard.

She looked around her formerly neat living room and sighed. Amaro had pulled some tables together and made a work area for himself, on which he'd planted two laptops.

"Yanmeng will be here in a few minutes," he said. "He went out for Chinese food."

"You two have taken over my place. You might as well invite Rosie to stay with us, too. How's she doing?"

Amaro looked pained. "She says it's a boy. She can tell by how hard he's kicking her. She wants to name him after me."

"What an honor. I'm sure she doesn't take that lightly."

"In her current state, she doesn't take anything lightly. Yesterday she called and yelled at me for fifteen minutes because she couldn't find her slippers. Turns out they were on her feet."

"Ouch."

"Yeah."

Yanmeng arrived with a large brown paper bag. Delicious smells arrived with him, but it was hard to pull her thoughts from the events in Washington.

Why couldn't I have stopped Cocomo's death? Am I that pathetic compared to Subedei? I should have thought, should have done, something different. His life slipped through my fingers and I don't even know much about him, except that he knew Hound.

She wasn't looking forward to telling Hound.

Maliha excused herself and went into her bedroom. At least that area looked just as she'd left it. In fact, the door to the bedroom had been closed, as if to give the room itself privacy from the two men.

She called Hound's phone number.

"Yeah."

"A man you worked with is dead," she said, without preamble. "Goes by Cocomo. I was with him when he was killed. You'll read about it in the news."

"Cocomo. Damn it, what happened?"

"He called me to D.C., saying he knew something about Nando and Hairy. I was talking to him in a plaza when his throat was slashed."

"Fuck! You okay?"

"I'm okay."

He didn't say anything for a minute and she wondered if he was going to blame her. When he spoke again, he'd put aside whatever grief he felt for another time, a private time.

A medic couldn't cry in the field.

"What did you learn about the coders?" he asked.

She told him everything she knew, which wasn't much, and asked him to look into Project CESR. He didn't ask who did the killing, and she didn't volunteer. He didn't express surprise that Cocomo, a man who'd hired him for classified work, had traded his influence for money. That meant he already knew or suspected that Cocomo was, in Hound's terms, a multifaceted person: adaptable to the circumstances.

Hound surely knew that Maliha fell into the same category, though not for money, and it hadn't bothered him to work for her.

He wasn't aware of her full background. He didn't know she'd saved him in Vietnam, so there was no problem with him thinking she was a young woman who hadn't even been alive during that war. For the time being, that's the way she wanted it. When his aging was apparent and hers wasn't, she'd have to decide what to do then. With Randy, too. Her girl friend was unaware that the voice on the other end of the phone, and the face across the luncheon table, belonged to someone who wasn't in her generation, by a long shot.

Or maybe my aging will be apparent sooner than I think. There's no telling what can happen.

"Be careful poking around on Project CESR. There are some big players in this."

"I figured that. Cocomo was a fucking big player himself."

He hung up before she could ask about that.

She took a shower to get rid of the smell of blood she imagined still clinging to her, although she'd washed and gotten rid of her clothing.

I used to tolerate the smell of blood. I'm changing in so many little ways—will I even recognize myself after another fifty years?

She stared at her face in the mirror. *Will I be here in another fifty years?*

A thought flashed through her mind: *Jake and I would have grandchildren by then. Great-grandchildren. Something of me would be passed on.*

It wasn't a new thought for her, but it was the first time she'd linked it to a particular man.

When she went back into the living room, wrapped in a thick terry-cloth robe, she found that the two men had started on the meal without her. The laptops were pushed aside to clear one end of a table. At her place there was a steaming bowl of rice and chopsticks. A teapot sat in the cleared area. When she sat down, she raised her cup and Yanmeng poured tea for her.

She gently tapped the knuckles of her two forefingers on the table, in acknowledgement of his service to her, as he was a senior serving a junior. It was a gentle joke between them, that he was her senior since he appeared older than she did.

It was a tradition that had originated 250 years ago in China. To keep from losing touch with his people, Emperor Ch'ien-lung dressed as a peasant and traveled in the countryside with his guard as his only companion. When the emperor served tea to his guard, the guard wanted to show his respect, but couldn't fall to his knees because that would risk exposing their identities. Instead the guard placed his two forefingers on the table, as if they were tiny legs, and bent them at the "knee" to indicate that he was kneeling and showing proper respect. Emperor Ch'ien-lung was a popular figure, and the knuckle tap remains to this day as an unobtrusive way to honor someone.

Maliha raised the cup to her face and let the wonderful aroma fill her nostrils. The tea was Lushan Clouds and Mist, her favorite, from a tearoom in California named Teance. The tea grew wild on the mist-shrouded slopes of Lushan Mountain in Southern China. She rested the tea in her mouth and savored its unique buttery taste.

She and Yanmeng picked food from the cartons delicately with chopsticks. Amaro used a plate and fork, dumping parts of three cartons on top of the rice on his plate. Attacked from three sides, the food didn't stand a chance.

Amaro cleared away the remnants of the meal. "Great food. Trust a Chinese man to find the best Chinese food in town."

"Hardly." Yanmeng sniffed. "It was the best in a three-block radius. I didn't feel like going any farther."

Maliha's fortune cookie said YOU WILL BE LUCKY IN LOVE. She slipped it into the pocket of her robe without letting the others see it.

In the living room, Yanmeng slid in a fluid movement to the floor, into a lotus position. Amaro stretched out full length on one of the sofas, and Maliha curled up in a soft upholstered chair.

"You first," Amaro said.

She took them through her invasion of ShaleTech. She included the safe and the control room, and minimized her narrow escape. She said nothing about meeting Jake in the barn—she still didn't know what to think of that herself.

Her heart was saying *Jake Jake Jake* and she told it to shut up.

She talked about Cocomo, her encounter with Subedei, and what little she knew about Project CESR. "Well, that's a thorough debriefing. Unless you'd like to question me for hours now with a bright light shining in my face."

It wouldn't be the first time.

"How's your leg?" Yanmeng asked. She'd mentioned that Subedei had put a throwing star in her thigh.

She pulled up her robe to look at the wound. It was clean from the shower, and she'd pulled the smoothly sliced edges together with a few butterfly bandages. She pressed a finger next to it experimentally and found that it hurt quite a bit. Ignoring pain was a plus in her business.

"No problem. I'll be fine in a day." She looked up to find both of her friends with their heads turned away. "Hey, what's the deal? It's just a cut. I've had much worse."

"It's, uh, the location of the cut," Amaro said.

"Prudes." She lowered her robe. "What have you got?"

"I've been digging for information on Project CESR," Yanmeng said. "Two words keep turning up in the same sentence. *Energy* and *national security*. That's as far as it gets."

"That fits with Cocomo being involved, since he was with the DHS," she said.

"I've been going over the photos you took in Greg Shale's office," Amaro said. "I want you to see some of them."

He went to the table, and the other two followed to look at the slideshow he'd prepared. A ledger page filled the laptop's screen. Yanmeng slipped on a pair of reading glasses, reminding Maliha that her friend was getting on in years— something she didn't like to contemplate.

"I compared these records with the company's annual

report that goes to shareholders and its Securities and Exchange Commission filings, the ones that don't have the glossy pictures like the annual report," Amaro said. "ShaleTech should issue a pair of rose-colored glasses with every report they mail out. They're reporting that profits from the sale of electrical, gas, coal, and nuclear power-control systems are at record levels."

"What are power-control systems?" Maliha asked.

"Motor controls. Circuit breakers. Transformers. Computers that manage substations and the software that goes with them. Things that go inside power stations that nobody knows or cares about except the people who work there."

"So those rooms I saw on the monitors are real control rooms somewhere."

Amaro nodded.

"In reality ShaleTech has a major new competitor that is siphoning off a good share of the market. The phony ledgers are claiming that ShaleTech has retained most of the market share now held by the competitor, Youngman Systems. ShaleTech is operating in the red. I wonder how many people know about it."

Amaro put up a succession of photos on his laptop that showed the interiors of clean, white rooms. He stopped at one and pointed at it with a pencil. "See that clock on the wall there? If Maliha was in Greg's office between two and two thirty in the morning"—he looked at her and she nodded—"then this room in the photo is in the Pacific time zone. There are a few other small clues in the photos to indicate they're scattered around the country. Clues like food wrappers and soda cups from regional restaurants. For example,"—he flipped through several more photos and stopped at one with a blue-and-white soft-drink cup visible outside the room through a window. He tapped at the image of the cup—"Culver's restaurants are mostly in the Midwest."

"Downers Grove. There's one right here in the western suburbs."

They both looked at her.

"What? I like them. If you've never had a ButterBurger, you're in for a treat."

Yanmeng's nose wrinkled. "This from the woman who's eaten in the world's finest restaurants?"

"I've also eaten roasted camel's feet. I'll take a ButterBurger over those any day."

The conversation deteriorated from there. Maliha left the two of them arguing about the weirdest foods they'd eaten and went to bed.

She was still unaccustomed to waking up with someone else in her condo—two someones.

When she left her bedroom in the morning, Yanmeng was doing a martial-arts workout in the living room. Amaro was sitting at the kitchen table, drinking coffee, eating croissants, and reading the *Sunday Tribune*. When he saw her, he pointed to his cup of coffee.

"Jesus Christ! Did you know that your coffee has been through the bowels of some jungle animal?"

"The secret's out." He'd evidently found an unopened package of coffee in the cabinet and read the description. "You've been drinking Kopi Luwak for a long time, you know, and thought it was good."

He sniffed. "I bought some decent coffee at the market downstairs, and a convenient way to make it, too. No need for mess and measuring." He sounded like he was parroting the clerk. "And I guarantee no animal shit it out before I brewed it."

She glanced over at the countertop. Her coffee things had been shoved aside, and there was a one-cup-at-a-time brewer in their place.

"The coffee comes in pods. I bought Hazelnut Crème. Want a taste?" He offered her his own cup.

Maliha was tempted to pick him up bodily and toss him into the hall. Instead she walked into the kitchen, pushed the new machine out of the way, and started her own coffee brewing.

"If you don't like the new coffee, you can just say so. My feelings won't be hurt." Amaro frowned in spite of his words.

Yanmeng, supposedly absorbed in his exercise, had a big smile on his face.

"I'll just leave this here," she gestured at the stainless-steel invader on her counter, "for you to use when you visit."

"Well, that's pretty fucking clear." Small puffs of red had appeared on Amaro's cheeks. "You didn't even try it. Don't expect me to do you any more favors."

She sat down and bit into a buttery croissant. At least he'd gotten them from her usual bakery.

"I want to talk about getting back into ShaleTech," she said between bites. "There's more for me to learn there. I believe there's a lot more behind that security door than that one small control room."

She drew a sketch on the back of the bag Amaro had used to bring his treasures home from the market. From memory, she drew the plan for the seventh floor of the building, starting from the elevator area where the guard's desk was. On the left side of the hallway leading from the elevator there were numerous doors, most of them with glass to see inside. She drew the positions of several labs that she'd seen through the small windows. The dojo and the dining room filled out the end of the left side of the hallway.

Yanmeng came over and stood beside her, and she picked up the unique smell he had after exercise, which she'd noticed all the way back when she'd first sparred with him. He didn't smell like the usual male sweat. Instead it was a smell like freshly turned earth, damp from a spring rain and now lying in the sun.

Even if Yanmeng lived to be an improbable 125 years old, that was just fifty years from now. That was about the time elapsed since she'd ceased to be Ageless and set her feet on the mortal path.

I have never let people be close to me, or me to them, until now. How will I deal with it when a friend I love dies?

Impulsively, she put her hand on Yanmeng's arm. He looked at her with a question in his eyes, but she just shook her head a little.

Not good to dwell on such things, especially now. I may

not outlive him, and it would be Yanmeng doing the griev-
ing, and Amaro and Rosie. And Hound. Jake, too?

That was such a foreign thought that it froze her in place.
Emotion must have shown on her face, because Yanmeng
reached out and caressed her cheek.

"All right, you two, cut out the mushy stuff. Or let me in
on it." Amaro tapped the diagram Maliha had drawn on the
paper bag. "What's on the other side of the hall?"

Maliha brought herself back to the discussion. She drew
Greg's office and the control room on the right side at the
end of the hall, opposite the dojo and dining room. She finished with an arrow from the elevator to the control room on
the right side of the hall. "There's nothing here. No doors.
Not so much as a mouse hole."

"So you think that almost the entire length of the hall is
connected to the back end of the control room, and not accessible any other way?" Yanmeng asked.

"Yes." Maliha's brow furrowed as she thought about her
time in the building. "When I was in the ventilation system,
there were no branches that headed in that direction. I'm
sure of it."

"So there's a self-contained area of the building there,
with its own heating and cooling and probably water, too,"
Amaro said.

"And electrical supply, probably," Yanmeng said. "Do
you know if the private area extends the full height of the
building, up and down from the seventh floor?"

Maliha shook her head. "No way to know. There are
windows on those floors, looking at the building from the
outside, but that's an elaborate setup there. They could be
dummy windows, just leading to an internal hallway or
atrium space."

Amaro's eyes gleamed. "Holy cow. A secret building
within a building."

"I have got to see this place," she said.

"Since you blew the door off the control room, there's
bound to be much heavier security there now," Yanmeng
said.

"There has to be an entrance other than the control room.

Or I should say, an exit. What if there was a fire or the control room was taken over by hostiles?"

"We need a blueprint of the building," Amaro said. "That's Kane County, isn't it?"

Maliha nodded. "Check public records. Another approach might be to look into who cleans that section. Dusts the desks, empties the trash."

"We've got our work cut out for us today," Yanmeng said. He went over to the kitchen counter and pointedly poured a cup of the coffee Maliha had brewed.

Amaro's lips pinched together. "I'm sticking to Hazelnut Crème. At least I know where a damn hazelnut comes from."

Maliha crossed her legs, a tough thing to do with any degree of modesty in a short, tight dress, but she wasn't aiming for modesty. She was in the office of Victor Carding, the owner of SecureClean, Inc. Victor's eyes shifted between her breasts and her thighs.

"I'm sure you appreciate the position I'm in, Mr. Carding," Maliha purred.

He's thinking of me in a different position, though. "The board won't approve a contract with SecureClean unless I verify the trustworthiness of the employees," she continued.

She'd approached the owner with a lucrative offer for a cleaning contract for a new building under construction about ten miles from ShaleTech. The building was real; her connection with it wasn't.

"I should think a list of our clients would be sufficient reference. We work in the most secure buildings in a six-county region."

Among them, ShaleTech.

"I'm aware of that." Maliha slowly recrossed her legs. "Our needs are comparable to, say, Nanoscale Instruments, Laymont International, or Shale Technology Services. How are the crews assigned to those systems verified?"

"The crews for Nanoscale and Laymont are screened for trustworthiness. ShaleTech has a higher standard. One thing to keep in mind is our low turnover rate among employees, far less than industry standard. We recruit with long-term retention in mind, and the pay and benefits are outstanding in this field. Our crews have years of experience and reliability under their belts."

"It sounds like our needs match ShaleTech's. Would our crew be the same people used in ShaleTech, or would you be recruiting new staff for our building?"

"There might be some minor overlap of staff until we could ramp up hiring. A few highly reliable supervisors, some handpicked staff, perhaps. I'd say there would be an overlap period of eighteen months or so. It takes that long to get the security clearance needed. You did say you'd be sponsored by the Department of Defense, correct?"

"Right. Then we'd be getting the least-experienced people, the new hires, rather than the most experienced. I don't think that would be acceptable to the board. Can you siphon off some of the ShaleTech staff permanently?" Maliha leaned forward and placed her hand on the desk, making sure Victor got a good look down her dress.

"That might be possible." There was a catch in his voice, as though he were agreeing to something else.

"Now we're getting somewhere. I'll need a list of the ShaleTech crew. The board might like to investigate them and ask for those who meet our specifications."

"We'd have to be farther along in contract negotiations for something like that, Ms. Ball." He tugged at his shirt collar with one finger. "The more that I think about it, I believe we wouldn't be able to provide such a list."

Maliha sighed, heaving her chest. "I guess I'll have to look elsewhere for my satisfaction." She stood up. "You do have competition."

"I wish I could offer more."

"I had plenty to offer, but you've passed on the opportunity."

She made sure he knew what opportunity he'd passed on as she walked out the door. It was the last he'd see of her gorgeous, swaying ass. The regret was palpable in the room.

Out in the parking lot, she phoned Amaro and said she'd been unsuccessful. She asked if he could hack into SecureClean's records and get the crew list for ShaleTech so she could work on finding a vulnerable employee. Maliha had centuries of experience in picking out vulnerabilities. She hadn't asked him to do it in the first place, because if the task could be accomplished by her in person, so much the better. She had a large network of informants in thrall.

At that thought a vision flitted through her mind of Manco, the archaeologist in Peru, lying dead in his office.

Unlike Midas, I have the death touch.

It was such a depressing idea that she stopped dead in the conversation.

"What was that you said? My cell reception's acting up." It was an excuse that had rocketed to classic status in a few years.

"I said, no need to bother. I got hold of the original blueprints for the building," Amaro said.

"Do I want to know how?"

He ignored the question. "The blueprints show a normal area there, with offices and labs that have doors to the hallway. So changes must have been made after the original construction and inspections."

"What good does that do us? I could have guessed that myself."

"Ah, but can you guess the architect's name? It's on the blueprints, and I'm in the process of tracking her down. I have a feeling Ms. Yolanda Preston might know something about those alterations. Who better than the original architect to do the customization?"

"Is this architect still alive? People who worked for Greg Shale seem to turn up dead."

"I'll have to let you know on that."

Chapter Thirty-Five

1967

China was in the midst of the Cultural Revolution launched by Mao Zedong. The Red Guard, a civilian army spurred on by Mao's wife, Jiang Qing, began a purge of those who showed any opposition to the Communist party. After the obvious targets within the government were gone, the Red Guard turned to artists, teachers, professors, even the families of the Red Guard youths.

It was a fruitful time for Maliha as far as moving the scale in her favor. She, along with brave Chinese who knew they risked all, established passageways to safety to get dissidents to Mongolia or Japan, similar to the Underground Railroad in America more than a century earlier. Few Westerners were tolerated in China at that time, so Maliha operated in a clandestine manner, living hidden in the homes of supporters of the underground movement and moving frequently.

Maliha was currently staying in the tiny apartment of Xia Yanmeng, a thirty-five-year-old teacher turned factory worker, and his wife, Eliu, a writer of children's stories who now wrote lyrics for songs like "Workers and Peasants and Victory" and "Revolutionary Youth on the March." They did what they needed to do to stay alive and keep the railroad running.

Yanmeng was a practitioner of the government-approved version of wu shu, acrobatic movements sometimes performed to music, that had replaced real martial arts in

China. Having fully trained fighters among the populace was too much of a threat to the government, so Maliha taught Yanmeng in secret.

The windows were tightly sealed, so that the light of a single candle couldn't leak out. Yanmeng and Maliha circled each other, treading softly, sparring in silence. Blankets padded the floor so that the elderly hard-of-hearing couple downstairs wouldn't hear them. Maliha could see Eliu's eyes gleaming proudly in the candlelight as she watched her husband practice the forbidden art: the elegant, traditional, and deadly art that was not wu shu. Yanmeng's body shone with sweat and joy as he blocked Maliha's attacks and sometimes landed a blow of his own. Grandfather had taught her that it is the responsibility of the fighter with more experience to protect the student from harm, and Maliha protected both Yanmeng's body and his dignity in subtle ways.

One evening, after a modest dinner, there was a loud knocking at the door. Yanmeng and his wife sat with eyes wide, motionless, rabbits in the grip of a hawk. They were the parents of a rebellious fifteen-year-old son, Xietai, a member of the Red Guard. Yanmeng and Eliu feared that he would reveal his parents' involvement with the underground. It looked like the time had come.

The knocking came again, more insistent. There was shouting, and the men outside said they'd break down the door if it wasn't opened immediately.

"You must open the door. Do it now," Maliha urged. "Don't resist, don't give them an excuse to kill you right here in your home." She pulled Yanmeng to his feet, aimed him at the door, and gave him a firm shove.

Then Maliha ran to the hiding place she used when anyone else came into the apartment. There was a hidden door in the cramped kitchen that concealed a compartment just big enough for Maliha to squeeze into. She pulled the door closed and waited in the dark, certain that her breathing was loud enough to give her away. In spite of her brave words, she wrestled with her own fear. Her heart beat a wild rhythm inside her chest, and she shivered as images from her imprisonment, trial, and burning came flooding back.

Hard as it was, the best thing to do was let them be hauled away, then make her plans to rescue them on her own terms. She needed a getaway plan for two people, needed to get them on the railroad and out of the country.

She needed time.

Maliha stiffened as the men surged into the room. There were only a few thin planks of wood separating her from the soldiers, with their gruff voices and pounding boots. Now that she gave in to the memories, she was fully back in her snug home in Massachusetts with the glow of a dying fire, the scent of herbs in the air, and her husband stumbling toward the door that shook with the pounding of fists. She reached in front of her to cradle the phantom weight in her womb, to protect it, and in her mind she felt the rounded form, a baby's foot kicking under her hands. It was a moment totally given over to the terror she'd felt then.

Then they were gone. The silence was frightening, incriminating. Had she done the right thing? Should she have fought?

Her friends were gone, and it was up to her to get them out alive.

Even though she put her plans together in record time, there was always the chance that Yanmeng had already died in prison, after "questioning."

Maliha, dressed as a prison guard, disarmed a second prison guard and forced him to take her to Yanmeng's cell. She ordered the guard to exchange clothing with Yanmeng. She winced when Yanmeng took off his shirt and revealed fresh seeping welts and burns.

The guard put on Yanmeng's prison uniform. "I'm going to take you through the hall at gunpoint, like a prisoner being taken to interrogation," she said to the guard. "Instead you will be leading me. Take me to Xia's wife. Her name is Eliu."

The man shook his head. "I can't. I know nothing about the women's section. I've only worked here for a few days. I don't know where she is."

The guard held to his story after a slash on the arm.

Yanmeng put his hand out to stop the questioning. "It doesn't matter. I'll find her myself."

Maliha knocked the guard unconscious.

"Your plan?"

Yanmeng hesitated.

"Hurry, friend. What is your plan?"

"You're not going to believe it, but here goes. I can see my wife and her surroundings in my mind. I've tracked her since we entered this vile place." Tears welled in his eyes. "Terrible things have been done to her. She's said nothing about you or the railroad. Please, we must get her out of here."

"This tracking—you're a remote viewer, then?"

"You know about it?"

"Only a little."

"How? Are you a scientist, or a viewer yourself?"

Maliha wasn't willing to say that her information was acquired during pillow talk with a high-ranking KGB agent, who'd said that formal study of the phenomenon in the Soviet Union was still a few years off but interest was building.

She dodged Yanmeng's questions. "It would be a useful military tool. My suggestion is to keep your ability hidden."

"It's not something I can do in the way they'd want me to, for spying. I need a connection to a person I know well in the remote location."

"Then lead the way. When we meet others, let me do the talking."

Yanmeng nodded. "Hold on."

He closed his eyes to concentrate. She waited nervously.

She was astonished to see his aura flare in the dimly lighted space: a wide band with whirls of clear yellow, white, and blue. It was a rare sight, indicating a person capable of moving into the lower level of the psychic plane, the state above the physical. That's what she did when she replayed the last minutes before a person's death, the ghostly imprint.

Yanmeng sighed and opened his eyes, which had an unfocused look.

"Got her. Let's go."

Chapter Thirty-Six

t turned out that the architect of Greg's building-within-a-building was alive, but living under a different name in Colorado. Amaro tracked her down through one of the simplest mistakes that "disappeared" people make. When her subscription to *Architectural Record* expired, she renewed it under the same customer number but with a change of both name and address. In order to make a disappearance viable, the person had to be willing to make a clean break with the past. That meant a new name, occupation, no contact with friends or relatives, and no connection to anything that belonged to the previous life. Few people were able to do it 100 percent.

Maliha, of course, was a pro at disappearing. She thought of it as shedding her skin to reveal a new one underneath.

The subscription change was almost ten years ago, the year after construction of the ShaleTech building was completed—at least, completed according to the filed blueprints. Yolanda Preston, now Pearl Burton, kept up the subscription during the intervening years. She worked as a landscape designer now, but couldn't close the door on her true love, architecture.

Yolanda lived outside Grand Lake, Colorado, in a small log cabin at ease with its surroundings of pine trees and mountains.

Maliha went to her home unannounced and knocked on the door. The door remained resolutely closed and the house was silent, but Maliha suspected Yolanda was inside. She just didn't want to answer the door when there was someone unfamiliar there. The shades on the windows were pulled all the way down, and heavy curtains hung behind them, to keep in the heat, or to ensure privacy, or both.

"Yolanda." Maliha's voice was raised to make sure someone inside could hear. "I'm here to talk to you about the work you did for Greg Shale, and I'm not going away."

Maliha sat on the porch and waited. It was a chilly mid-October day in the mountains. The cabin had a splendid view. She decided on the spot that she was going to get a cabin for herself.

When it got dark, she pulled her jacket around her. The smell of wood smoke emanated from the cabin, proof that someone was at home. The stars were beautiful and brilliant, so many more of them visible than in Chicago. She settled down and became as still as one of the posts of the porch. Around her, nocturnal animals played the game of predator and prey, tiny cries in the night marking the passing of the losers.

At about three in the morning the door opened, and a female voice said, "You'd better come in, then."

Maliha rose, stiff from the cold, and went inside. She was accustomed to setting aside creature comforts when the situation called for it, but she let the fire, visible through the glass of a wood stove, warm her. She hung her jacket on a hook near the door.

The cabin was one large, open room on the inside. A kitchen occupied one corner, with a gleaming stove, refrigerator, and freezer, and a display of pots belonging to a woman who liked to cook. A twin bed was pushed into another corner, the hearth had the third, and a small enclosure Maliha took to be the bathroom was in the fourth. Bookcases lined the walls, and in the center of the cabin stood an architect's drafting table with a tall swivel chair, a slanted surface, and a clamped-on lamp that meant business.

Yolanda was in her sixties, thin and wiry, spry from outdoor work. A cap of white hair contrasted with her dark skin, and her brown eyes sparkled with intelligence—and wariness. She was wrapped in a faded flannel robe. Maliha took an instant liking to her, and she'd long since learned to trust her instincts, even without the benefit of reading auras.

Except possibly with Jake.

"Hot chocolate?" Yolanda asked.

"Yes, please." Maliha pulled a chair near the stove and sat down, showing her appreciation for Yolanda's consideration. She'd shared a hearth with so many people in her lifetime who'd asked for nothing other than a few hours of good company. Sometimes Maliha had been there to kill her host. The thought profoundly saddened her, the thought that if she hadn't made the decision to forego immortality, she might be here to kill this woman.

Staring into the glass of the wood stove, she saw her face reflected there among the flames, a woman burning. Maliha looked away.

A mug of steaming hot chocolate was thrust into her hands, and Yolanda pulled up a chair to sit next to her. The two women said nothing for a few minutes, just blew on their chocolate and sipped from the mugs.

"How did you find me?"

"Magazine subscription."

"Damn. That was a weak thing to do. Are you here to kill me?"

Her words echoed what Maliha had just been thinking about a few minutes earlier.

An easy impression to get, considering the weapons I'm carrying.

She stood up and removed her waist pack, the throwing knives sheathed on her calves, the Glock from her shoulder holster, and the double-edged sword strapped on her back, and placed them all on a small table by the door.

"I'm a Boy Scout by nature. I like to be prepared. Is that better?"

Yolanda nodded.

"Let's talk about the Shale Technology Services building, outside Chicago. I know you drew up the original plans. Did you also design the alterations that created a self-contained wing?"

Yolanda hesitated for a long time, glancing at the weapons on the table. She may have been trying to figure out if she could get to the table before Maliha. Maliha said nothing and let the woman stew about her situation.

"My family is at risk."

"I can protect your family from Shale."

From Shale, positively. From Subedei, maybe.

Yolanda snorted. "It isn't that fool of a man I'm worried about. It's that bodyguard of his."

Maliha nodded. No sense holding back. "Very perceptive. He is the greater threat of the two."

"Told me I had to disappear and that if I said anything he'd rip the heads of my grandchildren off in front of me." Yolanda shuddered. "I think he meant it literally."

I know he meant it literally.

"Why are you talking to me now, then?"

Yolanda looked over at the weapons on the table. "In spite of the fact that you came in here packing all kinds of nasty weapons, I have a feeling about you. I don't think you're working for that bodyguard. In fact, I think maybe you had a run-in with him yourself."

"How did you know that?" Maliha wondered if Yolanda was reading her aura.

"I'm not blind. I saw you flinch when I mentioned him."

"I did?" She looked over at Yolanda, who nodded.

Well, hell. I'm supposed to be inscrutable.

"I figure anybody who's carrying all those weapons and has reason not to like that bodyguard is somebody I ought to cozy up to. I'd like to see my grandchildren again. With their heads on."

"Then I'll tell you I intend to kill the bodyguard, and Shale, too."

"More hot chocolate, friend?"

"Sure. I'll make it this time." Maliha got up to make the hot drinks.

"What can you tell me about the private area of the Shale building?" Maliha asked from the kitchen area.

"Shale called it the enclave, even though that's not an

architectural term. He meant it in the sense of a group that operates inside a larger community. He paid me generously to do the project, which I took on as a professional challenge. I thought it was a secure place to keep development safe from corporate spying. He had something a lot more sinister in mind, I think. Why else would he need a secret escape tunnel for himself?"

Maliha's heart skipped a beat, but this time she revealed nothing on the outside. She needed that kind of information, and she had to keep Yolanda talking.

"So what use did he have in mind for the enclave?"

"I have no idea. Once the construction was nearly complete, I wasn't needed anymore. It didn't occur to me that when the enclave area was completed, my knowledge of its details was a threat to him. I mean, look at me. Do I look like a corporate spy? I'm a grandmother, for heaven's sake. I've often wondered what happened to the construction bosses, but I don't have the nerve to check up on them. Anyway, that's the kind of stuff that happens in books."

"Why did he let you live?"

"In case he needed more modifications in the future. He didn't want to have to bring in somebody new and multiply the risk. And he had that bodyguard to keep me in line."

"Do you know anything at all about what Shale did in the enclave?"

"No. I do know that the power requirements he specified were extraordinary, and he's got a fantastic computer area in there. Had to have special cooling, fire considerations, and extra space for cabling. Everything had to be self-contained. There were only two connections to the rest of the building. There was a door from his office that was like stepping through the looking-glass into another world. And there was the elevator, a heavily guarded shaft on the north end of the building, accessible through a secure corridor."

"You mentioned an escape tunnel."

"Yes, that. Strangest thing I ever designed. We had to go through solid rock, sideways, lay track, utilities, air circulation considerations, everything. Like in a James Bond movie. Shale had a flare for the dramatic. He was very secretive about the whole thing. One member of his staff knew about it. His security chief, a genuinely nasty man."

"Chief Clark?"

Her eyes widened. "You do know the score."

"What did you mean by laying track?"

"For the high-speed escape pod. Holds one person. Like I said, James Bond stuff."

"Where does this tunnel come out?"

"On the ShaleTech property, in a building I designed to look like it's been there half a century instead of ten years. Looks natural in the countryside."

The realization smacked into Maliha. "A barn?"

Yolanda nodded. "You've seen it?"

"I've been in it."

"I was right about you. You are going to do something to help me. I'll bet you didn't find the hidden door." Her chin was raised and there was a note of pride in her voice.

The two women talked until dawn.

Chapter Thirty-Seven

Subedei was housecleaning. His home was on the third floor of an old hotel that had been converted to rooms for single men. He could live in a better place. He had plenty of gold, but this place suited him.

It had become so cluttered he couldn't walk around easily. In his sleeping corner, the furs had grown odorous after years of continuous use. They should have been shaken and left to air in a fresh, steady wind, tossed over a rope between two tents. He'd tried that once, by draping the furs over the fire escape, but had to take them down because a neighbor complained about the smell. He would have liked to plunge his fist into the neighbor's chest and rip out his heart, but Master Rabishu had instructed him to live quietly and not draw attention to himself, so that he could stay near Shale.

To him, that summed up everything that was wrong with living in Chicago: living quietly. He couldn't air out his furs and he couldn't build a fire on his floor to roast meat. For that matter, what meat was there? Bloodless hunks wrapped in plastic? He understood the strategy of this "living quietly" business, but it chafed.

When Subedei lived in North America, he liked to live in Montana or the wide plains of Canada, places with lots of space where he could ride a horse and sleep in a tent or on the ground next to his cooking fire. No one bothered him and he would go for years that way, until his master summoned him for a killing. It was even better when he was allowed to live in Asia. He had trod on the Great Wall of China as a tourist. The wall was made to keep his ancestors, the Hun clans of Central Asia, out of China. It gave him great satisfaction to stomp on it.

All of these things were minor nuisances compared to the bounty granted to him by his master: unlimited life in the powerful body of his youth with all his lusts for women and blood sated, and ample chances to devise strategies for winning wars—even if the wars weren't quite what he was used to.

All of it granted after he'd already been dead.

Having experienced both life and death, there was no doubt in Subedei's mind which he preferred and to whom he owed total allegiance.

The years he'd been in the city grated on him, but his work required him to be near the human Shale on almost a daily basis, and before that another human, who had failed to do the job Master Rabishu desired. After the failure, when Subedei was freed from the order to protect that man, he'd ripped off both the man's arms and watched him bleed to death. He wondered if the time would come when he would be able to do the same with Shale. He despised Shale for his pettiness and arrogance and weakness, but he kept him alive because his master wanted it that way. He also detected in Shale a sick cruelty much different from his own, albeit violent, approach to living. His killings were about retribution or pride or necessity, or done at the order of his master. As for Shale, Subedei had met up with that kind of sickness before, and the best thing to be done was to clean the air of foulness by killing the person. At least Subedei had his standards, and his code of conduct, whether they made sense in the twenty-first century or not.

Sometimes he found himself hoping that Project CESR—oh, yes, he knew all about it, even though Shale thought him ignorant—would fail. He mentally rehearsed various ways to dispose of Shale and found them all equally pleasing.

He and his demon master agreed on one thing. The renegade ex-Ageless woman would be his, and he'd have his way with her for a long time before turning her over to the demon. Subedei deeply understood betrayal, and she'd betrayed her master. That made her worthless in his eyes.

He'd have his way with her somewhere other than Chicago, though. Take her out to the high desert in the west, maybe, or the far north of Russia where the wind had some bite to it.

So the furs were the first things to go, stuffed into several plastic trash bags. Once he had a clear space on the floor, he could sort through other items, residue of past meals: bones, wrappers, greasy plates. More plastic bags were filled. When the room was clear except for Subedei's statuary and weapons, he hauled all the trash away. He returned to set what he considered a prime invention of the modern world—the bug bomb.

While his room was being cleared of pests that made him itch and ate his food, he left for a walk in the dark. Sometimes a mugger was foolish enough, or desperate enough, to accost him in spite of his bulk. Subedei was allowed to defend himself, even when he was supposed to be living quietly, and he did so with relish.

This time he was swept from the dark streets into the presence of his master. As the fog swept toward him in the formless place and the smell reached him, he fell to his knees and bowed his head.

"What do you desire, Great One?"

Tell me of Shale.

The voice flowed softly into his head. Subedei had experienced anger in that voice once, when he'd killed a target's family in addition to the target. Rabishu wanted the target's child, a daughter, to survive, embittered about the loss of her father. Since then, Subedei had operated with more self-discipline.

"Everything is on schedule. You will be pleased."

When all is done, I will reward you.

Subedei felt his master's clawed hand descend on his head and shoulders and rest there almost lovingly.

For success, you may live wherever you please, take

women, and hunt, and I shall not call upon you for a hundred years.

Suddenly a claw extended into Subedei's shoulder, piercing it like a knife. He grimaced but made no sound.

For failure, there will be consequences.

Reward and punishment were easily grasped by Subedei. "I understand. Can I ask a question, Great One?"

Yes. The voice vibrated with something that could have been affection.

"The traitor Maliha—when can I have her?"

Soon. But not yet.

When he was back on the sidewalk in the dark, Subedei wondered why he couldn't have the woman right away. Then he seized upon the reason, and nodded. His master was testing his discipline, after that time when he'd killed the daughter who was supposed to live.

Subedei shut away his lust for another time. He would pass the test.

Chapter Thirty-Eight

Maliha woke at dawn. Something had disturbed her, someone fanning air in her face, or a footstep deliberately creaking on the floor. She opened her eyes, sat up in bed, and then jumped from it, clearing the space to her door in one bound. Her heart pounding, her breath a leaden column in her chest, she opened the door and looked out.

They were all right. The two men had talked late into the night, and hadn't made it out of the living room. Yanmeng slept in the chair, Amaro stretched out on his side on her sofa, his face away from her. Both unbloodied. She swallowed, trying to break the block of fear that had appeared in her throat, fear for her friends.

Turning around, she confronted what had been her first image when she opened her eyes.

A sword was stuck into the second pillow on the bed, just inches from her head, and she recognized it as one she'd seen in Greg's dojo. It had blood on the edge, not her friends', she reassured herself. The sword was pinning a piece of paper with a single bold mark: the letter *S*.

Subedei had been in her home—again. It confirmed her feeling that he'd been in her bedroom before and put his hand on her. This time he'd stalked past her friends, entered her room, and arrogantly left her a message, a dare. And all of that in spite of the increased security and a motion detector inside the front door. She checked the security system's control panel. The motion detector had been turned off.

The rush of air I felt. On the way in he crossed the room before the detector could activate.

It made her physically sick first, and then very, very angry.

She yanked the sword from the pillow and crumpled the note. She wrapped the sword in the torn pillowcase and slid it under her bed.

How could I be so foolish, to allow Yanmeng and Amaro to be here, all of us together in a neat killing package? Two flicks of a knife and they both would have been dead. In my home, under my care.

A wail built up inside her, and she opened her mouth and screamed silently in her room.

Alone. I am alone in this battle with the Ageless one.

Dressed and steady, her fear suppressed, she went out to wake her friends. She roused them and they gathered at the kitchen table.

"Bad dream?" Yanmeng frowned. He'd once told her that he could see fear in a person. It was a form of viewing auras, but she didn't bother to explain it to him.

"You could say that. I have something to ask of you."

"We're here. Ask away," Amaro said.

"I want you to go to one of my safe houses."

"What? Leave you alone? Not a chance," Amaro said.

Yanmeng put a hand on his arm to quiet him. "When do we go?"

"Right now. You can leave all of your things here. You won't need them where you're going."

Her old friend stood up and dragged Amaro to his feet. "We're ready."

Maliha looked at Amaro. He was young and defiant. He'd taken the same selfless vow that Yanmeng had, and carried the same mark of it: the cyanide-filled suicide tooth in his mouth that Maliha had finally, reluctantly, agreed was a good thing, something that could save them much pain. He knew Maliha was going back to ShaleTech, and the protective instinct she'd felt from him didn't want to let her go alone. They'd talked it over just a few hours ago, before retiring, when she shared all the information Yolanda had supplied.

"Amaro, this is my job from now on. I have to know that you're safe and ready to be godfather to Rosie's baby."

Conflicting emotions played over his face. Finally he nodded. She told them to sit back down because there were some preparations to be done first.

"I have two safe houses in the Chicago area. I'd prefer to use a house far from this city, but there's no time. The one I want you to use is an ordinary-looking garage behind a house in Archer Heights." She gave them the address.

"The entrance is booby-trapped. You need a special key to deactivate the traps." She started unbuttoning her blouse. "You don't have to watch if you don't want to. Getting the key doesn't look very good."

Neither of them looked away.

She put a square of cloth on the table, and then used a knife to slice a cut about an inch long above her left breast. As blood welled and slid down her chest, she poked inside the cut with the tip of the knife until a thin disk smaller than the diameter of a pencil eraser slipped out. She put the tiny bloody wafer on the cloth, wiped it off, and dropped it into Yanmeng's outstretched hand.

"Back in a minute." She went into the bathroom, cleaned the blood off her chest, squeezed the edges closed, and put on a couple of butterfly bandages. Yanmeng had bought them for her and told her to get used to using them. Most of the time she didn't, but this time it felt important to do what he wanted. Looking in the mirror, she touched the spot between her breasts where Rabishu's mark was, where he'd taken her blood to sign the contract that marked her as Ageless. It was still faintly visible, a shadow on her skin, at least to her eyes.

Back at the table, Amaro was examining the crystalline wafer in Yanmeng's palm. "You're full of surprises. This is a beautiful piece of work. Where did you get it?"

She chose not to answer.

"It's a glorified bar code," she said. "You use this key first, on the wooden door." She fished around in her pocket and pulled out a conventional key. "Use that chip on the metal door inside it. Don't disturb the spike launcher. You should stay inside. If you have to leave for any reason, you must use the chip to get back in, or you'll be dead."

"Is this the only one?" Yanmeng said.

"Yes."

"So that means as long as we have the chip, you can't get into any of your safe houses."

Maliha shrugged. "I'm not planning to need them. When you leave here, travel seperately and don't go directly there. When you're inside, call me. There's a scrambled phone line. I want to know you arrived okay."

Amaro left twenty minutes after Yanmeng. He changed taxis twice, spent fifteen minutes drinking coffee in a diner, and took another cab. He gave an address a block away from the safe house. The taxi took him to South Archer Avenue and made a right turn on South Komensky, a tree-lined street fronted by narrow houses with deep lots. All the houses had garages at the back of their lots, so the row of garages in a neat line mirrored the appearance of the street.

An elderly couple lived in the main house, rent free, and used half the garage to park their car so it appeared to be a functioning garage. Their rectangular parking spot was carved out of the square footage of the garage and walled off with several inches of steel on Maliha's side and wood on their side.

Yanmeng was already there. Amaro opened the wooden door to the garage using the common-looking key he carried, revealing a blast-proof steel door inside the ordinary-looking wooden one. Yanmeng placed the chip next to a flashing light adjacent to the steel door and the door slid upwards.

Amaro retrieved the chip. They stepped into the dark interior, and the door came down behind them. Amaro clicked on the penlight Maliha had given him and used it to locate the light switch. Light flooded the interior and equipment hummed to life. Across from the door was a wicked-looking device that sported twelve sharp metal darts aligned vertically, what Maliha had referred to as the spike launcher. If someone managed to get in the door without the electronic key, the darts would fire and the person would be perforated from groin to head with a line of wicked arrows.

There were hidden cameras that gave a view of the perimeter, no windows, the reinforced walls and roof, and a comprehensive fire-extinguishing system. A hatch in the floor opened on a flight of stairs to a subterranean room that held a weapons cache; papers for several different identities, male and female; credit cards in those names in case they wanted to leave a deliberate trail; and a stock of cash, gold, and jewels. In the main living area downstairs was a communications setup with worldwide access, and water and food for a month—more if they scrimped. There were clean clothes for men and women that could lend a variety of appearances, and several cots stacked in a corner. The foyer, as Maliha had called the upstairs area, could contain a blast so that they'd be protected in the underground room.

Amaro went over to the communications console, which had two computer monitors built into it. On the counter in front of it was a bound book, an inch thick.

"What's that?" Yanmeng said.

"I don't suppose it's the *TV Guide*." Amaro picked it up and thumbed through it. "It's an instruction manual to operate everything in here." He plucked a sealed envelope from the back of the book and read the front of it. "This says . . . it says, 'To be opened only if I'm dead.'"

The two men stared at each other. Then Amaro opened a drawer and put the envelope in it, out of sight.

"Let's take a look at that manual," Yanmeng said. "We need to figure out how to make that encrypted phone call."

Chapter Thirty-Nine

Maliha didn't relax until she received the phone call from her safe house on a secure phone.

She didn't know all about Project CESR yet, but what she knew was alarming: It involved power stations and national security, and a minimum of five people had already died as a direct result of their knowledge. An Ageless servant was protecting Greg Shale, which meant that one of the seven demons had a strong interest in seeing Project CESR succeed.

She needed to stop the project and take out Subedei. To get Subedei to show up, all she had to do was threaten Greg, and that meant getting into the ShaleTech compound.

She doubted that she'd be invited in for lunch and a few rounds on the mat again.

Everything revolved around getting back into a place she had every reason to think would be heavily fortified this time around.

Maliha made and discarded plans. She ate a meal, made a decision, and called Hound on the landline in her condo.

"This isn't your usual phone number," he said when he picked up.

"This isn't a usual situation. Meet me at the big oak at one P.M. I have a mission for you."

"Aha, the game's afoot."

"In a big way. Hound, don't be followed."

"Yes, ma'am, I'll take that under advisement."

She turned out the lights and slept for a couple of hours, until it was time to leave.

The big oak was a tree that didn't live up to its name; it was neither big nor an oak. It was a code word for a location near a flowering crabapple tree in the Brookfield Zoo. Maliha arrived and sat in the open on a bench near the Roosevelt Fountain, observing the bare tree from a distance. No one else was paying any attention to the tree. Determined mothers pushed strollers under a brilliant blue cloudless sky, their visible breath streaming behind them like thin ghostly balloons. The strollers' pink-cheeked occupants were asleep at this time of day and tucked into enough coats and blankets to make sleeping comfortable in arctic climes.

Hound arrived not long after Maliha got there, and he sat on the other side of the fountain. He was reading a book, but behind the sunglasses, she was sure his eyes were doing the same thing as hers. He wasn't wearing his hat. He had on a sweatshirt with a zippered down vest over it against the cold, and a hood pulled up to keep his ears warm.

After several casual iterations of changing locations, they ended up crossing paths next to the flowering crab tree and then sitting on opposite ends of a bench.

"Haven't done this in a while," Hound said. "Almost forgot how."

"Sure, like you'd forget your middle name."

"Don't have one."

She blinked. "Just testing to see if that's you behind those shades."

"Un-huh. You're too tensed up. Relax a little. We're just enjoying a sunny day in the zoo."

He was right. Her body language was giving away more than she intended. She let herself relax until she was draped easily on the bench, as if she'd been poured there from the tree branches above them.

"Damn, you look good like that. Gonna jump your bones."

She laughed, in spite of the circumstances. Hound was good for her.

She kept the smile on her face and talked through it. "I'm

working on something big. I need a copter for a few hours tonight, a NOTAR, and a pilot to go with it."

A NOTAR—no tail rotor—helicopter design minimized noise by replacing the tail rotor with fins, like miniature airplane wings. It wasn't a true stealth machine, but at least it was better than the usual loud *whomp, whomp*.

"Sounds like you'll be dropping in on somebody quietly, without an invitation."

"Good description. You have somebody reliable, a guy who can keep his mouth shut?"

"Or what, you're going to have to kill him?"

She didn't say anything.

"You are doing something big. Yeah, I got somebody for that kind of thing. I need some money to rent the copter."

She passed him a bag from the zoo's gift shop that contained a stuffed tiger and some cash. "Twenty thousand, for the copter rental and the pilot. If you need more, I'll get it. I'll pay you your fee later."

Hound raised his eyebrows—the one he had left at least—at the suggestion of later payment. He tucked the bag under his arm. "This should do it."

"We might be taking fire on the way out. I need somebody who's cool with that."

Hound didn't say anything, just nodded. They set up a place and time for her to meet the copter that night.

"One last thing. I don't want you in that bird."

He got up and limped away. The ears of the stuffed tiger that was on top of the money stuck out of the bag and bounced along with his awkward gait.

"Where are you?" Jake said. "I tried to reach you at home."

Impulsively, she'd called Jake after her meeting with Hound.

"You could have followed me if you wanted to know where I was. Aren't the Feds good at that?"

"Yeah, I could have. But I didn't want to crowd you, after . . ."

"I'm going to be out of touch for a while. I just wanted you to know that I wasn't hiding from you or something."

"Why would you be avoiding me?" His voice warmed. He knew what she was talking about, but he wasn't making it easy. She played it straight.

"Because I don't know what to think yet." She'd called because she worried that with what she was heading into, she'd never see Jake again, and she wanted to hear the sound of his voice. Then she worried that she should never see him again anyway, and finally that she cared enough to worry.

She was unwilling to open up and talk to him. How could she? Her story wasn't typical. There was a tremor in her voice that reflected her ambiguity, and he picked up on it.

"Is something wrong?"

"No."

"Something you're regretting, about us?"

"No."

"Why don't we get together and talk about it?"

"I have something to do first. I told you I'd be out of touch. It could be a few days."

"You're making me worried. You're not going to do something stupid, are you? Like confront Greg about the drugs?"

"I'm not going after Greg about the drugs."

True, as far as it goes.

"Good, because I want to see you again. I think I . . ."

"See you later." She cut him off. She threw her cell phone into a trash can down the block from the pub. Her call might have generated enough curiosity that he'd try to track her with it.

A near-freezing rain fell as Maliha walked through the Ned Brown Forest Preserve, near I–90 and Illinois Highway 53. She was heading for the model airplane flying field, which had ample room for a helicopter's pinpoint landing.

Nearly twelve hours had passed since Maliha's impromptu phone call to Jake. Hound had told her that the pilot was a woman in her forties who went by the nickname "Glass." Maliha didn't question it; if Hound trusted the woman for her piloting skills under fire and her ability to remain quiet, then she did, too.

Crossing a rise in the land, she got a good view of I–90. Traffic was light, but her eye was caught by a blanket-wrapped bundle lying on the white line between two southeast-bound lanes. Something inside the blanket moved weakly.

Her sense of urgency pulled her toward the rendezvous point with the helicopter, but the blanket moved again, riveting her eyes to the spot. The bundle was large enough to contain an older child, a small woman, a large dog, or just trash blown by the wind that simulated movement.

A car zoomed by, swerving a little, just missing the bundle.

Shit. Shit! Not now! There couldn't be a worse time for this. A helicopter on the way that I paid big bucks for, my friends squirreled away in the safe house . . . everything's set. I'm on a timetable here.

She continued past the rise and got under the shelter of the trees, blocking the image from her mind. Then she heard a horn honk and the squeal of a car's tires swerving.

The situation on the interstate wasn't going to let go of her. If she didn't go check it out, she'd read about some poor person smeared all over the road in tomorrow's paper, and she could have stopped it. Even if the bundle contained a discarded pet, she would go out of her way to prevent such a cruel death.

Maliha took a deep breath and yanked her attention from the mission. She dropped the gear she was carrying and sped toward the highway. Several cars went by, just missing the bundle. She judged the approach time of more cars and dashed onto the pavement, a black figure slipping a little on a small patch of ice. She snatched up the bundle and made a rapid U-turn just in time to be missed by a truck in the far lane.

Frogger. I'm in a damn game of Frogger.

A horn blast from the truck and the wind of its passing beat at her. Facing the shoulder she came from, she could see a string of cars coming. Whatever was in the bundle struggled hard against her, nearly tipping her over.

"Hold still! I'm helping!"

The squirming stopped immediately, and the bundle was dead weight on her shoulder.

A chunk of pavement flew up at Maliha's feet, and she realized someone was shooting at her. The shots came from the forest preserve.

No fair. There's no shooting in Frogger.

Maliha took off running as bullets pinged the pavement around her, and cleared the traffic lanes just before the string of cars passed over the position she'd been in. She was off balance when she hit the grass and she rolled, clutching the bundle. She maneuvered to break the fall with her hip and side, sparing the bundle the brunt of the impact.

She took the bundle out of sight of the interstate. Her heart fell when she discovered that it was warm and wet on one side—whoever or whatever was inside had been hit, by bullet or vehicle. Maliha slit the blanket open with a knife. Inside was a teenage girl, nude, with her mouth closed with duct tape and her hands and feet tied. She'd been shot in the side and blood was flowing, but not enough for her to bleed out.

The girl had been left to become road kill, with someone watching with a rifle to finish the job if the traffic didn't. Maliha cut the rope around the girl's feet, and then she removed the duct tape.

"Fuck you, Eddie!" the teenager screamed. "You hear me, you rotten—"

Maliha slapped the tape back onto the girl's mouth and she squirmed in anger. Wood cracked as a bullet split off a piece of tree trunk inches from Maliha's head.

A shout followed the bullet. "I hate you, Cindy, you bitch! You're a lying slut! You're going to die!"

I knew it. I should have kept going. Now I've wandered into a foul-mouthed soap opera.

"Shut up, Cindy. Eddie's got a gun," Maliha whispered. "I'm going to cut the rope on your hands and I swear if you cause any more trouble, I'll kill you myself."

Cindy snorted but held still.

Sleet pelted down the back of Maliha's neck as she

leaned over and cut the ropes. She hauled the girl to her feet, trying to assess the seriousness of the wound.

The girl yanked the tape off her own mouth and shouted. "If you even look at Jennifer again, I'll cut your dick off!"

Maliha punched her. The girl collapsed like an over-cooked strand of spaghetti.

With Cindy slung over her shoulder, Maliha slipped farther into the woods until she came to the place where she'd dropped the supplies.

Let's see. Take the supplies and leave, or take care of the girl. It's a tough choice.

She left her gear and made her way toward the model-airplane field. A mixture of rain and sleet was falling now and she was worried about slipping. Even worse, she had to turn her back on the location where she thought the shooter was, and expected any second to get a bullet in the back or head. If the shooter was good, he'd have figured their general path and would be circling around to get in front of them. She could see the clearing up ahead. That would be their most dangerous time, when they stepped out from the cover of the woods.

She dumped her limp burden at the edge of the woods and ran to the center of the paved flying field. The down-draft and the somewhat muffled sound of the rotor told her that the helicopter was hovering, waiting for the signal to land. Maliha pointed a bright flashlight up in the air and blinked it twice. Sleet caught in the flashing beam seemed halted in midair. Then she got out of the way. The helicopter settled in the spot the flashlight indicated.

Maliha scooped up the teenager and took her to the copter, expecting to be dodging bullets or taking one. The copter was an obvious target that would attract the shooter's attention. Nothing happened, though. She wondered if Eddie had been frightened off by the thought of ending up dickless.

C'mere, Eddie, and I'll take care of that for you. Mentally she tested the edge of one of her knives.

The sleet let up into a cold, light drizzle. Maliha's braided hair lay on her back like a heavy, wet rope. She was pleased to see that Hound had taken her request seriously and hadn't shown up. The copter was a black Vietnam-era MD500 with its characteristic teardrop cabin shape.

"My name's Glass. You're late," the pilot said, irritation in her voice. Then she got a look at the nude, bleeding girl. "What the fuck?"

"Shooter's trying to kill her, if I don't do it first."

She boosted the girl into the door opening, and then got in herself. There were two seats in the cabin, and a modest amount of cargo space. Mounded along one side was a jumble of supplies. Maliha extracted a couple of blankets. Spreading one on the floor, she put Cindy on it and covered her with a second one. It was all she could do for now.

"Her name's Cindy. She's unconscious and wounded. If she wakes up, expect an earful. She's mad at her boy-friend."

"You mean the shooter?"

"Yeah, Eddie. She's jealous. He's been lusting after Jennifer. Just get her to a hospital somehow."

Maliha spotted several pairs of night-vision goggles in the supply corner, took one, and slipped it over her head. "Then come back for me. I've got some hunting to do here."

Glass gave her a thumbs-up, then she was on the radio, arranging for someone to meet her, someone who'd take the girl to the hospital. Glass couldn't just show up on the hos-pital helipad, shove her passenger out the door, and leave. If Hound was on the other end of that radio call, the wounded girl would be in good hands.

Once a medic, always a medic.

Maliha went to the door and hopped out, slapping the door closed behind her. She took off for the woods as the helicopter ascended. A bullet smashed into a tree seconds after she passed it.

Amateur. He's not correcting for my actual speed, which he's had a chance to observe, only the speed he thinks an ordinary runner at night should be going. Didn't try to take out the pilot, or he didn't get here until Glass took off. Either way he's too slow and inexperienced.

She thought about the setup with the girl-bundle on the interstate.

Sick, too. Really, really sick.

Maliha tossed a branch into the clearing. The shooter fired at it, and she picked up the muzzle flash of his rifle, intensely bright in her goggles, about a hundred feet to her right and fifteen feet off the ground. He'd gone up in a tree, and had his belly flat on a large branch and his thighs squeezing it.

The goggles she was wearing used the small amount of light that filtered through the forest from the headlights on nearby roads and multiplied it. The view wasn't as clear as it could have been because the fine raindrops in the air scattered light like tiny mirrors. Still, she saw everything well enough, from the rocks under her feet to the roll of duct tape on the shooter's belt to the fact that Eddie wasn't wearing night-vision goggles. He'd been expecting to shoot at the interstate, not look for his prey in the woods. She had the advantage.

Maliha crept through the trees, keeping an eye on the location of the shooter to make sure he didn't climb down and take a new position. He didn't, even after his muzzle flash had been made. He should have known his position had been marked.

She got close to the tree and put a spike in each of his thighs in rapid succession.

He screamed and fell from the tree. It was an inelegant fall, smacking into other tree branches with the sound of breaking wood, and rolling into the bushes. She hoped it was enough to finish him.

Eddie was still alive when she approached. She pulled away the rifle he was still gripping and yanked out her spikes, eliciting howls of pain. She fastened him to a tree with his own duct tape, his back to the flying field so he couldn't see what went on there. He had some serious internal injuries, she was sure, but he'd have to wait awhile for medical help. She had other priorities, such as getting on with the night's mission. If the Grim Reaper arrived during that time, well, it saved the expense of a trial. Eddie was too brutal to go on living. If he'd succeeded in killing Cindy, it would just be easier for him when his next girlfriend gave him some excuse. Or maybe Cindy wasn't the first.

Maliha backtracked to the spot where she'd dropped her supplies, retrieved them, and went back to the flying field. When she felt the downdraft, she blinked her flashlight. Right then, the carving on her stomach began to move, the balance began to shift, and she bent over in pain. A small figure made its way from one pan to the other. She had to get out of the way of the helicopter, so she forced herself to move while the footprints burned their way across her abdomen. She was panting with the effort by the time she reached the edge of the flying field.

Cindy was going to live. A goal scored, with assists by Glass and Hound.

Chapter Forty

When the pain of the figure moving across her body let up, she went back to the helicopter, got inside, and took off the night-vision goggles.

"That was a good thing you did," Glass said. "I have a teenage daughter. It could've been my girl out there."

Maliha nodded. She was settling down from the irritation that had gripped her since she spotted the moving bundle on the interstate. It had been a weird episode, but she was back on her timetable now.

She tried to put herself into the role of the mother of the girl she'd just rescued from the interstate. If Maliha hadn't come along at just that time, the girl would have died, for the principle reason of having made a wrong decision on her boyfriend.

One life lost and parents who would have to live out their lives with the pain of having a child die before them. So many lives had been taken by Maliha's hand during her servitude to the demon that the losses multiplied into rivers of grief when the loved ones of the victims were considered. The weight of it bowed her head and made her shoulders sink. What she'd undertaken to make up for all of that seemed impossible. The scale had a long way to go to reach balance. She had only one shard and the tablet in her quest to destroy the demons. She could die anytime, with both tasks unfinished.

Minutes ago, she'd been standing out there in the middle

of the road with a limp body slung over her shoulder and cars whizzing by. One false step on her part was all it would've taken to smear her—and the girl she carried— across the pavement.

It was right to go after her. And if I die, I've failed and that's my problem. The world will go on as it is, without me. If I'm going to do this and be true to myself, I have to accept the possibility of failure, and go out there and take risks to save people anyway. I have to live—and love—and risk it all every day.

Once put into succinct words, she could pull the concept around her like a comfortable shawl.

Time to focus.

Maliha needed every ounce of self-confidence for what lay ahead. There was no choice. She had to stop whatever Greg and Subedei were plotting. A handful of people had already died; she had no idea what the toll would be if she curled up and ignored the whole thing.

Her voice was steady as she gave Glass the destination coordinates and asked for a high flyover first.

"Can't be too high. We're not on any flight plan, so we can't get up there with the big guys." She pointed skyward.

"Whatever you can manage." Maliha unzipped her gear bag and set out night-vision binoculars.

In a few minutes, Glass said, "Coming up on it."

Maliha slid the door back, stretched out on the floor of the helicopter, and leaned her head over the edge of the door opening. Using the night-vision binoculars, she studied the compound as the helicopter made a pass over it.

About ten pairs of guards now patrolled the area between the two fences, none out of sight of another at any time. It made the doughnut area look like a giant carousel from the air, with the guards as the horses. Razor wire topped the fences. There was a sniper on the roof—guaranteed to be better than Eddie—who had a line of sight anywhere in the compound. The forest she'd run through on her way from the barn to the outer perimeter fence was saturated with foot patrols.

Her 5X binoculars revealed chains crisscrossed over the top of the vent covers to lock them in place. Loops of razor wire rimmed the edges of the roof, except for small openings where the sniper could take up a position. Brighter lights pointed up the sides of the building, so that anyone trying to climb up would be doing so in a spotlight.

The security chief, no doubt having had his ass chewed out about the break in, had stiffened physical security. The problem for him was that he'd done so in a reactive way, by examining what Maliha had done and setting up direct counters to it.

That assumed she'd do the same thing over again. Maliha had more ways of storming the castle than one.

Of major concern was the fact that there were a dozen limos pulled up close to the front entrance. Their drivers stood outside, smoking and talking. Greg was having a late-night meeting, and the attendees all were a) rich, b) security conscious, or c) both. Seeing the gathering of limos tweaked her anxious feeling that she was running out of time.

"I'll be dropping near that barn over there beyond the woods, three o'clock, about two hundred and fifty yards from the fence. You see it?"

"Yeah."

Glass took the copter for a run down nearby I–88 while Maliha picked out her gear from the bag she'd brought. She used a carabiner to lock her half-inch braided nylon rappel rope to an anchor in the floor. Tucking her hair inside her black killing suit, she put on the head covering that concealed her face, but didn't bother to put on one of the safety helmets lying nearby in the copter. She slipped on a harness, stuffed her gear in a belly bag and fastened it to the harness, and then rigged her descender. Finally, she put on leather gloves.

"I'm good to go."

The copter turned and headed back to the ShaleTech compound and the barn.

"When I'm down, find a way to notify the police about that sick shooter I left in the park. He's tied to a tree near the flying field. He'll need an ambulance, if he's still alive. I'll leave it to you to decide how long you want to leave him there."

"That would be until somebody spots his corpse tomorrow."

"His loss, the world's gain." It occurred to Maliha that Glass might be useful in the future. In spite of her nickname, she seemed to be made of steel. "Have you known Hound long?"

Glass looked over her shoulder and made eye contact. "We met before I was born. Our moms used to share a park bench. Hound says he touched my mom's pregnant belly when he was a kid, so I guess that counts as a meet."

"You aren't by any chance Mrs. Hound, are you?"

"Hell, no. Who'd wanna marry that freak?" She said it straight, but Maliha could see the look on her face in the dim light from the dials and switches of the copter's controls.

"Uh-huh. And is your daughter . . . ?"

"Not sure, but I think so. He damn well acts like Hannah's his. Kid came out normal, considering she grew up around Hound and me."

So Hound not only does classified government work, he also has an actual life. He's been holding out on me. No, that's not fair. I've never asked.

They each settled into their own thoughts about Hound.

Sitting in the cabin, she felt Yanmeng's touch on her shoulder. She stretched out her fist and made an *L* shape with her index finger and thumb. It was the agreed-upon signal for Yanmeng to withdraw. A few seconds later he touched her again: *Are you sure?*

She made the signal again, and felt nothing more from him.

Maliha double-checked the rappelling equipment and waited until the black copter, shielded in the mist, hovered near the barn. She tossed her rappel rope out the door, letting it slip through her gloved hands. She felt it hit the ground.

"Rope's down. I'm out of here."

She got a thumbs-up in response. Easing out the door of the copter, she rappelled down about a hundred feet, landed

outside the barn and disengaged from the rope. Ordinarily
a spotter in the helicopter, watching her descent, would disconnect her rope and drop it down after her, but she didn't
have a spotter. Maliha ran over to the side of the barn as
Glass took the copter up, trailing the rope like an umbilical cord. As soon as the copter was clear of the immediate
area, Glass would leave her seat just long enough to pull up
the rope. Trailing that line was an invitation to disaster, if it
should catch in a tree or elsewhere.

Inside the barn, Maliha unfastened her belly bag and
loaded up on weapons. She had the urge to pack on everything she'd brought, but she also had to stay quick, so she
had to be selective. The whip sword went around her waist;
throwing knives were strapped to both calves and thighs; an
axe and a small crossbow were slung on her back; a strap
was tightened across her chest with small knives, spikes,
and crossbow darts. A whole pack of throwing stars rested
on one hip, their weight reassuring, and a bag with tools and
explosives rode on the other hip. She didn't need to carry
any guns. Guards had guns, and she could always obtain
one that way.

She left some weapons in the bag and hid it under straw
that was there to make the barn look authentic.

Standing just inside the door, she paced off six paces on
a forty-five degree angle, swiveled ninety degrees counterclockwise, and measured another four paces, the directions
she'd gotten from Yolanda. She should be standing right on
top of the secret door. Brushing aside some straw, Maliha
examined the dirt underfoot. It was packed tightly from the
McLaren rolling over it. She reached behind her back for
her throwing axe, a sinuous one-piece streak of metal. Using
the axe, she pried at the dirt until she located the edges of a
hatch. She'd been off by a couple of feet because a pace is
such a subjective measurement. Clearing away the dirt, she
found she'd uncovered a hatch about three feet wide and
five feet long.

Tugging the recessed handle of the hatch, she lifted it
into a vertical position and it clicked into place there. She
squatted, reached inside, and pressed a button right below

the lip of the hatch. A dim light came on, enough for her to see a round shaft with a ladder going down about twelve feet. The whole arrangement looked like a sewer access, but based on Maliha's experience, it smelled a lot better.

She shined a flashlight down to the bottom of the ladder and then inspected the sides of the drop. Yolanda had said there were no surprises in the walls of the shaft itself, but that was ten years ago. The sides were gleaming and smooth, and Maliha would just have to hope there was no trap, like a blade that would swing out and slice a climber in half.

She focused the flashlight on the third rung of the ladder, and could just make out the thin line that perforated it. *Put your weight on it*, Yolanda had said, *and it'll give way and let you fall to the bottom and an alarm will show up on a special console in security central.* The console would give no indication of where the intrusion had taken place. All the regular staff could do was report it to the chief security officer. Shale hadn't wanted anyone to know about his private escape route, but it turned out that for his best protection, the chief of security had to know.

Maliha descended the ladder, skipping the third step.

At the bottom, in an area barely big enough to turn around in, was a steel door with a combination lock. If Maliha couldn't get through that door, it was going to be a very short mission. She couldn't blow it. Yolanda had assured her that even a shaped charge aimed at the door would create enough of a shock wave in the confined area of the shaft to break the third step and sound the alarm.

Her first step was using the fluorescing powder and the ALS, but the keypad revealed no fingerprints on the numbers of the combination. It must have been tested years ago, wiped clean, and left that way. Hoping that Greg was a creature of habit, she tried the same combination as she'd used on the safe in his office: 38248. No luck. She rearranged the numbers a couple of times and still there was no response. She was afraid the keypad would lock her out for having too many tries. Somewhere, in some computer's belly, her attempts were being recorded.

Maliha reached into her waist pack for C4. She was going

to have to take a chance on blowing the door. If an alarm was sounded right away, that would make things a whole lot harder but not impossible. She had her hand on the plastic explosive when she thought of something new to try.

The lock had been in place, untampered with, since the tunnel was built. Greg wasn't thirty-eight years old then. He was twenty-eight.

28248. She keyed it in, and the door rose to reveal a dark space that didn't stay dark for long. Light tubes were clicking on, beginning at the far end of the tunnel and moving toward her. There was a streak of light down the top of the tunnel and curved tubes running halfway down the sides. It looked like staring down a shiny, gigantic spinal column, with the lights as the spinal cord and branching ribs.

She stepped into the tunnel. It was seven feet high at its highest point, and about six feet wide. The tracks ran straight down the middle, taking up most of the room, but there was a maintenance walkway along one side. The tracks, Yolanda had said, were electrified, as the power source for speeding the escape pod along.

Her path was narrow. She had to walk sideways, her back against the wall. It was a weak position for an attack, no doubt intentional. She built up some speed, but it still took a long time to pass underneath the woods and the two fences and reach the place where the capsule was parked.

The capsule was streamlined, futuristic-looking, and bullet shaped. Peering in the windshield, she could see that it was made for only one person. Greg intended to save his own ass and no one else's if the shit hit the fan.

Beyond the capsule was a platform, a control console for the pod, and an elevator door. The elevator had a button to push that said UP. It seemed too easy, but she pressed it. There was a whirring sound as the elevator car came down from a higher floor, and then the door opened. Just like that. She checked the control panel by leaning a little bit into the elevator car. The controls were covered by a locked door. She could pick that lock, but . . .

She examined the UP button again. Concealed among the dark letters were small holes that looked like they might be a microphone. It must be voice activated, in addition to pressing it. Greg didn't want any riffraff coming up through the back door and surprising him. The elevator was keyed to his voice.

Maliha looked around for something expendable. There was a small fire extinguisher fastened to the side of the console that controlled the capsule. She unhooked it and brought it to the elevator. Without stepping in, she dropped the extinguisher from shoulder height onto the spot where she'd have to stand to pick the lock.

The floor dropped open and the extinguisher disappeared from sight into a black hole underneath it.

If I can take the Tablet of the Overlord from its location over a sucking sand pool, I can handle a trapdoor elevator car.

She used her crossbow to shoot a special dart into the ceiling of the elevator. Once it penetrated the ceiling, the tip burst open into a miniature grappling hook. She planted another hook about two feet away from it. The cords dangled down like a rope ladder with no rungs. Maliha held a lock pick in her mouth and then reached in and wound one cord around each arm. She did an aerial somersault that brought her face-to-face with the lock, twisting gracefully on the cords like a circus acrobat. She was upside down. She extended her legs to the ceiling to steady herself. She unwound the cord from her right arm, ending up standing on the ceiling, held up there by her left arm.

With her free hand, she picked the lock. The panel door opened to reveal another UP button, this one with no microphone. She pressed it and the car began moving upward. She didn't want to trust the floor, so she remained in position. She counted the seconds of upward travel: eight.

The door opened. Maliha swung out into a brightly lit space, landing with a knife in her hand. She was in a small room that appeared to have no way out.

Until she looked up.

The ceiling was at least twelve feet high. There was an outline of an opening in the ceiling, about two feet square. There was no handle, at least not on her side of the door.

She had one grappling hook dart left for the crossbow. There seemed to be no option but to use it. Maybe if she pulled hard enough, the hatch would open. Or maybe not, and she'd be stymied.

Wait! Think about it. Greg wouldn't use a method like that. He's not a crossbow kind of guy. There has to be something. . . .

The elevator door had closed behind her. There was nothing but a DOWN button on the wall, no holes for a microphone. She pressed it and the elevator door slid open. At the back wall, along the floor, was a small rocker switch. She hadn't seen it because she'd been hanging from the ceiling, facing in the opposite direction of the rocker switch. It was out of reach, and the trapdoor floor was still active.

Her cords dangled from the ceiling of the elevator. She wrapped her arms again and swung in. She lowered herself until her feet almost grazed the floor, and then began moving back and forth. After several tries, she hit the rocker switch with her foot. There was a mechanical noise from the room outside. She swung out through the door backward and released the cords, putting herself in the room as the hatch slid sideways above her. A rope ladder, a real one with actual rungs, fell down within easy reach. She climbed it, entering the dark area above the hatch. A string brushed her face. She pulled it, and a bare bulb illuminated the space.

She was in a storage closet. The smell of damp mops and furniture polish and pine cleaners filled the air. She put her hand on the door handle, turned out the bulb so that light wouldn't spill out of the room, and cracked open the door. She was in the middle of a long, dimly lit hallway. There were no cameras that she could see. Whatever was going on, Greg didn't want it on film.

The carpet was very thick and ran halfway up the walls. After the carpeting ended, the upper part of the hall was soundproofed with foam shaped into rows of small cones. Lights were set alternately in the floor and ceiling. There were doors every twenty feet. Ahead on the left was a door with a rectangular glass area, a window into whatever that room contained.

There were two guards, one on each side of that door. It wasn't hard to guess that whatever little party was going on here tonight was in that room.

The guards had to go.

Maliha reviewed her moves in her mind. The morality of killing guards who were not necessarily evil in themselves was something that bothered her. They were just standing there, paid employees, possibly supporting families. She had no proof that as individuals they were thugs or killers, and she went out of her way to spare lives in the absence of that proof. But tonight there was no opportunity to be a kinder, gentler Maliha; she couldn't have those guards alive and blocking her escape route if they regained consciousness.

She burst out of the door and crossed the space in few seconds. She lashed out with her foot underneath the first guard's chin, snapping his neck. Ducking below the window in the door, she punched the second guard beneath his ribs, doubling him over, then took his head in her hands and twisted. Both were dead, silently, bloodlessly, in less than ten seconds. She dragged the bodies back to the storage closet and pushed them to the side, out of her way.

In the hallway, her back pressed against the wall, she moved toward the door, then got down on hands and knees so that she wouldn't show up in the door's pane of glass. When she reached a lower corner of the glass, she raised her head to look in.

Chapter Forty-One

Greg was in his element, strutting in front of the people who were going to make him very wealthy.

Very, very wealthy. No more drug-smuggling schemes to raise cash. No more lying to bone-headed investors and shitty creditors to cover up the real way things are at the company, which is down the fucking toilet.

A couple of shaky decisions, a competitor roaring onto the scene, and the company he'd put a decade of his life into was spiraling downward to ruin. The people who knew about the sham he'd been perpetrating were dead now. An hour ago, he'd stood over the convulsing body of Edward Rupert, the CFO who'd fought the decisions Greg had rammed down his throat. He'd slit that throat and enjoyed it, too.

The senators, Homeland Security, Edward, Fawn, the coders—he'd cleared the runway for takeoff. All except for Marsha Winters, and she had to die, too. After first leaving it out of his report, Subedei had admitted that she'd been talking to the Homeland Security guy at the very time the guy got his throat slit. If she was talking to Cocomo, she knew everything, or at least way too much.

That had been a disappointment.

The little bitch. She wasn't interested in a charity donation, she was just sniffing around the whole time. Thought she'd get a book deal out of it or something.

He smiled. *Subedei said he wants her for his own. The*

man's got his appetites. Didn't take her out right then be-cause he wants more time with her, I'll bet.

His money worries would be over soon. The only question was how rich he was going to be. Then he'd fix up ShaleTech's financials to get himself off the hook, cash out neat and clean, and disappear. Somewhere there was a beach chair with his name on it, and a drink with a little umbrella waiting to be claimed. A lot of women waiting to be claimed, too.

I swore I was going to own the world by the time I was thirty-five. Well, I'm coming fucking close.

When the last guest was seated, it was time for the show to begin. He was in a semicircular theater. There were rows of seats, each raised higher than the previous one to allow an unobstructed view of him. Although there were at least fifty luxurious seats in the room, only a few were taken by the men—and one woman—who'd come in the limos outside. That alone had been a power trip, having these sinister leaders respond to his call.

A power trip. Good one.

Greg stood on a platform at the front. Subedei was nowhere in sight, probably out sniffing after the Winters woman. Greg hadn't wanted him at the presentation, anyway. What could go wrong? He was the only one in the room with a weapon; he'd made sure of that with the metal detectors. And he was very close to the door that led to his secret escape route. He could be out of the room and gone in seconds in case of trouble, and he had a little surprise for the occupants of the room if he had to take that route.

Tucked underneath a few of the seats were explosives set up for remote detonation using a switch taped under his shirt, near his belt. If he had to leave, he was going to leave with a bang.

Studying the faces of the attendees, he found that several of them had hoods that kept their features from being observed. Old habits, he supposed. The lights in the seating part of the theater were dimmed, the more to emphasize Greg in the front, and dim lighting appealed to those who chose not to flaunt their identities—nor had any need to.

One of the hooded men caught his eye. Something about the shape of the shoulders, the bulk across the chest—it could be Subedei, or just some other man with more muscles than brains. Greg was aware that although his invitation clearly stated "Principals Only," it was likely some of the people sitting in the audience were surrogates.

Since the day he'd arrived, the Mongolian seemed to be dancing to someone else's tune, not Greg's. At least Subedei didn't know the precise details of Project CESR, and Greg preferred it that way.

No matter. The need for secrecy would soon be over. Greg would be fantastically rich.

Do I need Subedei then?

He tried to picture his bodyguard in the tropical paradise Greg intended to call home, maybe sitting in a swimming suit and shades, lounging on the beach, holding a tequila sunrise. It was difficult to keep from laughing. There was never a clearer case of a man not fitting into the picture.

He might just meet with a little accident. Poison, maybe.

The platform was similar to the control room adjacent to his office. Banks of computers surrounded Greg. The wall behind him held huge monitors that displayed global maps, arranged in an arc facing the audience. He stepped up to speak, knowing that he had to establish credibility right away.

"My friends, thank you all for coming here tonight. I'm going to present to you a triumph of planning and technology, Project CESR. CESR stands for Critical Energy Supply Redistribution."

He tapped a button, and all the screens behind him worked together to display a single huge map of the United States.

"The United States of America is an energy-hungry country. Natural gas, nuclear, electricity whether produced by water or coal, alternative sources—it all comes down to power. Power for economic growth, national security, transportation, sanitation, and of course to warm houses. Power to keep the computers running. Power for lights."

He waved his hand and the lights in the presentation

room went off, including the glowing monitors. He left them in the dark for a few seconds, then waved again and turned on the lights. Most members of his audience were out of their seats. They settled back, frowning at the simple but effective demonstration.

"That was one tiny example of a phenomenon feared by every citizen of this country, indeed the world: the dark time. Our caveman ancestors feared it because the dark brought predators and death. We fear it for the same reasons. Riots. Hospitals gone black. Freezing cold. And we have our modern twist: massive technological and economic disruption. One could say that the more advanced a country is, the more susceptible it is to the dark time."

Greg was soaring. It was hard to contain his excitement. Heads were nodding in the audience. He could see his wealth going up by powers of ten.

"This country has at its disposal a vast amount of power. A problem is that sometimes it's not in the right place. Lights go out in New York, but in Florida, people are enjoying themselves at Disney World. Los Angeles has rolling blackouts during heat waves, but those in the Midwest are smug in their air-conditioning. It isn't just a matter of sweat, it's a matter of security. What if Los Angeles needed power and twenty medium-sized Midwest cities each had a little to spare that afternoon? Add up those small surpluses and route them to Los Angeles. *Poof!* Problem solved.

"That's what Project CESR does, on a nationwide scale. The Department of Homeland Security purchased CESR from me, and as of six months ago, it was up and running. If a major distribution station goes offline, the system compensates, and what would have been a huge problem becomes a harmless blip. Critical Homeland Security uses are guaranteed all the energy needed, at the expense of those air conditioners in Kansas City if need be. Even large-scale emergency generators are tied in, so that they can be switched on with power from another part of the country, preserving information, such as bank transfers in progress."

His audience looked like a bunch of bobbleheads. They were way ahead of him, this group of people who, for their own purposes, would like to see the United States brought to its knees.

"My friends, I am offering for sale to you today nothing less than the safety and security, the very future, of the United States. Think about having your finger on the control that can black out any city in this country on your schedule, or all cities at the same time. Power will trickle back, but you could take advantage of that lag and the panic it would cause. You would control the dark time."

When the lights had gone out in the building, Maliha had sprung up to do battle with whatever was coming at her in the dark. Nothing happened and the lights came back on, but her revved-up heartbeat and tensed muscles and the sick feeling in her stomach hadn't gone away. As she listened to Greg, she was horrified.

No wonder this man is protected by one of the Ageless. This plot would thrill any one of the demons. Millions of innocents dead for the twisted aims of a few evil men.

Greg echoed her thoughts.

"Millions dead from bombs planted by your agents during the dark time," Greg continued. "Less than three thousand deaths on September 11, 2001, put a serious dent in the American psyche. Imagine what the deaths of millions would do. Or if you prefer, set up small, surgical strikes meaningful to your cause."

The room erupted in questions.

"Wait, wait. One at a time, please."

A man impeccably dressed in a dark suit stood up. When he spoke, it was with a Latin-American accent. "You said DHS purchased this system from you. How is it that you still control it? I would need proof."

"As would I," another man said. Others voiced their concerns in a variety of accents. One of the men had a translator who spoke for him.

Greg extended his hands, palm down, and gestured for their silence.

"Of course I understand your skepticism. I'm prepared to explain and to demonstrate."

Greg pressed a button on one of the consoles, and the huge map of America displayed behind him on the monitors dimmed. Another layer was added on top of it, a spider-weblike network of lines.

"This is a representation of the total power grid in this country. It is simplified because the real thing is too complex to be shown in its entirety on flat screens like this." He gestured behind him. "The CESR grid exists in virtual reality, where those who monitor it can walk among the interconnecting lines in three dimensions and touch the nodes to display information. Power can be rerouted with a simple wave of the hand, as I did at the beginning of this presentation. Or rerouting can occur automatically, faster than any human can respond to emergencies. It is, in the truest sense of the word, awesome. As the developer, I had free access to the program code that supports this incredible system.

"A back door exists in the software, a secret entrance into the system that only I know how to use. It is extremely powerful. For example, I can keep the DHS from shutting down the CESR system via normal software methods. To shut it off, they'd have to disconnect the hardware from its own power source, a source that is amply redundant and draws upon all types of energy, from geothermal to fossil fuels. The back door wipes out all trace of its use. The only way to prevent repeated access is to disable the entire system, and that takes time—time that belongs to the highest bidder. The programming and physical setup to do this is unmatched anywhere else in the world, and I might add, was expensive."

Maliha could see from her vantage point that Greg had a screen in front of him with a miniature version of the same display covering the walls.

"That takes care of how I can do it. Now for the demonstration. Would someone call out a state?"

"California."

"Excellent. North or south?"

"South," a different voice said.

"County? Anyone familiar with a county in southern California?"

"Los Angeles. You have talked about it enough."

Greg shook his head. "Ah, better not. This is a demonstration. No need to tip our hand just yet. That would be too dramatic."

"Kern County, next door."

Greg was enjoying himself immensely, Maliha could see that. He was like a schoolteacher leading his classroom, with the subject being terror and the students already experts.

"Perfect. I remind you that you have collectively chosen the target for the demonstration, meaning that it's not a setup." He touched a spot on Southern California, and it blew up to display a giant image of Kern County on the wall behind him. "Let's see. Here's a good spot. China Lake, a community on the western edge of the Mojave Desert."

Information about the town flashed up on one of the monitors.

"A population of less than two thousand people at the last census."

Maliha was very worried, now that things had gotten so specific. What was Greg planning to do to the two thousand people? She stood up next to the door, staying away from the window in it. She tried the doorknob and found that it turned. As a test, she cracked open the door a quarter of an inch. She could get in anytime she wanted.

"There is something interesting about this small community," Greg lectured. "It is located right next to the Naval Air Weapons Station, NAWS, which has been a center for development and testing of airborne weapons for decades. I'm sure you know of it. Wouldn't want to touch them, would we?" He grinned. "At least, not as a demo. This will demonstrate the precision with which I can control the power grid. I'm going to black out China Lake but leave NAWS unaffected. One moment please, while I enter the back door."

Greg turned his back to his audience and worked at one of the computer consoles, one that had a shield over it.

"Ready. Here goes." He reached out and touched the dot that represented China Lake on the enlarged map of Kern County. A couple of grid lines leading to the town went dark, as did the town itself. There was silence in the room. Greg waited about thirty seconds, and then touched the grid again. China Lake lit up.

"You may all verify the effect. There are phones built into the arms of your chairs. Call whomever you wish, and we'll wait for the results." He sat down on a black swivel chair that was a twin to the one in the control room adjacent to his office.

Most of the fourteen audience members—she'd counted—picked up their phones. They dialed, and spoke softly into the handsets. Ten minutes passed as they, and Maliha, waited for confirmation.

The Latino in the dark suit stood again. "It is as you say. I offer ten million."

Chapter Forty-Two

"Ten million is a good starting bid," Greg said, with a grin on his face. "Who'll top it?"

A large man clothed in the garb of a sheik called out from his seat. "I will take the system for two hundred million U.S. dollars. The meeting is over."

Others rose to their feet, gesturing and yelling over one another's bids. Maliha had heard enough. Greg's scheme was going to be successful. There was no time to involve the Feds. She'd come here to confront Greg and Subedei— *Where is Subedei?*—and now was the time.

She couldn't see any guards in the room. She was sure Greg would be armed; she didn't know if the audience members were. Regardless, she was going to kill them all. She couldn't work up any sympathy for people who were bidding on the opportunity to kill innocent civilians to further their goals. Maliha pulled her whip sword from its sheath around her waist. She checked the placement of her throwing stars within their pack.

Then she examined her deep feelings. She had to be committed one hundred percent to what she was about to do.

No holding back. No fear. Subedei is here somewhere, I know it. I can't let him stand between me and saving millions of people. Go!

As ready as she was going to be, Maliha took a deep breath, threw the door open, and dashed inside.

The shrill alarm of a metal detector went off as she passed through it, jolting everyone in the room from their dreams of deaths and dollars. She went up one aisle of the theater, slashing the throats of those within reach of the whip sword. Its blades slipped through the air and bit with precision.

Four down.

The lone woman in the audience was the first to react. She leaped from her seat and ran for the door Maliha had just entered. Maliha caught her in the back with a throwing knife, and the woman stumbled forward, short of her goal.

Maliha kept in motion, not giving anyone a still target. A bullet flew by her. Greg or someone else was firing. She jumped to the top of the seat nearest her and ran lightly along the row of seat backs. A bullet hit one of the seats she'd just passed, exploding out the back with a burst of stuffing and fabric. The whip sword flicked again as men tried to move down the rows to get to the aisle. Each of the sword's blades took a life.

Seven.

Three men were heading down to the door. Maliha launched three throwing stars simultaneously. The stars split apart in midair and landed in the backs of their heads. They collapsed to the ground, forming a barrier to the door.

Greg had ducked behind a seat in the front row and was still firing at her. When she paused to throw the stars, a lucky shot of his grazed her side at the waist. An inch to the left and the bullet would have harmlessly sped by.

Damn that man. I'm going to . . .

She couldn't let the pain distract her. One of the men in front of her had stood his ground. As she approached, he flung a knife at her, followed by another. They were nearly invisible in the dim light because they were made of plastic. She lashed out with the whip sword, knocking one of them from the air. The other knife, deflected, slipped by her and nicked her thigh. She pulled the throwing axe from its position on her back and in one smooth motion sent it flying through the air. It split his face, and he went down, stunned. She unsheathed a knife and threw it at the seat Greg was hiding behind with tremendous force. It penetrated the seat and there was a scream.

Yes!

She kept up the momentum of her run and yanked the axe from the face of the dead man as she went by.

Eleven.

But at a cost. She was injured, bleeding, but couldn't let it slow her down. She locked the pain away with her strongest key and moved on.

Another of the men, a couple of rows over, launched a plastic throwing star at her. Intended to avoid triggering the metal detectors in the building, the plastic weapons had done their job. She hit the star with a throwing knife, propelling it back at him. Knife and star buried themselves in his throat.

Suddenly her heart nearly stopped. One of the men, in the shadows at the edge of the theater, was unaffected by the carnage around him. It was like the scene at the plaza in Washington, D.C., where she'd seen a motionless man, unmoved by death.

He came to life suddenly, with a crossbow that appeared from underneath his robes. He'd bypassed the metal detector somehow, because that bow gleamed with metallic menace. He notched an arrow and released it.

Move! Move!

Pulling out every remnant of speed in her diminished arsenal, Maliha jumped upward in a leap for her life. Instead of burying itself in her belly as intended, the arrow sliced her outfit and the skin on her lower leg, and passed by, trailing her blood like a comet's tail. Then the arrow embedded itself in the forehead of a man who'd been skulking low behind her, ready to attack with one of her own knives he'd yanked from a victim.

Thirteen.

She whirled in the air and landed in the aisle a dozen feet from Subedei.

Too close, can't be this close, he's faster.

To her surprise, he didn't take the advantage she'd given him. Instead he turned and sped for the platform. She fired a couple of darts aimed several feet ahead of him and they connected, landing in his hip. He ignored them, scooped up Greg from behind the seat, and ran for the door. He yanked on the handle, tossing aside the three dead men and the woman who'd piled up at the door.

Greg wasn't dead, but he'd been hit in the back with her knife. Subedei pulled the knife from Greg's body and threw it backward over his shoulder at Maliha.

She dodged it and went after Subedei. She couldn't let him get into the storage closet, into the escape tunnel, and away into the night. With grass under his feet outdoors, he could easily outrun her.

She got to the door. Subedei was headed the wrong way! He didn't know about the tunnel. Greg had kept the secret from his bodyguard. She had a chance.

Subedei threw Greg over his shoulder, with Greg's belly bouncing as he ran. The next thing Maliha knew, there was a tremendous explosion behind her in the theater room. Tossed forward by the force, she was thrown toward the opposite side of the hallway. While still in midair, she curled herself around the pack that contained the C4 she was carrying—this level of shock and heat could set it off, but she sheltered it with her body and was surprised to find herself still in one piece.

Trying to get away from the bombed-out room, she felt the clothing on her lower legs catch fire. Pain seemed to come from everywhere at once and the edges of her vision blackened. As though looking down the long tube of a telescope, she saw Subedei escaping, opening a door at the end of the hall and disappearing into it.

Maliha rolled before the flames crept higher, putting out the fire, and came to her feet. Precious seconds had been lost, and to one of the Ageless, seconds represented an overpowering advantage.

Maliha took off down the hall at the best speed she could manage. Part way down the hall, one of the doors opened in front of her and several guards poured out into her path. She didn't slacken her pace. She whipped four throwing stars at them, two from each hand, saw the stars separate and strike, and ran up the side of the wall to get around the last man. As she went by, she planted a dart in his heart. He fired his gun before he fell, but the shot went wild.

The pain of the burns tore at her as she ran. The skin on her calves was blistered and her two bullet wounds made themselves known with each impact of her feet, but at least she hadn't blown herself up with her own explosives. She wondered how much blood she'd lost, then decided it didn't matter. She was going after Subedei until she couldn't move anymore, and tried not to think how close to that condition she might be. She put her head down and ran. She couldn't let Subedei get away with Shale.

Or is it that I can't let Subedei get away?

She thought of his hands on her, of how close he'd come to killing her friends. There was no backing down now.

The door at the end of the hallway opened to flights of stairs. She was still in the enclave, so how was Subedei going to get out?

One of the doors is in Greg's office!

When she got to the stairs, she followed a hunch and went up instead of down.

Eight seconds in the elevator from the tunnel. Eight seconds, not enough to get to the Greg's seventh-floor office from underground in anything but a high-speed elevator, and the building wasn't tall enough to warrant it. The theater room has to be below the level of Greg's office.

Putting all of her hopes in that thought, she made her way up the stairs, leaning on the railing, moving as fast as she could. She passed three landings, then saw blood on a door as she passed it. She stopped and came back. Greg, still riding on Subedei's shoulder, must have brushed the door and left the blood.

Brushed against it when entering, or just in passing?

Resisting the urge to burst through the door—Subedei could be just inside—she eased it open. The hallway was just like the one below, which gave her no hint to go on.

She felt something like a hand descend onto her shoulder. She didn't recognize it at first, but then knew it must be Yanmeng remote viewing her and exerting more pressure than he ever had before. The hand gave her a slight push toward the hall. From Yanmeng's view above and around her, he must have seen Subedei just disappearing through the door a couple of seconds before she arrived.

This floor, then. She hoped Yanmeng would stop viewing her now. She didn't want him to see her die, if it came to that.

Ahead of her in the hallway she could see that Subedei had paused. He was holding Shale by the shoulders, his face pushed right into the wounded man's face. Subedei was talking to Shale in a low, deadly voice. If he remained distracted, she could overtake him. It might be her best chance. She quietly moved down the hall, flattening herself against the wall intermittently, then advancing further.

Suddenly Subedei whipped Shale up in the air and brought him down sharply on his knee. She heard the *crack!* of Shale's spine. She was close enough now that she could make out Subedei's words. He dangled Shale, still alive, in midair, clutching him by his head.

"You failed, human. Now you belong to me. I only wish I had a longer time to enjoy this."

Subedei twisted his hands, tearing off Shale's head. The body dropped limply to the floor. Subedei tossed the head away like a piece of garbage.

And then Subedei was gone in a flash. Maliha had been so intent on watching Shale's demise that she hadn't gotten close enough to launch an attack.

Damn, damn, damn! Staring like I've never seen a man die before.

She moved cautiously down the hallway. She had no idea which of the doors at the end would be the control room adjacent to Greg's office—the entry into the enclave. As she neared the doors, she heard something behind her.

She gave it everything she had, running up the side of the wall to get out of the path of certain death. Two knives whipped by where she'd been. Hitting the ceiling, she twisted—*damn, that hurt*—and came down hard, rolling on the floor and ending up next to one of the doors. The movement caused a spasm of pain in her blistered, wounded leg. She grimaced until it passed, and then she realized the center door of the three was open. He'd gone past her while she was rolling around in pain.

He's playing with me. He could have killed me right then. Or maybe he doesn't intend to kill me—yet.

Subedei's words came back to her. He'd told Shale that he wished he had more time with him. Time for what, she could imagine. She nearly gagged when she realized that part of that time would be spent ravishing her. He'd already made that clear in the darkness of her bedroom.

She didn't kid herself that she was going to outrun or outfight Subedei. If she took him out, it would be with cunning and luck.

The room she was looking into was dark. Subedei could materialize out of the blackness and jab her with a knife in the space of a heartbeat.

She reached inside the open door and ran her hand along the wall, looking for the light switch. She found it and flipped on the light. Fluorescent lights brightened the room, which was an office space with cubicles. The room appeared to be empty, but Subedei could be hiding in any of the cubicles.

A smear of blood on the floor encouraged her to enter. Subedei had probably stepped in Shale's blood. Cautiously, she made her way in, pausing at every cubicle entrance. Then she decided she was losing too much time that way, and just took off running. The room was about a hundred feet long. No boogeyman leaped out at her from behind the cubicle walls.

At the far end of the room, a door stood open. Subedei was inviting her in. Too late, she realized she was outlined in the doorway with the bright fluorescents behind her.

She felt the cold wind of Subedei's arrival but couldn't see him—he was moving too fast. Before she could move, she felt a slice on each of her arms. She did a backward handspring into the relative safety of the cubicle room, but she was bleeding from cuts that made it unlikely she could do that again.

Maliha was approaching the limit of her abilities. The

pain and blood loss from multiple wounds were wearing her down. Time was definitely on Subedei's side.

He knows it, and he's enjoying it.

She had to make a stand while she still could. She settled on the floor with a good view of the open door and fired her last grappling-hook dart into the ceiling. She had a plan, a desperate one. She reached into her pack, kneaded two blocks of C4 into a ball, and inserted a wireless detonator.

Come to me, demon's slave.

There was a commotion at the back of the room, where she'd entered. She heard the voices of guards, and then everything got very still. Too still.

A flashbang came rolling down the aisle between the cubicles. She couldn't wait, or she'd be helpless in a moment. She pulled on the grappling hook's rope and swung out into the aisle. If her weakened arms gave out now, she was exposed and would be dead in moments.

She kicked the flashbang back where it came from with all her strength. Whoever was back there took the full brunt of it.

While she was flying through the air on the rope, the flash went off behind her, and the bang struck her ears. The fluid in her ears reacted instantly, and she was disoriented and dizzy. Fighting against it, she pulled up higher on the rope and threw her feet out in front of her so her body was nearly parallel to the floor. That cost, dearly.

She went swinging through the doorway like a battering ram, and her feet connected in a satisfying way with solid flesh.

Subedei, aware of the flashbang, had stepped into the doorway after the blast to capture what he thought would be a helpless target. His head snapped back with the force of Maliha's body hitting him feet first. She continued past him and let go of the rope.

She was in the control room. Subedei moved to block her exit on the far side of the room. The door to the office was open—her path to safety—but the Mongolian was in the way.

There was nothing to do but attack. She ran at Subedei

and paid for her arrogance as he tossed a throwing star that struck her side.

Pain kills only if I allow it.

She saw the look in his eyes. He was lost somewhere deep in lust, his whole being focused on obtaining her.

The death of a thousand cuts. It has to end soon.

Swerving and ducking underneath his arm as he raised it to wreak more havoc on her, she smacked the ball of C4 onto his back, and then slid into Greg's office. She scrambled behind Greg's heavy desk and pressed the detonator button.

The explosion shook the floor and threw the desk—and Maliha—back into the wall. She took a crushing impact from the desk. An orange ball of fire, initially confined in the small area of the control room, burst through the walls and headed in her direction. Windows in the office shattered and flames curled outward. The heat of the explosion singed her hair even though she was curled behind the desk. When the wave of fire passed, she pulled herself up.

A chunk of Subedei's torso landed with a heavy splat next to her. Right then it was the most wonderful thing she could lay her eyes on. She picked the throwing star out of her body and triumphantly stabbed it into the bloody meat.

Maliha crawled out into the hall. She blinked and wiped blood from her eyes, because she thought she was so far gone she was seeing things.

In the middle of the hall was Grandfather, in a lotus position, floating a couple of feet off the floor. It was the young, powerful version of him that she faced.

Her heart sank and her stomach twisted inside. In her severely weakened condition—or in any condition as a mortal—the odds of taking out Grandfather were small.

To do the unexpected is my only chance.

She pulled together the threads of her tattered strength, and ran toward him. No explosives, no weapons left, it would have to be hand-to-hand.

When she approached him, the *shou* symbol on her left arm burst into flame. The pain was agonizing as the fire sank deeper into her arm. The symbol of her pledge was intent on disabling her, keeping her from attacking her master. She fought both it and the remembrance of burning alive that it triggered, and braced herself for combat, knowing that his first blow could be the end of her.

"Daughter," he said, "stop."

At his words, Maliha's feet felt as though she'd stepped in tar, and they tangled under her body. She crashed to the floor and slowly pulled herself up into a seated position. The fire popped out of existence on her arm. One thought screamed in her head.

My quest is over.

Grandfather gently floated down to the floor, and they were face-to-face. Sounds faded. A wall of silence surrounded them. Maliha concentrated on slowing her racing heart and breathing.

"You have killed Subedei, who was my son as you are my daughter."

There was no denying that. His blood had splashed on her. She remembered her pledge: I swear to honor you as my grandfather, to do nothing to bring shame to you or the school, and to never stray from the teachings of this school.

Does killing a member of the school qualify as straying from its teachings? Probably.

She met Grandfather's eyes, and found them unfocused, as if he were looking through her. She thought he might be reading her aura, but it seemed as though he was studying her blood flowing in its vessels, tracing it in and out of her heart, watching her lungs expand and contract, seeing everything she was made of, physically and emotionally.

"Let me tell you a story."

Time didn't seem to matter in the bubble they were in. She nodded.

"Five thousand years ago, I lived in the rich city of Ur in the land of Sumer, a powerful man content with my life. I was a priest of Anu. Already aged well beyond the usual number of years, I foolishly prayed to Anu to grant me a hundred more. When my health failed me, I grew bitter with Anu. He had not granted my prayer. I now know it was my pride that caused my bitterness, not any failing of Anu's. When my heart stopped, the last words from my mouth were a curse to Anu, to whom I had devoted my life. Wrapped in bitterness, I found myself in a strange place, surrounded by thick fog. It was there I met Rabishu, who turned my bitterness against me and took me as his slave."

He stopped. She could see memories whirling in his eyes.

"The demon trained me for years in the blank place. When I left there, I was a master of the killing arts, his first assassin. I serve him still, while waiting for the return of Anu to this world so I can beg forgiveness for the curse I uttered."

"Why don't you rebel? Join me. Together we can kill Rabishu and the others."

"If I break my contract, I return to the age I was at the time of my death. You have seen me. As a frail, blind, mortal man, I would have no hope of balancing the scale that Rabishu would carve on my body—a scale weighed down by five thousand years of killing. I would fail, and move from my wretched situation to a worse one in the demon's cage. My hope lies in the return of Anu."

"Are you going to kill me?"

"I want to know if you still honor your pledge of loyalty to me."

She searched his face.

So this is what it boils down to. If I say no, he kills me. I'm half-dead already, how could I stop him? If I say yes— what does that get me into? In all this time he hasn't asked anything of me, but as master of the school, he has the right to. He could order me to do something, and if I didn't do it, we're back to him killing me, or trying to.

"Will you call on me for your own needs?"

He shook his head. "Your pledge was unqualified when you took it, and must be unqualified when you affirm it."

He hates Rabishu as I do. Just go with that. The enemy of my enemy. . .

"I'm loyal to you and the school."

"Then I will pray for your success." It was said without much hope in his face or voice.

"There is one more thing. In the foulness of his mind, Rabishu may one day pit us against each other, master against disciple. If that happens, I will kill you. I must remain alive to serve Anu when he returns. I am his last priest."

Defiance sparked in Maliha and she remembered what she'd told Rabishu when she'd taken the mortal path. *You won't win. I swear you won't.*

The bubble faded. Grandfather got swiftly to his feet. When she blinked, he was gone.

With what strength she had left, she still had to get out of the building. That meant going out the front door, where there was certain to be an army of riled-up guards, or going out the secret way she came in.

Resigned, she levered herself to her feet to retrace her steps. She rushed through the burning control room and into the enclave beyond. The cubicle room was a shambles. The guards who had rushed up the aisle after minimal recovery from the flashbang had run straight into the explosion. Their tactic had backfired on them and resulted in their deaths.

She entered the stairwell and went down the flights of stairs, holding the railing, pausing to rest, continuing. Finally, looking out at the long hallway, she could see the blasted theater room and beyond it, the storage room she'd come through.

She went down the hall cautiously, her eyes scanning each door for any sign of movement. When she passed the blown-out theater-room door, a small group of guards had gathered inside, searching in case their boss had somehow survived. They spotted her and ran into the hall. She was ahead of them, and she had a short distance to go to get to the storage room. She drew an extra effort from somewhere inside, and hurried to the room. She banged the door open, passed the dead guards she'd left there, and dived into the opening in the floor where the rope ladder was. Bullets hit the wall in the storage room. Her body screamed with pain, but she had to keep going.

She grabbed one of the rungs of the rope ladder and stopped her face-forward descent. She couldn't swing there by her weakened arm for long, so she dropped the remaining six feet to the floor and landed on her feet. Her burned legs collapsed beneath her. Crawling, she moved to the wall and reached up to the elevator controls to press the DOWN button. Gunshots were fired down the rope ladder, then they stopped. She got to her feet, supporting herself on the frame of the elevator. She knew what was coming: the aerial act in the elevator car.

As the elevator door opened, a guard came down the ladder. She reached out for the cords dangling from her grappling hooks and pulled up quickly, trying to get out of the way of any shots. The man rushed after her into the elevator, sprang the trapdoor with his weight, and fell out of sight, screaming. The trapdoor snapped closed, giving no sign that someone had just plunged to his death. Maliha swung on the cords toward the elevator's control panel, slipping close to the trapdoor and recovering, and pressed the DOWN button with her elbow. The doors closed and she was on her way.

Eight very long seconds passed on the way down in the elevator.

When the door opened, the tunnel with its arched ribs of light was a welcome sight. She swung out of the elevator, letting go of the cords. After making an awkward, pain-filled landing, she went to what she assumed was the launcher for the escape pod. There were several buttons on it, but one had a diagram of the windshield of the pod lifting up. She jammed her fist down on it. Lights came on in the interior of the pod, and the windshield rotated up.

Let there be no more traps.

She forced her legs to move to the pod, crawled in, and sat in the semi-reclining seat. There was a similar button inside, showing the shield lowering. Greg had wanted the controls as clear and simple as possible, figuring he might not be in prime shape if he needed to use his escape route. She pressed it, and when the shield slipped down into place, a green button lit up. She pushed it, and the pod began to move.

Woozy, Maliha watched the lights overhead as the pod picked up speed and then slowed and came to a gentle stop at the other end of the tunnel. She got out of the pod, leaving a bloody stain on the plush seat, and went through the open steel door. The ladder to the surface was in front of her. She held on and pulled up step by painful step, remembering at the last moment to skip the third step. She dragged herself out the hatch and onto the dirt floor of the barn.

Not far away was the spot where she'd hidden the weapons she hadn't taken with her. With them was the signaler she needed to contact Glass to bring the helicopter back. The thought of having to climb up a rope into the helicopter was daunting.

Ten feet away. Just ten feet more feet and she could rest and wait for rescue.

A flashlight played over her. "Stop right there."

Maliha froze. She recognized the voice. It was the head of security, Chief Clark.

Chapter Forty-Three

When Maliha had ordered Hound to stay behind, he'd chafed at it. She was paying a good price for his service and he didn't like going against a client's order. He could get a bad reputation that way.

Still, this wasn't just any client. He wasn't in the habit of sleeping with many of his clients. None of them, in fact, except Maliha.

Without thinking a whole lot about it, he found himself in the helicopter with Glass waiting for the pickup summons. The copter was in the air just close enough to keep the building in sight through binoculars, and he saw the flare of orange leaking from windows on ShaleTech's third floor.

"Blast on level seven. I think that's our pickup call."

Glass nodded. She took them back to the barn and hovered the copter while Hound rappelled down.

He was at the door of the barn when he heard a voice that wasn't Maliha's. He dropped down and crawled in silently, taking up a post inside the door. He could see Maliha in the man's flashlight, and she looked bad. Really bad.

"The boss is dead and that fucking bodyguard is in a million pieces," the man holding a gun on her said. He was waving a radio, and was in touch with someone inside the ShaleTech building. "You did a first-rate job. Ordinarily, I'd try to hire you, but as much as I hate to admit it, you're a step or two above my ability, and I never hire anyone better than me."

His voice chilled Hound. It was the voice of someone who liked to see people suffer.

"That means I have to kill you. If I let you get away with this, I'd never get another top security job. Gonna be hard enough after that piece of work you did in there. 'Course you look three fourths dead on your own, so this is kind of a mercy killing."

Enough of this shit.

Hound pulled a gun and plugged the guy in the back three times. Then he walked up and put a couple more in his head, just to be sure.

He picked up the flashlight.

"It's me, Hound. I'm going to get you out of here. You owe me extra for that kill."

When the light hit her, he could see relief in her eyes. Then, from one breath to the next, she was writhing on the floor, her face contorted in a mask of terrible pain, clutching her belly. He'd seen it before, in the fields of Vietnam.

Dying!

He ran forward and knelt at her side, looking for whatever wound was sending her into death throes.

To be at her side when she died.

What he saw shocked him almost as much as her death would have. She'd ripped open the front of her outfit. In the flashlight's beam, a parade of small figures was moving across her belly, leaving a raw trough of burned flesh in their wake as their tiny feet moved. There was an animated scale on her body and it was tipping as he watched the figures climbing up into the taller of the two pans.

Maliha screamed as the last one dragged itself into the pan. He reached out to grab her shoulders, but she shimmered in front of his eyes as if something was pulling her away. His eyes couldn't quite focus on her, and his hands went right through her like she wasn't in the barn with him.

He wanted to pull her up into a fierce hug, to keep her there with him, to make whatever was happening stop, with the force of his will if nothing else.

When the shimmering passed, he sat back on his heels, keeping a hand on her to make sure she was there with him.

Damn. This woman's stranger than I thought.

Chapter Forty-Four

It had been nearly three weeks since the death of Subedei.

As Maliha's body healed, Hound told her what he'd witnessed. With no way to hide her true nature from a man who'd seen her belly scale in motion and watched her slip out of normal time, Maliha told him everything. It was a lot for him to absorb, and typical of Hound, he told her he'd get back to her on it.

When Yanmeng held a mirror up for her to study her face, there were noticeable wrinkles at the corners of her eyes and a generous sprinkling of silver hairs mixed into the black—but not too much different from the way she'd looked after saving Samantha Dearborn, when she'd taken a leap in age of about three years.

Maybe another couple of years this time.

She placed her age at about thirty. A slightly old-looking thirty. There was something else about her face, especially her eyes, that said she was on her way to wisdom as well as advancing in years. Her eyes reflected back at her the decision she'd made that risk be damned, she was going to live every day fully.

Rabishu said my aging would be uneven and that Anu would decide. Only two years for saving potentially millions, with a huge difference in the balance of the scales. Anu has favored me.

She wondered if Grandfather had prayed to Anu for her, and that this time his prayer was answered. She'd never know, but whatever the reason, she'd taken a big step toward denying Rabishu his plaything.

"Good evening, Ms. Winters."

"Same to you, Mr. Henshaw."

Maliha rode the elevator to the forty-eighth floor. It was late, and she was tired, but the thought of getting home propelled her at a good pace. At the door to her haven, she placed her palm against the biometric sensor and used the other hand to cover her eyes tightly against the brilliant light about to assault them. The door slid back. Stepping forward, light leaking in between her fingers, she crossed the foyer in an instant and slapped her hand against the switch on the far wall. Darts did not rain down upon her from the ceiling.

I might have to recalibrate that sensor as I get older and slower. I don't want to look like a pincushion. Bad for the complexion.

The spotlights snapped off and the door closed behind her.

"Lights, low."

She let her eyes rest on the soothing pastel painting in her foyer as they adjusted to the lack of spotlights. As she waited, she sensed that something wasn't right. This was her place that she knew intimately. Something, a light scent of . . . what?

She moved her hand through the air, waving it toward her face. She felt a little dampness, and smelled it, and soap, too. Yet she hadn't been here in nearly a month. It was as if someone had . . .

Taken a shower? Gotten in!

Maliha crouched. Her internal alarm was blaring. She was in a bad position, trapped in the dead-end hallway, and with the flash of the spotlights, she'd announced her presence big-time. She hesitated, then backed up toward the door. She could reach up and hit the switch to open the door, then dive out into the hall. Better to leave now, if she could, and return better prepared. The safe house had a large armory.

"You can come out now."

A familiar voice. Jake's.

Relief swept through her. Maliha straightened up on legs that became limp as the adrenaline rush dissipated. She leaned against the wall while her thoughts whirled in a pleasant orbit with the two of them at the center. Then she spotted the switch on the wall of the foyer and it reminded her of exactly where she was. As fast as her elation had arrived, it now fled.

Jake was inside her safe haven.

Why didn't he trigger the darts? Why is he still alive?

LEGENDS OF THE RIFTWAR

HONORED ENEMY

978-0-06-079284-8

by Raymond E. Feist & William R. Forstchen

In the frozen northlands of the embattled realm of Midkemia, Dennis Hartraft's Marauders must band together with their bitter enemy, the Tsurani, to battle *moredhel*, a migrating horde of deadly dark elves.

MURDER IN LAMUT

978-0-06-079291-6

by Raymond E. Feist & Joel Rosenberg

For twenty years the mercenaries Durine, Kethol, and Pirojil have fought other people's battles, defeating numerous deadly enemies. Now the Three Swords find themselves trapped by a winter's storm inside a castle teeming with ambitious, plotting lords and ladies, and it falls on the mercenaries to solve a series of cold-blooded murders.

JIMMY THE HAND

978-0-06-079299-2

by Raymond E. Feist & S.M. Stirling

Forced to flee the only home he's ever known, Jimmy the Hand, boy thief of Krondor finds himself among the rural villagers of Land's End. But Land's End is home to a dark, dangerous presence even the local smugglers don't recognize. And suddenly Jimmy's youthful bravado is leading him into the maw of chaos . . . and, quite possibly, his doom.